Flansburg's novel is the story of a heroic character's "fight or flight" journey which will leave readers captivated with relatable, heartfelt moments and lovable characters.

—Felicity Fox, author of *Where the Holidays Go*
www.thefelicityfoxhouse.com

Hope provides a unique perspective of how trauma and grief, if not processed, can have an impact on emotional health and relationships. Through relatable and authentic characters, *Piece by Piece* is a page turner and keeps readers enthralled until the end.

—Lynn A. Storey-Huylar Director, Safe Harbor,
a children's justice center

A heartfelt and honest account of the impact of abuse, *Piece by Piece* is a must read and offers readers inspirational insight on living a full, authentic life after overcoming trauma.

—Susan Walton, MSW Director,
Park County Department of Human Services

PIECE BY PIECE

Picking up the Shards of a
Soul Worth Saving

HOPE FLANSBURG

Dedication

My parents, Milton and Joanne Strang, for giving me a phenomenal childhood, the security in knowing a relationship with God, and the confidence to be my own person.

PROLOGUE

August — 1996

The tip of Jessie's tongue lightly touches the open gap on her crusted bottom lip. She blinks once and then twice, wondering how long she has been sitting there with her dry, blank eyes fixed out the window. Time, like her innocence, is no longer important.

With her knees pulled against her chest, she watches the charcoal clouds as they creep past, shadows from the luminous sky threatening a potential rainstorm. Deafening thunder drowns out the beating of her heart, the one reminder she is still alive.

After a moment she forces her burning eyes away and slips her aching, trembling body off the bed, onto the floor. Cringing, she picks up the ripped shirt and guides her arm through the torn sleeve. Exhausted from the small movement, she leans against the mattress and takes a heaving, unsteady breath. She swallows back a sob. Determined to leave before her attacker changes his mind and comes back to kill her, she drags herself to the corner where her pants and underwear lay in a heap. Wincing with each movement, Jessie carefully eases her bruised legs into the denim. Quivering fingers fumble with buttons while she watches her tears fall, wetting the floor beneath her.

Using the wall for support, she tries to stand, but her pounding head causes her to stumble. Defeated, she sinks to the floor. In a daze, she sees a spider from earlier, pedaling a few inches to the right of its original spot. The insect was her focus, her lifeline, and her sanity. When her attacker was on top of her, violating her in the most shameful ways, she prayed the spider would somehow grow big, like the insects in *James and the Giant Peach*. She wished it would spin a web large enough to catch prey and somehow come to her rescue.

As he continued to pound, dripping with the foul stench of sweat and cigarette smoke, Jessie didn't scream. She didn't even fight. She stared at the spider as it hung off a thread. It did not move. It appeared to watch her in return as if understanding her fear and sensing the hatred that was building inside of her.

Jessie would give anything to be that spider. The little insect had the power she seemed to have lost senselessly within a matter of moments.

Nervously, she picks at the torn clothes that hang lifeless from her body. He said he'd kill them both if anyone found out. Why hadn't her sister told her what was happening to her? Why didn't she reach for the gun when he put it down? What was Jessie supposed to do now?

She tries to wrap her head around the suffocating and irrational thoughts. Suddenly, nausea immobilizes her. She hunches over, vomiting on the chalk colored linoleum floor. When the dry heaving stops, she sags against the wall, shell-shocked and broken. Her tongue pokes the dried blood on her lip as the light in her soul begins to vanish.

• • •

His white knuckles grip the steering wheel as the truck stumbles along the dirt road toward the ranch. Rage swells in him like a wave ready to crash and break as he considers the violent confrontation he is about to face. Unwilling to consider the consequences, he pushes harder on the pedal, speeding toward his destination. Tires bump through ruts and puddles of mud, jostling him in the driver's seat. Releasing his vice-like grip, he wipes the sweat off his brow. The other hand remains locked around the pistol resting on his thigh.

The truck screeches to a halt in the driveway. The amber sun beams brilliantly through the mountain caps and across fields of golden wheat in the backdrop of the ranch. Everything around him holds the promise of warm, calm summer days, relaxing evenings, and the hope of a life well-lived. Any other day, the scene around him would remind him of a movie; someone else's life played out on the screen. Nothing prepared him for the news he overheard or how it transformed his entire world. He will not be underestimated. He will do absolutely anything to protect those he loves.

Noticing the familiar truck parked in front, a rush of adrenaline surges through him. Grabbing the gun, he leaps out and shoves it in his back pocket. His boots kick up clumps of mud while he sprints to the house. Violently, he pounds his fists against the front door and waits impatiently, his teeth clenched tightly. When no one answers, he curses and hits harder, rattling the wooden door with his strength. Twisting the knob and realizing it's unlocked, he opens the door, steps inside, and calls out angrily. Silence greets him.

Confused and desperate, he skirts around the back of the house and scans the rest of the property. Blood pulses in his temples as he paces back and forth, once again wiping his damp forehead. Anxious to find a release for the rage he can hardly contain, he spots a two-by-four leaning against the barn. He races toward it and wraps it in his large hands. With an agonizing scream, he repeatedly slams the side of the rafters until the wood breaks in two. With splinters piercing his skin, he collapses to his knees as sobs rattle his body.

He forces himself to be quiet when he hears soft whimpers. He trudges through thick muck around the corner of the barn and finds a crumpled figure on the ground next to the fence. Knowing it's who he has been looking for, he retrieves the pistol out of his back pocket. He pokes the body with his booted toe. He hears small, pathetic moans. With the force of his whole leg, he pushes the body onto its back.

Stunned, he steps away and slowly replaces the gun. After a moment's hesitation, he leans forward to look at the mangled figure. Blood and bruising cover every inch of his bloated face. A disfigured nose meshes into purple and yellowish bruised eyes, swollen shut. Several small gashes mark his cheeks, and he has a large, bleeding wound above his ear. More cuts and dried blood cover his hands. His knuckles are gnarled into fists at his side. White bubbly foam drips from the corner of his mouth, down his chin and onto his shirt. The man tries to move his lips, but no words are audible.

With a hand still lingering over the pistol in his back pocket, he wrestles with his conscience. He finds pleasure in knowing the man on the ground is suffering.

From what he can see from the man's wounds, it's not hard to assume his life is one that will not be worth living. His rage shifts slowly to pity. It would be easy to walk away and pretend he knows nothing. Sensibility and humanity get the best of him. He returns to the empty house, makes a phone call, and leaves before anyone knows he was there.

PART ONE

CHAPTER ONE

Jessie — May 2009

I attempt to distract myself with the book on tape while I drive the deserted Montana highway, dusk enveloping the night. Despite the twists and turns of the suspense novel, my anxiety crushes all my sense of reality. While I'm excited to reach the destination of my parent's house after the long drive, I'm consciously aware of what this means.

Exasperated, I turn off the narration and switch the radio to an AM station, hoping the latest headline news will trick my brain into thinking about something else. The distraction works temporarily until thoughts of the impending chaos of my life return.

Tapping the brakes of my car, I approach the outskirts of Helena and wonder what awaits me. It's been thirteen years since I set foot here. In all this time, I never had intentions of coming back. As my car moves through the business district of town, I take in all that is familiar with this place I used to call home. Realizing I have been holding my breath, I let out a long, deliberate exhale, and roll my shoulders and neck.

When I enter the subdivision where my parents live, the foreboding ache intensifies. I slow down to match the speed limit sign and avert my eyes from the community park fountain where my sister, Vicky, and I used to wade our feet as kids. I keep my gaze forward and avoid the school playground. Despite my hesitation, a door from the past opens, and I remember days when life was simple and sweet. I envision a younger me on a swing floating through the air, my legs pumping as I go higher and higher, pretending I'm flying toward freedom. The empty, hollow hole that's resided in my chest since I was eighteen years old begins to throb.

I try to redirect my attention back to my life in Seattle. Time has flown by in the five years since I followed my best friend A.J. to Seattle from Chicago. To maintain my sanity during medical school, I fantasized about owning a little café that served an assortment of baked goods for breakfast and sandwiches for lunch. It would specialize in flavored coffees, cappuccinos, lattes, and teas. Over time, I became an entirely different person with different dreams and goals, and with A.J.'s encouragement, I decided to pursue my dream. Thankfully, my education came from academic scholarships. If my parents footed the bill or I had student loans to pay, I would have completed my fellowship, received my medical license out of obligation, and been miserable my entire life. After dropping out of my first year of residency and relocating to Seattle, I started an intensive forty-eight-week culinary program, mentoring under a few of the city's finest. With A.J.'s financial investment, I was able to find the perfect property off of Puget Sound for my bistro. The restaurant became my life.

I knew my family worried about me. Lesser people would have disowned me, but despite the hurt I've put them through, they've shown me nothing but unconditional love. They haven't asked for much in return except to maintain a consistent and ongoing relationship with me. I admire them more than anyone in the world.

But now they need *my* help, and I can no longer be selfish or scared.

I smile when I pull up to the ranch-style, canary yellow house. Shifting my car into park, I step out to stretch and then grab two large suitcases out of the trunk. Making my way up the sidewalk, I look around as the first waves of nostalgia hit me. Mom's azaleas are blooming nicely in her stairwell planter. I scrunch my nose in disdain at the rosebushes planted in the exact spot where a large oak tree once stood. As I sit down on the cold cement step, I visualize the big trunk and large branches as if they are reaching out to embrace me in a welcome home hug. I was devastated when Dad told me he cut it down. The tree was more than the foundation to my treehouse; it was my entertainment and my imagination, but most of all, my sanctuary. I can recall the days Vicky and I spent in that tree as if it were yesterday.

• • •

"You bring up the blankets, Jessie," Vicky yelled from the top. "I have clothespins."

I cupped my hand around my mouth and shouted up to her. "What about the umbrellas? Mom said it's going to rain soon."

"I already have them and the bag of candy and pop."

I hoisted the blankets over my shoulder, holding onto them with one hand while climbing the rope ladder with the other. Breathing heavily, I crawled through the open wood slat into the treehouse.

"Just in time." My sister wrinkled her nose, pointing down the street. "Pull the ladder up. I don't want them here."

I looked past her finger to see Tyson and Zane riding bikes toward our house. Although I don't know the reason why Vicky doesn't want them here, I gathered the rope quickly, pulling one hand over the other to bring the ladder up before they arrived. Usually, we didn't mind playing with Tyson and his younger brother Zane. We've known them forever. They were practically our best friends. I think Tyson even had a crush on Vicky. However, there was something in my sister's voice. The nervous tension behind her frown told me she did not want them here. I chose to follow her command.

"Come on Vic! Jessica!" Tyson called from the base of the tree. "Let the ladder down. I want up."

Vicky's face turned red. "No!"

"Don't call me Jessica!" I snapped before turning back to her. "I thought you liked him," I whispered.

She gave me a dirty look. "I did, until yesterday."

"What happened yesterday?"

"Nothing. You're too young to worry about it."

I hated when Vicky used her age against me. I was only eleven, almost twelve, but I was just as smart as she was, even though she was fourteen. Her boobs were bigger than mine, but that didn't mean I was stupid. I saw how the boys looked at her. One day when Sam's friends were over, I overheard the things they were saying about her through the heat vent in my room, which was right above his. Though Sam claimed to hate both of us, he was a protective older brother and quickly shut them up. And Vicky, well, she wasn't dumb either. She knew how they talked about her. Her cheeks always turned a blotchy pink color when they came around.

Tyson pleaded for a few more minutes before he and Zane grew tired and took off on their bikes. Afterward, I noticed Vicky's hands shake when she popped the tab of a pop.

"What's wrong with you?" I asked.

"Nothing," she said sharply.

I watched as tears fell from her eyes, landing on the top of her aluminum can.

• • •

I blink to erase the memory and rub my eyes with the palms of my hands. I *do not* want to go here. Cracking my knuckles, I stand and poke the doorbell. Some may find it strange that I do not walk into my parent's house. Due to my lack of presence in their home for this long, it feels disrespectful.

My father answers the door in his moccasin slippers, sweatpants, and as usual, unbuttoned shirt. He wraps me in a long, tight hug. I swallow my emotions and cling to him. If all men in the world were like him, maybe I would not have so much bitterness in my soul. When he finally releases me, he steps an arms width away and nods his approval before returning to his recliner.

I leave my suitcases by the front door and walk through the large living room into the kitchen where I find my mother hard at work on the evening's dinner. She prides herself in taking care of her family. When her children left home, she continued to make a meal every night for her husband.

My parents, Libby and Mel Cody, have been married over forty years now. They have been the most excellent example of love, marriage, and family. The issues I have are not because of them. I realize I am probably as resilient and emotionally stable as I am because of the upbringing and security they gave me. Without them, who knows what or where I would be?

Mom stands casually at the sink rinsing dishes. With her long, silvery hair tied into a bun at the base of her neck, she stares aimlessly out the kitchen window as the blazing sun melts against the earth. I lean against the door frame and listen to her hum a familiar tune as she places a glass in the dish rack. I admire how young and vibrant she still looks, despite what she is going through. When I was younger, I wanted to be just like her. A part of me still does.

My parents provided me with a spectacular childhood. I find it rare for people to look back on their life with the ability to say it was great, let alone spectacular! In my experience, however challenging the last thirteen years have been, it's true.

While there is a slew of memories I have refused to dwell on, as I was driving home earlier, I found myself eagerly anticipating having a meal with *my* parents, in *my* house just like we used to. It might be old-fashioned, but our family meals continue to be relevant to me. On Fridays, we were allowed to have slumber parties and pizza. Saturdays we always came together to eat, no matter our activities or what was going on around town. Family came first. After, we were allowed to go roller skating, to the movies, birthday parties or hang out with friends. When I was young, I found it silly because we *always* had dinner together. During the week we would have chipped beef on toast, tuna casserole, meatloaf, spaghetti, or tacos. On Saturdays, the meals were extraordinary. Dad grilled steaks, and Mom would make a special potato surprise, which was always different. Sometimes she made scallops, or homemade French fries, or twice baked potatoes, or my favorite, cheesy mashed.

I smile at the absurd, yet simplistic evenings they were. The smoke from the drippings off the grill would drift from the back porch into the house and invade my nose, even when I hid under my tent of blankets. My sister and brother were huddled on the floor by the entertainment center arguing over who was going to change channels on the cable box. My dad with a cold beer in his hand, was stationed on the kitchen floor listening to country music. He was talking to my mom about his day while she cooked, swaying her hips from side to side, and singing along to the chorus of her favorite songs. I remember stealing glances from under my tent, enamored at the way my father grinned as she moved. I would burst into a fit of giggles when he jumped up, sweeping her into his arms to spin her around the room. I loved hearing her laughter and always thought one day a man was going to love me like that.

When we finally sat down to dinner, Dad would switch the television off but played the record player. To this day, I am soothed with comforting memories every time I hear Kenny Rogers, George Strait, or Willie Nelson on the radio. At the same time, it fills me with a sense of deep longing for the life I lost at eighteen. It's something I'm not willing to admit out loud, but I continue to crave it in the depths of my soul and won't stop searching until I find it again.

"Hi, Mom." I kiss her cheek as I wrap my arms around her waist.

"Oh, darling!" she exclaims, spinning around to hug me. She takes my hands in hers, steps back, her eyes shining with love the same way Dad's had. "You're gorgeous! You haven't changed a bit since our trip. By the way, your brother showed me how to download the pictures. I'll show you later this evening."

Although I don't come home, my parents always visited me. Two to three times a year, they travel the ten hours from Helena to Seattle to see their selfish daughter who refuses to acknowledge her previous life. I adore my parents and cherish our time together. As a token of my gratitude, I took them on an Alaskan cruise last summer. It was a dream of my father's, and luckily, I was in a financial position to make it happen. Despite the trip and all the other times we got together throughout the year, I still fight feelings of regret, especially now.

"How's A.J.?" my mother asks casually, pulling three plates out of the cupboard and setting them on the counter.

"Good. Working hard as always," I say, reaching around her to grab an apple from the fruit bowl.

Playfully, she slaps my hand.

"Dinner's in a half-hour," she scolds, turning back to the stove to stir what looks like a pot of gravy.

I sniff the air.

"Thought I smelled your chicken fried steak."

I bite into the apple as I walk into the living room. I ruffle my dad's hair as I pass the recliner. He grumbles lightheartedly in response. I take in the changes my parents have made as I walk through the house, pulling my suitcase behind me. Things have virtually remained the same except for different paint color and new carpet in the living room. The cherrywood dining table is covered with a burgundy runner, a vase of flowers accenting the middle with a votive of candles on each side. The built-in buffet that leads to the kitchen continues to house the beautiful wedding and anniversary crystals my mother has collected over the years. Despite having grandchildren, the new furniture they bought my senior year of high school has held up considerably well. The old appliances seem to be in mint condition, except for my father's television.

"When are you going to get a flat-screen?" I ask, walking down the hall.

"When I can't get any reception out of this one," Dad chuckles.

"That was about five years ago, wasn't it?" I call over my shoulder.

Smiling, I enter my old bedroom, but I stop short. I'm not sure what I was expecting. Maybe I wanted it to look as it did the day I left for college with pink walls, 90s band posters plastering every square inch of surface, stuffed animals hanging from the net above my bed, and piles of clothes scattered on the floor. When my parents visit, they bring boxes of personal belongings, so I guess I should have assumed the child who once occupied the room would no longer be detected. Although I can't blame my parents, it still makes me sad. I had to do what was needed to cope, and so did they.

I pull my cell phone out of my purse and dial A.J.'s number.

"Hey," I whisper.

"Hey, Babe," she replies in her soothing voice. "How was the drive?"

"Long. Dreadful. My anxiety was high."

"I would imagine. How are your parents?"

"Dad looks frail. Mom, perky and giddy," I laugh. "I just got here and thought I'd give you a call before dinner. I haven't had a chance to chat with them much. I'll find out more as the evening wears on, I'm sure."

I put her on speakerphone so I can listen to her tell me about work while I slip out of my jeans and into a pair of sweat pants. As I pull a pair of warm socks onto my feet, I hear my mother say dinner will be ready in five minutes. I promise to call A.J. tomorrow with more details on my dad.

After hanging up, I notice a kink in my lower back, a result from the long drive. Standing, I stretch my arms over my head and groan. I slowly reach over to touch my toes. Hanging upside down with my head between my knees, I catch a glimpse of three picture frames on the bottom corner bookshelf. It's our senior pictures. Sam, in his letter jacket, standing beside his orange Corvette. Vicky is in her volleyball jersey, carelessly holding the ball. I am in my cheerleading uniform, pom-poms in hand, class of 1996 scrawled in white letters across the megaphone I lean on.

Crouching down, I sit cross-legged on the floor to get a closer look. You can see the happy innocence radiating through my smile. Who could have predicted it would change in a matter of months?

It's Vicky's face I can't peel my eyes away from. I notice a distance in her hazel green eyes, a secret sadness she kept hidden. As resentment slowly makes its way into my heart, I still can't help but wonder why, and I know I may never receive a satisfactory answer to this question.

• • •

My uneasiness decreases when I join my parents for dinner. I feel as though I am teenager again when I am eating my mother's delicious cooking in my childhood home. I have the hopes and dreams of a young girl with the world and future at my fingertips. It's like nothing bad ever happened.

Dad tells me about his buddies at the coffee shop. It's the same group of guys he used to bowl and play softball with when I was a kid. They are now in their mid-to-late sixties. Most of them don't have the energy to bowl, and softball is something they watch their grandchildren play. Although they don't have the stamina for late nights, they meet at the coffee shop every morning, enjoying their retirement. They spend two to three hours talking politics and sports, and reminiscing over old hunting and fishing tales.

When Dad finishes talking, Mom tells me about Sam.

"He and Jillian finally moved out to the ranch a few months back."

"About time," Dad comments dryly. "It's ridiculous how long the renovations took."

My mother gives him a stern look. "Admit it-you loved having them here. But it was time for our own space," she adds with a sly grin. "Four months is a long time with those kids underfoot. We just aren't used to all that commotion anymore."

My older brother Sam was a jerk when we were growing up. He picked on me and Vicky ruthlessly. Now that we are adults, I couldn't ask for a better sibling. I was twelve when he left to attend college in Bozeman to study criminal justice. By the time I graduated high school, he was a full-fledged sheriff's deputy and engaged to Jillian. Now they have two kids. Tanner, their son, just turned ten, and Kelsey, their daughter, is close to eight. I adore my niece and nephew, but I wish I could see them more often. Although they openly disagree with my decision to stay away and have tried unsuccessfully to get me to change my mind, Sam and Jillian continue to offer emotional support. They are always willing to meet half-way each summer for a week of camping, hiking, and boating, and modern technology gives us middle-ground. I can have a somewhat connected relationship with all four of them through e-mail, Skype, and text messaging.

"Is he still talking about getting horses?" I ask, pouring ketchup over my potatoes.

"Already has them," Dad says with a chuckle. "And I'll be damned if you can get those kids off them on the weekends."

I am not surprised by this news. Growing up, Sam's first love was horses. Since we lived inside city limits, we were not allowed to own any. Fortunately, he had many friends who lived on ranches. In his spare time, Sam learned how to ride, rope, and train baby colts. Now, next to upholding the law, it continues to be a passion he wants to pass on to his children.

Mom and Dad take turns telling me the "who is what" and "what is who" of extended family and friends, while I grow more and more relaxed in their presence. After dinner, Dad gratefully goes back to his recliner and *Jeopardy!* while I clear the table. Alone with my mother, I finally have a chance to broach the topic of what brought me home.

"How is he feeling? And don't tell me he's great. I can see for myself how much weight he's lost. If you don't tell me the truth, I'll call Wilk myself."

With a half-hearted smile, Mom pats my arm.

"His spirits are good as you can see. But he's deteriorating fast." Tears fill her eyes as she sighs. "It's surreal. I mean, five months ago, he was as strong as an ox. Our trip to Alaska…" she drifts off. "I just don't get it."

Wrapping my arms around her shoulders, I pull her close.

"I'm not only here for him, you know. I'm here for you, too. I wish you would have told me sooner."

I could tell from the tone of her voice on the phone last month that something was wrong, but she wouldn't budge no matter how much I pried. Unable to shake the uneasy feeling, I called Sam the moment we hung up. He broke the news that Dad had cancer. He was evasive when I asked more questions. Determined to have answers, I called Dr. Wilkinson myself. He'd been our family doctor as well as Dad's best friend/poker playing/beer drinking/and hunting buddy for as long as I could remember. As a friend who was more like family, he had no problem giving it to me straight.

"It started in his prostate. It's spread to his lymph nodes and stomach. He's refusing treatment, and I have to tell you; I don't blame him. We caught it too late. His oncologist says there is not much treatment will do at this stage of the game. It is best to make him comfortable and happy while you can. Come home, Jessie. Your mom is going to need help."

Wilk, as my dad calls him, doesn't have a clue why I never return. No one does. I'm sure, despite the excuses Mom and Dad give, relatives and friends have witnessed how they jump through hoops for their self-centered daughter who doesn't seem to care enough about her aging parents to visit them.

Placing her hand on my cheek, my mom's eyes, full of gratitude, bore into mine.

"You always were a sneaky little one," she laughs, shaking her head. "I could not put you in that position, Jessie. Don't get me wrong. I'm over the moon that you are here, but I also know…"

"It's okay." Pulling away, I start to load the dishwasher. "How's Vic?" I dare to ask.

Again, Mom sighs. "She knows you're here."

I nod. "I would imagine. Sam tell her?"

"Yes."

"Did she say anything to you?"

"Just that she hopes to see you."

My shoulders tense. I haven't seen or spoken to my sister since I was eighteen years old. It's for the best. At least, that's what I convinced myself.

"She comes over a few times a week to sit with your dad. They read together, watch old World War II movies or M*A*S*H reruns. She drags him with her to pick the kids up from school once in a while. When they return, they have root beer floats or strawberry shortcake. She always was a daddy's girl, you know. This is hard for her."

I'm not sure how to respond.

Once again, my mom turns her attention out the kitchen window staring at the silhouette of the street lamp. A moment later, she wipes her hands on a dishtowel and clears her throat. "How long can you stay?" she asks.

"As long as you need me."

I see her eyes widen suspiciously.

"Employing great staff is a part of owning a great business. Phillip will run the front of the house, the kitchen can practically run itself, and A.J. is helping out. They'll be fine. If I need to make a trip back once in a while, I can. I'll do all the major business stuff from here on my laptop."

I see my mom struggle not to break down with relief. A part of me wants to hold her, to tell her to let it all out. She doesn't have to be the strong one anymore. For once, I can do it for her. But another part of me wants to escape. I'm not ready for any of this. On the drive here, I tried to prepare myself for the multitude of complex emotions I was about to face. At this moment, standing in the kitchen next to my mother talking about her husband—my father—dying, I cannot dig deep enough to find the strength I know she needs from me. Once again, I feel like a failure.

"What do you want to do tonight?" she asks, composing herself. "How about a movie? We can walk to the theatre. Your dad does okay for a few blocks as long as he can relax after. It's a beautiful evening out."

Instant panic leaves me speechless. Thinking about leaving the confines of this house terrifies me in a way I cannot comprehend or explain to her.

She senses my uncertainty. "We can hang out here and start a puzzle. We haven't done the one you gave us for Christmas last year," she suggests.

"That sounds great," I agree, sighing with relief.

• • •

Later that night, as I lay in the bed I grew up in, staring at the same ceiling I stared at numerous times, I listen through the open window to the reassuring sounds of nature. I hope they lull me to sleep. Still, I can't shut my mind off as the whirlwind of events from previous years continue to plague my thoughts as if taunting me to react. I try counting sheep. I try stretching. I even get out of bed for a glass of warm milk. Nothing works.

I consider calling A.J. but, she's asleep. It's not that she won't answer, but when I left, things were a bit awkward between us. Granted, it's her nature to be as helpful as possible, but she can be relentless in her attempts to fix me. I need her to be my girlfriend, not my therapist, especially about the topic that occupies my mind. How can I say to her, "I wonder what my life would have been like if...?"

As a young girl with a very vivid imagination, I daydreamed about getting married. We had an old, worn-out wedding dress shoved in the cedar chest with other childhood dress-up clothes. Lord knows how many times Vicky and I argued over who was going to be the bride, and who got stuck in one of Dad's old ties, pretending to be the groom. We spent hours pasting magazine cutouts into an old spiral notebook, planning our special days. We cut out everything from pictures of flowers to table centerpieces, wedding dresses, brides-maids dresses, and tuxedos. We made lists of songs for our dance playlist. As a teenage girl, my head was in the clouds full of romantic notions. I envisioned my marriage being one people could write songs about.

It is funny how dreams you've had your whole life can change at the drop of a hat. In college, marriage was the last thing on my mind. *Dating* was the last thing on my mind. I was content being single, although I did go through a destructive sexual phase in my early twenties. I didn't particularly like sex, but I had a lot of it. I wanted the power my sexuality gave me. My philosophy: screw them before they screw you, hurt them before you get hurt, and don't ever, *ever* put your heart on the line. I went through men, not like underwear, but more like a carton of eggs, one every few weeks. The free dinners, concerts, Chicago Bears and Chicago Cubs games were just an added perk. I enjoyed the dates, the attention, the drinks, and the drugs. It kept me from thinking or feeling.

I wasn't doing myself any favors. I was twenty-three when my roommate told me she was embarrassed to go to the pub with me. She said guys automatically assumed she was an easy pick-up because she was my friend. It became clear I had a bad reputation and significant issues.

I decided to try the relationship thing hoping that settling down would help me become *me* again, but quickly realized I didn't have what it took for commitment. Kenny, a personal trainer, complained that I was disconnected, drank too much, was unaffectionate and a "dead fish in bed." After six months, he found contentment and solace in the arms of another girl from the gym. Donovan, a fresh young attorney with political ambitions, tried unsuccessfully to mold me into what he deemed would be the perfect side kick and he, too, had a handful of extracurricular sexual activities on the side. It fizzled out fast. Then I met Joel, a sensitive, nurturing nurse at the hospital where I interned. He was sweet, compassionate, devoted, and adored me. We hit it off through our love of music, movies, books, and our mutual snarky sense of humor.

While I cared about him, something was missing. I could say I "sort of" loved him but wasn't as attracted to him as much as he thought I should be. He complained that I kept a thick, unbreakable wall between us. Sex made me uncomfortable and panicky. I found myself avoiding intimacy, and I became depressed. I smoked extreme amounts of marijuana to cope with my shortcomings. My drinking became extreme. The longer we were together, the more I separated myself. Joel, the poor guy, could not understand what he was or wasn't doing right. I didn't even understand.

In a desperate attempt to prove I was committed to our relationship, I moved into his one-bedroom apartment. It didn't take long for our dysfunctional interactions to bring out his dark side. If I had to guess, I think his anger was a part of his personality he struggled with even before me. Maybe our weaknesses are what drew us together.

After we had been out celebrating a friend's graduation from the University of Illinois, he hit me for the first time. We'd both had too much to drink and hadn't had sex for about five weeks. The moment we walked through the front door of our apartment, he pounced on me, his hands roughly shoving my skirt over my hips as he pressed my back against the wall. Although I typically cringed my way through sex, I was terrified by the rank smell of beer on his breath, combined with his aggressive behavior when he pawed at my underwear.

I shoved him away. Before I knew what happened, the force of his fist on the side of my cheek knocked me into the couch. Between the shock of getting hit and the buzz I had from drinking all night, I hardly realized it when he stormed out of the apartment.

The next day, full of apologies and "I love yous," he presented me with a two-carat diamond engagement ring. For a brief moment, I had the sweet, caring Joel back in my life. Deep down, I knew it was all a façade. I wore the ring because I loved it more than I loved him. I had no intention of getting married. I knew it was deceitful, even morally wrong, but for some reason, I could not be honest with him. We continued to play the game, cohabitating together for another six months. However, once a month or so, there were similar incidences. When I was not in the mood for his sexual advances, he became irate, pulled my hair, slapped me and called me horrible names. I was easy to throw around because I am petite and small-boned. He knew I was too submissive and scared to fight back.

I hated freezing, not standing up for myself. Most of all, I hated Joel. He was no longer "poor Joel" in my eyes. There was a temperamental volcano bubbling deep within me. It scared the hell out of me. At the same time, it began to awaken a part of me I didn't realize was there. The more Joel pushed, the angrier I became.

Thankfully, leaving him was not a dramatic production. I woke up one morning, decided I needed to move out and take control of my life. I didn't want to do something we would both regret. I packed what little I owned, changed my cell number, and moved in with another intern until I found a place of my own. Ironically, Joel never bothered me again. From that point on, I planned on living my life for myself. I was tired of feeling weak, like a pathetic doormat everyone could walk on. I was done with men. I despised every single one of them, *and* I was definitely done with sex. I started running to help with my anxiety and stopped smoking pot. When I did drink, it was only socially.

The next year, I put everything I had into getting through school. I lived, slept, breathed, and dreamt of the lectures, my monthly rotations in the E.R., general surgery, internal medicine, pediatrics, and OB/GYN. It's what I thought I was supposed to do, or probably even meant to do. Once again, like all the relationships I'd been in, I was going through the motions to become successful, but my heart and spirit weren't into it.

And I certainly hadn't planned on A.J. She morphed into my life and my heart when I least expected it.

Although she and I had never officially met, we'd heard enough about one another to feel like old friends when Phillip, our mutual friend, finally introduced us. By that point, I was stronger, more confident, and way more independent than before. At twenty-six, I'd given up on the dream of marriage, the beautiful house, or the kids, and settled into my old-maid status. I was even considering getting a cat.

A.J. was bisexual although we joke about how she looked more like a "stereotypical" lesbian with her short spiky, platinum blond hair, strong jawline, and athletic build. She didn't strike me as the type guys were usually attracted to, but with her large, catlike green eyes, I found her very intriguing. She easily attracted both sexes due to her personality. Guys loved her spunk, her flirtatious nature, her charisma and knowledge of business and sports. Women, on the other hand, were drawn to her compassionate advice and gentle, mesmerizing voice. She looked into a person's eyes when she spoke to them, hanging on every word. She made everyone feel like they were the only person that existed.

I was excited to have a new friend. It never occurred to me A.J. might find me attractive. We hung out the way I did with all my girlfriends. We shopped, went to dinner, frequented night clubs, and drank wine and margaritas. Things with A.J. were comfortable, and even though I told her I was not interested in a future with a man, I was pretty sure I made it clear I was straight.

One night over dinner, I confessed my lack of passion for becoming a surgeon and my secret dream of being a chef. She told me she had been offered a job at a firm in Seattle and asked if I was up for an adventure. She needed a roommate. Within a month, I quit school, moved, and started the culinary program.

A few months later, after a lively party at our apartment, we were cleaning up. While laughing and washing dishes together, I realized how lonely my life had been since age eighteen. Once I started living with A.J., the simple domestic things like cooking, buying groceries, and entertaining together was satisfying. It was the closest thing I'd had to a family in forever.

I felt drawn to A.J., and I couldn't deny the fact that she made me feel safe and content. She became my best friend and my confidant. Even though I had a variety of friends that I socialized with, I wasn't in the habit of allowing people close to me. It was different with A.J. She made it easy to share, and no matter what I wanted to do, she was supportive. She genuinely cared. In that moment of washing dishes with her, I found a spark of hope I had lost so many years before. The next thing I knew, she kissed me—and the rest was, as they say, history.

CHAPTER TWO

I squint against the bright rays of the sun. Warm light floods through the sheer polyester window drapes. Lost somewhere in my memories, I must have drifted off. It takes a moment to get my bearings. As I sit up and look around the room, I remember where I am. My heart slams against my chest as I wonder what the day will bring. Will I see my sister? Will I be able to leave the house? And if I do, who will I see?

Dressed in my favorite yoga pants and a loose T-shirt, I make my way to the breakfast nook, where I find my dad hovered over the newspaper with a cup of coffee. My mom is folding laundry while watching Matt Lauer interview Hillary Clinton on the *TODAY Show*.

"It may be nice to have a woman president one day. Don't you think, dear?" she asks me.

"Sure, but her?" I cringe.

"Better than that dimwitted Sarah Palin," Dad pipes in.

I laugh. "You weren't saying that when we were in Alaska. If I remember correctly, you thought trekking through the Alaskan wilderness with her might be quite enjoyable."

His face turns red. "Of course it would. Hunting, fishing, hiking—and she's not awful to look at, you know. But that doesn't mean I want her running our country."

"Well, then, it's a good thing she isn't running, isn't it?" my mother says, shoving an armful of folded towels at him.

He picks up his cup with his free hand and disappears down the hall into the bathroom.

My mother's eyes twinkle. "He can get quite ornery when he wants to," she says lightheartedly.

After pouring myself a bowl of cereal and a tall glass of orange juice, I join her at the small glass table tucked next to the bay window, in the corner of the kitchen. While she continues to listen to the daily news, my thoughts shift between the need to discuss Dad's care with her and the desire to map out a strategy for my life. It could turn topsy-turvy at any given moment. Instead, I chat about work, A.J., and Phillip, the simple things.

It was not easy telling my parents about A.J. Aside from running away thirteen years ago and my current status, it was one of the hardest things I've ever had to face. My family is my security and stability. They are the ones who loved me unconditionally despite the hell I put them through. How would I tell my family that I decided to be gay? Yes, I see my sexuality as a decision I made because I know I was not born homosexual. I spent too many years kissing my Eddie Vedder poster for practice and trying to convince my sister that Marky Mark was better looking than Jon Bon Jovi. Of course, there was Zane.

There is not some hereditary or DNA explanation for me. Maybe there is for others, but not me. Do I love A.J.? Of course. I can't say I necessarily want to be married to her, but that has nothing to do with the fact that she is a woman. I don't know if I want to be married to anyone. A lifetime commitment is no longer part of my plan. Either way, I'm not looking for anything or anyone different. I'm perfectly content where I am. I don't know if my halfhearted explanation is politically correct. I certainly will not win any activism awards, but for me, it works.

Well, it used to work, I remind myself, remembering the last few months.

I struggled with "coming out of the closet." I wanted to keep the dynamics of my relationship with A.J. a secret. I didn't know how to answer questions that were bound to come up. A.J. was patient with me. Eventually, I knew I had to give our relationship the respect it deserved.

My parents handled it better than expected. For the most part, they like A.J. She is an all-around easy-going person. My parents, as always, never criticized or judged, although I'm sure they had their unspoken concerns. It took Sam a little bit longer to come to terms, but he didn't make us feel ashamed. Given the fact that I had no contact with anyone from my past or hometown, it was easy to live my life without too much scrutiny.

"Is Phillip still dating that Rebecca girl we met last spring?" my mother asks, tossing a handful of folded dishtowels into a kitchen drawer.

"No. Rebecca moved to Ireland."

"What on earth is in Ireland?"

"An internship," I explain.

"Poor Phillip. Is he heartbroken?"

I chuckle, holding another spoonful of cereal up to my mouth. "Nah. You know Phillip. He's onto his next conquest. But he's been a bit private about this one."

Phillip and I met nine years ago. Feeling restless and bored with my college courses, I decided to take a baking class the University offered. I immediately fell in love with the art as well as my cooking partner. We both knew it was a platonic, sibling type of love. We've been inseparable friends since. Phillip was always a helpful voice of support and strength during my failed relationships. I watched him move from one emotionally unstable female to another more times than I cared to count. Two years after we met, our bond became stronger than ever when a motorcycle accident left him with a broken collar bone and a shattered knee. During recovery, when he was unable to cook, he became depressed and addicted to his pain medication. After getting fired from the head chef position at The Boiler Room, one of Chicago's finest dining establishments, I convinced him to check into Rehab. Phillip did a four-month in-patient program and has been clean and sober since. It didn't take much to bribe him to move to Seattle, where the three of us worked together to open the bistro. Phillip is the best manager I could ask for, and I'd trust him with my life. I never questioned leaving my baby in his hands when I decided to come home.

"What's on the agenda for today?" I ask, rinsing my bowl and placing it in the dishwasher. "Do we need to sit down and go over anything concerning Dad?"

Sadly, Mom shakes her head. "He has another oncology appointment on Friday. I'm heading to the grocery store later. Other than that, just typical daily chores around the house. I want to get the spare room in the basement cleaned out and painted. You can help me with that."

"The cleaning or the painting?"

"Just the cleaning for now. I need to go to the hardware store later this week and pick out paint. I brought some swatches home a few weeks back. You can help me decide on a color."

I welcome the idea of a project that will keep my body and mind busy while confined to the house. The thought of stepping out the front door horrifies me. Eventually, I will have to face going out in public, but today is not the day.

I follow my mother to the spare room downstairs. What had once been Sam's bedroom is now packed with a plethora of toys, a baby crib, a rocking chair, and boxes upon boxes of old clothes and shoes. I feel a slight twinge in my heart as I look around. Even though I wasn't here, I can envision my nieces and nephews as babies sleeping in this crib. Although I've never met Vicky's three kids, Mom always sends photos. From what I can tell, the six-year-old twin girls, Shelby and Sasha look just like Vicky with her curly auburn hair and hazel eyes. Her nine-year-old son Shane is the spitting image of his father. I wonder if my children would use the old oak crib if things were different.

"Look at all these!" I exclaim, kneeling to open up the pink Barbie case.

Inside are old Barbie Dolls. Vicky and I spent countless hours dressing them, fixing their hair and sending them on dates with Sam's G.I. Joes. I carry the case out to the sofa in the recreation room where I begin to paw through it, laughing as I do. I find my favorite metallic blue ball gown, the fluorescent green swimsuit, and all the shoes and accessories to match. Vicky was meticulous about organizing their wardrobe. She got angry with me when a shoe or hairpiece came up missing. In my disaster of a room, I could not find a darn thing, so she insisted we only play in her room where she could keep things neat and tidy.

Looking over my shoulder, I see my mother frantically packing more boxes and hauling them up the stairs.

"Are you taking those to the thrift store?" I ask when she returns.

"They're just old clothes. Out of style, out of date. No one here will ever wear them again."

"I'll help you."

Reaching for an open box, I cringe when I notice some of my old possessions lying on the top of the pile. There is the leopard skin vest and pale pink bodysuit I begged Mom to buy me to wear to my first high school dance. It should have been thrown away the day I bought it. Instead, I practically wore it out. I grin as I pick up the stack of flannel shirts. I am not ashamed to admit that I would still tie one around my waist with a pair of cut-off jeans and hiking boots.

"You are supposed to be packing, not unpacking," My mom says, playfully.

I continue to search through clothes until I reach the bottom of the pile where I find a little red and white bandana. Picking it up, I caress the rough-textured material between my thumb and index finger, and become flooded with memories.

• • •

"Vicky! Wait for me! Where are you going?"

I peddled as fast as I could to catch up, but Vicky was at least a block ahead of me. I saw her bike tires and the red and white bandana tied around her head, waving in the wind.

"Go home!" She yelled over her shoulder. "I'm meeting Tyson. You can't come."

Discouraged, I turned my bike around and rode home. It seemed like Vicky and Tyson were together all the time, and it sucked. I missed her. She was so different, more grown-up, and moody. She never wanted to play Barbies anymore and hardly climbed into the treehouse with me. She started wearing mascara and lip gloss and argued with Mom about her clothes almost every day. Mom said they were too tight, and boys would get the wrong impression of her. Vicky said she wanted to be popular more than anything, and claimed her friends dressed this way.

One night, Mom caught her sneaking out of the house after she was supposed to be in bed. She had four of Dad's beers in her backpack, and one of the *Playboy* magazine's Sam had stashed under his mattress. I have no idea what Mom said to her while they sat in her room for hours. When she emerged, she told me she was grounded for two weeks.

I was sitting in the treehouse by myself with an open book in my hand and a bag of chips on my lap. I heard a car pull up and two doors slam. Peeking over the wood slats, I saw Tyson's red Chevy Cavalier parked in front of our house. He'd bought it last month when he turned sixteen with the money he saved working on his grandparents' ranch.

"Hey!" I shouted as he and Zane walked toward the front door. "Up here!"

I threw down the ladder and watched as they climbed up one at a time. Wiping my orange hands on my jeans, I shifted my position to make room for them.

"Where's Vic?" Tyson asked as soon as his head popped through the floor opening.

"She took off on her bike to meet you," I said.

Zane grabbed my bag of chips and shoved a handful into his mouth while I stuck my tongue out at him.

"Zane and I've been at Landry's farm loading hay all day. We got off about fifteen minutes ago. We wanted to see what you two were doing tonight."

My stomach tightened into a knot. This wasn't the first time this had happened. Maybe I was the only one paying attention, but it seemed there were an awful lot of instances when Vicky said she was going somewhere with him, only to find out that Tyson did not know where she was. Maybe she was seeing someone behind his back, but she adored him, and I couldn't believe she was capable of dating anyone else.

"Oh, well I'm sure she'll be back in a little bit then," I explained.

"You going to the carnival?" Zane mumbled as chips sputtered out of his mouth.

I shrugged. "Thinking about it. You?"

"Dad's taking us," Zane replied. "Guess some country band is performing. He's going to announce them. You know, 'big Ron Stecks' needs to make sure everyone sees his boys and his doting wife hanging on his every word, proud to be a part of his family."

The sarcasm dripped from his words. It wasn't a secret that Zane didn't like his dad.

Tyson watched the street for any sign of Vicky, while Zane and I discussed the rides at the carnival. After fifteen minutes, Vicky still wasn't home. The boys stuck around for another half hour. After reassuring Tyson that we would meet them downtown around eight, they left, and I went inside to help Mom with dinner.

Dad was gone again. As an Insurance Adjuster, he traveled a lot and hated it. Mom hated it too, and all of us kids, we hated it even more. For as long as I can remember, he worked at the credit union. When something happened with the economy two years ago, he was laid off. He took this stupid job, and Mom went back to school to get her teaching degree. She had another year left of college, and until she was able to get a job, he was stuck on the road, gone for three or four days at a time, two or three times a month.

When I asked about Vicky, Mom told me she was babysitting for the Wheelers'. If that was the case, why didn't she tell me the truth? It's not like I would have followed her. I hated the Wheeler kids. Five-year-old Ethan had a never-ending runny nose. It attracted every dirt particle that flew through the air, and his sister Allie was a back-talking second grader. She thought she was smarter than me just because she was in advanced math, already learning fractions. No thanks.

I was watching *Beverly Hills 90210* when I heard the front door slam around seven-thirty. Mom peeked around the corner of the kitchen, hoping it was Dad, not hiding her disappointment when she saw Vicky.

"I didn't expect you for another hour or so."

"They got home early," Vicky grumbled, hanging her head low.

She darted past me to her room. I could tell she wasn't in the mood for company, but I didn't care. I was always a persistent kid, and I wanted answers. I was upset she lied to me, and besides that, I wanted to meet Tyson and Zane at the carnival.

Without knocking, I burst into her room. With her back to me, Vicky's shirt was over her head. The small red bruises and scrapes on her spine made me gasp.

"Get out of here, you little shit!" she yelled, frantically pulling her shirt down. "I'll kick your ass if you don't get out."

Her face was a shade of red similar to the small abrasions on her back.

"What happened? Why didn't you tell me you were babysitting?"

Between clenched teeth, Vicky's growl was deep. "I told you to leave. Did you hear me?"

I was scared. I'd never seen Vicky this upset before. Even her hands were shaking, and I saw tears in her eyes.

"Jesus, what's wrong with you?"

In her anger, she picked up her backpack and threw it at me. I caught it midair before it hit my head. I watched the red and white bandana fall to the floor. When I bent over to retrieve it, it was covered in dirt and straw and smelled like stale cigarette smoke.

My eyes grew wide. "Where were you? Were you smoking?"

"None of your damn business! I swear if you breathe a word of this to Mom, I will tell her about you stealing twenty dollars out of her purse to go to the movies with Zane when you were supposed to be at his grandma's branding. Now get the hell out!" she screamed, slamming the door in my face.

• • •

I feel my mom's hand on my shoulder, jolting me back to reality.

"You okay?" she asks.

With a nod, I force a smile.

I spend the next three hours packing boxes, tearing off wallpaper and cleaning out the closet. It is good physical work, but it doesn't stop my mind from wandering. Vicky hadn't talked to me for almost two weeks after that episode. As she asked, I did not mention a word to anyone. I wonder how many times over the last thirteen years, I regretted that decision.

It came as no surprise when at fifteen, Vicky and Tyson started going steady. It was even less surprising that Zane harbored a secret crush on me and vice versa. It was a secret because he was a player and had a reputation to uphold with his friends. There was no way I was going to risk our friendship or act as stupid as other girls who fell over their feet for the slightest bit of attention from him.

Even though he spent years teasing me mercilessly while we were growing up, I knew it was all in fun. I had thick skin, and besides, after school and on weekends, he was *my* best friend. We rode bikes to the swimming pool almost daily during the summer. We spent endless hours in the treehouse, burning up batteries on my portable tape player listening to eighties hair bands. Likewise, in junior high, we continued our private friendship but hung out in separate cliques while at school.

As we transitioned into high school, I fell in love with Zane. But I'd rot in hell before I'd ever tell him. Zane dated a different girl every few months, and none of them were serious. I hated the jealousy that came over me each time I saw him walking down the hall holding hands with his latest fling. Dawn Kilwicky was one of my best friends and the only one besides Vicky who knew I had a crush on him. When Zane and Dawn started dating, I stopped talking to her altogether. Zane never showed any interest in me other than friendship. Although I heard rumors some of the guys on the football team wanted to ask me out, not one of them had the guts to ask. According to Vicky, it was Zane's doing. One time, he found out I made out with Joshua Cline at a graduation party. Joshua showed up at school with a black eye the following week and never spoke to me again.

Tyson and Zane were popular, but others found them intimidating. I never really understood the intimidation part. I knew how kind and sincere both boys were. They hated to see people hurt and stuck up for the underdog at school. They had decent grades, but were suspended on several occasions for fighting. I saw why people did not want to be on the receiving end of their anger. They were big ranch boys, after all. They were solid, strong, and quick-tempered when pushed too far. People knew better than to mess with them, but on several occasions, an arrogant, cocky jock felt he had something to prove by picking on a smaller kid. It usually didn't turn out too well for the other guy when Zane or Tyson got involved.

The boys had demons of their own they suffered from. Their parents were Ron and Joan Stecks. They lived in our subdivision before we moved there. My mom used to joke if we were Mormon, Ron would be known as the neighborhood patriarch. He was the husband all women admired, had the job other men envied, and was the father all kids wanted to have. When in public, Ron and Joan linked their fingers together, he complimented her, bought her gifts, and bragged about his family. He coached the boys' baseball teams, he ran the Boy Scout Troop as the Leader, and enjoyed playing games with the neighborhood children.

Ron was the son of one of the wealthiest ranchers in the state but opted to go to college instead of staying home to ranch. When he eventually moved back to Helena, he opened and ran a successful sporting goods business. He intended the boys to take it over when he retired. As far as we knew, Joan never worked. She was a bit of a mystery to everyone and was often the subject of small-town gossip.

My parents were polite and friendly toward Ron and Joan. I wouldn't consider them close friends, but acquaintances. I don't ever remember my mother having Joan over for tea. We did not bake them a plate of holiday cookies, and though we were always invited, we didn't attend their New Year's Eve parties. My father loved to call Ron a "Sunday Christian." They respect-fully socialized at summer picnics and festivals in the park and even shook hands in church. But Dad, who rarely said a negative word about anyone, couldn't find a decent thing to say about the guy. Mom couldn't stand Ron. She said he was too flirtatious, with a fake charm. Strangely though, everyone else seemed to adore him.

Mom and Dad were right. I learned Ron was Dr. Jekyll and Mr. Hyde. Behind closed doors, he was overly critical and controlling, drank too much, and had impossible expectations of his sons. The expec-tations had severe consequences when the boys failed to meet them.

I was in fourth grade the first time I saw the welts on Tyson's back at the swimming pool. Tyson was fair-skinned with red hair and freckles. He always wore a tank top with his swimming trunks. On that particular day, he and Zane started wrestling on the grass over ten dollars to buy fireworks. Tyson was on top of his little brother, torturing him by poking his fingers relentlessly into his chest until he said, "Uncle!" In an attempt to get away, Zane hiked his foot over Tyson's head, flipped and pinned him in a headlock. During this, Tyson's back was exposed. I drew in a shocking breath when I saw the ugly scars that crisscrossed over his shoulder blade. Immediately, the boys stopped fighting and, a clearly embarrassed Tyson quickly adjusted his shirt. I didn't say anything, especially since Vicky hadn't noticed. I waited until later in the evening when Zane and I were hiding in the treehouse. He confessed there were times their dad took a leather strap to them but said it was rare and only happened when they deserved it. Zane swore he did not have any marks like Tyson. I didn't believe him. After that day, there were times I noticed him limp when he walked and cringe as he fidgeted at his desk at school.

The older I was, the more obvious it became that the dynamics in their household were very different than the ones in my own. Both boys loved being at our house. Even my mom used to sense the apprehension in them when it was time to go home. Zane told me when they were with us, there was a comfort and acceptance they'd never experienced before. In their own house, there was unexplained tension, a stormy current of uncertainty the three lived with all the while keeping up the charade of a happy family.

They both had caught their dad on *many* occasions with *many* different female employees in the storage room of the store when they were working after school. Zane did not believe his dad knew what they'd witnessed, but each time it occurred, Zane needed to tell someone, and I seemed to be the only person he could confide in.

There was a point in my childhood when I felt bad for Joan, but by the time I turned sixteen, I realized she was fully aware of Ron's extramarital affairs but chose to turn a blind eye. From that point on, I pitied her. The boys, on the other hand, were extra protective of their mother and spent much of their time trying to make her happy despite her miserable marriage and lack of ability to protect them. In time, Zane and Tyson's fear began to turn into anger.

"You're awful quiet," my mother states, handing me a folded piece of cardboard.

I shape it into a box and tape the bottom.

"Just thinking."

"Good thoughts I hope," she says, handing me another stack of clothes.

"Yes and no. Just reminiscing."

It's been years since I've allowed my mind to wander back to my youth. I thought the memories would bring pain. Instead, I feel sentimental. As we stack the boxes into the back of my mom's vehicle, I smile, thinking of my best childhood friends and the adventures we shared.

• • •

I ordered a treadmill before I left Seattle. I am thrilled when it arrives the following morning. I'm desperate to run, but I'm not sure if I will ever be ready to leave the house. I plan to put the machine downstairs, use my iPod, and sweat out my frustrations every morning for a good six to eight miles. When I run, I try to escape the world's problems, not solve them. One of my goals is to run a marathon. I've trained off and on over the last three years; every time I get close to signing up for a race, I chicken out. Maybe this is a good time for me to set the goal again. Since I'm on a roll facing my fears, maybe I'll finally cross this one off my bucket list.

Dad is pouring himself another cup of coffee as I drift through the kitchen, feeling energized and alive after my run.

"Jesus, you're soaked. What did you do? Stand under the sprinkler in the back yard?" he laughs at his joke.

I can't help but giggle. My dad has the corniest sense of humor, but innocently a comical one.

"Just running," I say, reaching over him for my cup.

He ducks out of the way. "Ew, don't get that on me. Last time I sweat that hard was when I chased your Mom around the block when she refused to kiss me. Wasn't that last year, Lib?"

Just then, my mom appears around the corner. "Good grief, Mel. You've embarrassed her."

"It's true, and you know it. I'd chase you anywhere," Dad says, slapping my mom on the bottom.

It's not unusual to see my parents flirt this way. I saw this charming love as I grew up. It is endearing. Today's exchange tugs at my heartstrings. My parents have a love of all loves, the type of relationship other couples' envy. Their marriage endures the test of time and all the different bullshit life can throw. Here they are, forty-some years after saying "I do" and they still adore one another. But how much time do they have left together? I cannot imagine my parents living without the other one. Tears sting my eyes as my mom wraps her arms around my dad's neck, pulling him into a kiss. This illness is truly unfair. Sadly, I am reminded there isn't much in my life so far that has been fair.

As I shower, my good mood turns sour—it may be a combination of my father's ailing health and feeling cooped up for five days—and I know, sooner or later, I am going to have to venture out of the house. As happy as I am to have the treadmill, I miss running outside, breathing in the fresh air, and getting my daily dose of Vitamin D. Plus, I want to go to my dad's doctor appointment tomorrow.

I notice my sister hasn't brought the kids by. I wonder if this was previously arranged because of my presence. I've never met them in person. I don't know what they think of me or if they even know about me. It is obvious Dad misses their company. He is polite and does not say as much, but each time the phone rings or he hears a car engine outside, the leans forward in his navy blue recliner to glance out the picture window. This makes me feel guilty.

I continue to wallow in self-pity as I finish my laundry then curl up on the couch with a suspense novel. After an hour of flipping pages without retaining the words, I decide to talk to Mom about Vicky. Searching the house, I find her and Dad on the back patio. They are sitting on the porch swing holding hands as they watch birds eat out of the feeder hanging under the roof. They don't hear me approach, so I stay behind the screen door and watch her lay her head on my dad's shoulder. He caresses the back of her hand with his thumb. I don't even realize tears are streaming down my cheeks until the phone in my back pocket vibrates. Startled, I wipe my hand across my eyes and bolt for the back bedroom. Once I hear A.J.'s voice, I break down.

• • •

As we drive home, my mom informs me my dad's doctor appointment was typical. She and Dad are exhausted from the emotional buildup of the day. Even though he made a choice not to go through treatment, they hold on to a glimmer of hope the oncologist will tell them the tumor has disappeared. My mom believes in miracles, and they stay positive together through prayer and avoiding negative thoughts. Unfortunately, I don't see through rose-colored glasses the way my parents do. This world is a shitty place, and everyone has to face a raw deal at some point. I have mine and Vicky certainly has hers. This illness is my dad's raw deal. There are plenty of others out there who do not deserve the grace that God supposedly hands out, but my dad deserves heaven and earth.

We carry the morning events around with us like a heavy blanket for the remainder of the day. Mom disappears outside to dig in her garden, and Dad sits in his recliner half asleep. I lounge on the couch with my book. As much as I love my books and the fantastic distraction they are from reality, I soon grow bored and restless. When Dad is asleep, I sneak the remote out of his relaxed hand and scroll through the guide page. I don't watch TV much, but I hope to find a distracting movie. After ten minutes of disappointment, I replace the remote, give Dad a quick kiss on top of the head and venture to the back yard. My mother is kneeling in the dirt, clipping dead flowers and pulling weeds.

"Want to help?" she hands me a pair of gloves.

I oblige and take the gloves. "It's hot out," I comment, collecting my hair in my hands and wrapping it in a ponytail.

She smiles but continues to dig. I can't tell if she is in the mood to talk or if she only wants the security and peacefulness of having me beside her. I stay quiet for a while as we work. The garden is more spectacular than I remember. She has outdone herself by adding Queen Anne's lace, tulips, and snapdragons to the already thriving rose bushes. The fragrance is heavenly. These things make me miss the stereotypical life I have always envisioned for myself. A.J. and I live in a two-bedroom apartment and do not get to enjoy the luxuries of flowers and plants. We don't even have a yard.

As I stand, I pick up my pile of weeds to throw into the gardening bucket. Glancing at my mom, I notice the strain of thought on her face and position myself on the ground next to her with my elbows resting on my knees. "You want to talk about it?" I ask compassionately.

"Yes. But it's you I'm thinking about, not your dad," she admits.

I nod. "Alright. Let's talk. I'll get us something to drink and meet you on the patio."

I return with two glasses of ice-cold tea. I hand one to my mother who is on the swing with her legs crossed at the ankles. After all these years, I can't get over how pretty she is. Despite the current chaos of life, she looks peaceful and content.

I dread what's coming and wonder how much to reveal. I made a choice all those years ago to protect them, but when I came home, I passed the point of no return. Mom knows someone hurt me. She does not know who or how or to what extent. She and Dad have their assumptions, but only Sam, Jillian and Vicky know the truth. I can't hide from my sister anymore.

Vicky crosses my mind every single day. I do not hate her or wish her ill will. Her happiness means more to me than mine, but that wasn't enough for me to stay. I could not pretend to approve of her choice, let alone stick around to watch her live a lie when I knew full well her soul and spirit continued to die a slow, painful death. I'm not sure how she kept up the charade all these years. Vicky was willing to self-sacrifice to please others but the bitterness and anger would have consumed me. I guess I'm too selfish, or probably too fucked up.

Though I told her face-to-face I was leaving, I still mailed her a letter. In it, I apologized profusely, saying the words I had trouble speaking in person. One day I hoped she could forgive me, and then I asked her to understand why I could never see her again. I explained I could not look at her or her husband without remembering the horror we endured or the nightmares that woke me from my sleep. Looking back, I realize it was a harsh request made out of fear, heavy emotions, trauma, and probably immaturity. Full of shame and stubborn pride, I never budged, and Vicky respected my wishes.

I see sympathy in Mom's eyes as I sit across from her on the wicker rocker. Nervously, I move back and forth in the chair, digging my fingernails into the small grooves between the thread of material weaved together.

"Vicky asked me if she could come over and brings the kids. She wants them to meet you," Mom says.

I remain silent. This isn't what I expected.

"Jess, don't you think it's time? Maybe it would be easier for you two if..." she trails off as if contemplating her next words. "Zane is living on his grandparent's ranch. He took over after they died. No one sees him. He's a hermit. I imagine he works his tail off but to be honest, I was surprised he even came back to town. I thought you might want to know since you are trying to avoid certain things."

The world around me spins slightly off-kilter as the palpitations in my heart increase rapidly. Anything concerning Zane is news to me. No one has mentioned his name for years, per my request. It doesn't mean I don't think about him or wonder where he lives, or if he's married, has kids *or* if he is happy.

I frown when I look at her. It is easy for her and Dad to assume Zane was the problem. I tried to protect him the best way possible, but it was a no-win situation. My parents may have hated him all these years, but telling the truth would have hurt him more in the long run.

I shake my head and refocus.

"I love Vicky. I miss her."

My mother frowns. "I know," she says quietly.

"I want to see her." I say the words quickly before I lose the nerve to speak them.

Mom is thrilled as she wraps me in her arms. As I untangle myself from her embrace, I ask that Vicky come by herself the first time. I am anxious to meet my nieces and nephew, but it will be easier on us-mostly me-if we take baby steps.

• • •

Later that evening, Mom takes Dad to a movie. After they leave, I attempt to wait patiently for my sister, but I can't sit still. Instead, I wander around the house looking at family photos lining the hallway walls.

My eyes narrow in on a framed photo of the five of us on Space Mountain at Disneyland. I was in fifth grade when we took this trip. Mom and Dad were sitting in the back-row, grinning from ear to ear. Sam was in the middle by himself making an obnoxious face. Vicky and I were cuddled together in the front seat screaming hysterically, our fear entirely genuine. I laugh as my heart expands. I loved my childhood. No cares or worries, just freedom, fun and lots of laughter. I shift my attention down the row of photos where I notice one of us white water rafting in Colorado. I had just graduated high school, and that was our last adventure together before our world turned upside down.

I hear the front door creak open and Vicky's apprehensive voice call out.

"Hello? Jess?"

A shiver moves up my spine. My first instinct is to run into my sister's arms and giggle like we used to as kids. Instead, I take a deep breath and step out of the hallway to find her closing the front door. A moment later, she turns to me, and we stare, both of us frozen on the spot. Vicky's thick auburn locks frame her eyes and ashen cheekbones. Just like our mom, she places a hand over her heart. Her green eyes grow wide and brighten with her smile. She looks mature, motherly, and grown-up. She's as pretty as I remember.

"Hi, Jess," she says softly.

"Hey, Vic," I reply nervously. "You thirsty? There's lemonade."

She shakes her head. "Dad keeps the soda in the fridge in the basement. Let's get that."

Not missing a beat, a soft laugh escapes my lips as we grin foolishly at each other. Mom used to insist that we were highly sensitive to soda, probably even addicted. We drove our parents and everyone around us crazy with our hyper, mindless chatter and silly conversations after only a few drinks.

I disappear downstairs and return a moment later with a six pack. Vicky is sitting at the dining room table nervously pulling on the edge of the table cloth. I hand her a can and then sit across from her. We stare at each other, neither of us knowing what to say or where to start. Finally, I ask her to tell me about the kids and we spend the next hour discussing them. I learn about the pregnancies, births, and personalities of all three children, their likes and dislikes, how they get along, their hobbies and accomplishments as well as struggles with learning disabilities and friends. I listen to every detail that comes out of her mouth, trying to envision each moment as if I was there, right by her side. How I wish I could have been and loathe myself for the things I've missed.

"They want to meet you," she claims.

I snort. "I can't imagine why."

"All these years, their bedtime stories are about our crazy antics as kids. They are always begging to hear more. It's as if they know you, Jess. They love you just as much as I do," she adds. "But mostly, they are curious about the person who sends the birthday and Christmas presents every year."

My eyes widen in surprise. "I didn't know if you would allow them to have them or not."

"Why wouldn't I?" she asks indignantly.

I shrug as my voice catches in my throat. "Do the kids ask? Do they want to know why they don't know me?"

"Yes. I'm able to pacify them with simple answers. But they are getting smarter as they get older."

I nod in response.

"Mom always gives me updates about your life with A.J.," she adds.

I feel my face go red at the mention of my girlfriend and can't help but wonder what Vicky thinks.

"Mostly she talks about your restaurant and how fantastic the food is," she continues as if sensing my discomfort. "It sounds wonderful. I can't tell you how many times I've wanted to hop in the car, take a trip to Seattle to try your food and see the life you made for yourself. I haven't because I figured that wouldn't be the best way to surprise you."

I tell her about my years in college, how I met A.J. as well as my decision to leave the medical field and open the bistro. She asks the question I knew would come; I didn't expect her to be so bold so soon.

"Do you love her?" Vicky asks.

"Of course," I whisper, staring at the label on my soda can, unable to meet her gaze.

"The way you loved Zane?" she says.

Vicky and I always had this type of relationship. The kind where no subject was off-limits. I was never able to hide anything from her and vice versa. It's one of the other complicated reasons I chose to run. In my desperation to be away from any reminders of what happened, I was furious with myself for not knowing what was going on with her. For the first time, she *was* able to hide something from me, and I was angry. I didn't see the truth that was right under my nose.

I lift my head away from the aluminum can and look Vicky squarely in the eye. In them, I see the mirror of my own heart; shards of broken, jagged pieces lying around waiting to be picked up and put back together. There have been several failed attempts. My pieces continue to collect dust, just waiting for the right moment when they can become whole again. It's then that I realize, even after all these years of being apart, Vicky still knows me better than anyone in the entire world.

• • •

Mom and Dad return three hours later to find Vicky and me laughing, surrounded by six empty cans as we sit on the floor of the living room looking through old photo albums.

"Remember Uncle Stephen snoring?" I shriek. "The night after Cousin Jay's wedding, we thought a bear was crawling through the window of the cabin. We were so scared we finally had to wake Mom up."

Vicky crumbles into a fit of giggles. "What about the next day when you were teasing him about it, and he flipped you off, right there in front of everyone at breakfast? I thought Grandma Marsha was going to die; she'd never seen anything so vulgar."

Delighted, Mom and Dad reminisce with us, but Dad soon reaches his limit. He gets up, shuffles to the kitchen to take his pills, and is off to bed. Mom tries to make it another half hour, but she too grows tired and calls it a night.

"I guess I better get going," Vicky says with a yawn as she stretches her arms above her head.

I feel an overwhelming wave of disappointment and panic. Vicky must feel it too because she links her fingers through mine.

"I'll call you tomorrow so we can make plans with the kids," she reassures me with a quick hug.

I watch through the picture window as her car backs out of the driveway. With the caress of her hand still lingering in mine, I rest my palm on my cheek as a tear escapes from my eye.

• • •

I can't sleep. It doesn't matter if I close my eyes or if I keep them open, the image of Zane lingers in every corner of my consciousness. I wonder if he is still as breathtakingly handsome. I remember his thick, chestnut hair pushed back in waves, soft blue eyes as vivid as the sky, and the air of mystery behind a smile that made him irresistible.

Damn the caffeine. Damn Vicky for asking me that question. Yes I love A.J. as much as I loved Zane. It's just different. Zane and I were silly kids.

For years, in the branches of our treehouse, Vicky and I daydreamed about our adult lives. She was married to Tyson, and of course, I was married to Zane. We fantasized about our houses, the traveling we would do, the holiday parties we would hold, even the names of our kids. Vicky couldn't wait to volunteer in the classrooms, make birthday cupcakes and conjure up creative Halloween costumes, like our mother had for us. I was determined to have boys so I could coach tee-ball and soccer and fill the weekends with hunting and camping excursions. We were sure we were meant for this life. The funny part is I think Zane and Tyson figured it was bound to happen as well.

Although Vicky and Tyson readily accepted their destiny and were willing to admit their love, Zane and I were stubborn. We tiptoed around it, claiming we were buddies when in reality, what we felt, the magnetic attraction between us became impossible to ignore.

Fantasy finally became a reality the night of our senior prom. His best friend Heath asked me to the dance the previous week. Zane, out of spite, asked Dawn Kilwicky even though they broke up. Somehow, we wound up double dating, which seemed to please Zane, but was awkward for the rest of us. The evening may have been more enjoyable if Dawn and I were still close friends but the tension limited all conversation. Poor Heath fidgeted uncomfortably under Zane's watchful eye. When he slipped the corsage onto my wrist and linked his fingers in mine, the scowl on Zane's face made Heath cower until he awkwardly removed his hand. Every compliment Heath gave was met with daggers. It didn't take long to realize if he kept a safe and healthy distance from me, Zane remained polite.

On our way to the dance, we cruised around town in the limousine Zane's dad rented for the occasion. I don't know who was more relieved to find the mini-fridge stocked with beers, Dawn or Heath. Within ten minutes, Heath chugged two and started on a third while Dawn popped the top of her second. I was sipping on mine when I noticed Zane pull a metal flask out of his tuxedo pocket. He took a small sip then held it toward me. When I shook my head, he passed it onto Heath, who was in the mood to chug anything. After three big gulps, Zane snatched it back and gave it to Dawn. Flirtatiously, she held the flask to her lips while peeking at him from under her long, dark lashes. When some of the brown liquor drizzled down her chin, Dawn giggled like a child and placed her hand on Zane's leg. Feeling confident under the influence of the alcohol, she began to stroke his thigh while leaning in to nuzzle the side of his neck.

Irritated and uncomfortable, I turned up the radio. I placed my mostly full beer in the cup holder, knowing my bad attitude combined with alcohol was a dangerous mix. Singing softly to myself, I stared out the window in an attempt to diffuse my jealousy but jumped when Zane touched my arm. As the electric shock raced through me, I noticed Dawn huddled in the corner of the back seat close to the door, pouting. I gave Zane a quizzical look, and he grinned sheepishly, shrugging his shoulders.

"I'll drink it if you don't want it," he said, motioning toward my beer.

I reached out to give him the bottle and his warm fingers wrapped around mine. He didn't release his grip. We locked eyes, and I was instantly mesmerized by the compelling urge to kiss him. Staring at his mouth and finding it difficult to breathe, I leaned toward him. Following my lead, his lips hovered only inches from mine when the limousine came to a stop.

The side door opened and the chauffeur announced our arrival. One by one, we climbed out. As the guys tipped the driver, I stood on the curb next to Dawn, unable to ignore the tear stains on her cheeks. A part of me sympathized because I knew Zane rejected her earlier advances. I scolded myself, swearing never to put myself in that situation.

Once inside, we quickly found a table of friends. The awkwardness that had been hanging over the four of us melted away and was replaced with laughter and loud conversation. Without Zane's knowledge, Heath had stolen the flask out of his coat pocket. Within a half-hour, it was empty. Completely drunk, Heath started playing grab-ass with me while Zane danced with Dawn after being reprimanded by a group of her friends. After several measly attempts to kiss me in his drunken stupor, I finally punched Heath in the jaw and escaped to an unoccupied table across the room.

Unable to take my eyes off the couple on the dance floor, I sulked. Why on earth did I let him have that type of power over me? Annoyed, I decided to get some air. As I made my way toward the door, I could feel the heat of Zane's lingering gaze on my back. I turned around and saw him with his arms carelessly placed around Dawn's lower back while he stared at me, his expression somber.

We broke eye contact when the song ended, and the Principal took his place on stage to announce the prom royalty. I was stunned when he called my name along with Zane's. Instead of reeling with excitement, I ached to go home. Two of my fellow cheerleaders embraced me in hugs and led me to the stage. Zane scanned the crowd. I froze when his eyes found mine and melted under his enchanting smile. I never felt as adored as I did at that moment.

Once the crowns were on our heads, I was in his arms for the traditional king and queen dance. Usually, Zane and I avoided physical contact other than a playful punch or a headlock here and there. During the dance, when he pulled me into his arms, I knew this was where I was meant to be. I was comfortable and content and I laid my head against his chest. His hand clasped mine, holding it close to his heart while the other hovered at the base of my spine, securing us together. One song led into two and two into three as we swayed in silence, unable to release our embrace, oblivious to everything around us.

I lost my breath when his warms lips touched my forehead. Placing a finger under my chin, he tilted my head until we were face to face. Overwhelmed with emotion, I could not speak. In his eyes, I saw hunger combined with tenderness and devotion, a reflection of everything I felt.

Without warning, the lights came on, startling both of us. Zane dropped my hand without saying a word. He took a step back and quickly walked away. Squinting from the glare, I looked around in confusion. When my eyes finally adjusted, my gaze landed on Dawn, who was red in the face and glaring at me. Heath was next to her, barely able to stand but stable enough to pull down his pants to reveal his pale ass.

A half-hour later, I still reeled with shock and disappointment. I stared out the window of the limousine as the chauffeur drove us home. There was an after-prom party, but we made a unanimous decision not to go. Heath was passed out in the front passenger's seat and Dawn, her arms crossed over her chest, moped in the corner across from me. Zane did not seem to notice. He stared out his window, lost in thought. When we stopped in front of my house, I grabbed my purse and anxiously climbed out.

Zane followed me.

"I'll walk from here," he told the driver, and then nodded toward Dawn. "Make sure she gets home."

Appalled, Dawn attempted to protest, but Zane slammed the door.

"That was rude," I told him as we watched the limo pull away.

He shrugged nonchalantly then linked his fingers in mine. I let him lead me to the back patio where we sat side by side on the swing.

After a moment of awkward silence, he spoke. "You know I love you, right?"

"Of course," I said nervously, staring at the night sky. "I'm your best friend."

"Not that way, Jess," his voice grew serious. "I'm *in* love with you. You are all I think about. I don't want anyone else. I want *you* to be my forever."

With the pitch black of the night around me, I lay in bed, remembering the way he placed his hand on my cheek to turn my face ever so gently toward him as he spoke. He seemed scared and hopeful at the same time. I have no idea what I said back to him that night. I only knew in that moment the world was right. Life with Zane is what I wanted, needed, and swore I could never live without. I loved him more than I thought was possible, and he loved me fiercely in return. We were young, carefree, and naïve. When all our dreams were coming true, in a matter of months, an unexplained turn of events would unfold, leaving in its path destruction and heartache. Who could have predicted that?

CHAPTER THREE

There is a reason I don't spend a significant amount of time alone. Between A.J., the bistro and our social life, I'm used to going a hundred miles a minute. My "to-do" list is so long I hardly have a moment to think about anything else. I like it this way. It keeps me from being what I am right now, bored, and restless. When I get bored and restless, I think. When I overthink, I become emotional. Avoiding emotion is what I've spent years perfecting.

The reality is I don't have A.J. here. I don't have the bistro, and aside from my parents, I have no social life. I try to come up with a variety of things to fill the void. I have no desire to take up yoga because that requires calmness and balance, and I don't possess those. Meditation is possible, but it sounds too healthy for my damaged psyche. I hang onto anxiety like an old, comforting friend. The last thing I want to do is let go of the intimacy of it.

Instead, I increase my running. I'm up to ten miles now. After the run, I eat a hearty breakfast with my parents, usually eggs, toast and sometimes bacon or ham. Once I finish breakfast, I sit down with a cup of piping hot coffee and watch Regis and Kelly. After that, I do laundry and help Mom with the cleaning. In the afternoons I read a book, this is my fourth in the last fifteen days. I dabble on the internet for work, and sometimes I e-mail friends. After an entertaining episode of *Ellen*, I help prepare the evening dinner before the five o'clock news. I imagine if I left the house, my life would be more adventurous, maybe even exciting. I could go to the gym or go shopping. The library or movie sounds appealing. Leaving the house would also be terrifying. I run the risk of facing people I once knew. People tend to ask questions I don't want to answer.

In the afternoons, for a change of pace, I'll sit on the back-porch swing watching butterflies and herons fly. Squirrels chase one another up trees and across branches, snickering as if they are playing a game of tag. The fresh air and surroundings should be peaceful and comforting, but they're not. It only gives me more time alone.

Vicky has been over twice since our reunion. She stayed for dinner on Sunday and asked me to join them at the park for an after-school picnic this coming Thursday. She promised me it would be her, the kids and our parents. Tyson would not be there. I told her I would think about it. I love being around her again. I love hearing her voice, laughing at her natural and easy wit, and watching the animated way she talks with her hands. Each time she leaves, desperate loneliness consumes me and does not subside until I fall into a deep sleep.

I find that I am crying more lately. Granted, I have a multitude of things to cry about because I avoided them for years. This endless stream of emotion is overwhelming and exhausting. A.J. is worried about me, so we try to connect as much as possible. Lately, she has been helping Phillip at the bistro during the day and works late into the night to catch up with clients. Though I try to stay awake and wait for her calls, I'm usually asleep around nine-thirty, and we wind up missing one another. Fortunately, she calls at eight tonight.

"Hey, Babe," she says into the phone. "You okay?"

My voice is hoarse, and I'm sniffling. "I just watched *Titanic* for the first time."

"You have never seen it before?" she asks incredulously.

I've spent all of my adult life avoiding romantic movies altogether, especially dramatic ones like *Titanic*. I don't tell her this. Instead, I relay the details of my day.

"How is Vicky?" she asks.

I can tell she is trying her best to appear supportive, but it's easy to detect her annoyance. A.J. knows bits and pieces of my past, including the fact my sister and I were estranged. She doesn't know why but knows enough to understand and sympathize with how excruciatingly painful it was for me to come home. As much as she loves me, she knows I am one fucked up person who has become an expert in self-pity and unable to move on from my past. A.J. lives her life appreciating the present moment. She doesn't believe in looking over her shoulder. She encourages me to go to counseling, claiming our relationship will be better if I get help.

I disagree. I guarantee it would tear us apart.

At first, A.J. wasn't thrilled with my decision to come back to Montana. It caused many arguments. Finally, she decided this may be an opportunity to heal old wounds. She waits patiently day after day, eager to hear me tell her something significant has changed. I don't think a relationship with my sister is what she bargained for.

Regardless, I tell her all that's happened. We chat for a few more minutes as she fills me in about the bistro, although I already know because I receive daily updates from Phillip. We say good night, and I turn off the bedside lamp, settle under the covers and think once again about the monotonous routine my life has become.

• • •

A bad dream startles me awake. I press a shaky hand to my cold, clammy forehead. In the past, when nightmares woke me, I forced my eyes open and stared at the ceiling until I was no longer scared. Other times, including tonight, when drenched in sweat with my teeth chattering, I have to turn on the light before I feel safe again.

Shivering, I touch my damp tank top and switch on the lamp. I can't recall the dream; the intricate details terrify me. I'm grateful for this strange, subconscious protection. I throw the covers off and walk through the hallway to the front door. I make sure it's locked. I move through the kitchen to the sliding glass door and check it as well. My breath begins to steady when I reach the kitchen. Opening the refrigerator door, I pull out a carton of milk and pour myself a glass. I drink it quickly and then return to the living room where I ease myself into my dad's recliner. Grabbing the remote, I press the power button hoping a little late-night television will relax me. After I settle on a rerun of *Friends*, I reach for the newspaper on the floor.

My hand starts to tremble the moment I open the black and white page and see the old advertisement for the sporting goods store. "Congratulations:

Celebrating Thirty Years 1979-2009," it reads in bold print. Underneath the headline is an article on the history of the store.

His image burns my eyes as the paper slips from my fingers. Bolting out of the chair, I rush to the bathroom, slamming the door behind me. I barely make it to the toilet before I vomit violently from the searing memory.

• • •

I stood in the doorway of the guesthouse, staring at the image of my sister on the television screen, trying to figure out why she was wearing a red negligee. I turned to run, but a large hand covered my mouth, pressing against my teeth so hard I was terrified they would break. The strong odor of cigarette residue on his hands and beer on his breath made me gag.

After he locked the door, he reached into his back pocket, retrieved the gun and pressed the barrel to my temple. My legs collapsed underneath me with gripping fear.

"Quiet or I'll kill you," he seethed into my ear.

Suddenly my head throbbed, and the room began to spin. Something trickled from my nose. As liquid pooled on my lip, I watched red droplets paint the floor beneath my feet. A moment later, he shoved me against the wall. I tried to run, but another blow stunned me. I couldn't focus on anything, not even his repulsive face, looming close to mine.

"You snoopy little bitch!" he yelled. "Did your sister tell you?"

I didn't know what he was talking about. When I tried to tell him there was a mistake, he grabbed my hair and yanked my body against his. His lips were on my neck, and I felt the pressure of his hard erection against my thigh.

"Wonder if you'll be as much fun to play with as she was. There were times I thought about your lips around my dick instead of hers," he sneered as his tongue invaded my ear.

"You're lying!" I screamed hysterically, clawing at his face.

Restraining my arms, he laughed.

"Vicky wanted me. She was a flirt, a dirty little whore. She liked everything we did and kept coming back, for Chrissakes! When I'm done with you, you're going to keep your big mouth shut, do you understand? If anyone finds out about this, I'll kill you both."

With one quick sweep, my pants were around my ankles, and my attacker ripped my shirt. I heard myself whimper helplessly as I stood in front of him naked and shivering.

Unbuckling his belt, he exposed himself and pushed his fingers inside me.

"Touch me," he demanded.

I sobbed uncontrollably as he pulled my hand to grip him. A second later, his hand cracked against my cheek.

"Slide it up and down, you idiot. Jesus, didn't Zane teach you anything?" he snarled maliciously.

As my hand moved, he quivered and inhaled sharply. Swallowing back tears, I stared at the wall where my eyes locked on spider dangling from a web like a trapeze artist. Desperate to abandon the part of myself that felt anything, I imagined shrinking to the size of the small insect and disappearing. Overcome with numbing exhaustion, I sank to my knees but remained transfixed as the spider danced through the air with strength and courage.

Where are my strength and courage? I wondered.

Another blow to the side of the head made my ears ring. Pulling me by the arm, he yanked me with him to the bed. Sitting down, he kicked his pants from his ankles until he was completely naked. When I didn't move, he pulled me onto his lap.

Bile constricted my throat, and I bit my lip to keep from screaming as he continued to use me for his pleasure. Withdrawing further into myself, I searched for my spider imagining her growing larger and more ferocious until her shadow hovered over us. Enraged, she would wrap a strand of silk around his neck and spin him into her trap until he could no longer breathe. I wanted him dead.

"I like it when you cry," he stammered breathlessly.

Pinching my mouth between his thumb and fingers, he forced me to look at him. Choking back sobs, I jerked my head away.

"Seeing you scared turns me on."

Roughly, he lifted me with both hands. I cringed as the pressure of him pushed against the most intimate part of me.

• • •

Disoriented, I stare at the bathroom ceiling, lying on my back paralyzed from the emotional assault. My legs shake violently as I push myself off the floor. First on all fours, then using the sink for balance, I make it to a standing position. I twist the faucet allowing the water to run cold while I lean on my elbows and spit. Cupping the ice-cold water into my hands, I splash my face and look into the mirror to find bloodshot, swollen eyes staring back at me.

Eventually, I stumble to my bedroom. With trembling hands, I lock the door and crawl under the down comforter. Curling into a ball, I weep quietly, rocking back and forth while I pray for the light of day when the demons from my past can no longer torment me.

• • •

I finally fall into a restless sleep, but when I wake at dawn, I know I cannot face the world. I send my mom a text message claiming to have the stomach flu. I take an old prescription of A.J.'s, an Ambien, and fall into a coma. I don't wake again until five in the afternoon. I am groggy and my stomach hurts from vomiting and a lack of food. My head feels as if it is about to explode.

As I lie there, staring at absolutely nothing, I feel utterly alone. The feeling is not unusual for me, but it's a strange sensation to be in my comfortable, childhood home, surrounded by the people who love me most and still feel this helpless. I contemplate calling A.J. but talk myself out of it. A more significant part of me is desperate to call Vicky, but I know that is an even more ridiculous thought.

Life is about choices, my father used to say, and I accepted the consequences of my choices a long time ago. But, throughout the night, I realize I didn't want to do this alone anymore. Unfortunately, isolation is a deep-seated habit that is not easy to break.

Later that afternoon, I shuffle into the kitchen for a bowl of cereal. My mother proceeds to tell me how awful I look.

"Are you sure you want to eat that?" she adds, eyeing my cereal bowl. "The milk could sour your stomach."

I nod, shoving a spoonful of cornflakes into my mouth. "I need substance. I think I just had a twenty-four-hour bug," I mumble between bites.

My mom feels my forehead and informs me I don't have a fever.

"Could it have been food poisoning? I hope it was. The last thing we need around this house is the stomach flu. I don't want to be rude, but please don't go around your father. He can't afford to get sick, honey."

"I won't," I reassure her.

When my bowl is empty, I place it in the dishwasher and tell her I'm going to go back to bed. Once I'm in my room, I call A.J. I hope hearing a friendly voice will bring some sense of normalcy to my world. When her phone goes straight to voicemail, I opt not to leave a message, but instead, I send a text.

Maybe I should call Sam. What I would I tell him? He knows what happened all those years ago, but we have not talked about it since the day I turned up at his house, broken, bloodied and half crazy. As appealing as it sounds to have a friend, I am not prepared to dump this on him right now.

Feeling defeated, I dig through my suitcase until I find my journal. A.J. gave it to me two years ago, claiming journaling could be therapeutic. I've carried it around with me ever since. I had good intentions to start it but haven't found the courage. Tucking two pillows behind my back, I sit up straight and begin to write. After I jot down a couple of words, my thoughts drift back to my brother.

• • •

"What the hell happened to you?" Sam shouted when I fell into his arms crying.

As he led me to the couch, Jillian ran to the bathroom and returned a moment later with a warm washcloth.

Careful not to hurt me, she dabbed at the cuts on my face.

Sam wanted to call the cops.

"Call Vicky," I said in a raspy voice. "When she gets here, I will tell you the whole story, but you have to promise me the cops will not be involved. Most of all, you can't tell Mom and Dad."

As Jillian rubbed ointment on my abrasions, Sam's booming voice echoed in the background.

"I don't give a shit what you are doing. You need to get your ass over here immediately. I'm not joking, Vic. It's an emergency. You either get over here, or I will come to find you and drag you."

Ten minutes later, Vicky arrived, pouting as she walked through the front door. Her face drained of color the moment she saw me.

"We need to talk," I whispered as tears seeped out of the corner of my eyes. "How long, Vic? How long has he been hurting you?"

I knew Tyson and Zane's father had an unusual fondness for Vicky. Ron's eyes would light up, and he smiled that big charming smile whenever he saw her. When picking teams for a neighborhood game of touch football or softball, he chose her first. He was just as flirtatious with her as with adult women. Ron poked her in the ribs when he was teasing her, holding her a little bit too tightly when he hugged her, and buying her favorite candy bar from the store while the rest of us shared one measly bag of M&M's.

I can't say I was jealous of Vicky's special treatment. I knew things about Ron that Vicky didn't, and frankly, he gave me the creeps. The other wives on our block and around town thought he was incredibly handsome. Vicky and her friends sighed and took second and third glances at him when he was around. I could not figure out why everyone was blind to his charms, especially Vicky. Maybe it was because she was the middle child, and it was no secret that she was daddy's little princess. Vicky was sensitive and had a tough time with the changes after Dad lost his job and started traveling. She probably liked the extra attention Ron gave her. Or maybe it was the stupidity of teenage hormones.

Vicky's eyes glassed over as she sank into the couch next to me.

"Not now, Jessie. My wedding is in a month. I can't handle this," she shook her head in a desperate plea.

"Do you know what he did to me? Do you?" I yelled as my entire body trembled.

Slowly, she laid her head on my lap and began to weep. I ran my fingers through her hair and cried with her. We cried for both of us. In quiet shock, Sam and Jillian sat on the floor across from us with their backs against the wall.

Once we had a chance to calm down, Vicky spoke.

She explained how it had started innocently enough. Ron offered to give her guitar lessons the summer after she turned fourteen, the summer Dad was gone more often than not due to the wildfires in California. The lessons were at the ranch on the outskirts of town where his parents lived. During lessons, the conversations they had were mostly about Tyson and Zane. He talked about how proud he was of them, how well they were doing in school, their sports, and his dreams for them to take over the business. After a few months, it became personal. He brought up her relationship with Tyson. He wanted to know if Tyson treated her like a lady, if he bought her flowers, took her on dates, and held her hand. Vicky, being as naïve as she was, loved this inside connection to Tyson and it encouraged her that Ron thought she was worthy to date his son. He even said so. His compliments seemed genuine, and Vicky almost looked forward to her lessons each week. Plus, she enjoyed the company of the grandparents as well. There was always freshly baked banana bread, cookies, or a pie waiting for her when she arrived.

By the end of fall, instead of having lessons at the main house with the grandparents, they strted meeting in the guesthouse Ron renovated. Vicky hadn't thought it strange, and by this time, she trusted him. It was after her first lesson in the guesthouse he kissed her cheek goodbye. Again, she hadn't thought anything odd about it. She'd seen him kiss many a cheek in the neighborhood, men, and women. Three weeks later, Vicky started to get uncomfortable. While she practiced her cords, Ron rubbed her shoulders, claiming her tight muscles affected her playing. While doing this, his hands shifted around her back until he was playing with her bra straps. When he asked her if she'd ever been fitted correctly for a bra, Vicky was caught off guard and didn't answer.

"I'm only doing this for your sake. With your bust size, it's important you are comfortable," Ron explained innocently.

Cupping her breasts, he went on to describe the correct way a bra should fit. He gave her fifty dollars and told her to go to the department store to buy herself a matching bra and panties. He said to bring them to the lesson the following week so he could make sure she got something Tyson would love.

Vicky chose to ignore Ron's behavior. She convinced herself he truly was looking out for Tyson's best interests. After all, he knew his son better than anyone. She did as he asked, and the next week pulled the newly purchased items out of her backpack. Delighted, Ron praised Vicky for her efforts, and as if nothing unusual had happened, her lessons returned to normal. Her apprehension disappeared over the holidays. But, not long after the New Year, he started to inquire about her sexual activity. With some coaxing, she finally confided that she and Tyson had fooled around, but wanted to wait until she was sixteen, in a little over a year, to lose her virginity.

"Well, that gives me plenty of time to teach you a thing or two," he said with a wink.

Vicky had thought he was teasing, but it wasn't long before Ron was sharing advice on what men wanted and preferred. He always reminded her, "Don't tell Tyson a thing. He should be pleasantly surprised."

For the most part, Vicky tried to ignore his comments and focus on her lessons. One day, when she showed up to the guesthouse, Ron had a pornographic movie playing in his VCR, which made her angry. Appearing shocked by her outburst, Ron pulled her into a hug and explained how surprised he was that her parents hadn't allowed her to watch one. He went on to say it was a parent's responsibility to have age-appropriate conversations about sex so kids wouldn't be blindsided or wind up in uncomfortable situations.

His words made Vicky feel stupid and confused. Yes, her parents had informed her about the birds and the bees, good touch and bad touch. Though they preached to their kids about the importance of waiting to have sex until marriage, Mel and Libby were not ignorant. They also discussed safe sex, good boundaries, and self-respect. They never had conversations about the intricacies of the act, how to have it, what to do, what not to do, let alone allow them to watch pornography. Vicky could see Ron's point, and she couldn't help but wonder if her friends' parents were having those discussions, or if more of them were like her own. Either way, she was too embarrassed to ask.

The following week, as she was putting her guitar away, Ron caught her off guard by kissing her long and passionately on the mouth. It took a moment for the shock to register. When it did, Vicky shoved him away. Ron pinned her against the wall, laughing. He locked his fingers around one of her wrists and pulled her hand down to the bulge in his pants. When she tried to slap him, he laughed louder and harder. Vicky realized she was dealing with a very demented and dangerous man.

He placed a hand on the wall above her head and bent down to kiss her. She felt powerless and terrified. He used her closest relationships as ammunition against her. He threatened to tell those she respected and loved what she'd been doing at guitar lessons. He whispered words like promiscuous, flirtatious, and trashy as his hands explored her body. When he told her this was her fault and no one would love her if they found out she was a whore, she broke down and cried.

This was the beginning of a year and a half of sexual and emotional abuse. Vicky continued to meet him at the farm once a week, and after hours at the sporting goods store. To keep the secret, Vicky became an expert liar. Despite what Ron claimed, Vicky swore they never had sexual intercourse. There was fondling, heavy petting, oral sex, and digital penetration. He lived out his wildest fantasies with sex toys, videos, and pictures of her dressed in lingerie.

Vicky continued to date Tyson through these eighteen months. As she hoped, she lost her virginity to her one true love on her sixteenth birthday. Interestingly enough, a few weeks later, Ron told her he was no longer available to give lessons. He hadn't touched or threatened her since.

When Vicky finished telling her horrific story, no one knew what to say. Sam still wanted to make a report, but Vicky and I were adamant that the police could not be involved. Vicky didn't want Tyson to find out, especially right before their wedding. As for me, I was now damaged goods, a shattered mess that could never look Zane in the eyes again, let alone be loved by him. Too many lives could be ruined by what Ron did to us.

Sam finally called our parents. He told them Zane and I got into a heated argument at a party the previous evening. I was going to stay at his place for a few days to get space and clarity. They informed Sam that Zane has been calling relentlessly, and even stopped by the house several times looking for me. Sam did his best to reassure my mother that Zane and I were fine.

We were far from fine. I would never be able to see Zane the same way again. How could I hold his hand, kiss his lips, or allow him to put his hands on me without the sick, twisted memory of his father invading my thoughts? And what about Vicky? No matter how much I begged, my sister was still going to get married. She said she would rather deal with Ron once in a while, rather than face a lifetime without Tyson. I could not fathom her logic. She would have to see her abuser day in and day out while hiding the truth from her husband. Ron would always control a piece of her.

Over the next two days, Jillian nursed my wounds. Once I made the transition back home it was as if nothing physically happened but my fractured mind would never be the same. Slowly, I fell into a state of depression and detachment. I went to my job at the ice cream parlor every day, finding enough internal strength to fake a smile and engage with customers. In the evenings, I hid in my room. I was intent on destroying myself and all the relationships around me. I didn't deserve any of them. Though my mother was concerned, she respected my privacy. She figured the "thing" with Zane would eventually blow over.

Zane continued to call, but I continued to avoid him. We were both accepted to Montana State University in Bozeman and were looking forward to starting the fall semester together. However, over the days of isolation, my mind began to shift, and I came up with a different plan that took me far away from Zane, my hometown, and the hideous nightmare I endured.

CHAPTER FOUR

I stay in my room journaling and sleeping for the next day and a half. I venture out for meals, still pretending to be under the weather. The last thing I want to do is worry my parents.

Eventually, I get texts from A.J., but it's random snippets here and there. When she finally calls, she explains how busy the restaurant has been due to Memorial Day weekend. I immediately offer to come home.

"Don't you dare!" she snaps. "Look, I've got to go. I'll call you later." She hangs up quickly, which surprises me because of the unpleasant attitude she had about me coming here in the first place.

Although I am slightly annoyed by her quick dismissal, I remind myself this is a game A.J. is famous for playing. In the past, when she is angry, she tends to get caught up in a tornado of tasks and activities to avoid interacting with me. She stays at the office later than normal, schedules appointments she had initially put off, and happy hour with clients take priority over our quality time together. It's her passive-aggressive way of punishing me while protecting herself. Even though I'm hurting too, I typically apologize out of shame and desperation for her company and to ease the tension between us. An apology is exactly what she wants. We don't talk about the situation that brought us to this point or come up with compromises moving forward. We go on as if nothing happened. In time, A.J. shifts back to her usual, joyful self. I repress my frustrations while making a mental note not to make the same mistake.

Although this is our typical cycle, because of the geographical distance between us, I am gaining an entirely new perspective. Engaging in A.J.'s typical neediness requires more energy than I can expend at the moment.

Feeling restless, I crawl out from under the covers. I lift the blinds to open a window and allow fresh air to reclaim the room. After a cleansing shower, I finally feel more like my old self. Granted, I haven't been one hundred percent my old self since I was eighteen. I usually held at a steady sixty-five percent. The two previous days, I was only at ten percent. Now, I am at least a fifty. If I am trying to stay positive, this is progress.

Quickly, the days return to the routine I initially established, except Vicky comes over daily. I made an excuse to bail out of the picnic, considering the emotional wrecking ball I encountered earlier in the week. Although I am anxious to meet her children, I know I am not up for any more heavy emotions. She doesn't ask why and reassures me we can reschedule.

During her visits, we spend most of our time on the backyard swing talking and catching up on years missed. I relay more stories of life in Chicago and Seattle—the parties, the nightlife, and of course, the bistro. I answer questions about my staff as she absorbs every detail. In return, I want to know all there is about her life. I smile as she shares dramatic, but hilarious tales of parenting, adventures they have had with my brother's family, and the juicy gossip about people we knew. It is as if no time has passed at all.

"Dawn Kilwicky married your prom date," she says, trying to sound nonchalant.

I laugh. "No kidding!"

"She tried to get her claws into Zane after you left, but he wanted nothing to do with her."

I feel the heat crawl up my neck. Do I want to know? Of course, I do. But am I ready to know?

"I imagine there were tons of girls interested. He was a catch." I hesitate for a brief moment. "So, which one of the vultures landed him if it wasn't Dawn? Or did he find someone at the university?"

"Neither," Vicky says. "He never married."

I'm not sure what to do with this information, so I stare at my brightly colored toenails as they poke out the tips of my sandals.

After a few moments of silence, Vicky continues. "He went to Bozeman, got a degree in Forestry as he planned. After his grandparents died, he moved home and took over the ranch. He doesn't come to town often. We see him once a month if that. He is a wonderful uncle, and the kids adore him. Tyson drops them off once a week to help at the ranch and ride horses. But nothing has ever been the same between them, and Zane can't seem to look me in the eye. We make enough small talk to get by, but I am guessing I remind him too much of you. Two hired hands live and work out on the ranch, but other than that, he's pretty much a loner."

I absorb her words as questions bounce on the tip of my tongue, but I remain silent.

"Mom and Dad still think he is the cause of you leaving. I imagine that keeps him away as well," she says.

Standing up, I walk over to the fence where I rest my elbows on the wood slats and watch vehicles pass by. "Does he know I'm here?" I ask.

"I don't think so. The kids were out there over the weekend, but at the time, they didn't know you were in town. I can't ask them to keep it a secret though, Jessie. I have to tell Tyson as soon as he gets home from fishing on Sunday," she replies.

I'm not sure what terrifies me more, Zane knowing I am here, or Tyson. My feelings for Tyson are platonic, brotherly love. There were countless games of tag football in the park, riding bikes to the pool on hot summer days, and playing King of the Hill or having snowball fights after a blizzard. When the neighborhood kids got together for games in the evenings, the four of us always stuck together. He and Zane were at every birthday party, and we walked to and from school every day until Tyson was old enough to get his driver's license. Even then, he was gracious enough to give Zane and me rides to the junior high on cold days.

"It's going to be okay, Jessie," she reassures me. "Tyson will want to see you, I promise."

"What on earth does he think happened all those years ago, Vicky?" I snap, turning away from the fence to look at her. "He hates me for leaving before your wedding and definitely hates me for leaving Zane. What could you have possibly told him that would make him understand why I left?"

"I didn't," she confesses. "Zane did."

I am shocked. "Zane? What? What did he tell him?"

"He said we needed to trust you, and though it seemed to be a selfish choice, it wasn't. Tyson doesn't hate you. He worries about you," Vicky reveals.

My head spins. After everything I put Zane through, he stood up for me. Why would he do that? The last time I saw him was the evening before my nightmare began. It was exactly four weeks before we were supposed to leave for college. We sat together on the front porch of my house, listening to the sky rumble in the distance. With our fingers linked carelessly, we discussed plans to meet at his grandparent's ranch the following afternoon.

• • •

"Supposed to be more thunderstorms tomorrow," Zane said nonchalantly, tilting his head upwards.

"Good," I smiled, nudging him with my shoulder. "That will make the day all the more romantic."

Shaking his head, Zane laughed while I caressed the back of his hand with my thumb. "I've got the picnic already packed," I told him.

Winking, he planted a tender kiss below my knuckles. "I'll take care of everything else."

Looking at his watch, he sighed and pulled me up with him. A light kiss grazed my lips as he pushed a chunk of stray hair behind my ear. Wrapping my arms tightly around his torso, I laid my head on his chest and closed my eyes, inhaling the earthly scent of him that had become familiar and comforting.

"Jessie," he whispered.

My eyes opened to see him staring at me hungrily, as his finger gently touched my lips.

"Tomorrow I'm going to show you how much I love you. I promise, one day I'm going to make you my wife."

The certainty in his voice warmed me to the core. Unable to speak, I pressed my lips to his allowing my actions to express what words could not.

A moment later, he reluctantly pulled away from me but continued to make promises as he slowly walked to his truck—college, traveling, the wedding, and kids, our whole life. The world was at our fingertips, and the idea of spending my life with my best friend could not have been sweeter.

I showed up at the guesthouse the following day five minutes before noon. Zane wasn't there. Instead, I encountered Ron, red faced, and angry. I kept praying Zane would show up to rescue me. He didn't and to this day, I have no idea what kept him from meeting me. If he had been there like he promised…

While I stayed at Sam and Jillian's, it was easy enough to avoid him. It was also easy to allow my parents to think that my depression was over a break-up. They had no idea there had been the death of the "me" that I once knew, or that I was in the process of making changes that would alter all of our lives.

While everyone was preoccupied with planning my sister's wedding, I was making phone calls, applying for grants and loans, and frantically filling out applications. Within two weeks, I was a new student at a college over one thousand miles away.

Vicky kept her distance because I knew her secret, and she knew I was upset about the wedding. If she was angry with me, I didn't care. I wasn't mad at her for what Ron did to me. I was angry she didn't come to her family for help when it was happening to her. She let him bully and intimidate her into keeping it secret. At the same time, I also understood how helpless she must have felt.

I packed my car on a Monday afternoon before my parents got home from work. I planned to leave early the following morning. The wedding was less than a week away, and I felt a sharp, panicky desire to be as far away from the event as possible. It made me sick to even think about. Ironically, Vicky showed up when I was loading the last box.

She didn't yell or throw a fit because I wasn't going to be her maid of honor, and she didn't give me a guilt trip about the loved ones I was leaving behind. Instead, she wrapped me tightly in her arms while we both sobbed. Eventually, she untangled herself, kissed my forehead, said she loved me and left. I was inconsolable for the next hour. When I finally regained my composure, I decided I could not wait until morning. I placed the goodbye note on the dining room table for my parents and then made a quick stop at the post office to mail another. I left for Chicago without saying goodbye to anyone else.

• • •

"Jessie?" Vicky's hand touches my shoulder, and I jolt upright and wipe my eyes.

"Sam and his family have been over for dinner at least once a week since I've been home," I quickly recover.

Vicky's silence tells me she is not ready to end the conversation. Reluctantly, she respects my wishes.

"He told me. He wants to talk to you about the possibility of a family dinner in a few weeks."

"A family dinner will be good," I agree before picking up my tea glass and disappearing inside.

A moment later, Vicky follows. She continues to chat, but I barely listen while unloading the dishwasher. I'm still disengaged when I start chopping vegetables for dinner until she mentions Shane's baseball practice later that evening, and his natural talent for sports. The idea of watching a baseball game sounds appealing. I remember many times we rode our bikes to the baseball diamond for Tyson and Zane's games. She spends the next fifteen minutes convincing me to tag along to pick up the children from school. I finally cave when she bribes me with ice cream. Reluctant, but also desperate for a change of scenery, I crawl into the passenger seat of her SUV and strap on my seatbelt.

Fidgeting, I twirl the string of my hooded sweatshirt around the tip of my finger as my eyes dart from one side of the road to the other. Without thinking about it, I look apprehensively into every car we pass on the drive.

Vicky places her hand on my bouncing knee. "You don't have to worry about seeing him."

During our interactions thus far, we have been careful not to broach the subject of what drove me away, but I knew this was bound to happen.

"What?" I ask, feigning innocence.

Vicky sighs. "He's in a nursing home, Jessie. There was an accident before the wedding. He was climbing onto the barn roof at the ranch when he fell. He broke his nose, shattered his cheekbone, and cracked a few ribs. He also suffered a traumatic brain injury. There were rumors of foul play. No one knows the truth."

Speechless and confused, I press my fingertips into the corners of my eyes.

She continues. "He was in the hospital and couldn't come to the wedding. To be honest with you, I don't know if he would have anyway. He and Tyson were barely on speaking terms at that time. A week later, he went to a rehabilitation facility, but he suffered a stroke there, so he was sent to a long-term care facility. He's had two more strokes over the years, and the last one left him completely disabled. Joan only goes to see him once every six months. When she does, she reports that he still has some recognition, but he can't speak or move and will always need full-time care."

Vicky smiles mischievously. "She is so much happier with him out of her life. It's as if she can breathe again. She comes and goes as she pleases, takes trips with friends, belongs to a book club, and attends a yoga class once a week. After all these years, she finally bought herself some decent clothes that flatter her body. Remember how she always wore those ugly, oversized sweaters and baggy slacks in drab colors? You should see her. She looks ten years younger with highlights in her hair and manicured nails."

I don't know whether to laugh or cry. "He wasn't at your wedding?"

"Nope," she says.

"If that wasn't a stroke of good luck. No pun intended." I can't believe I am joking about something this serious, but I feel as if a massive boulder of shame, fear, and anxiety has been lifted from my heart. "Why didn't anyone tell me?"

Vicky shrugs. "Mom and Dad had no idea it would matter to you, and you and I didn't have contact. I wanted to tell you when I first saw you but figured it would come out in time."

"What about Sam?"

"I don't know, Jessie. I'm sure he has his reasons."

We pull up to the school and park behind a line of cars. I lean forward in my seat to peer out the window at my elementary school. As we sit in silence, waiting for the bell to ring, my head is full of a torrid of memories and endless questions that I know will have to wait.

I watch the front doors intently, envisioning myself as a student running through them, backpack slung over my shoulder, excited for what the weekend had in store. I can't help but wonder if Shane, Shelby, and Sasha's lives are as carefree and filled with joy as mine once was. I search the sea of faces and inhale when I spot them. Even though I've seen pictures over the years, I didn't realize how much the twins looked like me at that age, and Shane was a beautiful combination of his mother and father.

Vicky places her hand over mine. "They are going to love you, and you are going to love them. I promise."

They climb through the door one by one—eyes growing wide, full of anxious enthusiasm—and begin talking at once as Vicky starts the engine.

"Mom said she was going to surprise us with you one day this week," the twin I believe is Sasha exclaims.

"Is it true that you and Mom use to sleep in the old treehouse out front during rainstorms with only blankets for a tent?" Shane inquires.

I nod.

"That is so cool!" he says.

"That is dangerous," the other twin scolds. "You could have been struck by lightning, but I'm glad you weren't. Otherwise you wouldn't be here now."

The interrogation continues for the fifteen-minute ride. Suddenly, there is silence as we pull into the drive-through of the ice cream parlor. Shane reads the dessert menu to his sisters, and I look over my shoulder to stare at the three of them. Vicky chuckles beside me. Once we have our treats, we drive the short distance to the park where the kids leap out and run to the nearest picnic table. A few moments later, Vicky and I join them. Since they are devouring their ice cream as if they hadn't had a meal all day, I take the opportunity to ask questions about school, interests, friends, and relationships with one another. They engage delightfully between bites, but it is apparent Sasha is more reserved, allowing her brother and sister to speak for her more often than not. When they are full and happy, laughter fills the air as they climb on the playground equipment. I watch in awe, enamored by the miracle of these beautiful children and the fact that in only a short time, I have fallen in love with all three of them.

• • •

Later that night while sitting in bed, I journal and spend a whole thirty minutes writing. I usually have a difficult time labeling my emotions because I'm an expert at avoidance. Tonight, with a collection of emotions coming from all directions, I'm grateful to get them out of my head. After the day I've had, I find it easy to let them flow.

I first write about my father. It's painful to watch the process of his deterioration. His weight loss is significant, his appetite comes and goes, and the color in his cheeks have gone from the familiar rosy red to an ashen grey. Mom informs me he no longer sleeps well because the pain medication gives him insomnia. Last night, after he went to bed, I was shocked when she approached the subject of medical marijuana. She wants him to be as comfortable as possible during the time he has left. She asked if I could get some when I go to Seattle in a few weeks. She is not sure Dad will even agree to use it since he still has negative opinions about the drug, but she would like to have some on hand just in case.

My thoughts then shift toward Tyson. It's a relief to know he does not hate me, so I'm not as terrified to see him. Maybe I am a little terrified of the questions, but it is not sending me into a panic like before.

I frown as my mind replays the conversation I had with Vicky. I was blind-sided to learn what happened to Ron. I spent years afraid, constantly looking over my shoulder, wondering if he'd ever make good on his threat to hunt me down, especially after he realized I stole the VCR tape of Vicky when I left the guesthouse that day thirteen years ago. I had the evidence that could send him to prison. If only I had known he was incapacitated.

I don't want to think about the alternatives, but I can't help it. Zane constantly spoke about taking over his grandparent's ranch one day. He thought it was something the two of us would do together. The plan was for us to attend the university and when I had my medical license, we'd move back to Helena to live on the ranch, and I'd have a private practice in town. I guess it surprises me he followed through with his part of the plan. If he doesn't have much contact with our family, why didn't he start a new life for himself somewhere else without the memories? Why didn't he ever marry?

He wrote me about twenty letters. He gave them to Tyson, who gave them to Vicky, who passed them on to Mom. Even though Mom believed he was responsible for my leaving, she still made sure I received every note. I returned all of them without opening one. She said she would keep them if I changed my mind. Over the years, on my darkest days, when I was feeling sorry for myself, I was tempted to have her mail them to me. But I never found the courage to ask. I knew they would take me to a place I didn't want to go.

Other than that, Zane had no way to get in touch with me. I did eventually get a cell phone, but the only people who had my number were my parents and Sam. And I trusted they would not share it with anyone.

I set up a Facebook account a year ago to search for him. I couldn't help it. I was curious and maybe a bit hopeful. At that time, he did not have a page. I checked again before I came here, but still nothing. I have been cautious with my profile. Those who don't know me well won't find me. I've been able to keep my page contained to friends from my new life and hardly anyone from my old life. But I have a gut feeling if he tries to look me up, he will know how to find me.

I don't know what my reaction would be if we did connect on the social media site. I think seeing pictures and having access to him would be painful yet exhilarating. Would I reach out and message him? Would he even respond? I've played the same scenario in my head a dozen times.

This is what adds confusion to my already complicated life. No one in thirteen years has made me feel the way Zane did. As hard as I try to push him out, he continues to linger in the back of my mind. I try to deny it, but no other man, and certainly not A.J., has filled my empty heart.

CHAPTER FIVE

The upcoming family dinner at Sam and Jillian's on Saturday is significant to my parents, and because we don't want anything to spoil it, Vicky invites me to her house for a glass of wine a few days beforehand. She feels it might be best for Tyson and me to become acclimated with one another again before we are thrown into a big family gathering. I agree.

"He wasn't surprised you are home considering the issues with Dad," she claims. "*And* he's glad you're here."

Despite her reassurance, I'm nervous as I drive to their house. Dad's directions take me to a new development on the north side of town where I park in front of a Neo-Colonial home. I find it eerily strange that Vicky has a grown-up house that I have never been to, with an adult husband. Though I've seen her with her kids, it's still hard for me to picture her as a mother. These milestones were supposed to happen gradually, not all at once, years later.

With the loaf of banana bread Mom baked earlier that day in one hand and a bottle of wine in the other, I shuffle up the sidewalk. My heart palpitations increase as I poke my finger into the doorbell and wait. I look around the front yard and attempt to take in the small details, but have difficulty breathing, let alone the ability to pay attention to anything else.

Behind the door, I hear high pitched squeals of delight before an argument breaks out about who will greet me first. When the door opens, a victorious Shane stands on the other side grinning. Before I can move, the twins shove him aside, wrapping their arms around my torso and ushering me into the house. In the kitchen, I find Vicky and Tyson cleaning up the remnants of their dinner. Vicky smiles warmly and places a glass of red wine in front of me as I crawl onto the bar stool. Before we even make eye contact, Tyson herds the kids into the living room. Curiously, I watch as he hustles after them, picking up shoes and jackets while dodging complaints. Finally, he gives all three of them a stern warning. They quickly quiet down, shifting their attention to a movie playing on the television.

I would recognize him anywhere, but he is not the boy I knew from my childhood. He was always tall, lean, and well-built, but he seems more intimidating now than he was in high school. His always fascinating ginger hair, is now mixed with grey and his jawline, more mature and defined, is covered with an appealing five-o-clock shadow. His skin, except for a stream of freckles across his nose, is fair and when he smiles, his eyes still twinkle bright blue.

Before I realize what is happening, he returns to the kitchen to pull me into his arms.

• • •

Three hours later, after Vicky and Tyson have carried sleeping kids to their rooms, we sit on the sofa talking, reminiscing, and laughing. There are moments of awkward silence due to the obvious reasons, but we easily maneuver back to more light-hearted topics. The humorous tales of child-rearing never end as I encourage them to tell me more. Tyson shares his love of hunting, fishing, and snowmobiling, while Vicky shows me around their beautiful four bedroom home. It's the perfect size for the five of them, warm and inviting. Tyson asks thoughtful, polite questions about life in Seattle. I avoid bringing up A.J. He appears hesitant but eventually explains how he took over the family business.

Vicky tactfully changes the subject back to the kids' summer activities until we finally stumble our way into discussing Dad. While we know the outcome of his prognosis, it doesn't make it any more realistic than the first time I heard the news. Tyson does not even try to hide his emotion as we talk about the ongoing preparations. He stands up, wipes his eyes, and leaves the room.

"He's taking this hard," Vicky says, gazing at the closed door her husband escaped through. "He cares about Mom and Dad more than he did his parents. We've tried to model our marriage after theirs."

She leaves the sofa and moves into the kitchen where she picks up a dishcloth and starts wiping the counters. I follow her, setting my empty wine glass in the sink. She continues to talk, but I am distracted. My mind should be on my father and the words coming out of her mouth, but instead, I focus on the comment she made about her marriage. I look over my shoulder to make sure Tyson hasn't returned to the room. "How do you do it?" I whisper.

She looks at me quizzically.

"Seriously, how do you do this marriage knowing you're keeping a huge secret?"

Frowning, she glances at the clock. She walks across the room and disappears behind the same door Tyson used moments before. I gather my belongings preparing to leave, figuring I made her angry. But, as I hoist my purse over my shoulder, she returns.

"Tyson asked me to apologize and to tell you he's looking forward to dinner with the family in a few days."

She grabs her mug of tea, and I follow her through the sliding glass door onto the back patio. She relaxes into the glider, patting the seat next to her, motioning for me to sit. I hesitate at first but then sink down beside her.

I can tell she is trying to decide what to say. I wait while staring into the darkness of the night sky, the silver crescent of the moon glaring above the treetops.

"Ron and I never had intercourse," she reminds me.

"But that doesn't make it any less—" I start to say.

Vicky interrupts. "You're right. What he did was horrible, inappropriate, and yes, it tormented me. A part of me will always have issues," she admits. "But I never had issues with Tyson. I can't explain it, Jessie. All I know is when I look at Tyson, I only see my husband. I don't see any connection to Ron at all. Your fear is when you are with Zane, you will hear Ron's voice, feel his hands touching you. I understood when you left that you could not live that way. I also knew you were worried he would find out you weren't a virgin anymore. How would you explain that?"

My eyes burn with unshed tears. How easily my sister puts into words the scars that hide beneath the Band-Aid I refuse to rip off.

Vicky tells me about the triggers she suffered when her children began getting invites for sleepovers. She had a hard enough time manipulating play dates when they were younger, but slumber parties were another thing entirely. Vicky did not trust other adults even if she'd known the families for years. While she carefully supervised all three kids, she was more controlling of the twins than Shane. The fear she carried around practically suffocated her.

"I still have panic attacks around cigarette smoke," she reveals.

This information shocks me. I too, suffer from shortness of breath and become drastically dizzy or nauseous every time I walk through a cloud of smoke or smell it on someone standing next to me. All this time, I chalked it up to asthma. It never dawned on me it could be something more.

"I haven't picked up a guitar since the day my lessons ended. I don't think I ever will." Vicky said.

I frown. "I understand that. It's too bad because you were really talented."

"Maybe I'll take up the drums one day," she smiles, sadly.

Vicky says she was able to hide her erratic behavior from Tyson, but it was not easy. Her anxiety and insomnia kept her awake most nights. She tried to supervise the children carefully, but it turned into obsessive, overprotective parenting. She became a mother who was always looking for the dark, scary guy lurking around the corner. She became more irritable than usual, and her fuse was short. She and Tyson fought over the smallest things. Her fear was debilitating at times, and she found that she was disengaged more than she was involved.

"I couldn't rationalize my fears," she went on to explain. "Ron was out of our lives, but at every birthday party, family gathering, or school event I became paranoid and anxious that he would miraculously recover and want to be a part of the family—a loving, involved and overly affectionate grandfather. I made myself sick with worry, wondering how to protect my kids, my marriage, even my husband."

Finally, a close friend, unaware of the full story but noticing signs of trauma, suggested she see a counselor.

"It was the most terrifying thing I've ever done, Jessie. If I didn't love him or my kids as much as I do, I don't know if I could have gone through with it. Ron ruined me. He ruined *our* relationship. I was damned if I was going to let him ruin my future with the man I loved. I refused to give him that much power over me." Vicky said.

Tears stream down my cheeks as I stare blankly at the shadows in the sky.

Vicky sighs as she placed her hand over mine. "It's worth it, Jessie. I have my life back. Don't get me wrong. It's always going to be a part of who I am, but I don't let it define me. I'm free. I want you to be free, too."

Vicky doesn't understand. Ron groomed her, molested, manipulated, and touched her in ways she should not have been touched. But Vicky's trauma was different than mine. He did not beat her. He did not brutally rape her. He did not hold a gun to her head. The last thing in the world I want to do is relive that nightmare over again until l am normal. What if I can never be normal?

As if reading my mind, Vicky speaks again. "You wouldn't have to do it alone. For the first time in a long time, you don't have to be scared."

The world seems to fall away at her words. Although it feels like I'm tipping on the brink of insanity, I desperately cling to the security of my sister's arms and cry while she holds me.

• • •

After my hysterics died down, Vicky led me to the spare bedroom where I crawled under the covers and quickly fell asleep. Now, as rays of sun peek through the drapes, I look at the digital clock on the nightstand. It reads ten-twenty-eight. I drag my tired body out of bed, groaning as I make my way to the living room where I find the house quiet and empty, a note lying on the kitchen counter.

> *T and I at work. Called parents to let them know you spent the night. Help yourself to whatever. Please lock the front door when you leave. See you tomorrow at Sam's.*
>
> *Love U!*
> *Vic*
>
> *PS: Think about what I said.*

I make myself scrambled eggs, a side of toast, and a mug of hot green tea. As I sit at the center island to eat, I stare out the large kitchen window and think about the conversations I've had the last few weeks. I feel my life is more complicated than it was the day I traveled here. Frustrated, I toss my dishes into the dishwasher and slam it shut. Locking the door behind me, I drive home.

I hear my mother's frantic yell the moment I walk through the front door.

"Call 911!"

I rush to the livingroom where I find her hovering over my father, who is on the floor, vomiting into the trash can.

"What's wrong?"

"Call emergency! Now!" The fear in her eyes terrifies me.

Frantically, I dig my cell phone out of my purse and dial emergency, then I text Vicky and Sam. Feeling helpless, I stand against the wall and wait until I hear sirens. I watch as the EMT's load my delirious father onto a gurney and into the ambulance. My mom crawls in, stone-faced, behind him, and the paramedics close the door. I rush into the house, throw on a new pair of running pants, a T-shirt and tennis shoes. I make sure the stove is off, and all is in order before jumping back into my car.

Vicky and Sam are already in the waiting room by the time I arrive, and Mom is in the emergency room with our father. I collapse into one of the brown leather chairs next to my brother.

"This happened one other time about a week before you came home," Sam states. "Mom said he was out of sorts this morning when he woke. She could hardly get him out of bed and when she finally did, he started throwing up and didn't stop."

The emergency room doctor comes out forty-five minutes later informing us that Dad is comfortable and resting. They want to admit him overnight, but it looks like the vomiting was a reaction to his opioids, the pain medication he started taking after his last appointment. In the meantime, they are discussing other pain options and anti-nausea pills. Even though Dad does not want any preventative treatment for his disease, everyone wants to make sure he is as comfortable as possible during this process. I decide this is a good time to tell Sam and Vicky about the conversation I had with Mom about medical marijuana.

Sam snorts.

"I think it's a good idea," Vicky admits. "It sounds like Mom agrees. How do we get Dad on board?"

"We could just make him brownies or cookies every day," Sam chuckles.

"Is that legal?" I ask, feeling ignorant. "Would we need his approval, or would we be drugging him illegally?"

"Hell if I know," Sam states. "This whole medical marijuana stuff is new to me. I don't want to know how you get it here. Whatever you decide, I'll play dumb.

"You are going to Seattle in a few weeks, right?" Vicky asks.

"Exactly," I say. "Phillip may be able to get me something I can bring back. Maybe a cream? Hell, I don't know. I haven't smoked pot for years."

Vicky and Sam stare at me in disbelief. "*You* smoked pot?" Vicky asks.

I wave my hand in the air. "A discussion for another day and another time."

After tossing around more ideas to help our father, we shift our attention to the episode of *Days of Our Lives* playing on the television in the waiting room.

"Christ," Sam mumbles.

Vicky and I giggle. When I was in junior high, we used to record the soap opera and rush home every day to watch it after school. The overdramatic plot twists and ridiculous love stories kept us intrigued, hooked, and forever romanticizing.

"You still watch this stuff?" I ask Vicky.

She cringes. "No. When would I have time?"

Vicky teaches part-time at a Montessori school, then rushes to pick up her three kids and evenings are full of various activities. She told me it's been years since she's even had time to sit down to read a good book, let alone watch television.

"Me either." I cock my head to the side as I stare at the screen. "Was the acting always this bad?"

"Yes!" Sam exclaims, clearly exasperated. "It was horrible. You two refused to let me watch anything else until it was over. Jack and Jennifer, Bo and Hope, Marlena and John, or Roman or whoever—it drove me insane!"

Vicky's raises an eyebrow. "Seriously, Sam? You were paying enough attention to know the characters names?"

Sam's flushes.

I point at him. "You were," I laugh. "Admit it. You were getting all hot and bothered over those steamy love scenes too!"

"Was?" Jillian comments with a sheepish grin as she walks into the waiting room. "Don't let him fool you. I still catch him watching an episode every once in a while when he is on swing shift."

"You three go to hell," Sam grumbles, crossing his arms over his chest as he sinks into his seat.

We update Jillian as we continue to wait for Dad to be transferred to a room. Mom joins us briefly but does not want to leave him alone long. I should call A.J., but I realize I don't want to. I decide to get some fresh air while Vicky takes a trip to the cafeteria, and Sam paces the hallway talking on his cell phone. Once I'm outside, I begin a brisk walk around the building, which turns into a jog then shifts into a run.

Thirty minutes later, between the late May heat and adrenaline, I am a sweaty mess. As I turn the corner to the hospital, I realize I am much calmer than I was before my run. I stop in the first-floor bathroom, throw cold water onto my flushed face, and dry off with rough paper towels. I make my way to the cafeteria to get an iced tea. I scan the room and realize that I have not worried once today about who I may see.

I send a quick text message to my siblings to see if anyone needs anything from the cafeteria. My phone beeps and I glance at Vicky's reply. Dad is in room three-fifteen, and she asks me to get Mom an iced tea and a bag of chips. I pull a large plastic cup from the dispenser. Suddenly, my gut starts to twist, and I feel the hair on the back of my neck stand up. I turn around anticipating to find someone standing close behind me, but the nearest person is more than three feet away, pouring dressing on a salad, oblivious to me. Yet, I can't shake the strange sensation someone is watching me. With a shrug, I put ice into the cups and then pull on the handle of the iced tea dispenser filling one at a time. After fitting the lids, I choose five bags of chips to ensure there are snacks for everyone. I pull cash out of my pocket and pay.

I cuss under my breath as I clamp two bags of chips between my teeth and juggle the other items in my arms. I hustle to the elevator. Before I entertain the idea of balancing a cup on my head to free a hand to push the button, someone beats me to it.

"Let me get that."

I inhale sharply as my pulse begins to race and the cup in my hand shakes.

The voice, though much deeper and deliberate, is unmistakable. Despite feeling lightheaded, I keep my eyes transfixed on the almond colored tiles that seem to tilt sideways. The weight of the burdens in my heart and my arms become excessive. My emotions are over-whelming. As desperate as I am to run, a larger part of me is inclined to stay. Even though I shiver, I am not cold. Instead, it's as if the heat from Zane's penetrating gaze is scorching a hole through my skin.

Taking a step toward me, he grabs the cup that topples out of my grasp.

"Don't," I hiss, jerking away, but not soon enough.

He catches it with a bandaged hand before it hits the floor and explodes.

Finally, the ding of the opening elevator door rescues me. Grabbing the cup, I hastily bolt into the safety of the metal frame and forcefully press the button with my pinky finger. Exasperated, I lean against the back wall, willing the doors to shut. Timidly, I lift my head and stare into the eyes of the boy I used to love. My throat tightens, and seeing him for the first time makes my legs go weak. For a brief moment, the years between us slip away and just as he steps forward to say something, the elevator door closes.

• • •

When I reach the third floor, I can hardly focus on where I am or what I am supposed to be doing. I need a few moments to compose myself. I find a waiting room at the end of the hall, set my belongings on the coffee table, and close the door. I feel like I'm going to crawl out of my own skin. I pace the floor and rub my arms until they turn red. A few years back, A.J. bought me a punching bag for my anger and aggression. It hangs in our spare bedroom, and I've never used it, but I'd give anything to have it now. Instead, I seek safety in an overstuffed chair where I stare at the stark white wall.

My vibrating phone jolts me back to reality. It's a text from Vicky wanting to know where I am. I scoop up my belongings, feeling guilty. When I find the room, I give my dad a quick kiss on the forehead, hand Mom the iced tea and toss the bags of chips onto the end table.

"The doctors feel confident about releasing Dad first thing in the morning, but I am going to stay the night. This chair here," Mom pats the seat underneath her, "pulls out into a bed. Jessie, would you mind going home and getting a few things for us?"

"I'll go with you," Vicky suggests, grabbing the list out of Mom's hand. "Tyson will meet us here after he gets the kids from school. We can stop and pick up chicken and potato salad for dinner. Does that sound okay, Mom?"

"What? Huh?" Distracted, my mom turns from where she is adjusting Dad's bed covers and waves her hand. "Whatever you two want, dear."

We walk in silence to the elevator while my paranoid eyes dart around. The last thing I need is to be blindsided by the same someone I'm unprepared to see.

"What's your deal?" Vicky asks once the steel doors begin to close.

I lean my head back against the cold metal and look up at the ceiling. "I saw Zane, and he saw me."

"Fuck," she says as she imitates my pose.

We drive home without discussing it. While Vicky makes necessary phone calls to the pharmacy and Dr. Wilkenson, I pack my parents' belongings into the small suitcase I find on the top shelf of their closet.

When I return to the living room, suitcase in hand, Vicky is talking in hushed whispers on her cell phone. She quickly ends the conversation and hangs up when she sees me.

"That was Tyson," she explains. "He got an unexpected visit at the store from a very angry Zane. He demanded to know why we haven't told him you were in town."

The irony of this makes me laugh. "Poor Tyson. What did he tell him?"

"He hasn't had a chance to tell Zane about Dad, so Tyson explained everything. Needless to say, he is reeling from that news, too. I am not surprised by his reaction."

"I guess not. But he seemed a lot less disturbed than I was, unless he hid it better," I add.

"I think he's had a lot of practice," Vicky admits sadly. "You know he's not going to let this lie. He'll want to talk to you. Are you prepared for that?"

Tears pool in my eyes. "No. But I don't have a choice, do I?"

We stop by the local grocery store to pick up fried chicken, potato salad, fruit, and drinks, before we head back to the hospital. On the drive there, I tell Vicky what transpired.

"I don't know if I would have known him if I hadn't recognized his voice," I explain as I tug the seatbelt away from my chest.

I tell her how I imagined this moment over the years—how I would react, what I would say, how I would feel. The only thing that came close in the interaction is how I felt. There was a horrible pain that seared my heart, but there was also a mixture of shock and thrilling exhilaration. It was almost baffling how his energy made me feel like a carefree young girl who stumbled upon someone with whom she felt a mystifying connection. I was tempted to reach out, to re-introduce myself and strike up a new friendship.

We meet Tyson and the kids at the front entrance of the hospital. Our arms are full of grocery bags. He shoots an awkward smile my way as we walk through the lobby.

Sam and his family are already in the room when we arrive. Dad is awake but groggy and appears over-whelmed with so many family members congregating in the tiny space all at once. After I give him a quick hug, Sam suggests we take the food to the waiting room. Vicky lingers behind while the rest of us, including Mom, make our way down the hall.

Walking beside her, I glance out of the corner of my eye and for the first time, notice how exhausted Mom looks. When I reach for her hand, she squeezes mine in return.

We find Sam rummaging through the food containers spread across the table while Jillian hands each of us a paper plate. Once dinner is dished out, we chat lightheartedly about the kids' end of the year school programs, track meets, and awards ceremonies. Mom is unusually quiet while she picks at her food. She has been stoic through all of this, but today I sense a final acceptance of what the future holds and can see the grief is weighing her down.

"Mom," I say, standing up. "Let's go for a walk."

Without a word, she sets her plate on the end table and follows me down the stairwell into the fresh night air. Once we are outside, she looks up, smiles, and closes her eyes, inhaling deeply. I notice the stars brightly illuminate against a clear, black sky when I gaze upwards. When she starts to walk, I grasp her hand, and we stroll along the cracked sidewalk, the heaviness of our unspoken words surrounding us.

I spot a picnic table a few yards away tucked privately under a tall oak tree. "Do you want to keep walking?" I ask. "Or should we sit?"

"Let's sit." Mom's voice cracks.

Her shoulders start to shake before we make it to the bench. It has only been on rare occasions that I have seen my mother cry. In her era, her family did not openly display emotions. I'm sure she allowed her deepest feelings to surface when she was alone with Dad, but not ever in front of us as kids.

By the time we were adults, she'd softened and no longer hid her feelings in front of us. Like the time she told me Vicky was pregnant. We were on a camping trip.

Dad, Sam, and Jillian took the kids fishing. Mom and I were cleaning up after breakfast when she delivered the news. I was stunned. I was thrilled Vicky was having a baby, but I was also sad. I couldn't imagine not sharing something so wonderful and intimate with my sister, or not being the one to throw her a baby shower and help pick out the theme for the nursery. Instead, I had to live vicariously through others and my imagination. When Mom saw the look on my face, we wept together.

But this is different.

I sit quietly with my arm wrapped around her and rub her shoulder as she quivers uncontrollably. She rests her head against mine. I run my fingers through her hair and kiss her forehead as she used to do to me as a child.

"What am I going to do without him?" she whispers. "When you kids grew up and moved out, it was him and me against the world. He's my partner. My best friend. I can't believe this is really happening."

My eyes burn back tears. I try to picture myself in my mother's shoes, wondering how I would feel if something like this happened to A.J. Annoyed, I remind myself that my relationship with A.J. is not even comparable to the love my mother and father share.

"It's fuckin stupid," my mom snaps.

I chuckle at her awkward attempt to curse.

Wiping her tears with the back of her hand, she lets out a small laugh. "I've never been good at using that word," she admits.

"It's okay. It's not that great of a word." I reassure her.

She links her fingers through mine and shakes her head. "I thought I was doing okay, that I could handle this but lately, Jessie, I'm cracking. I'm not as strong as I want to be."

She places her hand on my cheek gently turning my face toward her. "I know it's been difficult for you, but thank you for coming home. You have no idea how much it means to both of us having you here. I watch him watch you. His eyes shine seeing you and your sister together," she breaks down again.

By now I'm crying with her. "I can't imagine not being here," I tell her. "I just wish…" I trail off.

"Don't," she hisses. "Don't you dare do the guilt thing."

"Someone has to," I comment, sarcastically. "You and Dad never did."

Mom pulls her shoulders back, her eyes wide with shock. "You wanted us to punish you? To hold a grudge?"

I shake my head. "I'm grateful you didn't, but my God, Mom, you two have been unbelievably understanding. I've been selfish and now with this…"

She places her index finger on my lips to stop me from continuing. Silently I watch as she pieces her thoughts together. "You had your reasons. But I know your heart. Even when you were a teenager, I knew you. You were happy, focused, driven, and in love. Our family was solid. Whatever or whoever hurt you enough to make you leave and never come home, I may not have liked it, but I understood. You wouldn't have left the way you did unless you had to. It ripped my heart out, but I never blamed you. It could have been so much worse. We never really lost you or wondered where you were. You were always here." She pats her heart.

In my head, I wrestle with the idea of telling her the truth about Ron. I can't do it now with Dad in this condition. It would be selfish, and the emotional burden would be too much for either of them to bear. Logically, they would know there was nothing they could have done, but the guilt would eat them alive. I stay quiet as a flood of emotions surface within me.

In my silence, Mom continues. "It was hardest on Vicky. It's like a part of her was missing. I could also see that in you. I guess you two just got used to it, but I never did. Now everything can be like it used to."

The stresses of my dad's health and running into Zane earlier leave me feeling like I've been sitting on a fragile bubble. Mom's words are the pin that makes it pop, and I am unable to control the flood that bursts out of me.

"We never got used to it!" I rub my temples and stare at the ground. "No, everything cannot go back to what it was. It was like a death, even though I was too stubborn to grieve it."

She places her hand on my arm, but I yank it away and stand up.

"I'm a mess, Mom. Do you understand that? I'm a dysfunctional, can't deal with life, emotional mess. All of this," I shriek, motioning to myself. "All of this I fake really well. On the outside, I function at work, with friends and with A.J., and now here at home. I pretend I'm motivated when I am exhausted. In my shell of a body, I walk like a zombie through my life. But inside is broken, dead."

I start to cry harder. "I hate it. I was happy for eighteen years. One day, my outlook on life, my trust, my faith in love, and my family, even my confidence disappeared. I've tried desperately to create the same sense of security and safety I had growing up. It's impossible. Frankly, it is exhausting to wake up every day to do it all over again. I do it because I know there is more to life. Despite how numb I feel most of the time, now and then I get a spark of hope to sustain me to move forward. Hope brought me home and being here with all of you, that hope is more alive than I thought possible."

In the shadow of the street light, I see her face full of empathy, but for some reason, this unnerves me.

"What I need you to understand is as much as it excites me, feeling alive is terrifying. I lost everything, including myself, in a matter of days. There is a lot of misery and loneliness in this world I hide behind, but it's the only way I found to survive, and it's not an easy way to live. I crave the opposite, but it's foreign. I'm trying and will continue to try. But I need you to be patient. It's going to be one step forward and two steps back at times. But I'm determined, and I refuse to stop."

I cringe as she takes a step toward me.

"As a mother, I wish I could take your hurt away, but I can't," she frowns.

Feeling defeated, I sigh. I desire for Mom to do just that, take the hurt away. Instead, I change the subject. Wrapping my arm around her shoulder, I pull her close and apologize.

"We came out here so I can support you and look what happened. I turned it into a bitch session for myself."

"It was much needed. We are both a mess and just piss ass tired," Mom laughs, gently rubbing my shoulder. "Come on, let's go back in and check on your dad."

CHAPTER SIX

This recent episode was hard on Dad, and we are more aware of his decline now than ever before. Since being discharged, he spends more extended periods in bed or his recliner. Upon waking, he slowly shuffles to the table where it takes him about a half hour to eat his scrambled eggs, oatmeal, or applesauce. He misses his heartier meals, but his stomach cannot tolerate them. He doesn't complain much, except when he drinks hot green tea instead of coffee. He calls it a sissy drink. Because of his digestive system, anything other than bland foods will have him in the bathroom all morning, which he learned zaps his energy for the rest of the day.

After breakfast, he makes it to his chair, where he tries to stay awake for the *TODAY* show. But he's exhausted and quickly falls asleep. I stay with him while Mom runs errands. I catch up with Phillip and A.J. about business. A.J. is distant but cooperative. Phillip is his same old fun-loving self who can always shift my mood from bad to good. If we hadn't been such emotional basket cases when we met, maybe there could have been potential for a heavy romance. There is no denying he is a charming, attractive man who is also devoted and trustworthy. He is the one person in the last decade who made me feel alive without any expectations or strings attached. But the two of us together romantically would be like adding vinegar to baking soda, a chemical reaction ready to combust.

After his nap, Mom helps Dad in the shower and with dressing. Since he hasn't lost his mischievous humor, he has no problem letting us know how much he enjoys this part of his day. About a month ago, Sam installed a handicapped tub and shower in their master bathroom that Dad can walk into without worrying about falling. Between the two of them, they have enough strength to complete these tasks but there will soon come a time when Mom cannot do it alone, which is why she wants to hire a home health nurse.

By lunchtime, Dad is exhausted again and only has an appetite for a fruit smoothie with a protein supplement. He spends most of the afternoon napping off and on with Mom reading a book or napping beside him. I use these opportunities to spend my days enjoying summer with the kids.

Sam's family lives on fifteen acres ten minutes outside of town. Since moving four months ago, they purchased three horses and are up to their elbows in decorating projects. I go there on Tuesdays and Thursdays to feed the horses, go for an occasional ride, and help with whatever they need—painting a fence, putting tile in the bathroom, weeding the garden, running kids to activities if their parents are stretched thin.

I attend Shane and Tanner's baseball games every Monday evening and Saturday mornings. On

Wednesdays at one, I take the three girls to gymnastics, and afterward it is routine to stop for ice cream and play at the park before I take them home. On these evenings, I stay and have supper with Tyson and Vicky.

Tonight, Tyson has a brisket on the grill. I sit on a cushioned Adirondack chair on their back patio with a cold beer in my hand, listening to Vicky complain about the girls' gymnastics coach.

"She says to me, in front of the girls mind you, that they are not showing as much talent or passion as she would have hoped. Cassidy is outshining them and has become her star pupil."

"Uh-oh," Tyson mumbles as he gets up to check the meat.

"So I asked her, 'Where do you live?' She looked confused but said 'Helena.' 'And where do you teach?' I asked. 'At the YMCA,' she answered."

Again, Tyson chuckles.

"So, I stepped close to her and said, 'You do realize these girls are only six years old, correct? You do realize as parents, we do not bring them here with dreams of becoming Olympic athletes. We bring them here so they can socialize, be active and part of a team, figure out how to follow direction and respect authority in other adults, such as you, their coach. Most importantly, we bring them here to build self-esteem and confidence. I really hope that the comments you just made in front of my children are never repeated, and I hope you take time to reflect on how you are approaching your role as a YMCA gymnastics coach. The program has never been known as competitive, but instead as a program that promotes values. You may need to see if your expectations are in the best interests of the children involved or if you have another agenda. If this program has changed and I am unaware, I would like to have my children removed immediately so they can find a program that better suits their personality, ages, and interests.'"

It is now my turn to be speechless. The Vicky I grew up with had a stereotypical middle child personality. She was the laidback, easygoing girl next door one would call a passive peacemaker who avoided conflict at all costs. I, on the other hand, was the feisty one never afraid to stand up for injustice. It's hard for me to picture her telling anyone off.

"Listen to you!" I exclaim.

"There are certain things a momma bear will not tolerate," Tyson laughs. "She's gotten in touch with "her inner fight" since the day those cubs were born," he adds with a wink.

I completely understood. What that woman dared to say about my nieces made me want to scratch her eyeballs out, too. I can't imagine the anger it would stir up in me if it had been my children.

Tyson disappears through the side gate to call the kids for dinner. Vicky returns from the kitchen with the salad and corn on the cob while I grab drinks. The kids rush through the gate and into the house to wash their hands. A moment later, they calmly return to the table after their father reminds them to settle down.

Nostalgia washes over me as we eat. Family dinners are one of the routines I miss the most in the new life I created. When I was on my own, I typically ate when and where I landed, in front of the television, in my room studying or fast food on the go in my car. When A.J. and I moved in together, I attempted family dinners by setting a lovely table and encouraging her to sit with me. But A.J. filled her plate and sat in front of the television to watch the evening news. Though we were together in the same room, it wasn't anything close to what I'd envisioned for my life.

After we eat, all three kids start their chores while Tyson, Vicky and I linger on the patio, relaxing after a long and busy day.

"I envy you," I admit. "This is an amazing life and a wonderful family you two have made."

Tyson stands, "I'll finish helping the kids," he says.

"I didn't mean to drive him off," I say after he disappears.

Vicky frowns. "You didn't. He knows when we need privacy."

"I wanted this, you know."

Vicky nods sadly. "I remember."

There was a time when I shifted the blame of my circumstances onto Vicky. In my mind, if she hadn't kept what happened between her and Ron a secret, I wouldn't have been put in the situation I was. I wanted someone to pay for what happened to me, and she seemed the logical choice. Looking back, I can honestly say I wanted to punish her, and I did by creating the rift between us. It's not something I'm proud of, and it took me a long time to resolve the resentment I carried. One day, I realized Vicky was no more responsible for Ron's actions than I was and placing blame was unfair and spiteful. Almost immediately, my anger toward her dissolved.

That was before. Now, witnessing the life she has created and the person she's become, I feel regret. As happy as I am for my sister, I recognize a bitterness that boils beneath the surface of my happiness. Jealousy is a living thing. It grows, moves, and shifts, taking on a life of its own. I have a feeling if I don't get a grip, mine could spiral out of control destroying the very relationship I am trying to rebuild.

• • •

Two weeks later, on Saturday evening, A.J. meets me at the airport. It's good to see her, but when she embraces me in a hug, I recoil at her touch. The hurt in her eyes is apparent, and immediately, I feel ashamed even though this has been an ongoing issue in our relationship. A.J., though respectfully discreet, is very open, loving, and affectionate. I, on the other hand, am not, even in the privacy of our own home.

She needs more from me. We've had lengthy discussions and many arguments regarding it. I try, but I am not comfortable. I spend much of my time reassuring her that it has nothing to do with her. It was the same with Joel and other guys I dated. I try to make up for my shortcomings in different ways like buying little gifts to let her know I am thinking about her as well as keeping my schedule open and flexible to prioritize our time together. I enjoy her company. A.J. is entertaining, adventurous, and can always make me laugh.

I make a mental note to try harder to meet her needs while I am here.

We make small talk as we retrieve my luggage from baggage claim, and I breathe a sigh of relief as the car exits the airport terminal. On the forty-five-minute ride home, I talk endlessly about what has transpired over the last month with my sister and her family. I fill her in about Sam, Jillian, and the kids and cry as I tell her about Dad. She reaches for my hand, and this time, I don't pull away. It's a loving gesture of comfort, not a sexual one, and this I can handle.

I grab Kleenex out of the glove compartment, dry my eyes, and shift my attention to the bistro. She explains that things are going as smooth as possible. Phillip has stepped up and taken on a big part of the responsibility. They hired a new server, and all of our regular customers ask about me. Along with the bookkeeping, she helps

out in the front of the house when she can, claiming
it's been a nice distraction with me gone.

I laugh. "You hate serving."

She smiles. "I know, but it's been fun. It doesn't feel
like work when it's your own place. It's more like having
company over."

It's close to midnight when we pull into the garage,
and though I am exhausted, my anxiety is high for a
multitude of reasons. Anticipating this trip back to
Seattle was rough. Everything leading up to it brought
me to tears—sitting next to my dad watching the evening news, helping my mother bake peanut butter/
pecan cookies, witnessing Tanner's first home run of
the season, and then sitting with my three nieces last
evening putting together a jigsaw puzzle. My heart
physically hurt at the thought of leaving.

"You're coming back this time," Vicky reminded me
as I clung to her embrace the day I left.

When Mom dropped me off at the airport, I was
nauseous. I broke into a cold sweat as I watched her car
pull away. And now, as I look around the two-bedroom
apartment where I've lived for the last four years, though
everything is strangely familiar, I feel completely out
of place.

When we first moved, A.J., who has immaculate taste,
decorated according to her style. I tagged along hunting
thrift shops and antique markets for the perfect lamps,
throw rugs, wall hangings and accents. She asked what
I liked, and I was honest in my opinions, but ultimately,
the final decision was hers. The space is small, but she
decided colors such as "lemonade yellow," "swimming
pool aqua," and "vanilla ice cream ivory" allowed in
natural light to make the space appear larger. Every day
all year long felt like summer. I didn't mind it. It's not

what I would have picked for myself, but at the time, I felt as if it were her move. I was simply a roommate.

After being away for two months, coming back gives me an entirely new perspective. My eyes search for something that shouts out "Jessie lives here." None of the furniture is mine. If I recall correctly, A.J. had most of it before we moved. There are a few books on the bookshelf and, of course, my cooking appliances in the kitchen. Other than a few random framed pictures of the two of us and a sweater hanging casually on a hook by the front door, it's as if I don't even exist.

Why haven't I noticed this before?

When A.J. rubs my back and lightly caresses my cheek with her lips, I feel my muscles tighten. I dreaded this. I know she wants some intimacy, but I don't have it in me, and I can tell she senses this.

"I made up the spare bedroom," she says dryly, picking up my luggage and carrying it down the hall. "It's late, and we both need a good night's sleep."

Ignoring the scowl on her face, I disappear into the room. My sleep is restless, and the next morning when I find her at the kitchen table eating breakfast, I still feel anxious.

"You okay?" she asks casually while spreading butter on her toast.

I grab a box of cereal out of the pantry and pour the kernels into my bowl. "Of course."

Though I can see she has more that she wants to say, A.J. clears her throat and plasters a smile on her face. "So, what is on your agenda? You're home for how many days?"

"I fly out Wednesday evening. I am hoping we can go for a run. After a shower, I want to go into the bistro to check inventory, look over the menu, and see if there is anything that needs to be updated or changed."

"Jessie, you do all of that plus more from Montana. It's the luxury of technology!"

This is true. I've been able to dip my hands into the daily activities of the restaurant. I can see all the accounts, I update the website weekly, and if any problems arise with orders or vendors, Phillips contacts me directly. I'm just a phone call away, and so are they.

"So why go into the restaurant when it's closed today?" she asks. "You can spend Monday and Tuesday there. Let's do something fun! Maybe we can go on a hike instead of a run, have lunch and then see a movie. It sounds like you have not been to one in ages."

"I just left the house for the first time not too long ago, remember?" The simple thought of it makes me miss my family. My eyes fill with tears. I wipe them away, but not before A.J. notices.

Clearly frustrated, she runs a hand through her short spikey hair. "Why did you come home, Jess? Seriously. You didn't need to."

"I wanted to see you."

"Really?" She arches an eyebrow.

She wants to discuss *us*, but I don't want to get into it with her right now. It's hard enough being here as it is, let alone plunging face-first into a fight.

I stand up. On my way to the kitchen sink, I affectionately caress her arm.

"You're right. Let's go for a hike. It's a beautiful day. I need to be outside and to be with you. Lunch and a movie sound great too. Afterward, I need to do a little shopping, if that's okay."

The hike is therapeutic, as are the conversations A.J. and I have. Regardless of what is transpiring in our relationship, I know that A.J. has been very worried about me. We stay off the subject of our relationship but discuss the challenges that have come along with my trip to my childhood home. A.J. knows I was sexually assaulted as a teenager by an adult male, hence the reason I never go home. She realizes it has literally paralyzed me in many ways and causes my nightmares. She is aware that my parents have no clue, but that's the end of it. Despite her genuine concern and prodding, I have never shared anything else. As I trail a foot behind her up a steep incline, I finally give her his name, explain Ron's accident, and reassure her the fear of running into him no longer consumes me.

On a lighthearted note, I share more details about my nieces and nephews and explain how nice it is to be with my family without hiding. A.J. mostly listens but pipes in now and then with questions as if she is trying to get to know them through the stories I tell.

Three miles into the hike, we stop and sit on a rock. We pull out our water bottles and drink to quench our thirst.

"You should come back with me for a few days," I suggest but regret the words as soon as they leave my mouth.

A.J. wipes her forehead with the back of her hand and stares over the mountain at the breathtaking view. "I don't think so, Jess. Not yet anyway."

I am briefly relieved, yet the sadness in her voice concerns me.

"Why not?"

She shrugs. "Do you realize this is the most I've ever heard you talk about your family or your childhood? It feels like this big mystery. I think you need more time before you drag me into it."

I nod in agreement, but there is no missing the resentment in her tone.

We finish our hike and then head home to shower and change for our afternoon out. Though I feel revived and rejuvenated, A.J. is more quiet than usual on the drive to the store.

"Let's have Phillip and a few others over for dinner tomorrow night," I suggest, breaking the silence.

"If you want."

I send Phillip and two coworkers a group text message. After we go over the menu, A.J. casually asks how long I plan to stay in Montana. I don't know what to tell her because I don't have an answer. The oncologist gave Dad six months to a year to live, and that was four months ago. Mom, Vicky, Sam, and I have discussed hospice options when the time comes, but that could still be months away. Yes, he is fading, but he continues to hold his own. Realistically, I could stay in Seattle, fall into the routine of my life, and return when he takes a turn for the worse—but the thought of that makes my heartache.

The rest of the day is relaxed and somewhat enjoyable, regardless of the cloud of negativity that continues to hang between us. Honestly, the cloud has been there for a while. It made going home when I found out Dad was sick that much easier. A.J. and I had fallen into a familiar but dull pattern, and we hadn't been getting along well. I figured the break would do us good, make us appreciate one another more and find our way back to each other.

A.J. knew getting involved with me was a risk. I was honest with her from the start about my intimacy issues and lack of emotional availability. She also knew a relationship with another woman had never been on my radar. It quickly became apparent I was a project for her, someone she wanted to fix. I didn't mind much at first. It was nice to have someone care about my best interests, but it didn't take long before I became annoyed with the constant "hero syndrome." I'd pretty much gotten used to taking care of myself, relying on no one and surviving. It took time for me to start depending on her, and even when I did, it wasn't enough for her. Do I trust her? Of course I do, but it doesn't mean I need her to fix me.

When she offered to front the money for the bistro, I was shocked and hesitant at first. I have a lot of pride and didn't want to rely on someone to help me make my way in the world. When she explained it would be a financial investment, not a handout, I felt much more comfortable with the decision. Being business partners works well for us and being best friends, roommates, and companions in life works too. But lovers? Not so much.

We don't fight about money. We don't fight about work. We don't even fight about friends. We fight about my past. She desperately tries to dig and I shut her down every time. She believes if I deal with it, I will become more available, intimate, and carefree. She wants to get married and have kids. I don't want any of these things. Giving up my dream used to make me sad, but I found acceptance with it. A.J. has not. She spends a lot of time trying to convince me otherwise. I spend a lot of time ignoring her.

I had been sleeping in the spare bedroom for three months before I left. On the surface, A.J. and I carried on like we were the best couple in the world, but in the privacy of our home, we did not interact much. We talked about surface things—work, friends, hobbies, etc. However, the deep bond we once shared was slowly disappearing into the shadows of seclusion.

I think we had high hopes this break would bring us closer. With everything going on in my life—and she's been busy herself—we've started losing touch, and our entangled cycle continues to spiral. This is more apparent to me now than ever before.

I try to stay present and engaged with A.J. as she tells me more about work, but my thoughts drift back to my family.

After Dad came home from the hospital, he insisted we still hold our big family dinner. Mom thought it was too soon. Sam, Vicky, and I convinced her to let us do all the work and decided on a traditional Easter meal since we were not together to celebrate the previous month. Vicky volunteered to cook the ham, and I would tackle the potatoes as well as apple and cherry pies while Jillian promised to put together some creative salads and a vegetable tray. When Sam was leaving for the liquor store to buy beer, I slipped two twenties into his pocket, suggesting he pick up champagne as well.

The entire family congregated at my parents' house mid-morning, fussing over ingredients, mixing bowls, vegetables, and sauces while munching on a batch of cinnamon rolls my mother underhandedly whipped up before I was out of bed. While we cut, sliced, basted, and sipped on mimosas, Tyson and Sam put up the badminton set in the backyard to start a tournament. As we cooked, we listened to the commotion and laughter through the kitchen window. By early afternoon, Dad was sitting contently on the swing with his feet crossed at the ankles, a can of soda propped in his hand and a satisfied grin on his face as he watched his grandkids play.

Apparently, I wasn't the only one with a talent for cooking. I watched in awe as Jillian creatively designed roses out of radishes and sunflowers out of cucumbers. It was the most beautiful relish tray I'd ever seen. Vicky even stunned me with her knack of making sauces and gravies. The seasoning and spices she added to the fat drippings made my mouth water in anticipation. The goal of having us cook the meal was to give my mother a much-needed break from the stress, but it was impossible to keep her out of the kitchen. I poured her a glass of champagne, added a little orange juice and gave her the duty of peeling potatoes while she sat at the kitchen table.

The house smelled heavenly. The ham and pies were in the oven, the salads in the refrigerator, and an array of hors d'oeuvres—stuffed jalapeno peppers, stuffed mushrooms and, of course, the relish tray—was spread out on a card table on the back patio. We relaxed, munched, and watched the badminton competition in full swing. It was family against family—Sam and his kids against Tyson, the twins, and Shane. Sam's crew was up seven to three.

I was taking pictures on my cell phone when Sam thrust his racquet in my face. Tyson tossed his to Vicky before following Sam to the cooler where they each grabbed a cold beer. They collapsed onto the grass, exhausted.

Tanner, Kelsey, and I played Vicky and her kids. It only took a matter of minutes to realize Vicky and I were horrible at badminton. It didn't stop us from engaging in many fits of giggles at the snide remarks being made from the spectators on the sidelines each time we swung the racquet and missed. After a competitive half hour, Vicky's family finally beat us. By this point, the kids were tired of hanging out with adults. They took off on the bicycles kept in the garage. Dad was also worn out, so we suggested he relax inside before dinner. Sam and Tyson helped him in, and it wasn't long before he was asleep. When Mom laid on the couch beside his chair to watch an old western movie, the rest of us disappeared downstairs for a game of pool.

The two married couples divided into teams, so I found a comfortable spot in the corner of the sofa where I could watch.

"Jillian and I want to take the kids camping in August before school starts. Will you still be around to go with us?" Sam asked while determining his next shot. With a quick *thunk*, the striped ball bounced off the side and into the corner pocket.

I hadn't given much thought to this question. I figured I'd stay as long as my parents needed me. But I also had a life in Seattle and a girlfriend I probably needed to get back to. Truly, I didn't want to be anywhere else but here, at home. It surprised me that I still thought of this as home. I'd built up a pretty big, strong wall to keep the memories in my head away from my heart. The moment I returned, the wall started to demolish, and despite the horrid memories, I felt more at peace here than I anywhere else I had tried to escape to.

Now I am back in Seattle, which is technically home, and what weighs on my mind the most is how I am going to balance the two lives. One life I created out of the need to survive, and the other is a part of my core, my roots, and even though I pushed it away, it's the life I've missed and the one I longed to find.

Now that I have, I'm desperate not to let go.

• • •

I sleep in the following morning. We were out late the evening before. First, the movie and then dinner where we ran into mutual friends who joined us for drinks. Last, we stopped at the twenty-four-hour grocery store. A.J. and I have a pleasant and lazy morning relaxing comfortably on the couch watching the first two *American Pie* movies on DVD. Finally, by midafternoon, we decide to prepare for our guests.

The music blares in the background as we tidy up the house and begin dinner—chicken cordon bleu, bacon-wrapped asparagus spears with tomatoes sprin-kled with taleggio cheese, strawberry feta tossed salad and a simple chocolate mousse for dessert. A.J. and I have always complemented one another's style in the kitchen, and we easily fall into the old pattern, but the conversation is strained. I figure she is tired of hearing about my family, and the more she fills me in on the goings-on of our social circles, the more I realize I don't want to hear the drama. I try to hide my disinterest, but I do not care that Seth cheated on Rhonda six months after their elopement, or that Veronica was offered an engineering job with an oil and gas company in North Dakota, leaving her fiancée behind. When the doorbell sounds announcing the arrival of Phillip, Alicia, and Roberto, two other wait staff from the bistro, I don't know who is more relieved, her or me.

Phillip wraps his burly arms around my waist and whips me into the air. The moment my toes touch the ground, he gives me a sloppy, playful kiss on the lips. I am thrilled to see him and return the embrace with more enthusiasm than he expects. After giving Alicia a hug and Roberto a quick peck on the cheek, I pour everyone a glass of Malbec. We move outside to sit on the deck and enjoy the warm evening temperatures before the sun disappears beyond the horizon.

"How are your parents?" Alicia asks, popping a goat-cheese-stuffed olive into her mouth.

I have always liked and respected Alicia and Roberto. We have worked together the last few years and occa-sionally hang out socially. I trust them with my restaurant almost as much as I trust Phillip. Due to the dynamics of the work environment, there isn't much about my life they don't know, except for the obvious secrets of my past I've kept hidden from everyone.

As I update them on what has transpired, A.J. disappears into the kitchen to check on dinner. I watch Phillip's eyes follow her and frown. He must notice her unusually quiet demeanor this evening too.

Fifteen minutes later, we transition to the dining room table and continue to make small talk as we eat. They entertain me with the variety of colorful stories about the bistro—the new female coffee distributor who has been hitting on Phillip nonstop, the newly hired college students, and our regular customers. When Alicia recalls a story about her five-year-old daughter's kindergarten graduation, I realize how much I miss my brother's and sister's kids. As I think about what they may be doing this weekend, I feel a sharp ache in my chest. I rub my hand over my heart and take another sip of wine.

"When do you think you'll be back permanently?" Roberto asks nonchalantly, tipping the bottle over his glass.

I avoid the question at every turn, but it continues to rear its ugly head. I contemplate my answer as I watch the deep red of the wine creep its way just below the lip of the glass. My heart says never. I know it's not realistic but the thought of coming back to Seattle forever makes me sick to my stomach. Refusing to make eye contact with A.J., I clear my throat.

"I'm not sure yet. Dad could still have another five or six months. If he takes a turn for the worse, I would like to be there to support my mom when the time comes. It's a very heavy and confusing decision for me."

Out of the corner of my eye, I catch A.J. and Phillip exchange an unusual look and feel myself become instantly defensive. Phillip is *my* sounding board. *My* best friend. I understand they have been working together quite a bit. If A.J. is having a difficult time with the dynamics of what may or may not be going on between us, it's only natural she would talk to Phillip. It still frustrates me. I can't wait to spend time alone with him when I can finally let my hair down, relax, and get some logical feedback about my life.

What feedback am I looking for? Someone to tell me it's okay to give up life in Seattle and move back to where I grew up—to the place I ran away from, never discussed, and never returned to visit? Do I want someone to tell me it's okay to want to see Zane, talk to Zane, and possibly...?

I clasp my hand over my mouth and gasp, shocked at my thoughts.

A.J. narrows her eyes suspiciously. "What is it?"

"Nothing. I just bit my tongue," I lie.

After dinner, we spend the rest of the evening on the patio. Phillip and Roberto sip on cups of coffee while A.J., Alicia and I have one last glass of wine. Conversation remains lighthearted and pleasant, but I find my thoughts are miles away with a boy who is now a man. For thirteen years, I shoved that boy into the back corner of my mind. Tonight, it's as if he pushed his way to the forefront, refusing to be ignored anymore. I smile as I let myself hope for the first time without shame or fear.

Roberto yawns announcing the end of our evening. When I glance at the clock, I see it's close to midnight. I link arms with Roberto and Alicia, and walk them to the door giving each a hug and promising to see them at the bistro before I leave on Wednesday.

Slowly and quietly, I close the door while straining to hear the whispers between Phillip and A.J. from the kitchen. Confident they are talking about me, I tiptoe closer. I am dismayed when I round the corner to find them in what looks like an intimate embrace. When they untangle themselves, A.J. has tears in her eyes, and Phillip gently rubs her shoulder. Typically, this gesture would not surprise me. Phillip knows the right amount of love and tenderness to give without being inappropriate, and there were numerous occasions where I had found comfort and reassurance in his big, burly arms after a bad day. Many women have. But not A.J. In the years the three of us have hung out together, I don't recall them hugging one another in greeting or when saying goodbye. A.J. and Phillip got along marvelously, and I consider them good friends, but if I recall correctly, they were never ones to engage in playful affection. I guess I never thought it strange.

Until now.

• • •

The next morning, I get up early to go for a run before the temperatures soar. Though sleep came quickly to me the night before, Zane was the last thought I had before I drifted off and the first one that popped into my head the moment I woke. I need time to myself to process this and can't deal with A.J. beforehand.

My encounter with Zane at the hospital shook me up pretty good. It didn't take long for my old detachment mechanisms to kick in, and like I'd done a million other times in the past, I forced myself to forget. I'd learned over the years not to fantasize, not to hope, and not have any expectations. Last night, when my mind drifted somewhere it had not gone in a very long time and I couldn't control it the way I had in the past, it caught me off guard.

I adjust the headphones in my ears and scroll down my music list on my iPod until I find Rob Zombie. He will get my adrenaline pumping and work through any panic that's creeping its way into my psyche. I start at a slow pace, but within five minutes, I'm at a steady rhythm with my feet caressing the pavement and my mind reflecting on a young girl once in love.

• • •

Zane kissed my lips gently at first, but a moment later, he pulled me against him, deepening the embrace with more fever and passion than ever before. His hand moved down my breast while the other snaked its way up my inner thigh. His fingers fumbled with the lining of my panties, and I moaned as he gently pushed the silky material aside. Although we spent most of our time together pushing the limits of our intimacy, this was the furthest I had ever let him go. I knew he didn't want to stop, but when I turned my head to catch my breath, he pulled away.

I knew he did this for my sake. I loved him desperately but couldn't understand why I was scared to take the next step. We talked about the future, and there was no doubt we would be together forever. Zane was everything I'd dreamed of, plus more. He loved me in everything he did—carrying my books to class, bringing me lunch during cheerleading practice, or holding the door open every time I climbed into his truck. No one ever touched his truck, but Zane trusted me enough to take it to pick up my graduation dress at the mall. We spent countless hours on horseback rides and hikes discussing our lives, our dreams, our ambitions, and our fears. Our souls connected. I saw Zane as the perfect man. For the most part, he was quiet and reserved, yet confident, and even a bit mysterious, although he could easily become riled up if his buttons were pushed. His willingness to be vulnerable in my presence showed me he could trust and open his heart if and when he felt safe. I couldn't say he had always felt safe in his life, but he worked hard to overcome the circumstances that tried to tear him down. Zane was willing to do what it took to give me the world.

So why couldn't I give him all of me in return?

"You okay?" he asked, placing his finger under my chin, tilting my face until our eyes locked.

"I don't know what is wrong with me."

Zane chuckled. "Nothing is wrong with you, Jessie. You're normal. All girls go through this."

"How do you know?" I eyed him suspiciously.

Even though I tried to sound lighthearted, the innocent comment pierced deep into my heart. Zane was not a virgin. He told me when he lost his virginity as a tenth grader to a girl he met while visiting friends at Montana State College. There were three others after that. I wasn't impressed then or now. His experience with women intimidated me. The experience I had with other boys was minor in comparison. What if I couldn't live up to his expectations? What if I had no clue what I was doing? When I told him these doubts, I felt ashamed and stupidly oversensitive and started to cry.

He wrapped me in a hug.

"That is why I love you, Jessie. I get to have all of you for myself. I don't have to share or even wonder what you've done with someone else. We get to figure this out together. So what if I've been with a few girls? It's not like I'm an expert. This is different. You are the only one I'm ever going to remember or care about the rest of my life. I will be your first, your only, and your forever."

• • •

By now I'm running so hard and fast, I begin to hyper-ventilate. I stop, yank the headphones out, bend over, and place my hands on my sweaty knees as I catch my breath. I'm dizzy, but I don't feel like I am going to pass out. Instead, I count to fifty then slowly straighten up. I link my fingers behind my head, and I pace down the sidewalk, taking long deep breaths in through my nose and out through my mouth.

As I am walking back to the apartment, I can tell my mood for the day has been drastically altered as Zane's words plague my thoughts.

"I don't have to share or even wonder what you've done with someone else. I will be your first, your only, and your forever."

I've subconsciously known all this time how Zane's innocent statement in the heat of passion is the link to my decision to leave, yet it's as if years of turmoil suddenly make sense in a new and dramatic way. I find myself wondering, for the very first time, what would have happened if I hadn't left. Could I have told Zane the truth? Would he have still loved me? I'd never entertained the idea of it because all the "what if's" were torture. I'd never given the alternative any consideration. What did I do instead? I ran.

To be honest, I'd been running for years. Since I've been home, I've taken the time to slow down and look back. It's been painful, but I am still here. I survived. It didn't kill me. I haven't run away again. It's as if the answer fell straight from the sky and hit me on the head, much harder this time, probably to make sure the message gets through.

I rush into the apartment to find A.J. at the dining room table, her laptop open in front of her as she lifts a bottle of sparkling water to her lips.

"I'm going home," I announce, tugging off my tennis shoes as I walk down the hall.

I pull my tank top over my head and reach over the bathtub to turn on the shower. She appears a moment later leaning against the door jamb.

"Your flight doesn't leave until tomorrow evening," she reminds me.

I shake my head. "I can't wait until tomorrow. I'm going to the airport and taking an earlier flight."

In the reflection of the mirror, I see her jaw drop. I ignore the reaction, strip down to my bare nakedness, crawl into the shower, close the curtain behind me, and allow the pulsing warm water to massage my body. I quickly wash and condition my hair, scrub away the grime and sweat and wrap up in a warm cotton towel. I get ready while packing my belongings at the same time. The urgency is all-consuming as I hustle around the apartment, collecting my things. A half hour later, I walk out of the spare bedroom, pulling my suitcase behind me. A.J. is standing by the kitchen sink, frowning and tapping her fingernails on the granite counter-top.

"What's going on?" she demands.

As much as I want to avoid her, I can't. I owe her an explanation. When I start to talk, she interrupts me.

"Phillip is coming over."

I am surprised. "What does Phillip have to do with this?"

"We agree that someone needs to talk some sense into you," she says. "It's time for an intervention."

I laugh at the absurdity. Now I know what the whispering and tears must have been about the night before. There is a knock at the door, and A.J. shoves past me to answer it. Again, I watch in strange disbelief as she gives Phillip a warm embrace. I shift uncomfortably as his hands linger a little bit too long on her lower back.

The grip on my suitcase handle tightens when they turn to me.

"Are you going to take me to the airport, or do I need to call a cab?" I ask irritably.

"Let's not be so hasty," Phillip suggests, gesturing to the couch. "How about we sit down and talk about this first."

I laugh. "Have you suddenly become my therapist?"

The two of them exchange a knowing glance, and I sigh.

"Fine. Let's talk," I say, sitting in a chair at the dining room table.

Phillip starts. "Why are you going home? You've only been here a few days, haven't even been to the bistro yet and you're ready to leave? We just got you back, can't we enjoy you for a while? Jessie, we miss you!"

I smile. Good ol' Phillip always knows how to make me feel special.

"Look, none of this is easy to explain," I begin. "I hardly understand it myself. Ever since I've been home, my home in Montana, my past is staring me in the face. It taunts me, teasing me and begging me to remember." I shove a hand through my hair in frustration. "As cliché as it sounds, I truly did open a can of worms."

"You mean about the rape?" Phillip asks.

I arch my eyebrow and give A.J. a dirty look.

"I told him," she admits. "I'm sorry. But for crying out loud, Jessie, he wanted to know what the hell was going on with you. I'm not the only one that is picking up this strange vibe."

"You've been encouraging me to do this for years, A.J. and now that I am, you want me to stop?"

"It's not that I want you to stop. I'm worried. You're completely removed from life here. You hardly call. Even though you are engaged with the bistro on a certain level, you're still absent. It's like you have lost all passion for what you once used to love. Like you don't care about any of us anymore."

"Maybe I found some new passions," I declare bluntly.

A.J.'s face goes white. "Your family," she whispers.

"Yes. What is so wrong with that? The both of you have family. Why can't I?"

"Jessie, you do," she says defensively. "We get together with your parents and brother's crew a few times a year. It's not like you haven't had anyone."

Exasperated, I shake my head. "A few times a year? You don't get it, A.J. My family was my life. The most important people in the world to me. We were close, and we were happy. A few times a year has not cut it in the big scheme of what my life was supposed to be. I had dreams, big dreams, and they did not include leaving Montana. I was accepted at Montana State. Vicky and I were going to stay close and raise our kids together. Yes, I wanted kids, lots of them. I was supposed to marry Zane, move home and live..." I trail off after realizing what I said.

Wide-eyed, the two of them stare at me as if I'm a stranger.

Finally, A.J. speaks. "*Who* is Zane?"

I puff out a breath. "My high school boyfriend."

"Why haven't you ever told me about him?"

I feel my jaw clench tightly. "There was no point. He was dead to me."

"Dead because?" Phillip prods.

The stillness in the room is disturbing. It feels like needles are poking every nerve in my body, and I taste the bile in my throat as I force myself to voice the uncomfortable truth.

"Zane is Ron's son."

• • •

Phillip and A.J. gang up on me and guilt trip me to stay. I cave and decide to take my original flight the following evening as planned. Even though being here is borderline unbearable, I figure it's the right thing to do.

I limit my time with A.J. as much as possible. She wants to have endless discussions about who I was before her and why I didn't trust her enough to confide the mysteries of my past. As I listen to her rant, I grow irritated as she personalizes the situation instead of showing any sign of compassion.

"I didn't tell anyone," I defend myself. "There was no point living in the past."

"What about the pain this is causing me? I don't know who you truly are!" she exclaims.

I want to tell her that *I* don't even know who I am anymore, at least not in Seattle. In Montana, I feel more like myself than I have in a long time. Instead, I sit in silence as she continues to rant.

"Thank you for at least telling me about Zane. It helps me understand, a little bit, why you are so screwed up," she states sarcastically. "This is such a fucking mess!"

"It's my fucking mess."

A.J. glares at me. "I am your partner."

I try to remind myself she has a right to be upset. As much as I'd like to convince myself that I've done nothing wrong, I know she has a point.

"It's never going to be the same," she says, dabbing her eyes with a Kleenex.

"I don't expect it to be the same. What I expect and what I want it to be is real. I'm tired of running away from the things I love. I'm trying to find a happy and realistic compromise so I can have the best of both worlds."

But as the words leave my mouth, I know I am once again deceiving her.

CHAPTER SEVEN

Phillip takes me to the airport late Wednesday afternoon. A.J.'s goodbye is cold and distant. She asks me to text when I arrive safely and then, without even a hug, she disappears into her bedroom, slamming the door behind her.

The flight is short; it's early evening when I land. Vicky and family are waiting for me as I walk down the terminal, and I see the kids bounce on their tiptoes, looking over the heads of strangers, anticipating my arrival. When my gaze meets their eager faces, the affection I feel for this family absorbs my entire being.

Breaking free from the crowd of people, I run into their arms, clutching them tightly to me. When I release the kids, I turn to Vicky, embrace her warmly, and give Tyson a quick peck on the cheek. He offers to take my luggage while the girls grasp my hands and skip along beside me. We take turns jabbering as if we haven't seen one another for months instead of only a few days.

A half hour later, we pull into the driveway of my parents' house. A peaceful, content sensation washes over me, and for the first time since last week, I feel like I can fully breathe.

Mom is on the couch working on a crossword puzzle while Dad sleeps beside her in his chair, his slippered feet propped up and his favorite blanket tucked beneath his chin.

"Let me make some tea," she suggests, placing a soft kiss on my cheek before retreating into the kitchen.

Tyson puts my suitcase into the bedroom while the kids, after a stern warning not to wake up Grandpa, rush out the back door to kick the soccer ball around. At the dining room table, I relax, resting my feet on the chair next to me and inhale the fresh peppermint when Mom sets down the steaming cup of tea.

"How was the trip?" she asks, sitting across from me.

"Trip was fine. The bistro is the same as always. Phillip's taking care of everything. How about a movie tomorrow night?" I suggest, changing the subject. "Maybe bowling or a picnic in the park again would be good. Something we can do with Dad," I say excitedly.

The euphoria I feel, though a bit terrifying and unusual, is also thrilling.

Mom exchanges a curious glance with Vicky then places her hand on my arm.

"Everything okay with A.J.?"

I sigh. "Yes and no."

For the next half hour, I confide—for the first time—in my mother and Vicky. I tell them, without too much detail, about my stressful and unhealthy relationships with men, and how my friendship with A.J. turned into more than what I had anticipated or expected. I explain how much I enjoy her companionship and how our work partnership thrives, but even before I came home, our personal relationship was dying.

"To be honest, I don't think it was ever alive. A.J. hoped it would turn into something phenomenal. But it wasn't real. It was convenient. While she was shaping and molding me into who she wanted me to be, I was resisting just as hard. I didn't exactly handle things the way I should have. I kept a lot of important parts of my life from her; therefore she is confused, insecure, and bent out of shape."

It's apparent by the look on both their faces that Mom and Vicky are full of questions. Neither asks, and I am grateful for their discretion.

Regardless, I try to give them some resolution. "I don't know what any of this means. All I know is when I was back in Seattle, I wanted to be here. When I'm here, I have no desire to be there. It's time to make changes in my life."

• • •

The following weekend we go to church with Mom. It's not how I want to spend my Sunday morning, but Vicky reminds me about our conversation the week before saying it would be a smart place for me to start making changes. When I get defensive, Mom informs me the church is now a non-denominational Christian Center, and the new pastor shares messages on spiritual transformation and a relationship with God. Apparently, he's a very engaging speaker. This is the only reason I agree to go.

I grew up in this church, but I feel a bit awkward and out of place walking through the large wooden doors. The last time I was inside these four walls was the Sunday morning of my high school graduation day.

Fifteen minutes later toward the end of the announce-
ments, I'm struggling to stay awake when Vicky elbows
me in the ribs. Realizing everyone is standing, I follow
suit, mumble my way through a vaguely familiar hymn,
and recite the prayer. When the pastor starts to speak, I
grab the bulletin, pull a pen out of my purse, and start
doodling. I feel childish under the heat of my mother's
gaze. I tuck the pen and bulletin away and sit up straight
in an attempt to pay attention.

My mom was right. I'm pleasantly surprised to find
the speaker is animated with a decent sense of humor.
His message is upbeat and spirited, not preachy like I
recall from my childhood. It's the strength of his words
in between his playful antics that touch my heart.

"God's forgiveness is available for everybody. Many of
us have been through unimaginable things, experienced
tragedy and pain, and suffered more than anyone should
suffer. Many of you feel like your life is over, and the
dreams you once believed possible are dead. I'm going
to share with you four statements from God. He loves
you. He will protect you. He has a plan for your life.
And He is well pleased with you."

It feels as if his gaze has x-ray vision and is penetrating the very core of my soul as he continues.

"I want to ask, which of those statements is the
hardest for you to believe? Do any of them jump out at
you making you think 'that can't be true?' I know many
of you believe these statements are suitable for other
people but not you. Do you believe you are too bad,
too broken, and therefore disqualified from being with
God? Do you believe when you do something wrong,
He punishes you? Many of us think our circumstances
must be a result of our sin. This is not true. God says,
'Blessed are the empty, broken people who look inside
and find emptiness and heartache.' People believe they

have nothing to offer to God, but He welcomes you to come as you are and live life with Him. Why not tear down the wall and let Him travel this journey with you?"

I shift uncomfortably in my seat. I know it's not rational thinking, but I feel like everyone is staring at me as if they know my secret and the pastor is speaking directly to me.

"I want you to hear me when I say that resurrecting dead stuff is God's specialty. He wants to breathe life into it what's broken. He understands when things are not fair. He wants to walk through life with you right now so He can make it right. God knows if we could fix our lives on our own, we would. But what do we do? We look for comfort in other people, other things, everywhere else but in the right place, in God's Kingdom. The circumstances of our lives are not a statement upon God's love for us. God doesn't love us because we have done the right things, and God doesn't hate us because we have done wrong things. God loves us in spite of our circumstances, and He loves you through the circumstances."

For some inexplicable reason, my hands start to shake, and the warmth of the room constricts my breathing. At the end of the sermon, I stand with the congregation for another hymn but get dizzy. Feeling feverish, I lightly touch my forehead while my eyes burn with unshed tears. Vicky links her fingers through mine, and this seems to ground me for the moment. At the end of the song, I quietly excuse myself to the bathroom, but before I get there, I change my mind and hastily march outside instead.

Before I know it, I'm shaking my fists at the sky and screaming as the rage burns my throat.

"Where were you? You want me to believe you love me and protect me? That's a lie! Do you know what happened to me? You left me! How can you have a plan for my life? Have you seen my life? I am dead and unfixable. You are pleased with me? Do you have any idea what I put them through? I've screwed up everything that matters. Why did you let that happen?"

I fall to the ground and yank fists of grass out of the earth. My sobs grow hysterical as I throw it in the air around me.

"You say you forgive? Why? I'm *not* worth it," my voice grows weak. "I left Zane and my family behind so they didn't have to find out how disgusting I am. I don't deserve *their* love, and I don't deserve yours."

I'm on my knees, gasping for air when I feel a gentle touch on my back. I collapse into Vicky's arms, and as she holds me, I reflect again on the words I heard minutes before. Only this time, instead of the gut-wrenching mindset I've stubbornly held onto, believing God left me, I find the message brings me an inkling of clarity. Is it possible there is a plan for my life? If so, what is it?

Suddenly, the words come to me as clearly as if I said them myself.

Find peace from your pain and suffering. Use it to serve others. To serve me.

With a long deep breath, I wipe the tears away and shade my eyes from the sun, so I can look at Vicky.

"What did you say?"

Puzzled, she stares at me. "I didn't say anything. I'm just sitting here."

I glance around her, expecting someone else to appear in my line of vision. But it's only the two of us.

"You okay?" she asks.

I nod and sit back on my heels as I contemplate the very unexpected, yet perfectly timed words I heard.

"It's been a long time since I've been reminded what it's like to have a relationship with God. How could I have forgotten and convinced myself that He abandoned me? How could I have abandoned Him?" I ask.

"Mom and Dad engrained that love in us from the time we were born. They taught us we are loved, no matter what. It's easy to forget when we feel broken, especially after trauma. I've been in your shoes, and I know how easy it is to question. Easy to want to blame." Vicky says.

"You know, Vicky, you are a pesky little know-it-all who always appears at the perfect moment to plant your seeds of wisdom," I tease.

"I have a lot of built-up big sister wisdom just waiting to leak out. You better watch yourself," she smiles.

Standing up, I wipe the dirt off my knees. "This is the first time I've done that. Getting mad was liberating," I admit.

"What on earth are you two doing?" My mother calls from the doorway of the church. Welcoming the interruption, we meet her at the car.

"Have you been crying?" she asks, looking at me curiously.

I give Vicky a playful shove. "We were bored to tears," I say as we break into hysterical laughter.

• • •

My therapist's name is Bethann. We delve into the core of my issues during my third session. She suggests we do something called Eye Movement Desensitization and Reprocessing. In simple terms, I won't forget the trauma, but it will decrease my triggers and the negative beliefs associated with the triggers that are controlling my life. While this sounds fantastic, a strong desire within me wants to give it a voice. I feel talking about my shame will lessen its power.

"If you are comfortable and feel ready, we can start," Bethann says. "Tell me only as much as you want. We can still work on the trauma regardless of the details you share."

After we discuss the importance of my internal and external supports, coping skills, and how to keep myself safe if I feel too emotionally elevated, we begin. For the first time ever, I tell my story. To help set the stage, I tell Bethann about Zane.

"It hurts. Sometimes the pain is so intense I feel like I'm having a heart attack," I say, rubbing my chest.

I shift uncomfortably in my seat while picking at my cuticles. I don't know if she wants the details, but I forge ahead anyway. I close my eyes and picture the scenario in my head, my senses fully alert. I see the VHS tapes scattered on the floor and my blue cheerleading bag in the corner by the bed where he kicked it. I recognize the torn shirt that hangs off my shoulder. I shiver, recalling the cold, damp temperature of the room. I hear the thunder outside, smell the stench of cigarettes on his breath, and even remember the little spider dangling the corner of the ceiling. I feel the cold circular barrel of the gun pressed against my head and hear it tap against my front tooth when it's shoved in my mouth.

When I finish, I don't cry, but I start to shake uncontrollably. I stare at my fingernails again, afraid to see the reaction on her face.

"Let's take some deep breaths to keep you grounded," she suggests.

Once I am calm, her gentle voice interrupts my thoughts. "What is the negative belief you have about yourself right now?"

At her words, it feels as if a massive boulder has slammed into my chest. Sheets of tears rain onto my hands as they rest, limply in my lap. I can't answer her question without gasping for air.

"We can stop here if you want," she says, holding out a box of tissues.

"I am weak," I finally say, ignoring the tissues. "He made me feel dirty, gross, and helpless. I knew the first time he hit me what else was coming. I thought if I could get ahold of his gun, I'd kill him. But that scared me more."

My thoughts grow quiet as I close my eyes.

"Do you want to stop?" Bethann gently asks again.

I shake my head emphatically. "It's Zane."

"What about Zane?"

Numbly, I stare at her.

"He won't love me if he finds out. How could he love a girl that was fucked by his father?"

CHAPTER EIGHT

By August, my dad is holding his own again. He is not getting worse but not getting better. His weight loss is dramatic as expected with his bland diet and loss of appetite. We continue to meet his needs and very rarely steer away from the routine of his day, all appreciative of the time we get with him. He remains in good spirits when we are together and thrives on the company. When he is not napping, we can usually get him outside with us as we toss around a volleyball or watch the kids ride their bikes.

Right now, his pain is minimal. While I was in Seattle, I was able to get my hands on a few bottles of cream that contains THC. It came highly recommended by one of the bistro's customers who has fibromyalgia. One evening when the nerve pain was intolerable, I handed Mom the bottle.

"Dad, I have a muscle cream that may help. It's like that junk you used when you had sore muscles and backaches when I was a kid. Only this doesn't smell as wretched. I've used it a few times after running injuries, and it works wonders."

He agrees, not questioning my motives, and allows Mom to massage it on his muscles. Within an hour, he is relaxed. Now each time he feels the persistent pain coming on, he asks to use that "miracle cream of Jessie's." What he doesn't know won't hurt him, and at this stage of the game, it's about keeping him comfortable.

I am worried about my mother, though. The role of caretaker is taking a toll. Dad is still capable of using his walker or a cane, so physically she is not too worn out, but emotionally she is broken. Recently my siblings and their spouses began rotating evening shifts to give her a much-needed break, but she can't escape the poison of deep grief that continuously invades her heart.

Late at night after Dad is in bed, she sits in the living room by herself staring out the picture window. Sometimes she cries. Other times she talks to God. I doubt Dad ever hears her as they have a noisy ceiling fan in their bedroom that helps him sleep. My room, on the other hand, happens to be on the other side of the wall, so I hear her sobs.

Knowing how private my mother is, I usually leave her alone. Tonight I decide to check on her. I don't know if she hears me approach, but her hand clasps mine when I touch her shoulder. After a moment, I wrap my arms around her, rocking back and forth the way she had done with me countless times as a child.

We sit like this for several minutes until I finally ask, "Are you scared for Dad to die?"

Immediately she shakes her head.

"Just sad. I'm sad that I have to figure out how to do my days differently than I have for the past forty years. I'm sad my partner won't be by my side anymore, and we won't do the things we had planned. Half of my heart will be gone. But I'm not scared. I know where your Dad is going. God loaned him to us for quite a while, and I am grateful for the time I've been able to enjoy him. Our ultimate goal is to be with our Father. He's is calling your Dad back earlier than we anticipated and I'm just going to have to wait patiently to join him. As I wait, he made me promise to cherish the days I have left with all of you. I intend to do that."

I feel the tears on my cheek before I even realize I am crying.

"You two have always had so much faith. How?"

"The alternative seems worse. I wouldn't want to do this life without it. My faith provides me with companionship, grace, forgiveness, and an abundance of love. It brings peace and comfort during hard times. And as you know, there are plenty of hard times."

With a faraway look in her eyes, she speaks. "Hope is a golden cord connecting you to heaven. This cord helps you hold your head up high even when multiple trials are buffeting you. God never leaves your side and never let's go of your hand. Hope lifts your perspective from your weary feet to the glorious view you can see from the high road. The road traveled together is ultimately a highway to heaven. When you consider this radiant destination, the roughness or smoothness of the road ahead becomes much less significant."

"That's beautiful," I whisper.

In the iridescent glow of the moonlight sparkling through the picture window, her smile widens, and I've never seen her look more beautiful.

"It's a devotional I memorized before your Dad and I got married. It's what gets me through the hard days. Your dad has to take the road sooner than me, but we are going to wind up at the same destination. I look forward to the destination. It's worth hoping for."

I curl deeper into her as I think about the words. How peaceful it must feel to be that confident in something. I don't ever recall having a spiritual connection the way my mother speaks about hers. Maybe I did at some point but was too young to recognize it for what it was.

With my head on her shoulder, my eyes grow heavy. As I begin to drift into sleep, I can't help but wonder if the peaceful contentment and security from my childhood I have spent years chasing, without ever catching, is what she spoke about today.

• • •

I have not heard from A.J. much over the last month. I'm not sure if this means our relationship is over or if we are cooling off. It is irritating she won't talk to me, but the demise of our relationship is not. Regardless, Phillip and I continue to communicate every day. He isn't bothered about my past or that I am rekindling relationships with loved ones. It's a refreshing relief to have his support and an open ear anytime I need to talk to someone outside of my family about my family.

My phone rests on the bathroom counter. I have Phillip on speakerphone while I finish getting ready for my counseling appointment. Casually, I invite him to come to Montana for a visit so he can finally meet the rest of my family. He declines. He does not think it's a good idea without an invite for A.J. I can see his point of view, but I treasure our friendship and force the issue.

Although it's clear he is disappointed, Phillip stands firm. "Right now, I have to interact with A.J. almost daily. I can't afford to be the one who pisses her off even more."

Reluctantly, I drop the subject. We swap recipe ideas and say goodbye when I realize I'm running late for my appointment. I didn't sleep well last night anticipating my session. A piece of me dreads the emotions this will bring, but I'm anxious and ready to put this part of my past to rest, finally.

An hour and a half later, Vicky is trying to catch up to me as I rush across the parking lot. She offered to give me a ride today, knowing the work I was going to do would be intense.

"Want to talk about it?" Vicky asks.

I shake my head. "I just want to get home."

I am utterly exhausted moving years of mental and emotional baggage out of my body instead of carrying it around. I am also heartbroken. I didn't allow myself permission to be sad about what Ron did to that eighteen-year-old girl. It made me feel vulnerable, and the idea of being weak in any way terrified me.

When we arrive home, Vicky follows me inside. I thank her and head straight to my room, leaving her to explain the appointment to our parents. As I shut the door, I overhear her say "rough session...she'll be okay...exhausted."

I lie in bed thinking about what transpired over the last hour. I have no idea what any of this is supposed to accomplish, but my brain is numb, so analyzing it is virtually impossible. Shutting my eyes, I drift off to sleep.

• • •

The alarm on my phone wakes me up at six-thirty the following morning. I'm shocked. I slept through the entire night without getting up once. The alarm stops when I slide the red X to the right. With half-opened eyes, I see I have four text messages from A.J. She's irritated I asked Phillip to visit. I don't want to deal with the drama, but I send a brief reply reminding her she hasn't been speaking to me. After hitting send, I silence my phone and pull the covers over my head. Yawning, I close my eyes and pray for another hour of sleep.

• • •

A knock on my bedroom door wakes me.

"Come in," I say, groggily.

My mom peeks in her head in. The creases in the corner of her eyes show worry.

"It's almost lunchtime."

I grab my phone off the nightstand. It is eleven forty-five. I sit up, rub my eyes, and apologize.

"It's okay," she smiles. "I just wanted to make sure you were still alive."

I pull on sweats and a T-shirt before following her into the living room where Dad sits in his recliner sipping on his smoothie.

"Aw, Mom. I should have been up helping you. How are you doing, Dad?" I ask, throwing myself on the couch.

"Perfect," he mumbles over his straw.

Judge Judy is over, and he is onto *Dr. Oz*, but before I know it, I am drifting off again, the voices on the television seeping into my subconscious. Mom shakes my shoulder a few moments later.

"Take a shower, Jessie. It will wake you up. Vicky's called a few times."

The last thing I want to do is talk to Vicky. Right now, the thought of carrying on a conversation with anyone irritates me. Instead, I make peanut butter toast and take my plate along with a steaming cup of coffee into the bathroom. I draw a bath anticipating the glorious relaxation. After I sink into the hot water, I lay my head against the porcelain tub, placing a damp washcloth over my eyes.

A knock on the door startles me, and I jerk awake. My mother's concerned voice echoes from the other side.

"Jessie?"

I step out of the tub onto the bathroom rug, wrap a towel around my chest and another around my head. I wave at Mom as I move through the hallway back to my bedroom.

"I'm going to go take a little nap," I say.

• • •

The next two days are similar. Though I sleep hard and heavy all night, I'm exhausted when I wake up. I do my best to help Mom, but I fall asleep beside Dad on the couch once he is settled. I have no desire to go anywhere or do anything. I am completely content and comfortable in my sweat pants, hanging out with my dad, both of us zoned out on television all day long. My brain is mush. I don't think about anything, and I hardly care about anything except helping Mom when I need to. I don't have much of an appetite. I sleep about sixteen hours a day, and my lips are numb. I find this comical, but before I have time to consider why my brain shuts off again.

I overhear my mother talking to Vicky on the phone. "Is this normal?"

I can't hear Vicky's reply, but my mother seems to be less concerned when the conversation ends.

It's dinner time when Vicky shows up to find me lying on the couch. I don't have the energy to give her much of a reaction. She lifts my blanketed legs, sits down and rests them on top of her lap.

"I'm so tired," I tell her between half-open eyelids. "Is this how the rest of my life is going to be? If so, damn you for making me go see that counselor. This sucks worse than before," I complain.

"Are you still sad?" she asks.

I lift my head off the pillow and gaze at her quizzically. "I don't feel a thing. It's like I've smoked a whole closet full of pot."

Vicky curls up her nose. "I wouldn't know what that's like."

I force a smile. "I wouldn't either. Not a whole closet full anyway."

She laughs and rubs her fingers along the tight muscle in my calf.

I groan. "Now that feels like heaven."

"You *should* be exhausted. You've been carrying around this heavy burden for a long time. This is your body's way of saying 'Thank you, I needed a break, and now I'm going to rest.'"

"Whatever," I tell her.

Closing my eyes again, I can hear everyone whispering as I fall into my deep, dreamless trance.

● ● ●

Vicky is at the house the following morning at eight. I'm actually out of bed, showered and eating breakfast when she arrives. Mentally I'm still tired, but my body does not feel as horribly weak as it had.

"Let's go for a ride," she suggests. "I already talked to Jill, and she will get Hedwig and Scabbers saddled up for us."

I grin at the unique names Kelsey and Tanner chose for their horses. All my nieces and nephews are huge *Harry Potter* fanatics. Until two months ago, I'd never read the books, so I didn't understand the fascination. Then they had me watch four of the movies. I am now halfway through reading *Harry Potter and the Prisoner of Azkaban*, and it's a bit ridiculous, but I've become a Harry Potter junkie too.

"I don't think I'm up for a ride," I say.

"Nonsense. It doesn't have to be a long one. It's time to start moving your body again, to get out of the house and show the world what your bright, smiling face has to offer."

"You are way too chipper for me to deal with this morning."

An hour later, we are pulling up the dirt drive. I see Jillian in the pasture tightening the cinch on Hedwig's reigns. She waves to us as we walk toward her.

Their farmhouse was built in the late nineteen twenties. Though it's been remodeled and upgraded over the years, it still holds some of its original historic charm. The captivating Queen Anne Victorian property boasts stained glass windows, chestnut trim, cast iron radiators, and even a claw foot bathtub. The front porch faces a running stream, and the house backs up to national forest open space. I envy the home and envision myself sitting on the porch, drinking my morning cup of coffee as I listen to the sounds of nature.

"You coming with us, Jill?" Vicky asks.

"Nah, I took Hermione out early this morning," she says, wiping her gloved hands on her already dusty jeans. "I've got a cake to get into the oven for tomorrow's back to school open house. You two have fun. Come in for a drink later. Sam stocked up on beer and wine."

After she disappears, we stash our bottles of water and snacks in the side pouches of the saddles then mount the horses and set off out into the pasture. It is a beautiful day for a ride. Morning dew glistens with sunlight on the auburn ground, and there is scarcely a cloud in the pale blue sky.

I was worried about my energy level, but Vicky pumped me full of Vitamins D and B12, so I feel pretty decent. As we steer the horses toward the bed of the creek, we stroll side by side as Vicky fills the silence with constant chatter. Shane has decided to try out for football this fall, and the twins want to join Girl Scouts. She talks about Tyson's frustration with his upcoming hunting trip in October because the guy he usually goes with didn't draw a tag. Tyson doesn't want to go by himself, so she is considering taking the kids out of school so they can all tag along.

Yellow sunflowers, white yarrow, and daisies scatter the field. I feel at peace and comfortable with the tranquil beauty around us. We find a narrow spot to cross the creek, and make our way through the meadow.

Vicky graciously listens without interrupting when I tell her about my appointment.

"Not to sound cliché...but how do you feel?" she asks.

"I don't know. All I do is sleep. Ask me next week."

We remain quiet, lost in thought, as we continue our ride. I glance up to see the sun disappear behind a white cloud giving us brief relief from the heat. Vicky breaks Hedwig into a gallop, and a few seconds later, I join her. The horses are in a full run as we race to the end of the field where small crested buttes begin to scatter the horizon. A private property sign hangs on a wooden fence post where the creek falls over a bed of rocks and trickles into a fishing pond.

I realize why this area looks familiar. The week before my sixteenth birthday the boys brought us to this spot where we fished for rainbow trout. Vicky caught five big ones about eight inches long, but I only caught one lousy fish the size of my index finger. The boys did not let me live it down.

"Mom knows I was molested," Vicky says, breaking into my thoughts. "So does Tyson."

Confused, I turn in my saddle to look at her.

"What do you mean?"

"When I was in counseling, Bethann encouraged me to have them attend a session. They came separately and I told them. They still don't know who, though."

"Oh my God," I murmur.

"I'm sorry I didn't tell you sooner. I was waiting for the right time, but there never seemed to be one. Mom cried a lot. She started seeing Bethann privately herself to work through her grief and guilt. I assume Mom thinks the same thing happened to you. I don't know if she ever told Dad. Tyson was weird. I expected him to be angry, to want to kill someone. I think on the inside a part of him did, but outwardly he was compassionate, more attentive, and even though we never discussed it again, it drew us closer."

"Are you angry with me?" Vicky asks hesitantly.

"No," I sigh. "I've wasted a lot of my life being angry. Besides, so many times over this summer I wanted to break down and confess to her. You did me a favor," I say. "I guess it explains why she isn't asking many questions about why I am going to counseling."

"You know Mom. She's always respected our privacy. We never gave her a reason not to. But I think that was her biggest regret, not being more nosy or at least sensing that something wasn't right."

"Why do you think she still blames Zane?"

Vicky shrugs. "I honestly don't know."

She glances at the clock on her cell phone. "We should probably turn back. I've got to work at least a few hours today."

"Would you care if I stayed out here a little bit longer? I know the way back. I'll hang out on the farm and Jillian can give me a ride into town when she takes the kids to swimming lessons."

Vicky makes sure I am okay and apologizes again. I reassure her, and when she turns Hedwig toward the farm, I steer Scabbers closer to the pond where we trot along the bank. A few moments later, I dismount and with the reigns still in my hand, lead the horse toward three huge boulders. I climb to the top of one where I sit, watching the breeze ripple over the water. Eventually, I lay back and stare at the sky.

How *do* I feel? I am somewhat relieved and less exhausted, but still sad. I'm sad for the young girl who lived inside a tragically shattered glass bubble. I am sad someone completely unimportant broke her and changed her for the worse. I am sad she spent years tiptoeing through life, not making waves and running from the things that scared her the most.

The sun warms my face, drying tears that formed wet lines down my cheeks. I've gotten comfortable with crying and I welcome it, because every time I do, I feel a little bit lighter.

I climb down from the rock and stick my hand in the murky water creating waves that fold on top of each other until they disappear on the outer edge of the pond.

I sense him before I see him. I know his eyes are on me, watching me, studying me. I stand, rubbing the goosebumps on my arms and turn around. He is astride his horse about a half a football field's length away under a grove of aspen trees. Though I can't see his face clearly, I know it's him by his posture and the way his shoulders pulled back when I turned around.

In a gesture of friendship, I raise my hand. For a moment I'm hopeful, but my heart quickly sinks when he pulls on the reigns and gives his horse a slight nudge with his foot. They gallop in the opposite direction, and aching with disappointment, I watch until Zane is only a spot in the distance.

PART TWO

PART TWO

CHAPTER NINE

Zane — 2009

I spot other hunters in the bottom of the aspen-covered draw that runs down the mountainside, and I decide to make a loop through the sagebrush instead. I'm only a few hundred yards into the tall brush when I spot two does and a small three-point buck. I walk the hill and find a spot to sit where I can glass the countryside. Resting my elbows on my knees, I lift my binoculars to my eyes and size up two more bucks about five-hundred yards away in the bottom of the draw. One buck is bedded down and appears to be another three-point, but the bigger of the two looks worth the shot. After about five minutes, I decide I better take a chance before another hunter beats me to it.

The terrain of the sagebrush hills is working nicely to my advantage as I sneak down and then up the backside of the ridge to close the distance within two hundred yards. As I get closer, I lie down and snake to the top on my belly. As I top the hill, I see the larger buck standing right behind the smaller one. In front of me, about ten yards away, I notice a small boulder I can use for cover. I slither along the ground undetected, but as I reach my shield, the bigger buck slowly walks further up the draw away from me.

I rest my rifle across the rock, hold my breath, and pull the trigger. The buck falls in an instant and doesn't move. I feel my excitement mount as I hurriedly approach. The deer is massive with exceptional forks, the best I tagged so far, and it will provide me more than enough meat for the year.

As dusk approaches, I'm covered in sweat and blood. The deer is boned and gutted, stored in a cooler and loaded onto the four-wheeler. I head back to the camper where I pack the meat on ice until I get back to the ranch tomorrow where the guys will help me process it.

I heat a can of soup over the open fire, exhausted but still reeling with adrenaline. I lean back in my lawn chair and stare at the dark, ominous sky as I tip the beer bottle to my mouth, appreciating the cold liquid as it slides down my throat. It never ceases to amaze me how vast and bewitching the universe can be. The clarity of the stars, breathing the open, fresh air and nothing to hear but the occasional coyote calling out brings me a sense of peace.

Although I love the challenge of the hunt and the meat that feeds me, it's the peace that draws me out here by myself year after year. I used to hunt with Tyson and Mel, but not anymore. I've grown to like the solitude, the isolation.

I laugh at the irony. It seems I have enough solitude and isolation in my life, but for some reason, it's different out here. I have a love/hate relationship with the ranch.

When I am there, I am restless, always looking over my shoulder for my father to show up barking orders and smacking me across the face for doing something stupid, or I'm looking for Jessie's return. The demons of what happened thirteen years ago still haunt me, and until I have closure, it's possible they always will. Out here I can get away from it. Out here I find calmness and contentment that has eluded me my entire life, except for those moments I had with Jessie.

I've been hunting for three days, and for some unexplainable reason, I am anxious to leave. I told the guys I would be gone for the week, so they are not expecting me back anytime soon. Yet, there is an uneasy feeling in my gut, as if there is something I did not take care of that I need to get back to. I cannot figure out what it could be. The ranch is in good hands. I spoke with Tyson and checked on my mother before I left, so they know where to find me. Unless my father died, there is nothing I can think of that would matter. Frankly, that wouldn't matter to me, either.

When I'm hardly able to keep my eyes open, I kick dirt on the fire and stare aimlessly at the golden embers until the last flick of light is out, leaving me alone in the quiet, black night. With a sigh, I open the door of the camper, crawl inside and lock it behind me. Despite how tired I am, sleep escapes me. I can't shake the unsettling feeling that my life is going to be turned upside down once again. I know it's coming, maybe not tomorrow or next month, but this time I want to be prepared.

• • •

Six months later, as I recall the peculiar anxiety I experienced my last night of hunting, I wonder if my subconscious knew she was home. Concluding that her image is a figment of my imagination, I shake my head in hopes to clear it and blink my eyes, not once, not twice, but three times.

She is real, distracted as she balances two cups, the bags of chips and her wallet in her arms, but nevertheless, she is real.

I looked for her face among the crowds for thirteen long and painful years. I hoped for a glimpse, a glimmer that eventually there would be a day when fate would bring her across my path once again. I still remember how it felt to love her. Night after night, year after year, I've tortured myself holding tightly to the space she left in my arms, her image etched in my mind. Each morning when I opened my eyes, the harsh reality of my dreams, or rather my nightmares, would remind me that she was still gone.

After years of watching and wondering if she was going to appear out of thin air, it happens when I least expect it. I look down at the bandage covering my throbbing right index finger and wince. It was a stupid accident that would not usually have brought me to urgent care. I could have stitched it up myself, but I left my first aid kit in the sagebrush of Colorado. I was anxious about loading my deer onto the four-wheeler before dark. I forgot to pick the kit up and was back in Montana before I realized it. I didn't think to replace it until today as I was sharpening the dull blade on the ax I was using to chop down dead trees. As I was running the file across the blade, I sliced my finger on the edge. A good chunk was missing, and I could not get the blood to stop. I cursed and—realizing I had no choice—hopped into the truck and made the much-dreaded drive into town.

I don't come into town much anymore for a variety of reasons. I've made a conscious effort to avoid the hospital altogether and walking through the front door today brought back a multitude of uncomfortable, but not regrettable memories.

After my hand was stitched, I was anxious to be on my way, but my phone vibrated in the back pocket of my jeans. I don't get texts from many people, so when I do, I know it's either ranch business or life or death. I stopped in the corridor by the cafeteria to find a message from Dawson asking me to pick up five bags of feed. As I sent my reply, I noticed a vaguely familiar movement out of the corner of my eye. My heart stopped when I whipped my head and saw her. She was standing by the drink dispenser fitting a lid onto her cup. At first, I thought my eyes were playing tricks on me, but with every move she made, I realized it wasn't my imagination.

I quickly assess where she is headed and position myself by the elevator doors. As she draws near, I can't help but think this has to be fate.

Desperate to see the eyes hiding behind the wisps of hair framing her face, I will her to look at me, but instead, she remains distracted by the unbalanced load in her arms. Before I can think, I push the elevator button and then I speak. My hand shakes as I reach out to catch the falling cup. Her knee-jerk reaction discourages me, so I step away. Right before the elevator doors slam shut, her beautiful, captivating sandstone eyes briefly hold mine. They are not hot with anger but instead shimmer with affection. For a moment, my heart doesn't hurt.

• • •

A short time later, I screech to a halt in front of the sporting goods store. I storm through the front door, demanding to know where my brother is.

Baffled, the sales clerk places her half-eaten sandwich onto the counter and hesitantly points to the back office. I make my way up the stairs two at a time, never thanking the clerk, and I enter the office without knocking.

Tyson is shocked to see me. I rarely frequent the sporting goods store. He tells whoever is on the other end of the phone that he will call back.

"Why the fuck didn't you tell me she was in town?" I explode.

His face pales as his brows knit together in frustration. He gestures to a chair, but I'm too furious to sit. I pace the length of his office.

"I just found out. I'm sorry, Zane. I should have told you it was a possibility," he says, his expression pained.

I glare at him as he sinks into his chair. "Mel's got cancer. He and Libby kept it to themselves until a couple of months ago. It's inoperable, and he's doesn't want treatment. So, she came home. That's all I know. I saw her for the first time the other night. She and Vicky, as you can imagine, are spending a lot of time together."

Too shocked to stand, I opt to sit. With my elbows on my knees, I lean forward, placing my head in my hands.

"You've got to be kidding me. Mel?"

Tyson shakes his head sadly.

"Shit!" I shout as the truth settles around me.

Mel is one of the best men I've ever known in my life. As a kid, I loved being at Jessie's house more than I could stand being at my own. She had a real family who liked to be around one another. Tyson and I could hardly wait to finish our chores to go over there, and we never refused Libby's invites for dinner.

Mel was a man's man. People used to say that about my father, but anyone who truly knew the man my father was, which wasn't many, knew he was nothing but a wolf in sheep's clothing. No, he wasn't a man. A man didn't cheat on his wife continuously. A man didn't take his anger and insecurities out on two young boys who wanted nothing more than his love and affection. A man didn't belittle and terrorize the people he claimed to love behind closed doors, and then intimidate them into pretending they were one big happy family in public. A man didn't hurt, disrespect, and manipulate the people in his life for business, financial or personal gain, or sexual gratification.

Mel, on the other hand, was the man I wanted to be. I watched and admired him from a young age. Whether he was mowing his lawn, tinkering on his truck, helping Libby with her gardening, or playing tag football with his kids in the front yard, he was genuinely happy. He was present at every one of his kid's activities, showering them with encouragement and support.

Everyone liked Mel, and he was always willing to lend a helping hand to anyone who needed it. When the widowed Mrs. Miller needed new shingles on her roof, Mel was the first to volunteer free labor plus he drummed up funds from others in the neighborhood to help pay for supplies. Tyson and I were more than willing to help as long as we got to spend time with him. We felt like we were hanging out with a favorite uncle when we were in his presence. He was laid-back and optimistic, he laughed, he joked, but he also had expectations of Tyson and me that we desperately wanted to meet.

My father wanted to whip us into being men. Mel, on the other hand, taught us how to be a man by setting an example. He taught us to enjoy hard work, trust the decisions we made and that it was okay to have a sense of pride in a job well done. When we became teenagers, it was an unwritten rule that every weekend, no matter what project he was doing around the house, Sam, Tyson, and I were by his side. He let us help change the oil on the car, replace the engine in an old Ford truck, rewire worn-out electrical lines in the garage and fix the kitchen sink plumbing. Every fall, when it was time to stock up firewood, he let us tag along with him and Sam to one of the local farms. For a whole day we cut down dead trees, split and loaded it into the back of that old Ford truck. Into the evening, we delivered firewood to probably fifteen different houses of elderly couples, single mothers, and other families down on their luck. With his guidance we learned how to shoot, clean, respect, and care for a rifle. When I was twelve and Tyson was fourteen, he paid for us to take a hunter safety course at the YMCA when our dad wouldn't.

At first, our dad found Mel's interest in us irritating, claiming he was using us for free labor. Tyson and I knew better. What my dad made us do was free labor—mow the lawn, wash the cars, pull the weeds in the garden, rake leaves, pick up dog poop, paint the house, and clean the garage. We didn't mind the work. It pissed us off he sat on the back porch, a beer in one hand and a cigarette in the other observing and criticizing, unwilling to lift a finger. Our mom finally convinced him that as long as we kept up on the chores around our house, it didn't hurt to help Mel as well. Even though he continued to bitch, he never stopped us from going.

Mel was a mentor, a surrogate father, and his kindness toward us was life-changing. I don't think he ever realized it, but our time with him shaped us into the men we are today. Tyson is the husband and father our dad never was, and the one I would like to be.

My heart tightens when I meet Tyson's gaze. He nods with understanding, quickly wiping away the moisture from the corner of his eye. He pushes out of his chair to face the window. After a moment, he clears his throat.

"Jessie needs time, so give that to her. Between coming home and her dad, if you jump into the equation, it may be more than she can handle. She is fragile and distant, and not sure what to make of us welcoming her home with open arms. She's getting to know the kids. So far, they seem to adore her and vice versa. I think in the long run, that relationship is going to be the key to keeping her here."

"Are *you* ready for this?" I ask Tyson.

He pinches the tip of his nose as he turns around to face me. "Do I have a choice? It was a blessing when Vicky went to counseling. It was a relief not to have *that* secret between us, but I couldn't bring myself to tell her what I already knew. She's braver than I am. When the truth comes out, I'll have to deal with it."

I walk to my brother, clap a hand on his shoulder and pull him into a tight embrace.

"We are in this together," I remind him.

"Always have been," he returns my hug.

• • •

I shut off the radio and drive back to the ranch in silence. The sky is breathtaking as the sun casts a purplish-orange haze onto the early evening clouds. Fields of golden stocks sway as a breeze gently whispers through the air. My thoughts are briefly interrupted when I realize how lucky I was to inherit the ranch. While I do get frustrated at times, this is my heart, my soul, and my life.

My father was born and raised on the ranch but had no attachment to it or his family. He had been a highly intelligent child and did not hesitate to let everyone know he was not cut out for the labor work of ranching. He was determined to have a well-deserved life that did not consist of riding horses, bailing hay, branding cows, or selling pigs. When he spoke about his childhood, he said how stupid, ignorant, and annoying his parents were, and how superior he was. After high school, he moved as far away as possible, to New York City, where he got his bachelor's degree in Agriculture Economics, and his master's in Business Administration. He landed his first job on Wall Street in the early seventies although no one seemed to know what his career was. He eventually met my mother while she was waitressing at a breakfast diner he frequented. After a quick elopement, they lived in a small Manhattan apartment for two years.

The details of what happened in New York are sketchy because each time it was brought up over the years, the story changed. By the time our mother was pregnant with me, they were back in Helena living on the ranch. My dad was miserable, and everyone around him paid the price. Grandpa tried to connect him with Montana's state secretary of agriculture, but according to Dad, he couldn't work with her because she was a raving lunatic. According to my grandpa, Dad burned too many bridges in New York and couldn't land a job in his field.

Grandpa, who was not naïve to his son's less-than-stellar reputation, offered up a compromise. He co-signed on a business loan to open the sporting goods store because he knew Dad was a smart business man. Grandpa agreed that as long as Dad paid the loan, he could run it how he wanted and Grandpa would keep his nose out of it. Likewise, he asked Dad, who liked to pretend he knew all there was to know about everything, to mind his own business and leave the ranching to him. From there, a partnership began with as much respect as possible.

Surprisingly, Dad held up his end of the bargain, as did my grandfather. It took him five years to pay off the business loan, and once he did, he rarely associated with my grandparents, and didn't have anything to do with the ranch except use it for his extracurricular activities.

Ironically, even though my father hated Helena and most of the people who lived there, he put on the persona of the ideal community member. He joined the Chamber of Commerce, he was on the church council and the school board and, much to our dismay, he coached little league baseball. He was loved by all except those related to him.

It still boggles my mind how two supportive, giving, and kind people like my grandparents raised such a spoiled, narcissistic asshole like my father. I thought there had to be some explanation as to why he was the way he was and expected to hear horror stories of the abuse inflicted upon my father by his parents. I heard nothing about emotional or physical abuse, neglect, or manipulation by either of them. Granted, being an only child may have had something to do with it, but my guess is he was born with a heart of stone and ice in his veins. Despite the nurturing love and encouragement my grandmother showered him with, he could not—would not—give it in return.

My grandparents didn't come to our house often because my dad treated them horribly. Tyson and I adored them so Mom made it a priority to take us to them every other Saturday. It was there that we were free to be ourselves.

On the early morning horseback rides, Grandpa told stories of his childhood on the ranch. Even then, I craved the lifestyle. Grandma always had a big lunch waiting after we fed the animals and finished the chores. In the afternoons, there was usually another project. If the weather was bad, the four of us stayed indoors or sat on the front porch putting together puzzles or playing cards. Grandpa taught us poker, pitch, gin rummy, and even some fun card tricks. The routine was comfortable, and the normalcy of it was something Tyson and I craved.

Over the years, my grandmother treated a few black eyes, many swollen lips, cuts, and abrasions as a result of our father's anger. I saw the pain in her eyes, a result of disappointment in her son and a strong desire to protect us, but she never asked questions or confronted him about it. Grandpa didn't say anything either. I think they were as afraid of him as we were, and they couldn't talk to my mom. She was as much his victim as the rest of us were.

The older Tyson and I got, the angrier we became. Thankfully, the more involved we were in activities at school, the less we were home. By the time we were in eighth grade, it was just a place to sleep. Dad left the house around seven in the morning, so Tyson and I made a point not to get out of bed until we heard his vehicle pull out of the garage. Once he was gone, we showered, got ready, grabbed a granola bar, and headed out the door. Between after school practices, hanging out with friends, and doing homework in the library, we usually didn't get home until seven, after our parents had eaten. We ate leftovers, then we did our chores before disappearing into our rooms. The less interaction we had with him, the less often we were the target of his temper.

At first, we worried he would take it out on Mom, but thankfully, he didn't, at least not with his fists, although she continued to be his emotional punching bag. Our mom was passive, quiet, and detached. She attempted to put on the same show as Dad, but she didn't have the skills nor the inclination to do it well. She was pretty enough and kept herself looking attractive to please him, but she didn't have the personality to draw people to her the way Dad did. Others saw her as his mousy, introverted wife and found her very uncomfortable to be around. She didn't have friends, and as far as we knew, she didn't keep in contact with her family. She never talked about them, and I don't recall ever meeting them. Her life revolved around caring for the three of us. Our house was immaculately clean, our laundry done, and great meals were always on the table. In grade school, she volunteered in the classroom, and by the time high school rolled around, she was at every single sporting event and award ceremony. Dad showed up once in a while to save face with the members of the community. God forbid someone question good ol' Ron Stecks about the touchdown his son made at Friday night's game and find out he didn't know a darn thing about it. It would ruin his reputation as the father of the year.

I never understood what Mom saw in him. Sure, he was a handsome guy. He was still charming toward her at times. We saw it—damn, the whole town saw it whenever they were together in public. Maybe little bits and pieces of that gave her enough hope. There was a time when I wished she was stronger or assertive enough to take us and get far away. I've come to a peaceful understanding that he probably picked her because she was a young, easy target. Despite the circumstances, she was a good mom, she did the best she could, and I love her. I try to see her about once a week, and sometimes she comes out to the ranch for dinner. She is still introverted, but she does have friends. Since Dad's accident, she joined a book club. She actively volunteers at the church cooking for weddings, funerals, and baptisms. She fills in when the church secretary is out of town and helps plan fundraising activities for the youth group. I wouldn't say she is a hands-on, nurturing grandmother, but the grandkids are the lights of her life and she tries to be at all their activities. This is the happiest I have ever seen her.

My truck rolls onto the dirt road heading to the house as the pink and purple sunset fades behind the mountain. Weiser, my black lab, runs out to greet me as I jump out of the cab. I pat his head and rub his belly before opening the passenger door to grab the fifty-pound bag of dog food and gingerly toss him a pig's ear. He retreats onto the porch where he gnaws on it, oblivious as I carry supplies from the back of the truck into the barn.

I'm sweating by the time I finish unloading the two by fours, sheets of drywall and bags of feed. Weiser is still working on his treat when I return to the porch with a cold beer. I lean back in the rocking chair, kick my feet up, and stare at the metallic sky. Thunderclouds rumble as the distant flash of light threatens a storm.

The old farmhouse my grandfather's father built in the early nineteen-thirties was a mess by the time I inherited it, but I didn't want to tear it down and rebuild. It holds great memories for me and has been in the family for decades. The part of me that held onto hope for Jessie's return was sensitive enough to understand the horrific memories here. I spent the first few years remodeling, replacing, moving, and making it different yet as traditional to the values of my grandparents as possible.

Aside from tearing down the guesthouse and replacing it with the two log cabins that Brent's family and Dawson now live in, I restored the old barn and built a new one on the south side of the property away from the house. I moved the pig troughs behind the stable where they can't be hit directly by the wind. It's a little further of a walk, but it's nice to sit on the front porch of the house and not be inundated with the rank smell of manure.

In my head, I rewind the events of the day as I take a long swig from the bottle, savoring the hoppy, earthy flavor. Though I'm emotionally and physically exhausted, I know sleep will be restless. I can't help but think about Mel. If it weren't for him and the intervention of my grandparents, who knows where Tyson and I would have wound up — a juvenile detention center probably.

Hormones plus the pressure of school and friends mixed with angry, defiant, resentful preteen boys were not a good combination. We became experts at toeing the line at home, so by the time we got to school, we were bombs on the verge of detonating. We had a reputation as trouble makers, and fights became a weekly occurrence.

The only time we were suspended in eighth grade, our sadistic asshole of a father made us beat one another with an electrical cord. We knew we needed to whip each other hard enough to leave a mark or he would take over, which would be ten times worse. No punishment was a real punishment unless a red welt appeared, he always reminded us. While sipping on two fingers of whiskey, he watched from the corner of the basement while Tyson released the cord as hard as he could against my bare back. I heard him whimper as the wire struck my skin, and I jolted forward in pain. Dad made him do this five more times, and then it was my turn. Even though there was a two-year age difference between us, I was a bit broader than Tyson and equally as strong. Afterward, Dad seemed satisfied and left us alone, but the next day at school, we could hardly move.

Our grandfather picked us up that day because our parents left for a business conference. When he commented on the stiff stride of our gait, we hung our heads in shame mumbling some half-assed story about lifting weights in gym class. Later, when we finished helping him coral one of the pregnant heifers back into her pen, he affectionately slapped Tyson on the back. Tyson grimaced in pain and squirmed out of his reach. Grandpa demanded to see our backs, and we had no choice but to obey. Silently, he escorted us back to the house where Grandma once again tended to our wounds while he made phone calls. To this day I'm not sure how my grandfather convinced the principal to cooperate, but whenever we got into trouble at school, the school called either him or Mel, never my parents.

Once again, it was Mel who opened our eyes to the choices we were making. Although he never directly came out and asked what went on at home, we knew he was aware. A few months later on a fall evening after helping him rake up dead leaves in the yard, he sat down with Tyson and I and handed us a soda. By this time, it was apparent to everyone, including Mel and Libby, that Tyson and Vicky had a thing for each other.

"You boys have become as important to me as my kids, and you are my family. I want to keep it that way. In this family, we love. We don't treat others the way your dad does. You boys are good friends with my girls, they care about you, and again, I want to keep it that way. For the sake of family and friendship, I think you need to reconsider some of your behavior."

Mel had a way of saying things without actually coming right out and saying the words, yet we always understood his message. This conversation was all it took for us to change. He said the kindest words any grown man, besides our grandfather, had ever said to us. How this man, who was not our biological father or even a blood relative could care for us the way he did, gave life a whole new meaning. We began channeling our aggression into sports instead of fights. We still had a reputation, but from that point forward, there were no more physical altercations.

The chimes hanging from the porch ceiling ring as the wind picks up. Reluctantly, I get to my feet and stretch my back before going to the kitchen. Inside, I rummage through the fridge until I find the leftover pot roast and mashed potatoes. I spoon the meal onto a plate, and I stick it in the microwave and punch a few buttons. As I wait, I am tempted to pour myself a shot of whiskey but decide against it knowing the hard alcohol is not a good mix with my current temperament. Instead, I pop the top off another beer.

Taking my food outside, I eat in silence and allow my mind to wander to the place I have been avoiding all evening.

Jessie's hair is a softer, pale blonde instead of the dirty dishwater she had growing up. Although she's a little thin, she still has her sexy athletic build. I'd know her anywhere by the way she moved, but it surprised me how she kept her head down and lips pinched in a scowl as if she was intentionally trying to ward people off. The Jessie I knew wouldn't have done that. The Jessie I fell in love with had a smile for everyone she met. She could strike up a conversation with a stranger and leave the stranger better because of the vibrant energy she possessed. Her purpose in life, although she probably didn't realize it, was to make others feel better with complete disregard to what they offered in return because she felt good enough, worthy enough and loved enough as it was. She wanted to give that back to the world. To this day, I never met anyone that came close to having those qualities.

I tried. Lord knows *how* much I wanted to forget her. I'm embarrassed to admit in college I drank myself into oblivion on a few occasions and wound up on the floor of my dorm room covered in my bile. Eventually, I tried to get back into the dating scene, hoping to find someone kind, intelligent, and pretty, and I did find it. But they lacked in areas Jessie didn't. She wasn't only beautiful and smart; she was also animated and enthusiastic, but stubborn as hell, yet determined, humble, and desirable. God, she was so damn desirable. There wasn't another woman in the world who could twist my stomach into knots the way she did. I wasn't willing to settle and I'd rather be alone than live my life comparing another woman to Jessie.

I stayed in Bozeman after college, working for Montana's Game and Fish Department, waiting for life to provide me with direction. I spent my time hunting, fishing, playing softball on Tuesday evenings and drinking beer with the guys. A part of me waited and hoped that Jessie would hunt me down and tell me she couldn't live without me, while the other part floundered in misery, realizing I needed to move on without her.

It was the summer of my twenty-fifth birthday when my grandparents passed away, two months apart. They hadn't been in good health since my senior year. After my dad's accident, and without Tyson and me around anymore, they declined quickly. Four months after their death, it wasn't shocking to find out Tyson and I inherited the ranch. We met with the lawyer and agreed that I would buy out Tyson's half. He had recently purchased a new house, and Vicky was pregnant with the twins. He was content running the store. I, on the other hand, had nothing. Tyson agreed on one hundred dollars for his half with one condition—that I allowed his kids to know and love the ranch the same way we had growing up. It was an offer I did not want to refuse.

It was bittersweet moving back to Helena. After all, it was my plan with Jessie all along. Still, I thrived on the challenge. There were two hired hands, Brent and Dawson, who had been doing most of the work for Grandpa in his last years that I chose to keep on. Brent had a wife and a kid. Dawson was a single guy in his mid-thirties. I trusted them, and they had done right by our family. Besides, I could not run the place by myself with fifteen hundred head of cattle, fifty pigs, and five horses. For the first time since Jessie left, I was able to throw myself into physically and mentally exhausting work. Every night when I closed my eyes, instead of the restlessness and insomnia, sleep came easily.

Now she is back, and all the shit comes with her.

I lost my appetite and put the uneaten portion of my pot roast on the ground next to Weiser. He happily licks the plate. I rub behind his ears when he finishes. Afterward, he playfully runs along beside me as I stroll around the property to lock up. When I'm finished, I turn off the porch lights, bolt the front door, and head upstairs. While I brush my teeth, Weiser scratches and circles his dog bed until he is comfortable enough to nest in. Soon, he is snoring, and as I crawl under my covers, I hope I can rest that peacefully.

CHAPTER TEN

A month has passed since I saw Jessie at the hospital, and I still don't know what to do. What does she want or even need me to do?

Unbeknownst to Jessie, Sam and her parents helped Vicky, Tyson and me keep tabs on her through the years. They shared updates with Vicky, who shared with Tyson, who then told me. From the sounds of it, she kept to herself and lived under the radar of any drama or excitement. In my mind, no news was good news, and I continued to hold out hope that she would come home. My hope shattered with the news that she quit school and moved to Seattle with someone named A.J. to open up a bistro. I want to say I am unselfish and could wish her well if she were to find happiness, but that isn't my personality. It was unbearable to know she was living a life without me and possibly with some other man—until I found out A.J. was a woman.

Brent and I were putting drywall up in the new shop the day Tyson came over to deliver the news. Realizing Tyson wanted privacy, I asked Brent to get another bag of nails from the back of the truck.

"So, A.J. is her business partner, then?" I asked, setting my hammer on the bench.

"I'm not sure," Tyson said evasively, leaning against the wall. "They live together."

"What do you mean you're not sure? If they are roommates, what is the big deal? Is she dating someone else she works with?"

Tyson's face turned a dark shade of red. "Look, Zane. No one knows the whole story, or if they do, no one is saying. But it sounds like A.J. may be Jessie's girlfriend, partner, lover…get my drift?"

At first, I laughed, but the somber expression on my brother's face told me he was dead serious.

"No way!" I shouted. "There is no way in hell. I know Jessie. It's not possible."

"You don't know her anymore," Tyson informed me quietly. "She's changed, Zane."

"Fuck you!" I yelled before punching my fist through the slat of drywall. Picking up the hammer, I tossed it across the floor. A dumbfounded Brent returned with the nails as I stormed out of the shop. A moment later, I heard Tyson's truck rumble down the driveway.

It took a beer or two, but I eventually calmed down and convinced myself I knew the truth behind the whole scenario. It was a ruse, a scheme for her to continue to dodge everything she'd been avoiding since the day she ran away. Once this reality set in, I was less worried about her moving on with another man or forgetting about me. But as the years passed, a helpless feeling crawled into the empty space that had once housed my dreams.

I'm in the barn when I hear the school bus rumble up to my drive. It drops Shane, Sasha, and Shelby off every Monday after school. They help me with chores, and then we go horseback riding before Tyson picks them up after work. This weekly time with them seems to fill a quarter of the void in my soul, and I can connect with the *me* I was before Jessie left. I sort of like that guy.

Two hours later, we are putting the saddles away after our ride when we hear Tyson's truck. He rolls his window down to tell me Vicky has a PTA meeting, so he and the kids are on their own for dinner. The kids beg us to let them go for a hike in the woods behind the house before they have to leave. We agree, and I hand Tyson a beer as I squat down beside him on the front porch step. He reaches into my bag of sunflower seeds and shoves a handful into the side of his cheek. We sit quietly at first, taking in the brisk evening air and the smell of freshly watered hay fields. I watch him spit shells onto the grass in front of us and think back to the first time he came to see me after I moved in. It was an evening similar to this, and if I recall correctly, we were also eating sunflower seeds but well on our way to the end of a six-pack of beer and ready to start on another.

We hadn't spent a significant amount of time together since his wedding. The last real conversation we had was when we made a pact to keep what happened quiet until we had some time, space, and distance between us and the events that transpired. Unfortunately, time and distance formed an unintentional wedge. He was busy with a new wife, the business and pretending as if he hadn't a care in the world. I was busy nursing a broken heart that most thought I'd never recover from. Maybe they were right. If only they knew that there was so much more to the story than just a broken heart.

I never stopped caring about my brother. We have a bond that can never be broken and will protect each other, always. I guess, at the time, it was easier to ignore one another than face reality. It's also too painful for the three of us—him, Vicky, and me, to be together without Jessie. She was the missing link. Instead of attempting to fill the void, we chose not to try at all. There was too much that wasn't being said, too many secrets, and it was better if I stayed away.

I saw them for the first time in years at my grandfather's funeral and then again two months later at my grandmother's. Like a moth drawn to the flame, I could not keep my distance.

"We miss you so much," a very pregnant Vicky sobbed as she hugged me.

With eyes full of sorrow, Tyson clasped my shoulder, and I knew he felt the same. There was an immediate infatuation with two-year-old Shane that made it impossible to tear myself away from him ever since. Two months later, when the twins were born, I remembered what it felt like *not* to have a heart of stone.

Less than a week later, Tyson was at my door, beer in hand.

We sat up until midnight rehashing everything. It wasn't a pleasant conversation, but thankfully, the beer helped. When the beer was gone, we turned to whiskey. Since then, Tyson makes it a priority to pick up the kids and come over by himself once a month.

Vicky doesn't know any of this because, for whatever reason, we decided it was best if we kept our interactions private. I continue to keep my distance from her. I can't bring myself to engage in the happy family dynamics when there is such a huge piece missing. Maybe it's my stubborn pride, and there are days when I wonder if I shouldn't just suck it up, but when I start to bring myself to accept the invite to a family dinner, I only withdraw further.

I do miss the relationship Tyson and I used to have. We spent our lives doing everything together, hunting, riding ATVs, sports, his friends were my friends and vice versa. We had never been jealous or competitive with one another. In fact, because of the bullshit we dealt with at home, I think we supported each other that much more. I had his back, and he had mine. He was my brother, my best friend, advocate, and confidant. No one understood our lives better than us, and because of the circumstances before his wedding, we shared an unbreakable bond.

Tonight Tyson tells me the latest about Mel. It is still hard for me to wrap my head around the news. When he finishes his beer, I hand him a bottle of water. He takes a drink then informs me about Jessie's trip back to Seattle the previous week. Again, he does not give me much to go on except the basic, everyday details of her life.

"She started seeing a counselor," he admits.

I take a long, hard swig of my beer and nod as I squint into the setting sun. I'm tolerant of life without Jessie. I wouldn't say I'm happy, but I'm not miserable. I feel uncomfortably content. My life is dull and uneventful, but I am doing what I love. Now she is back in town, and my heart aches to see her, to talk to her, to touch her.

Hope is a strange thing. It gives you something to desire, a dream to work toward, or a goal to achieve. When the dream is within arm's reach, and it seems that everything you want may possibly become real, fear takes hold. Hope suddenly becomes your worst nightmare because if you get everything you want, there is a higher possibility that you may lose it.

And losing Jessie again would be unbearable.

• • •

If I thought my days were dull and monotonous before, by the end of summer, they are worse. Jessie's face pops into my head the moment my eyes open after a restless sleep. As I move through the morning routine feeding cattle, pigs, and horses, I replay every memory I have of her and sometimes find myself laughing. Where I was reserved and serious, Jessie was animated and entertaining. Whether she was hopping around in her cheerleading uniform practicing routines, dancing around the room, or recapping a Saturday Night Live skit, the complexity of her spirit and fierceness of her soul made the desire to be around her even more intense.

Brent and Dawson eye me suspiciously when this happens. I realize they do not see me laugh often except when Tyson's kids are around. Other than that, my demeanor is steady and no-nonsense.

My afternoons are the same as the mornings. Whether I am building a fence, replacing horseshoes, rounding up cattle or a variety of other chores, all I think about is Jessie. It's pathetic. I'm like a lovesick puppy. I get distracted fantasizing about the fun we would have at our nieces and nephew's activities, family dinner nights with our siblings, or on camping trips together. I imagine giving her a tour of the ranch and taking her fishing. For a moment, the pieces of my heart feel mended. Just as quickly, when I realize the dream slipped through my fingers, I become angry. The reality makes my days drag.

My temperament is all over the place. Brent and Dawson keep their distance, but I imagine they think I've lost my mind. As the sun starts to set, I mumble my goodbyes before disappearing into my house. Tonight, I throw a turkey pot pie into the oven. While it cooks,

I turn Pandora to the Rolling Stones station and sit at my desk, staring at the laptop while allowing my tense shoulders to relax.

I've had a computer for years but don't use it much. Brent has a business degree and takes care of the financials so other than e-mail, reading the news and surfing the internet when I want to buy something, nothing else on the computer serves a purpose. Last year curiosity got the best of me, and I broke down and set up a Facebook page under a false name. I log on every couple of weeks to see if I can find her. But I have never been able to. My guess is she stays away from it as much as I have.

I check out the latest pictures of my brother's kids, "like" a few of them, check my e-mails and then log off. I don't know why I waste my time, I guess it's another bad habit I can't break.

I glance around the house wondering what Jessie would think of the changes and if she'd be comfortable here. I kept the antique character of the doorways and window moldings but sanded and stained them a dark cherry. I gutted and remodeled the kitchen. Along with the front door, I replaced windows throughout and added a sliding glass door that leads to the deck. There are new cupboards in the same cherry color as the molding, granite countertops, and new stainless-steel appliances. I kept the original kitchen sink and was able to find a similar one at an auction. Now there is a large upgraded double sink.

A more than enthusiastic Tonya helped with decorating. She went to several websites and came up with a variety of ways to incorporate my grandparent's belongings around the house. The shelves on the wall are from their wooden pallets, the coffee and end tables were once the kitchen cupboards, and a variety of memorabilia line the top of the new ones. Old rugs were dry cleaned to bring out the color that hasn't seen the light of day in forty years. One rug adorns the kitchen floor while the other is in the middle of the living room. I also pulled out the orange shag carpet and replaced it with a wood laminate that wraps through the kitchen, into the hallways and bathroom. I added new carpet and painted the master bedroom and knocked out a wall which led to my grandpa's office and turned it into a huge master bath and walk-in closet. My next project will be the downstairs bathroom. The pink and blue tile, blue sink and metal silver faucets need to be replaced.

I hired a crew to put up new siding and repaint the outside after I replaced the roof. It is the same brick red color that matches the barn, another tip from Tonya. The porch is my favorite place of all. My goal was to keep the integrity of the original exterior of the house, so I secured the old beams, sanded, stained, and then added on, wrapping it around the side of the house to the back where it transforms into a deck. I have my morning cup of coffee here to watch the sunrise, and in the evening, to watch it set.

The buzz of the timer on the stove goes off, and I hop up. As I am pulling the pie out of the oven, there is a knock on the front door.

"Yoo-hoo! Zane, it's me, Tonya!" I hear her announce through the screen door. "I brought you some zucchini bread."

"I'm in the kitchen," I call out.

I like Tonya. She is a pretty, petite brunette with short spikey hair and big brown eyes. Originally from Alabama, she met Brent when he was stationed there in the Air Force. With her Southern drawl and soft, inviting voice, she is easy to be around. She is friendly and welcoming, not overbearing, loud or annoying like some Southern women I have been around.

I pull the top off my pie, mesmerized by the steam, while Tonya places a loaf wrapped in tin foil on the table.

"The girls and I baked today. Figured you'd like some." She smiles brightly.

Charlie, who was a toddler when I met her, is now nine and loves to bake. Her four-year-old little sister, Zoe attempts to help but from what I have seen, winds up wearing most of the batter.

"That's nice of you. Thanks," I return the smile.

I take a seat at the table and dig into my meal. She looks around the kitchen for a moment and then back at me. "Would you like to sit down?" I gesture to the chair across from me. "You hungry? I can get you something. Maybe a piece of your bread?"

"Oh no thanks," she says as she pulls back the chair.

In silence, she watches me eat.

"Would you like a beer? I don't have any wine. Not many women around here to drink wine," I joke.

Again, she smiles warmly. "Well, that's sort of why I am here."

"For wine?"

"No. To check on you. The guys are worried, and you know how guys are. Shoot, they're never going to ask you themselves, so I volunteered."

"You've been talking about me?" I raise my eyebrows.

"Of course. We always discuss family, especially when we worry about them."

I return to eating my dinner.

"I'm not going to ask you if everything is okay. It is pretty apparent it's not. We have been out on the ranch with you for almost six years now, and we've never seen you this troubled. Like I said, we are family. If there is something we can help with, I know you may not want to tell the guys, but I'm a good listener. I do give pretty good advice."

My first inclination is to be annoyed. It's not like Tonya to be intrusive, but I know her heart is in the right place.

Exhausted, I rub my hands over my face, and then shove them through my greasy hair. I look at Tonya, thinking how nice it would be to talk to someone besides Tyson to get a different perspective. Of course, I can't tell her the whole story. I lean back in my chair and take a deep breath.

"I had a girlfriend in high school," I blurt out. "It's long and complicated, and I can't get into it, but she left not long after graduation. I have not seen or heard from her since. Now she is back, and I'm a mess."

Tonya places a hand on her heart as if she can feel my pain. "Oh, Zane. You still love her?"

"Never stopped. But like I said. It's very complicated."

"Love always is. Can I ask why she left?"

I frown. "Someone hurt her."

"Someone you know?" she whispers.

I hesitate briefly. My voice shakes as the words come out. "Yes, someone I knew all too well."

Tonya doesn't ask any more questions. Instead, she wants to hear all about her. I spend the next hour raving about the woman I put onto a pedestal and never took down.

"And she felt the same way about you?"

I nod. "A lot has happened in thirteen years, though. We don't know one another anymore."

"True. You have to be logical about that. It wouldn't hurt to try to get to know one another again, would it?" Tonya suggests.

"You make it sound simple. Unfortunately, some dynamics play a bigger part in making it anything but simple. Her sister is married to my brother," I admit.

Surprised Tonya shakes her head in dismay. "It is complicated."

Her head would spin if she knew the rest, but I've said enough. As I stab my fork into my now cold pot pie, Tonya stands up. She pats my back as she passes me on her way toward the door.

"Things have a funny way of working out the way they are supposed to."

I used to believe that, but after years of disappointment, I find it hard to have faith.

"You let us know if you need anything. Otherwise, we will respect your privacy."

She knows me all too well. "Thanks, Tonya. Tell the girls thanks for the zucchini bread. I'll have a piece for breakfast in the morning."

After she shuts the front door, I sink into my chair wondering why the hell I told her a damn thing. In all this time, I hadn't spoken a word to anyone about Jessie. Frustrated, I toss my dinner in the trash, grab a soda out of the fridge and walk out to the front porch where Weiser is laying on his back breathing heavily as he sleeps.

There is no moon to reflect any light so aside from the stars that speckle the ebony sky the land in front of me is pitch black. Regardless, I stare out wishing Jessie's figure would somehow materialize out of the obscure shadows. Some days it's hard to believe this much time has passed. Others feel like an eternity.

For years now I've been unsettled about how I handled the circumstances before she left. If I had any inclination she was going to run away, I would have been more persistent when she was hiding at her brother's. I was trying to give her space. I couldn't imagine what seeing me would stir up, and the last thing I wanted to do was hurt her. What if she hated me? What if she blamed me? At the time, the thought was a relentless reminder that encouraged me to keep my distance. Besides, if I had seen her, what could I have possibly said to take away her pain?

I've replayed the scenario in my mind a dozen times. There is not a perfect answer. We all fell victim to the same monster. As fiercely protective as Tyson and I were, the two people we love most in the world wound up having their lives destroyed by him.

• • •

The next day I am up earlier than usual to start my chores. While I laid awake in bed the evening before, a memory came back to me of a time I took Jessie fishing not far from the land Sam bought. I haven't been there since that day, but I have a strong inkling to check it out, so I go for a ride mid-morning when the sunlight shines brightest over the meadow. My horse needs exercise, and I could use a change of scenery.

I've often thought about driving over to Sam's place to pay a friendly visit like ranching neighbors sometimes do. I never have, and a part of me envies Tyson for the fact that he was able to stay connected. I avoid going into town as often as possible unless I have to buy supplies, so I don't run into many people I know, but I have seen Sam at the feed store. He is friendly, makes small talk about the ranch, and tells me about his kids. We briefly discuss Vicky and Tyson's family before going our separate ways. I'm never sure what to make of it and try not to give it too much attention, but it nags at me. Sam was like a brother. The whole family was the family I never had. When Jessie left, I lost everyone I cared about.

Ironically, I only ran into Mel once, never Libby. I was coming out of the liquor store with a six-pack of beer a couple of months after I took over the ranch. He was climbing out of his truck but stopped short when he spotted me. The look on his face held sorrow, disappointment, and anger. For a brief moment, neither of us moved. I desperately wanted to say something to break the apparent tension, but I froze. It seemed like minutes, but I'm sure it was only seconds later when Mel got back into his truck and drove away.

Shaking away the memory, I saddle up Rosie, the last Saddlebred my grandfather bought before he passed away. I tell the guys I'm taking off but plan to be back by early afternoon. They are less apprehensive around me today, which I imagine has to do with my conversation with Tonya. I know they won't bring it up, but it's still awkward that they know private details of my life.

I give Rosie a gentle kick with the heel of my boot, and she takes off through the meadow toward an aspen grove. The leaves are a rich gold with an accent of sunrise orange. It won't be long before we get our first frost and the leaves fall, leaving nothing but bare branches. I feel my adrenaline surge as I run Rosie hard the first fifteen minutes. By the time she slows down for a drink of water from the creek, we ease into a leisurely stroll.

As I make my way to where I took Jessie fishing, I am flooded with bittersweet memories.

● ● ●

"It's just a worm. Shit, Jessie, just two years ago we were in the backyard with your dad after a storm digging up night crawlers. You didn't have a problem then."

She made a face. "That was different. All I had to do was dig them out of the ground and put them in a big tub with all their little friends. I wasn't sticking a hook through them. That is just malicious."

"Are you going to be able to handle taking the hook out of a fish's mouth if we catch one?"

She grimaced.

Laughing, I took the pole from her. "You sure you want to do this?"

When she smiled, there was a twinkle in her eye. "I can think of other things we can do instead."

I felt myself grow stiff merely hearing the words leave her mouth. It wasn't second nature for Jessie to flirt, so the fact that she even attempted made me love her more. Without a moment's hesitation, I tossed the pole on the ground and pulled her into my arms. I kissed her slowly at first, sucking on her bottom lip, one hand on her lower back and the other thrust into her mass of thick hair. I made sure there were no rocks or sticks beneath us as I eased her gently onto her back. My lips devoured her neck while my hand hungrily searched for the bare skin under her shirt.

When I found her mouth again, my tongue explored her welcoming warmth, as I pressed my body deeper into hers. We'd been exploring each other like this for a few months, and though my limits were tested, I was always able to refrain. Jessie wasn't ready, and despite how badly I wanted her, I was willing to wait.

I rolled onto my back. Jessie laid her head on my chest and caressed my arm with her fingertip. Breathing heavily, I stared at the pale indigo sky, watching the clouds as they moved in front of the sun, giving us a brief reprieve from the heat. My fingers traced the curve of her shoulder as she shivered under my touch.

I saw her eyes were closed, the steady rhythm of her breath indicating she was almost asleep. I didn't want to disturb her. I stared at her delicate features, stenciling the perfect, breathtaking image into my mind.

I clearly remembered the day her family moved in across the street. Tyson and I were excited to hear they had kids our same age, seven and almost nine, only to be disappointed they were two girls. But it wasn't long before the four of us were riding bikes around town, to the movies, to the swimming pool and playing in the treehouse Mel built for them that first summer. Jessie and Vicky were better to hang out with than any of our friends. They didn't mind playing night games in the cemetery after dark, climbing trees in the park or going to the ranch with us on weekends where we chased baby pigs and milked cows. On the occasions my dad decided to be a decent parent and interact with us, they were right there getting grass stains on their knees while we played touch football. There was no drama, they didn't whine or complain, and unlike boys, they weren't trying to compete with us. They loved every adventure we came up with and were always willing to tag along on our explorations.

I was fourteen years when I realized I was in love with Jessie. Lord knows I wasn't going to tell her. Why would a girl with good grades, looks, personality, popularity, and a wonderful family want anything to do with a punk like me. I had a temper, was kicked out of school for fighting, my grades were less than desirable, and my only ambition in life was avoiding my home. My parents had money, but they were both jack asses. Other than being good at sports, I had nothing to offer. It was one thing to be best friends, but to be a boyfriend? Probably not. I saw how other guys looked at her. I didn't want to admit it, but a lot of them were decent.

By the time we were sophomores in high school, I hated hearing other guys talk about her. Jessie was naïve and innocent, but other guys fantasized and talked shit anyway. I made it clear Jessie was off-limits. Therefore, she didn't get asked on many dates. My worst fear was one of those decent guys would come along and not just want to get down her pants but want to give her what she deserved, and what I couldn't.

On the other hand, I had a new girl every other month but refused to commit to anyone. It was stupid, but it was the only way I could rationally keep my mind off Jessie, which never worked. She was still the one I wanted to spend time with, the one I wanted to tell everything to and the one I laid in bed at night thinking of. My desire for her was so strong, it overwhelmed me at times. It was challenging to be away from her, and when we were together, it was almost impossible not to touch her.

I watched her eyes flutter open. She stared at me somberly until I kissed her again. I was crazy in love with this girl and would move heaven and earth to have a future with her. Was it even realistic? A doctor married to a park ranger who wanted to own a ranch? Jessie made me want to be a better person. We were young, and some considered us naïve, but with her by my side, I had no doubt anything was possible.

• • •

Rosie's jolt startles me back to reality. I grab the reigns in an attempt to steady her as she prances in a circle when she hears another horse in the distance. It's rare to run into others when I ride, but I did venture off my usual trail onto someone else's property. I can see the horse, but the rider seems to be absent. Curious, I guide a now calm Rosie across the field but pull her back when a female figure appears from the other side of a large boulder. She is about fifty yards away, but I can see her clearly when she looks in my direction. Her face holds no expression or recognition.

I have conflicted emotions. My heart wants to go after her, but my head recognizes the reality of the impossible circumstances.

Defeated, I turn Rosie around and ride for home.

• • •

"Did you talk to her?"

I asked Tyson to come over after work. I'm going out of my mind and need someone to talk to about my brief encounter with Jessie.

I think about how her once bright and cheerful eyes seemed flat and lifeless, and shake my head. "Damn it, Tyson, she just looks so, I don't know the word. Not like Jessie."

Tyson sighs. "I don't know what you expect."

I feel helpless. "I don't know either."

"Look, I know you want to be with her. We want that too. I think you have to let things play out the way they are supposed to. I know I am ready to face my wife if and when the truth comes out. Are you willing to do the same?"

"I have to be. It's the only way we can move forward."

"She didn't leave town because she hated you. But there is a possibility if she learns the truth, she will, and Vicky may hate me too." Tyson hangs his head and rubs the back of his neck. "What did you bring me over here for, Zane? Therapy? To rehash the impossible?"

I open my mouth to speak but close it just as quickly realizing how ludicrous it will sound if I ask him to set up a chance meeting.

"Jesus, Tyson, I'm going nuts. The longer it goes on, the harder it is. I didn't have a choice before because I didn't know where she was. I couldn't just call her up or drive over to talk sense into her. She disappeared into thin air. Now I know what room she is sleeping in and in the morning, I know what chair she sits in to eat her breakfast. The fact that she is at your house, and at the kids sporting events, it's taking all I have not to show up."

Tyson picks up a deck of cards from the end table and shuffles them in his hands. He sympathizes with me because he knows how easily it could have been Vicky that ran away all those years ago.

"You know, I hate to sound like a parent, but I'm going to. While you are waiting, it wouldn't hurt to talk to someone. It's not as if this hasn't affected you. Jessie is going to need your support, and a jaded asshole with his own issues isn't going to help."

I kick my feet onto the coffee table in front of me, and I lean further into the couch, resting my head against the pillow propped up behind me. "I already have," I mumble.

He tosses a card at me. "What? When?"

I explain how I managed to pass my college courses for the first two years, but by the second semester of my junior year, I was flunking out. I couldn't concentrate and was having horrible nightmares. I went on a drinking binge and had sex with every girl who showed interest. My roommate and a professor finally intervened. They gave me two options—either get help or get kicked out of school. College was my only saving grace, and if Jessie ever came home, I was determined to follow through on every promise I made. I went to counseling for a year and a half until I graduated.

"If I hadn't, I wouldn't be rational enough to handle this now," I admit.

There is a hint of fear in Tyson's eyes.

"Don't worry. I told the therapist enough to help me without divulging the details. What about you?" I ask him.

He smiles with relief. "After I went to therapy with Vicky, the counselor gave me the name of a pastor. I went for about a year under the pretense that it was to help me support her. It made a big difference, but I also realized there are some things we have to learn to live with."

"Be stupid to think otherwise," I say, somberly.

In the quiet of the evening Tyson continues to shuffle cards. I spin the lid from my beer bottle between my thumb and forefinger.

"You ever wonder what happened to that gun?" Tyson's question breaks the silence.

I jerk my head up. His eyes are a reflection of the worry that constantly nags me.

"Every day. I keep waiting for that piece of evidence to bite us in the ass."

Tyson slaps me on the back as he stands to leave. "We'll get this figured out, little brother. Dad tried to destroy all of us, but we aren't going to let him. You and I are stronger than he ever imagined, even to this day."

After he leaves, I attempt to watch an episode of Friends. It's my favorite, the one where Rachel and Ross get drunk and elope in Vegas. Again, it brings me back to Jessie. She used to remind me of Rachel—her spunk, her fun-loving spirit, her spontaneity. The similarities end there. Rachel was a high maintenance girly-girl who belonged in the city. Jessie is a beautiful tomboy with a little bit of sass who belongs on my ranch.

Irritated, I turn off the television and stare at the ceiling. I need to go to bed. I dread closing my eyes because sleep is either going to elude me due to the never-ending thoughts of Jessie, or the memories of my father. I received the help to keep the nightmares at bay for a long time, but since Jessie's been home, it's all in the forefront of my mind.

What hurts me the most is my intentions with Jessie were good, but somehow, I managed to screw it up in the most incomprehensible way. Once again, I find myself wondering what would have happened if there was a different turn of events that day thirteen years ago.

· · ·

I looked around my grandparents' house for old blankets with no luck. Jessie was going to be here any minute, and I wanted to have everything ready. I ran to the guesthouse, surprised to find it unlocked. I turned the knob, stepped inside and glanced around, seeing it for the first time in years. It wasn't what one would expect as a hideaway for my dad's affairs. It was simple, small, and dingy.

My grandparents didn't know what Dad used it for, or if they did, they turned a blind eye as they did for his other indiscretions. Unfortunately, Tyson and I found out by accident one day when we were working at the store after school. We overheard his secretary, the one he was having an affair with, on the phone telling someone when and where they would meet. The following day we rode our bikes to the ranch and crawled into the loft of the barn to wait. From the window we watched him arrive with two women, his secretary, and her friend. We got as close as we could, and it wasn't long before the sounds of their tryst were loud enough to be heard through the walls. We immediately took off, knowing if Dad caught us, we would get the worst beatings of our lives.

The small house doesn't look much different from when Tyson and I played here when we were little. My grandfather meant to remodel it, but once my dad took over, our playtime ended, and remodeling was an afterthought. On the wall closest to the door was a window with cupboards on either side and underneath it a kitchen sink. There was a small stovetop but no oven. Two mini-fridges were stacked one on top of the other. I pulled open the door of one to find it stocked with beer. The other held wine coolers and pop. A large mattress covered with a fitted sheet and comforter was shoved against the far wall. The bed was made with two pillows carelessly tossed on top. Next to the bed sat an old nightstand with two drawers, a rustic lamp and an ashtray filled with cigarette butts, some with traces of red lipstick on the end. The area was littered with *Playboy* magazines, candy wrappers, and pop cans. Kitty-corner from that stood a small wooden entertainment center with a twelve-inch television and VCR. A small kitchen table sat in the middle of the room, surrounded by three wooden chairs. A door to the back of the cottage led to a tightly cramped bathroom hardly bigger than an outhouse, with running water.

I found a pile of blankets on the floor in the corner of the room. I took the top two and started to leave but stopped, returning to the nightstand to look for condoms. Opening the drawer, I saw two boxes. I wanted to take a whole box, but knowing how anal-retentive my dad was, he would notice. Instead, I grabbed four packets and shoved them in the back pocket of my jeans. I was about to close the drawer when I saw a black VCR tape shoved in the back. What caught my eye was the white sticker stuck to it that read, "Vicky-1991."

Intrigued, I removed the cassette from its case and shoved it into the open slot of the VCR. After a couple of minutes, my temples began to throb as the reality of what I was seeing became disgustingly clear. Vicky was dressed in lingerie, had heavy black makeup on her eyes, and her lips were painted blood red. My father was demanding with his instructions as he touched her body. With much coaxing and some threats, she was compliant, although there were tears in her eyes and her lips quivered in fear. Hastily, I ripped the cassette case apart and threw it on the floor. When I glanced at the collection of videotapes next to the television, I realized there was a label on each one with a girl's name. I recognized some from school.

I threw the tapes to the ground. Blinded by rage, I grabbed one of the wooden chairs and slammed it against the wall where it shattered into pieces. My stomach churned. Dazed and lightheaded, I ran to the bathroom where I heaved violently into the toilet. After I regained my bearings, I stormed out the door, not even bothering to shut it behind me. I hopped into my truck, forgetting Jessie was meeting me any moment.

Numb and shaken, I didn't know what to do. I couldn't confront my father. If I did, I knew I would kill him. I drove around town then onto country roads attempting to piece the nightmare together. I hated my father before, but the poisonous feelings that pumped through my veins didn't even compare. The contempt and fury started to overpower me as my driving became erratic. When I couldn't handle it anymore, I jerked the truck to a stop in the deserted parking lot of the high school and slammed my fists against the steering wheel while I screamed in agony.

Exhausted, I laid my head on the wheel and began to cry. How could he do that to her? To anyone? Only a cruel, sadistic tyrant would target his own son's girlfriend.

I hardly noticed the roar of thunder or the flashes of light, but the rhythm of the raindrops against the roof lulled me into submission. I didn't know how much time passed, but when I finally glanced at the clock on my dashboard, it read six-thirty.

Berating myself for losing track of time, I shifted my truck into reverse and punched the gas pedal. My tires squealed as I drove off. Five excruciating minutes later, I sighed with relief when I pulled into the dirt drive. Jessie's car was not there. In my haste, I practically fell out of the driver's door and sprinted to the guesthouse. But my stomach tightened when I noticed the shut door, and when I reached for the handle, it was locked. I ran to the window. Balancing on two logs of wood, I hoisted myself up to look through the open blinds. On the floor next to the bed were her jacket and cheerleading bag. Squinting my eyes, I studied the room a bit closer, and that is when I saw streaks of blood spread across the unmade bed.

● ● ●

Morning sunbeams bounce through the front picture window warming my face. I rub my hand over the rough stubble on my chin and sit up slowly, peeking out the small slit of one open eye. The clock above the stove reads seven-twenty. Dazed, I realize I must have fallen asleep on the couch after Tyson left. Feeling groggy, I force myself to climb the stairs and into the shower.

I get dressed, grab my morning cup of coffee and a piece of zucchini bread and head out the door to meet the guys at the barn.

"Look at you, Sleeping Beauty. We were wondering if you were going to waste your day away," Dawson says. "We have a mare over there that is ready to give birth any moment but was waiting for you to assist her."

I scowl and peek into the stall where Shadey is lying uncomfortably, almost too big to move. I knew it was coming, but I guess with everything else on my mind, I forgot how soon. Birthing animals is not new to me, but it's also not my forte. Brent, on the other hand, went to Vet Tech School and worked at a large animal veterinary clinic for four years before he started full time at the ranch. I depend on him when it comes to pregnant livestock. He's not my right-hand man. He is *the* man.

I am in a fairly decent mood this morning considering the day I had yesterday. I guess a good night's sleep will do that. The three of us banter back and forth until we go our separate ways, Brent and Dawson cleaning out the horse stalls and sticking close to Shadey while I head over to feed pigs.

I'm in the middle of mucking slop when my mind starts to drift again. Tyson warned me, once we unseal the past, a person has no control over the memories that crawl out.

• • •

I finally found Jessie's car parked in front of Sam's house. I couldn't bring myself to go to the door. In a crazed state, I rushed home praying the entire time that my father was not there, knowing a confrontation would be the worst thing that could happen for either of us. When I saw the empty garage, I snuck inside. Ignoring my mother, I packed most of my necessary belongings into two colossal suitcases, and a few boxes and loaded them into my truck.

"Where are you going?" she asked, startling me.

I looked up to find her standing in the bedroom doorway, a hand on her hip.

"If you want to be married to the fucking sadistic pig, you go ahead, but I am not going to be subjected to him ever again. I'm staying with Tyson until I leave for Bozeman."

By the time I showed up to Tyson's apartment, I was an incoherent mess.

"Dude, what is going on?" he asked, opening the door at my insistent pounding.

"I need your phone," I said, moving past him.

Frantically, I dialed Sam's number. When no one answered, I tried Jessie's home phone, but no answer there either. I left message after message begging someone to return my call.

"Jesus, Zane. Calm down," Tyson grabbed my shoulder.

Reactively, I shoved him against the wall, ready to fight. He placed his fists in front of his face, and I knew by his stance he would have taken me on. I stepped back, shaking uncontrollably and crouched onto the floor where I wrapped my arms around the back of my head.

I needed him to help me help them, but I dreaded saying the words that I knew would destroy his life. Somehow, I managed to get it all out.

With his fist cupped over his mouth, Tyson sank to the couch and stared at me as if he'd never seen me before. His silence was as unbearable as the pain tearing through me.

"I knew what he was doing to Vicky."

Shell-shocked, I jerked my head up to meet his gaze.

"You knew?" I choked out.

"I heard him on the phone one day. He was having one of those conversations where he uses that voice when he is talking to one of his girlfriends. Out of stupid curiosity, I picked up the extension in my room and heard Vicky's voice on the other end. She was crying."

Shaking his head, Tyson looked at the ceiling and cursed loudly, his face red with fury. He proceeded to tell me how he overheard our father encourage Vicky to lie to her parents and played on her relationship with him. When she refused, he threatened her, claiming everyone she cared about would find out she was a slut, Tyson wouldn't love her anymore, and she'd be lucky to find a guy who wanted a trashy and weak-minded girl.

"Zane, I felt exactly as you do now, helpless and crazy. I took Vicky with me that night to the Varsity basketball game and made sure Dad knew I was with her all evening. Afterwards, I hovered over her like a vulture making sure she was never alone. When I had time to look back and piece everything together, I was sick. He groomed her the whole time right in front of us. I hated myself for not protecting her."

Tyson explains how a week later, he snuck into Mel's safe and took a pistol without asking. To his father's surprise, he confronted him at work in his office. He steadily pointed the gun while reminding Ron that thanks to Mel, Tyson had plenty of experience handling one, while Ron had none.

He told him if he ever looked at her, touched her, or paid the slightest bit of attention to her he would hunt him down and make it look like one of his whores shot him in a jealous rage. Ron had his excuses, saying he never actually fucked her. He was preparing her, and if anything, his son should be grateful. Something in Tyson snapped. He grabbed the side of the desk, flipped it upside down and shoved Ron against the wall, his hand around his throat.

"It was in that moment as I hovered at least a foot over him, I saw real fear in Dad's eyes. I reminded him I knew too much about his personal and business affairs and would have no problem ruining his life. As far as I was concerned, my worthless excuse for a father was dead to me. That's when I quit work and moved out."

Tyson went on to explain how a month later, Dad showed up at his apartment, tail in hand asking Tyson to come back to work. Of course, Dad was asking because he had no desire to be there. He wanted the income to keep flowing but wasn't invested in its success. He had golf to play, women to screw, whiskey to drink, and friends to impress, and Tyson was the only one he trusted. Tyson agreed on the condition that their relationship was strictly professional and other than work-related conversations, they had no purpose in each other's lives.

It seems the agreement was the start of Tyson slowly taking over the reins. When I asked how he could stand being in the same room with him knowing what he'd done to Vicky, Tyson claimed he rarely saw him, and all communication about store decisions was through letters. Tyson thought keeping a paper trail was the best way to keep Dad true to his word. It was a win/win situation.

I paced the short length of his living room.

"Jesus, Tyson, this is wrong on so many levels. It's not a win/win situation. He molested your girlfriend. Lord knows what he just did to mine!"

"This is my fault, Zane. I knew he was a monster, but that was almost three years ago. As far as I know, Vicky hasn't told anyone, and it wasn't up to me to reveal her secret. It's my job to love her and to help her feel safe despite what Dad did. It never occurred to me there were other girls too."

"He's capable of anything. Jessie went to the ranch to meet me and probably saw the door to the guesthouse open. The videos were scattered all over the floor, and I left one playing on the television. Dad could have found her in there and assumed…"

Crushed by the combination of frustration, anger, and helplessness, I punched the wall. A lightning bolt of pain seared through my arm as I ran out of the apartment, taking the stairs two at a time. Outside, I sprinted down the block hard and fast desperate to escape the truth.

• • •

"Uncle Zane?" A sweet innocent voice surprises me. "Are you okay?"

I didn't realize I had squatted to my knees in the mud staring in a daze at absolutely nothing. I look over my shoulder to find worried expressions on the faces of Shelby, Shane, Sasha, and Vicky.

"Everything alright?" Vicky asks. "We honked as we pulled up, but you didn't hear. I figured you might be listening to music, so we called your name a few times. You were like a statue, stuck in the mud," she says, making an awkward joke.

I take her outstretched hand and pull to a stand.

"I'm good. Lost track of time, I guess. You guys ready for a ride?" I direct the question to the kids.

They squeal in delight and run toward the barn. Vicky and I follow but walk at a slower pace.

"Jessie told me she saw you on her ride yesterday."

Her directness surprises me.

Wiping dried mud off my elbow, I nod.

"Eventually you two are going to have to talk."

I give her a skeptical look. "Why? She's probably going to take off again. I'd rather spare myself the pain."

A grimace passes over her features but is replaced with sympathy. In silence, we continue to walk toward the barn.

Finally, she speaks up. "If I have anything to do with it, she won't be leaving again. It was painful for all of us. But to be honest, I don't think she wants to leave again."

"I'm sorry, Vic. I get easily irritated these days. I didn't mean to take it out on you."

Soon we reach the open door of the barn and find the kids saddling their horses.

"You feel like riding with them?" I ask.

She thinks about it for a moment. "Only if you go."

With a shrug, I grab two more blankets and saddles. As I dress up the horses, I point out where Vicky can find an extra pair of boots since she didn't bring hers.

Ten minutes later, we ride in a straight line with Shane leading and the twins in the middle followed by Vicky. I bring up the end. Earlier, while lost in my memories, the sunshine disappeared and was replaced by a cold misty overcast. With the day now gloomy, we don't have a sense of urgency as we glide calmly along the trail.

Vicky and I listen in amusement to the kids' endless chatter. Sasha and Shelby giggle as they take turns discussing recess adventures with two boys in their class, Ethan and Will. Apparently, the boys chase them on the playground threatening kisses. They caught Sasha that afternoon, but Will was too embarrassed to actually kiss her. Ethan did instead. Shane reassures his mother, who is clearly shocked, that he saw the whole thing and a terrified Ethan only kissed the back of her hand. He changes the subject, proudly telling us he passed his multiplication quiz and has moved on to division. After that, it will be fractions. He informed his teacher last week that he wants to be a mechanical engineer.

"Do you know what a mechanical engineer does?" Vicky asks, grinning.

"No. But I overheard Dad telling Susan at the store that I was so smart I could be a mechanical engineer. She looked impressed, so I guess it must be important. I want an important job."

Vicky and I laugh out loud. By this time, we rode off the trail into a grassy field and are side by side, the horses are trotting at a steady pace.

"Buddy, whatever job brings you joy in life is going to be the most important one you do," I say.

"What if I want to be skydiver? Would that be important?"

"Would it bring you joy?" I ask.

"I don't know. I've never done it. Maybe."

Again, I laugh. "How about when you're older you try a variety of different things and find which one brings you happiness. Maybe it's baseball, football, sky diving, engineering, ranching, heck, there is a whole world out there of really cool things. You never know, there may be more than one most important thing."

"That's a great idea, Uncle Zane. How come you only have one important thing?"

Curiosity gets the best of me. "What's my important thing?"

"Ranching."

"I like hunting too. And fishing."

"Yeah, but you don't do those for work."

"Agreed, but look at your dad. He has the store, and then he has your mom and of course he has you. He does three really important things."

"I know what important thing you can do," Shelby pipes up.

"What is that, kiddo?"

"Aunt Jessie," she says excitedly.

The other two eagerly agree while a nervous laugh escapes from Vicky.

"Mom, remember? You and Dad were talking after dinner the other night about Aunt Jessie and Uncle Zane. You said they used to be in love."

"But *you* said so!" Shelby demands when her mother gives her a stern look.

"Shelby, honey. I thought you were in the other room doing homework."

She pushes out her bottom lip. "I needed a glass of water, and I heard you two talking, so I listened. There are so many secrets. You and Dad. You and Jessie. Dad and Zane. Grandma and Grandpa. I just wanted to hear what is so important that it has to be secrets. Now we know."

Holding onto the reins with one hand, Vicky rubs her eyes with the other.

"Okay, I see your point. In the future, please ask me if you are wondering what the adults are talking about because sometimes we have discussions, and we don't want little ears to worry. It doesn't make them secrets. As far as Uncle Zane and Aunt Jessie, that is none of your business. It's none of my business either."

"Okay," Shelby says though it's clear she's not entirely convinced. "But I think Uncle Zane should make her important. When we were at Grandma's last week, we were looking at pictures with Aunt Jessie in her room. Uncle Zane was in a bunch of them. He had his arms wrapped around her, and in some, they were kissing. When I asked her why, she started crying."

Sasha's eyes widen with excitement. "Yeah! Then she said she never loved anyone like she loved him."

CHAPTER ELEVEN

On Halloween, Brent and Tonya bring the kids over in the late afternoon before going into town for the annual Festival in the park. Zoe is dressed as a cat and says nothing the entire time but "meow." Charlie, much to her mother's chagrin, is a zombie.

"No matter how many times I remind Brent not to watch his scary movies in front of the impressionable nine-year-old, somehow all she wants to be is a zombie," Tonya glares at her husband.

I don't get many trick or treaters, but I do keep candy on hand for moments like this. Reaching into the bowl, Brent grabs a Tootsie Roll and shrugs as he pops it into his mouth.

Once they leave, I watch the new Poltergeist. It does not hold a candle to the original version, but regardless, I'm intrigued. Half-way through there is a knock at the door. I grab the candy bowl and open it to find Tyson's entire clan dressed as Star Wars characters. Vicky is a perfect Princess Leah. Tyson growls his best Chewbacca impression while Shane swings his Darth Vader lightsaber at me. I can't help but laugh as both girls struggle to move in their uncomfortable R2D2 and C-3PO costumes. Kelsey and Tanner are with them. They make a great team as Luke Skywalker and Han Solo.

I usher them inside. I know I won't get any other trick or treaters, so I divide all the candy between them. Tyson shuffles over to the fridge where he grabs a beer, and looking over his shoulder, he asks Vicky if she wants one.

Baffled, Vicky shakes her head. "When did you get comfortable enough to just help yourself?"

Tyson, whose face is covered with a Chewbacca mask, ignores her, but when she turns to me, I quickly hand her a Kit Kat bar.

"Uncle Zane, why don't you come to the Festival with us?" Shane says as if it's the best idea in the world.

Tyson coughs and Vicky immediately looks uncomfortable as she tries to redirect Shane.

"Uncle Zane isn't wearing a costume," Tyson points out.

I raise an eyebrow. "So what? Not everyone at the Festival wears a costume."

"Oh, and you would know this because you have been to the Festival in…how many years has it been now?"

I ruffle Shane's hair. "Thanks, kiddo. I'll pass on this one. I'm in the middle of Poltergeist, so it's best if I stay here and see if any ghosts jump out of my TV screen."

In unison, Tyson and Vicky sigh.

I'm puzzled by their reaction, but when I overhear the twins discussing Aunt Jessie and her friend A.J.'s pirate costumes, I am enlightened. Once everyone leaves, it doesn't take long for me to change my mind.

• • •

I rifle through my closet and come up with the one costume it's remotely possible to wear—hunting gear. I pull on my brown Real Tree pants, coat, matching ball cap and gloves, and step into my hiking boots. If nothing else, at least I will be warm. I smear streaks of green camouflage paint across my cheeks, nose, and forehead, and call it good enough.

Last time I dressed up for Halloween was our senior year of high school when Jessie decided we would be Fred and Wilma Flintstone. Though we were not dating at the time, it was easier for us to attend together like we always had. A whole group of us was going, so it seemed natural for the two of us to pair up in costume.

A short while later, I parallel park next to the curb. As I walk through the tight crowd of people, I realize nothing about this entire situation is natural. Here I am about to make the boldest move of my life while wondering if it's also another mistake.

The one good thing about Halloween is it's easy to be inconspicuous if a person chooses to be. With my hat and face paint, I can walk through crowds without drawing too much attention. No one expects to see me in public. I bump into a few people along the way and offer my apologies while I look for the familiar faces of my family. I finally spot them next to the haunted maze thirty yards away.

Everyone who was at my house, along with Sam and Jillian, Libby, Jessie, and an unknown face who I assume must be A.J., are assembled around the maze watching the kids enter. I lean my shoulder against a large oak tree and observe, mostly curious about Jessie and her girlfriend. The girlfriend situation is the main reason I opted to make an ass out of myself by coming here in the first place. From Tyson's perspective, the two were on the outs. It disappoints me she is here let alone coordinating Halloween costumes with Jessie. I wish Tyson would have said something so I wasn't blindsided again.

I still have a difficult time believing that Jessie is a lesbian or even bi-sexual, as my brother kindly suggested. What Jessie and I shared was a once-in-a-lifetime love. People spend years searching for our type of love, and many live without it. Maybe it's my ego, or false hope, but I know neither of us will find it again. My guess is Jessie decided to play it safe. Though I hate the idea of the woman I love sharing her life with anyone but me, I can somewhat understand. It was likely more than she was willing to risk to get involved with another man on that level.

A.J. is attractive, but she is definitely what a person would consider the stereotypical lesbian where Jessie is feminine and dainty. While they are both dressed as Pirates, they could not be any more opposite. Jessie is in a purple barista-style skirt cut high on her thigh, exposing a matching lace garter belt. The off-the-shoulder white blouse with black corset hugs tightly underneath her breasts. Her big eyes are outlined in black, which only makes them more inviting, and her lips are bright red. She carries a hook in one hand while a fake parrot rests on her shoulder.

A.J., on the other hand, reminds me of Smee from *Peter Pan*. She wears red pants cut in jagged edges at the calf and a black-and-white striped prison shirt while a black bandana covers her short spiky hair. She has a patch over one eye and, other than a fake scar someone drew on her cheek, she wears no makeup.

Like a stalker, I remain aloof, watching from afar. I can't take my eyes off Jessie. She looks beautiful, radiant. As she engages with her family, I see the carefree, confident girl I love. Her interactions with A.J. strike me as odd. Granted, I am not familiar with many lesbian couples, and maybe it is wishful thinking on my part, but there appears to be tension between the two. There's a good two feet of distance between them at any given time. When Jessie speaks, while everyone else responds, A.J. frowns or glares, and vice versa. The rest of the family does not look as comfortable with A.J. as I imagined considering she's been in Jessie's life for quite a few years. However, this is the first time Vicky and Tyson have met her.

After each activity, the kids turn to Jessie anxious to share their experiences. She gives them her undivided attention appearing to be just as excited. They lead her into the Frankenstein bounce house where she jumps and giggles like a young girl. The three nieces encourage her to get her face painted, and the boys mock her when she shoots baskets with them—until they are speechless when she wins.

It does not seem that any of this sits well with A.J. She stands by herself, scowling at the interactions around her. Likewise, her reaction does not go unnoticed by Libby and Vicky who are huddled together, animated whispers flying between them.

My constant companion, the dull ache in my chest, intensifies. I crave to be the one tagging along with the family, sharing jokes, and creating memories. Every inch of me aches to walk next to Jessie, drape my arm around her shoulder, press my lips to her cheek, and be the one to make her eyes shine.

For one brief moment, I consider doing just that and claiming what was once mine.

Annoyed with myself, I exhale slowly. I saw what I came to see. As I stroll toward my truck, I decide to stop for a caramel apple. As I stand in line, I recall the Halloween when I was in fourth grade. A week before the actual holiday, Jessie's family had a pumpkin carving party. It was a tradition, but the first time Tyson and I were invited.

Mel and Sam spent the afternoon putting up fake tombstones and skeletons in the front yard. Bats and ghosts hung from the treehouse, and cobwebs covered the windows. When we walked through the front door, the first thing I noticed was the dimmed lights and lit candles. Halloween music blared from the stereo as the entire family stood around the dining room table. Old newspapers were spread out and covered with pumpkins, freshly picked from the patch earlier that day. A variety of cutting utensils, spoons, paints, markers in every color, and stencils were placed in the middle of the table. Chili boiled on the stove while cornbread baked in the oven. For dessert, we made caramel apples. We'd never experienced anything like it and said as much.

"What does your family do for Halloween?" Libby asked, kindly.

"We each get twenty dollars, and Mom takes us to the store to buy our costumes. Zane and I trick or treat with the neighbor kids. After, we go to the Festival as long as we have a ride home with another parent," Tyson said.

"Your parents don't go trick or treating with you?" Libby inquired.

"Nope. They're not home. Dad has meetings, and Mom goes with him. We are in bed when they come home but Dad is loud and drunk."

"Have you ever carved a pumpkin?" Mel asked, slicing a hole into the top of the one he was holding.

"No, sir," Tyson replied with a shake of his head.

"What about Christmas and Thanksgiving?" an innocent Vicky asked.

Nonchalantly Tyson described the typical Thanksgiving at our house. Mom made a big dinner. Dad invited friends who had no place else to go, saying it was the charitable and Christian thing to do. They loaded their plates and sat in front of the television watching football, guzzling beer, and smoking cigarettes while Mom, Zane, and I sat at the table eating by ourselves. Christmas was similar. While the three of us stayed home watching movies on Christmas Eve, Dad went to the bar with friends. Mom watched us open presents Christmas morning while Dad nursed a hangover. By mid-afternoon, he was ready to eat the fantastic meal my mother prepared but hardly acknowledged any of us. He didn't lift a finger to help, but a few of his buddies showed up again after. While they drank and watched sports, Tyson and I spent the day in our room with our new toys while Mom locked herself in her room, either crying or sleeping.

It was more than we ever told anyone about our home life. It was the first of many times Mel and Libby's faces showed concern and empathy. From that point forward, we became a part of their family. They always extended an invitation to my mother. She never accepted, but it didn't stop Tyson and me from going. As hard as she tried to give us a normal childhood, she was emotionally checked out, so I think it was a relief for her to pass the responsibility on to someone else. For years we tagged along to sing Christmas carols, and to cut down and decorate the family tree. On the Fourth of July, we attended the parade and watched fireworks, and every Halloween until I graduated high school, we sat at that dining room table carving pumpkins and eating caramel apples.

The bittersweet memory, like so many similar to it, brings back a strong desire to have a cozy home, the big family, and make my own holiday traditions. Everything I was able to experience thanks to Mel and Libby.

I grow restless as the line moves slowly. Finally, I make it to the open window and ask for three caramel apples—one covered only in nuts for myself, and the other two with nuts and chocolate sprinkles. I'll drop them off as a special surprise for Charlie and Zoe. The young girl behind the window puts two in a bag while I bite into mine. The sweet sensation practically melts in my mouth. As I turn to leave a long sticky string drapes over my hand. When I lean forward to lick it off, my eyes lock on the face of the woman standing in front of me.

"Guess some traditions never die," Jessie says timidly.

Stunned, I brush the back of my hand over the string of caramel that hangs off my chin.

Her eyes twinkle, but there is no mistaking the nervousness in her voice. "I'm surprised to see you here, and dressed up, too!"

"I'm surprised to be here. When everyone stopped by the house talking about the Festival I felt, sentimental," I admit. "I haven't been here since…"

Damn it! Of all the stupid things to say.

I shift my eyes over her shoulder where I see the entire family standing by a group of teenagers bobbing for apples, watching us like vultures. With arms crossed over her chest in anger, A.J. is scowling. Sam, Jillian, and Tyson cannot hide their grins while Vicky reassuringly puts an arm around her mother. At the same time, the kids return from wherever they have been exploring and stop to stare.

Following my eyes, Jessie turns around.

"Looks like we have become a bit of a spectacle," I tell her. "Best I go."

She nods. I turn to leave and make it no more than five steps when she calls out apprehensively.

"Zane! I, uh, maybe we could…?"

Twisting around, I step toward her and hold out the bag. She takes it and peeks inside. When she looks back at me, the infectious smile radiates from her soul.

"You remember," she whispers.

Without a word, I maneuver through the wave of people back to my truck. It takes half the trip home for my heart to stop pounding. I guess Charlie and Zoe will have to go without. I can't help but smile to myself. Who would have thought that Jessie's favorite, caramel apples with chocolate sprinkles and nuts, is the one thing to finally bring us together?

• • •

There hasn't been any significant accumulation of snow yet, but in the two weeks leading up to Thanksgiving, mornings at the ranch start with a heavy dusting of frost and a haze that clears by mid-morning. By the afternoon, temperatures are comfortable enough to be outside if dressed appropriately. So far, we haven't had the terrible gusts of wind we usually have this time of year.

Today is unseasonably warm as I stand by the coral dressed in a flannel shirt, jeans, steel-toed boots, and a pair of work gloves. I had to strip my coat a few hours ago after pitching hay. Now I relax as I watch Dawson, with Brent's help, break in Shadey's new filly. Tonya and her girls walk from the end of the drive where they met Charlie at the bus stop a few moments ago. They hold hands, skip and sing songs as they approach. When they reach the coral, Tonya lifts both girls onto the lower rung of the fence so they can see the baby colt. The girls giggle as they take turns saying hello while holding tightly to the bars and swaying back and forth.

I watch them in amusement.

"I met someone today," Tonya says with an air of mystery in her voice. She pulls a bottle of water from the backpack she has flung over her shoulder and takes a sip.

I press my lips together. "Okay?"

"I met Jessie! She's a para-professional in Charlie's classroom two days a week. I spoke with her and Vicky this morning."

Confused, I stop her before she can continue. "She got a job?"

"As I was saying, she said she was growing restless and needed something to keep her busy. How convenient is it that she is in Charlie's classroom? Oh, Zane, she is adorable *and* delightful," she gushes, resting a hand on my arm.

"Oh, and she mentioned since she will be staying here indefinitely, she is working on a plan. This is step one, probably temporary, but it gives her time to come up with something concrete," she winks.

I'm not sure what to make of this news. It's been two weeks since Halloween, and I hoped Jessie would make an attempt to reach out. Although I know full well I could have reached out too, I'm not confident it's what she wants. She was friendly, but I'm not sure it means anything. She got all awkward and said, "maybe." Since that night, I've been trying to figure out what "maybe" means. Nevertheless, I am thrilled to hear she is planning on sticking around. Indefinitely, Tonya said. That has to be a good sign.

"That's a lot of information for someone you just met," I say.

"When have you known me not to make someone feel welcome?" she states innocently in her Southern drawl. "Maybe you should make her dinner."

I shake my head and grimace. "She has no desire to come out here."

Tonya looks perplexed.

"She hates this place," I explain. "She won't ever step foot out here again."

"So, *take* her to dinner or a movie. Do you need me to figure this out for you? Seriously, how long has it been since you've had a date?"

"She's the last girl I dated," I divulge.

"Oh," she replies, clearly embarrassed. "Ugh, this is awkward, but Zane I've seen cars parked here overnight."

I give her a knowing look.

"Come on, Tonya. Don't be naïve. Just because a girl spends the night does not mean I dated her or cared enough to wine and dine, take her to the movies, or buy flowers."

She snaps her fingers, and her eyes grow wide.

"Flowers! Send her a bouquet, but not roses. They would scare her off. A nice small bouquet of say, sunflowers or a mixed arrangement for Thanksgiving. Maybe a centerpiece for the holiday."

Her enthusiasm is contagious, and I laugh.

"I'll think about it. If I decide to do it, you can help me. Lord knows I haven't the first clue."

• • •

I dream of Jessie often. Sometimes it's brief glimpses of our childhood together. Riding bikes, playing night games, walking the hallways of school together holding hands, or sitting in the treehouse. Other times, she is walking through the front door of the house, calling my name, searching for me. The image of her face, beautiful as ever, materializes in the snapshots of my subconscious, and when I reach out, it's as if I can feel the softness of her skin and the warmth of her touch. If it were possible, I'd stay in this state forever rather than face the morning without her. The euphoria of the dream accompanies me through the day in the hopes of having her with me again when I close my eyes at night.

It's rare, but once in a while, I still have the nightmare. This dream is surreal, a back-and-forth contrast between the reality of the truth as it happened and the illusion of my psyche. But the panic I feel remains consistent.

This is what jolts me awake now. Surrounded by complete darkness, I sit up and suck air into my lungs as my shoulders heave with fear. I blink, desperate to shake the vision that invaded my mind. As my eyes adjust, I take in my surroundings but find I cannot stop the anxiety that ravages my body. I throw off my covers in frustration and turn on the bedside lamp. My hands continue to shake. Even though I'm aware a trigger is coming, I can't stop this one from catapulting me into the past.

● ● ●

She's gone. Her letter blindsided me. Of all the outcomes I'd tossed around in my head, this was one I hadn't seen coming. I crumpled the piece of paper in my hand and stared disoriented out the window of my brother's apartment.

Tyson planned a pre-wedding camping trip to the mountains. He thought it would be a good idea to get out of town for a while, give Jessie some space and let me clear my head. We were supposed to leave early this morning but had to change the oil on the ATVs. We finished loading the four-wheelers onto the trailer when Tyson asked me to check the mail. I was surprised to find an envelope addressed to me in Jessie's handwriting.

I heard Tyson's muffled voice repeat my name, but he sounded far away as if he was underwater. Maybe I was the one underwater, drowning. I tried to answer but choked on my words because saying them out loud made it real. I didn't want this to be real. His hand on my shoulder shook me out of my trance.

Shoving the paper at him, I dropped to the couch as he flattened it out and began to read. Within moments the color drained from his face. As the severity of the situation sank in, my shock turned to rage, and like a caged animal, I exploded. Roughly, I grabbed Tyson by the collar. I screamed profanities, and I shoved him against the wall. Unable to control myself, I punched a hole behind him, missing his head by inches. When I let my guard down for the briefest of moments, he tackled me to the ground where he put me into a headlock. It only took a moment for me to succumb to the over-whelming despair. When I was calm, Tyson let me go.

"You aren't to blame," I said, standing up. "There is only one person responsible. He's going to pay."

Moments later, I was digging the keys out of the front pocket of my jeans and crawled behind the steering wheel. As I revved up the engine, the passenger door opened.

"What are you doing?" I growled.

"I'm coming with you. You aren't the only one who owes him."

When we pulled up to the ranch, his truck wasn't parked in its usual place by the guesthouse, but instead sat at an awkward angle taking up the entire drive. There were no other vehicles in sight. I spun my truck around and barely came to a complete stop beside the barn when I shifted into park and jumped out.

We found Dad in the sitting on the bed, organizing the VHS tapes, and smoking a cigarette. I think it was fear that flashed in his ice-cold eyes when first he saw us. It was gone the next second, replaced with malicious irritation. Slowly, he crushed his cigarette in the ashtray and stood up.

"Looks like you have a new hobby," I made sure the accusation was clear.

Undaunted, he glanced at the tapes scattered on the bed and then down at the one he held in his hand.

"You two up for movie night?" he scoffed.

My first blow hit him in the nose, and blood splattered when it cracked on impact. The second blow connected with his mouth as his head snapped back. Tyson took a couple of jabs to his ribs which caused Ron to double over in pain, but he stayed on his feet. He took a swing and caught the corner of my right eye. I threw an uppercut to his chin as Tyson kicked him in the stomach.

By this time, blood impaired his vision, and he was gasping for air. Tyson and I watched the pathetic sight of him stumble around the room swinging at nothing. I hoped more than anything he felt the intensity of our wrath. He tried to speak, but the words came out muffled as he spit chunks of red saliva onto the ground. Finally, he gave up, gasping heavily, he placed his hands on his knees.

"You two little shits," he gasped.

Tyson gave one last kick which caused him to tumble to the ground where he clutched his stomach. I grabbed Jessie's duffle bag and unzipped it to find her jacket shoved inside. While I held the bag open, Tyson gathered the VHS tapes and tossed them in, and without a glance back at our father, we hurried to my truck.

I heard the blast as I tossed the bag into the back seat of the cab. The first shot barely missed me. The second shattered the windshield. I shouted a warning to Tyson, but he was already on the ground army crawling his way to the other side of the barn. I crouched behind the bed of the truck. Peeking around the corner, I saw my father's battered figure slowly stumbling his way toward the barn wielding a pistol. A moment later, he disappeared around the corner where Tyson was hiding.

I had to reach him before he got to my brother. I burst into a sprint. I was about to tackle him, but he turned and aimed the barrel straight at my head. He was filled with poisonous hatred, and I knew it would not faze him to pull the trigger.

"If you would have left well enough alone, you would not be in this position," he said menacingly.

A noise from behind startled Ron. Reactively he turned and discharged the gun into the air. At the same time, Tyson appeared from around the corner. He was swinging a two-by-four with intense momentum and strength, and he delivered a blow to the back of Ron's head. I heard the loud crack and he dropped the gun. I watched my dad's eyes go lifeless as he collapsed to the ground in a pool of blood.

• • •

I shake my head in an attempt to dislodge the memory, but it's as if I'm reliving it in real-time, and I struggle to separate the present from the past. I am disturbed by my thoughts and decide I may as well get up as trying to go back to sleep will only bring an onslaught of the same. Unfortunately, after an hour of chores, I realize the physical labor does nothing to stop the hypervigilant paranoia or the flashbacks I continue to have.

I have no doubt my father would have killed both of us that day. I don't regret our actions to protect ourselves, the girls we loved, and other young women he terrorized. But I do have regrets. And I know Tyson does as well.

It took a split second after the plank of wood fell out of his hands for us to run to my truck. We briefly argued about going back to retrieve the gun, but there wasn't time. Our gear was already loaded at our apartment, so I only had to back up to the trailer where Tyson jumped out to attach the hitch. We were on the road and setting up camp in the mountains within the hour.

For three days we didn't talk about it. We rode four-wheelers and fished in silence. We drank beer and ate our dinners staring into the flames of the campfire, heavyhearted, and lost in private thoughts. When we returned, it was Vicky who delivered the news that our father was in the hospital.

How does a person begin to explain the complicated emotions that came with our actions? Ron was our father, but I didn't love him. I realized this around the age of fourteen. Nothing my father showed came anywhere close to love. He derived some sick sense of pleasure from abusing us emotionally and physically. That is not love. There was a time when I craved his attention and approval. I wanted kind words, affection, and validation from him more than I wanted anything in the world. He knew this and controlled me with it. That is not love. Ron was a narcissistic monster, and it wouldn't matter what we did or didn't do. It was never going to change.

It was Mel's love that helped me come to terms with this. Mel, who gave selflessly and pure of heart, didn't merely say he loved us but showed it in his actions in the way he respected, valued, and appreciated others and their individuality. It was in his example that I learned what love was and blood was not thicker than water. Yes, Ron was my biological father, but can you truly love someone you despised so much you wanted him dead? I don't know about others, but for me, this was black and white. Ron Stecks became a name, someone I had to deal with until I graduated high school and could leave home. He was no longer someone for whom I had any emotion.

My impassiveness was apparent as I sat in my truck outside the entrance of the hospital the following day. Obligation to my mother made me feel like I needed to check on him. Guilt made me wonder how extensive his injuries were. Curiosity and dread made me want to know what transpired after we disappeared to the mountains. Rumors swirled around town—a suicide attempt, a drug deal gone awry, retribution for a gambling debt, a betrayed husband's revenge. But nowhere in the fragments of the stories was the mention of a gun found at the scene.

I told myself I wasn't crazy. There was a bullet hole in the windshield. I watched the gun fall out my dad's hand. I also know we left it on the ground when we took off. What happened to it?

For two hours I wrestled with my mind. When we left him at the ranch, we knew there was a possibility he may die. What sickened me most about the entire scenario is I had a father who was capable of such horrendous actions that at eighteen years old, I was put in a position to even make that horrific choice. Yet, a large part of me found satisfaction in knowing I played a role in putting him where he was.

I walked into the lobby of the hospital that day but turned around and left without seeing him ever again.

I will always wonder what would have happened if I had walked into his hospital room. Would seeing him tied up to tubes and monitors been my last memory of him? Probably not. I have a feeling the grim expression pasted on his face and the sound of his skull crushing will haunt me forever.

PART THREE

CHAPTER TWELVE

Jessie and Zane — 2009

As early morning dawns and rays of light peek around grey clouds, Jessie inspects the property, startled by the changes. When she first pulled into the driveway of the ranch, she wondered if she took a wrong turn. When she saw the house, she recognized it as the right place despite the significant differences. In an attempt to go unnoticed, she parked by the highway and hiked in. In her winter coat and snow boots, she clomped through the soft, heavy falling snow, hoping it covered her tracks.

Now, Jessie finds herself disoriented as the wet flakes moisten her lashes. Vicky told her Zane made massive changes, but the layout of the structures is not as she remembers. She tugs her stocking cap securely around her ears, and then takes a deep breath, adjusting her gloves as she looks around.

Shaking her head, she wipes her face with the back of her hand and continues to walk. She isn't even sure why she had the urge to come here, but once the idea came to her, she knew nothing could stop her. She is hopeful she will find what she needs and be gone before anyone catches wind she is stalking around the property at this ridiculous hour of the morning.

Even though she is having a hard time seeing, her senses heighten as she draws closer to the house. Her body is flooded with warmth as she recalls the first time her parents brought her here. She smiles when she remembers assisting Zane's grandmother with the baking while the boys painted a fence, stacked hay, or cleaned the barns. There were countless games of cards on the front porch, many days of horseback riding, and as teenagers, night games with their friends. It's a shame one awful memory could destroy many happy memories.

Her grin vanishes at the thought. There it is, what she was waiting for, the fear she needs to face. Jessie squeezes her eyes tightly as she inhales deeply, the cold air stinging her lungs. As if she was punched in the stomach, the ground begins to spin. She bends over, she places her hands on her knees and counts to ten, slowly reminding herself she is in the present, not the past. The threat is no longer here.

It takes a few minutes for her heartbeat to steady. When it does, she wiggles her gloved fingers until they tingle ever so slightly, the sensation a relief. She moves past the house and rounds the yard admiring the work on the new porch. Suddenly she gasps, her face breaking into a grin. About fifty yards away sits a small green-house surrounded by abandoned corn stalks and rotten, frozen pumpkins covered in snow. The idea of having a greenhouse to grow vegetables for the restaurant gives her a rush of euphoria. And then she remembers as of next Monday, she will no longer be a restaurant owner.

She focuses on the task at hand and shoves the bistro and all its complications out of her head. Instead, she turns to peer through the row of pine trees and juniper shrubs that separate the house from the barn and feels her heart spike again. Zane's grandfather planted the trees when the boys were just toddlers. Thirteen years ago, they were as tall as the roof of the front porch, but now the sky-high, thick branches practically hide the rest of the ranch from the house.

Jessie hikes the twenty or so feet through the brush and snow but is stopped short. Her astonishment slowly turns to disbelief when two small log cabins come into her line of vision. They stand erect in the same spot where the small, white shack use to be.

$$\bullet \; \bullet \; \bullet$$

When a rancher lives alone outside of town for as long as Zane has, he can always sense a disturbance. While lying in bed sound asleep, by some strange force of nature, his eyes fly open. Gut instinct tells him something is not right. Quickly and quietly, he jumps out of bed, throws on sweat pants, a T-shirt and leaps down the stairs. The house is still dark. He leaves the lights off, not wanting to draw attention, but grabs his shotgun from the rack in the living room.

He is just about to open the front door when he spots movement out of his peripheral vision. Through the wide windows, his eyes follow Jessie as she walks around the house. He stands still, holding his breath as she treks through the trees to where the guesthouse used to stand. He places his gun back on the rack, reaches for his coat and shuts the front door softly behind him.

Grateful for years of tracking big game, he meticulously traces her footsteps stopping about thirty yards behind her. He wonders what is going through her mind. He shifts his position so he can watch her but remains unnoticed as she sinks onto her heels in the snow, her face expressionless. After a few minutes, she wipes away tears with her gloved hand.

As much as he would like to wrap her in his arms, Zane decides what she needs is privacy. He returns to the house and begins his day but stops to peek out the window every few minutes to see if she is still there. He showers and brushes his teeth before he throws a load of clothes in the washing machine, and he's ready for coffee.

He pours himself a cup and pours one for her too. He looks out the sliding glass door and spots the bright purple coat standing out against the white of the snow. She has not moved. He throws on his coat back on, grabs a blanket off the back of the couch, and heads outside. If she hears him moving toward her, she doesn't let on. When he reaches her, a fresh layer of snow conceals the top of her hat and shoulders. She seems lost in a daze. When the sunlight peeks through a cloud reflecting off the snow onto her face, he notices her teeth chatter.

She reaches for the warm ceramic mug without turning when he hands it to her. She takes a sip and sighs. He gently sweeps the snow off her shoulders, places a hand under her elbow and helps her to her feet. Without protest, she follows him inside the house with the blanket draped around her.

He helps her out of her coat and hangs it on the rack behind the door. In a zombielike motion, she moves to the couch and sits swaddled in the blanket. With a blank expression on her face, she watches as he loads wood into the fireplace. When he strikes a match, the flames roar to life crackling and sparking, immediately warming her cold bones. Weiser, anxious to check out someone new, sniffs her suspiciously. She briefly pats his head, but when she drops her hand, he returns to his bed and nestles in. She continues to sip her coffee as she stares absent-mindedly into the dancing fire.

Zane makes himself comfortable in the chair opposite her but finds he can't shift his gaze from her face.

"Are you hungry?" he asks, breaking the silence.

She turns to him, appearing startled as if finally realizing where she is and who she is with.

"I can make eggs and toast. You're still shaking. It may be good to get some food into your stomach."

She rubs her tired eyes, blinking a few times.

"Yeah," she says slowly. "Eggs would be good. I can help," she offers standing up.

"No, you sit here. Relax and get warm. Your lips are still blue."

She sits back down and stares at him.

"Thank you," she whispers.

He nods before disappearing into the kitchen. He makes another cup of coffee and sips on it while watching a spoonful of butter melt in the skillet. He cracks four eggs, two for each of them, sprinkles them with salt and pepper and slips bread into the toaster. While he waits, he wonders if it's time to have the much-needed conversation.

The idea of it terrifies him. He exhales sharply and shoves a hand through his unkempt hair.

The toast pops up, startling him. He butters it and takes two plates out of the cupboard. He slides the over-easy eggs onto them, grabs two forks out of the drawer and walks back into the living room. He balances the plates in one hand, his coffee cup in another, and he approaches the couch.

"You need more coffee?" he asks, setting their break-fast on the coffee table in front of him.

When he doesn't get an answer, he glances over his shoulder to find Jessie sprawled out on the couch fast asleep with Weiser curled at her feet.

• • •

After feeding the cows and pigs, mucking the stalls, and fixing two busted horseshoes, he decides he'd better give Vicky a call to let her know where her sister is.

"I wasn't worried," she reassures him. "I knew she was there."

"Someone could have warned me," he replies gruffly.

"Someone did. Tyson called you last night."

Zane shakes his head as the pieces fall into place. Tyson did call. His questions were a bit strange and out of character, but his brother was showing more of an interest in the ranch lately, so Zane didn't question his motives. When he mentioned Jessie's desire to visit, Zane was thrilled. He didn't realize they meant sooner than later.

"Why so early?" he asks.

"She thought it was the best time of day for pri-vacy. She was adamant she needed to go but wouldn't explain why."

Zane knew why. Vicky knew why as well, but this dance around the truth was their pattern.

He reassures her that he will have Jessie call when she wakes up, shoves the cell phone into the back pocket of his jeans and climbs the stairs of the porch.

Jessie stirs when he purposely lets the front door slam shut behind him. Disoriented, she pushes herself up, pulling the blanket around her shoulders.

"What time is it?"

"Close to noon," he says, once again sitting in the chair across from her. "I ate your eggs."

She smiles. "Probably a good thing. Cold eggs are nasty."

"Want me to make you some more?"

"No, that's okay. I've put you out enough." She stands up and folds the blanket. "Thank you for the coffee, and the blanket, and something to sleep on."

"Having you here will never put me out, Jessie," he says somberly.

She can feel his gaze on her as she places the blanket over the back of the couch. She heads toward the door and removes her coat from the rack.

"So that's it?" he asks.

She holds onto the door for support as she slips her snow boot over one foot while balancing on the other.

"What's it?"

"You show up here at six in the morning, sneak around my property crying, drink my coffee, sleep on my couch, and now you are leaving? Why?"

This is what she had hoped to avoid by coming out early.

Or was it?

She pulls her shoulders back defensively and turns to him.

"This is part of my childhood. I loved this place. Since I've been home, I've been facing the things I ran away from. I figured it was time to come here."

He knew this was as close to the truth as he was going to get.

"Does facing the things you ran away from mean me too? Had you bargained on me seeing you?" he adds.

"I don't really know. Look, Zane, I knew there would be a point and time when I could not avoid you any-more. I don't know if that's today or next week or next month. But, coming here wasn't about you. It was about something else, and hopefully, that would bring me to the next step where I *can* face you."

"I've been patient. I've given you space." Exasperated, he takes a step toward her. "Damn it, I've respected you since the day you left!"

Torment shadows her delicate features.

"I'm sorry," he whispers, taking the step back.

Jessie shakes her head as her eyes glisten with tears.

"You have nothing to be sorry about," her voice cracks. "You did nothing wrong. I'm the one who is sorry. Zane, what I did, it's unforgivable. I know that."

He holds up a hand to stop her from continuing. "No. You're wrong. It's..." he trails off. "I want to spend time with you. I miss my friend."

"I'm not the same person I used to be. I'm different."

"We both are."

Jessie nods. "I better go. I've got to help get Dad to his appointment this afternoon."

Zane holds her coat as she put her arms through the sleeve. After she zips it, he and Weiser follow her onto the porch, but before she can leave, he places a hand on her arm. Her eyes are full of sorrow when she meets his gaze.

"Don't look at me like that," he jokes. "How about coffee?"

"What?" she asks as Weiser licks her hand affectionately.

"Friday afternoon. Let's meet for coffee."

"Okay," she nods. "Let's meet for coffee."

• • •

Libby paces the waiting room as Jessie slumps in a chair. Mel has been with the doctor for twenty minutes, and as they anxiously wait, Jessie reveals that she made plans to meet Zane.

"You are doing what?" Libby hisses.

Embarrassed, Jessie looks around the waiting room. "Shh! You don't need to make a scene!"

With a determined look in her eyes, Libby takes a seat next to her daughter and grabs her hand. As she is about to speak, they are interrupted.

"Libby?"

Following her mother's gaze to the other side of the room, she sees Dr. Wilkenson's nurse standing in the doorway, summoning them.

The nurse escorts them down the hall. Inside the examination room, they find Mel lying down, a paper-white robe wrapped tightly around him and a blanket draped over his legs. Wilks holds onto his arm reassuringly while adjusting an oxygen mask.

Mel's eyes shift from the ceiling to his wife and daughter as he forces a smile through the plastic.

"His stats dropped significantly, and he was struggling to breathe. I'm going to send him home on oxygen," Wilks says. "I'm still okay with him going home because of the care you have there, Libby. However, I do think you and the kids need to have some serious conversation about hospice." With his head low, Wilks squeezes his friend's hand, his voice trembling as he continues. "It's only a matter of time now."

Jessie's chest tightens as she places a hand on her mother's shoulder. Through the thin jacket, she feels her go rigid.

Mel pulls the oxygen away from his nose and mouth and looks up at Wilks.

With a shaky and unsteady breath, he says, "No hospice. I will...be home." With tears in his eyes, he gazes at Libby. "The...home...we...made."

Unable to hide his own emotions, Wilks wipes his eyes and leaves the room while Jessie swallows back the lump forming in her throat.

A few moments later, two nurses arrive to help Mel into his wheelchair. In the parking lot, one assists him into the car while the other loads the oxygen tank, his new companion from this point forward.

It's a somber ride home. No one speaks, each lost in thought, unwilling to share the private, intimate reflections of their hearts. Tyson is already there to meet them when they arrive thanks to the text message Jessie sent.

Mel is exhausted and falls asleep quickly once he is settled in bed. Libby checks the oxygen tank and prepares his medicine while Jessie pulls a pan from the cupboard to start dinner. She keeps herself busy peeling and slicing potatoes, hardly noticing Tyson when he wanders in to join her. He takes a soda out of the refrigerator, and he leans on the kitchen counter.

"Hear you have a coffee date tomorrow," he snickers, trying to lighten the mood.

Jessie glares at him out of the corner of her eye as she maneuvers the paring knife more aggressively.

"Jesus, can't everyone just mind their own damn business?" she murmurs.

He slams the soda can on the counter, and he snaps back. "No, I can't mind my own business. He is my brother, and I don't want to see him get hurt."

In stunned silence, Jessie drops her chin shamefully and takes a deep breath.

"I'm sorry. It's been a long day. Can we please not talk about Zane or anything serious for a while? I need light and easy."

His expression softens as he takes a sip of his drink. A moment later, he says, "So what's the deal with you and A.J.? Did you finally dump her?"

He impishly laughs when Jessie narrows her eyes and playfully throws a handful of potato peels at him.

• • •

Jessie plugs the nine-digit number into her phone and moves her thumb across the keyboard to send Zane a text.

Hi. Been thinking…and don't know if coffee tomorrow is a good idea. At least not right now. I hope you understand. Jess ☺

Tyson's comment impacted her more than she expected. What did she think was going to happen? Maybe they would reminisce and catch up on old times. Would they try to get to know one another again? She was not a young girl anymore. She made life choices that impacted a lot of people and caused more pain than she wanted to acknowledge. After what she did to him, how could she even consider dragging him into her shit show of life? She left for a reason, to spare him more heartache and frustration. It wouldn't be fair to dangle a carrot in front of him for her own ego-driven agenda without considering the consequences.

Later, while getting ready for bed, she hears her phone ding. She is filled with nervous anticipation desperately hoping Zane will ask her to reconsider. It's not him, but she smiles anyway when she reads Phillip's message.

Hey beautiful! Sure missing you. We have last-minute details to go over before finalizing the sale. Want to come here or should I come to you? I could use a weekend away! Been super busy and A.J. is riding my ass!! Where are you when I need you? ☺

Yes, come here! Dad is declining, so I don't want to leave. ☹ *They put him on oxygen today. Would you mind staying*

*at my sister's? I don't want Mom to worry about visitors.
I can stay there with you.*

*Damn, Jess. That sucks. You need anything? Of course,
I will come there and yes, I will stay at your sister's. I can
get a hotel if need be.*

*Thanks. I don't need anything, just to see you! No hotel
room. Slumber party at my sisters! But don't hit on her.
Tyson will tear you limb from limb!* ☺

I promise to bring my best behavior. No flirting???

No flirting!!!!

Jessie plugs her cell phone into the charger and flips
back the covers of her bed. She checks her text messages one last time, slightly disappointed that she has
not heard from Zane. It's better this way, she tells herself. The last thing she needs to do is send him mixed
messages.

Yet, as she closes her eyes, she cannot shake the
image of him or deny the shiver of excitement running
through her with the possibility of a date. She places
her hands on her chest. She waits in silence, motionless.
Then she feels it—steady, strong, and alive. She almost
forgot what it is like to connect with the desires of her
heart. This must be what it's like to wake up to life.

● ● ●

"I've decided to sell the bistro to Phillip," Jessie
announces the following afternoon.

Vicky stopped by the house to grab a sandwich while
running errands. Although she was already aware of
Jessie's plans, her parents are stunned.

"Why?" Mel asks.

"I don't belong in Seattle. That season of my life is
over. I want to stay here." Tears spring to her eyes as she
continues. "I spent years searching for a home. I tried

to create it in many different scenarios of my life, but I couldn't get it right. Now that I am here, I realize I craved exactly what I ran away from. I'm in my thirty's, and even though I don't have a family of my own, you reminded me I always have one."

She goes on to explain her plans to reinvest the money into a bakery in Helena. In the meantime, she wants to run a small catering business out of her parent's kitchen to save on overhead costs and have more cash for a down payment when she finds a location.

Ecstatic, Libby and Vicky start talking at once, sharing ideas of how they can help. Vicky can connect Jessie with parents she knows, and of course, the PTA for school events and fundraisers. Libby will contact her PEO group, the women's ministry, and Bunco club.

"Both Linda and Susie have daughters getting married next summer. You could do their wedding cakes, and I'm positive they will have bridal showers too. I've got to get a piece of paper and start making a list!" Libby exclaims, disappearing from the room with Vicky skipping after her.

Jessie turns to her dad and shrugs her shoulders. There is a twinkle in his eye as he wags his finger, motioning her to him. She helps him adjust the strap of the oxygen mask around his head, and then he pats his chest. As she did when she was a little girl, Jessie gently lies her head on him. A moment later, she starts to cry.

While the tears fall, he runs his fingers through her hair as she remembers a lifetime of moments with him. She and Vicky cuddled in his lap watching Saturday morning cartoons, her dad pushing them on swings as they sang their favorite songs while Sam played imaginary drums on the slide. How he tossed them in the air, onto the couch and spun them in circles until they laughed with dizziness. He jumped with them on the trampoline and chased them around the backyard with a hose to cool them down on hot summer days. It wasn't unusual to find him outside with them building snow forts or making snow angels in the middle of winter.

She places her hand on his heart and feels the thump. She can't imagine a day when it does not beat anymore. Filled with intense agony, she knows she is not ready to lose him. He is her stability, her strength, her rock. He blessed her with a nearly perfect childhood, and the type of unconditional love people only wish for. She circles her arms around his fragile body, and she pulls herself closer.

"I'm so sorry, Daddy. I'm sorry for how much I hurt you, Mom, everyone," she cries.

He affectionately rubs her back and pulls the oxygen mask away from his lips. "You make me happy, *and* I'm proud of you."

"Dad, I made so many mistakes."

He shakes his head. "You are not responsible for someone else's choices."

"I could have handled things differently. I could have…"

"Maybe. Maybe not," he interrupts in a weary voice. "I'm sure we all could have handled things differently. You gave your mother and me the best gift of all tonight, kiddo. Let's enjoy that."

He closes his eyes, and though Jessie can't bear to let go, she knows he needs to sleep. She pulls the blanket up to his chin and kisses his cheek before leaving the room. In the kitchen, Vicky and Libby are preoccupied with marketing and business ideas for Jessie, they hardly notice her swollen, bloodshot eyes.

"Are you working with a realtor?" Libby asks.

"Yeah. Sue Jesperson. I'm going to look again next week. By the way, I invited Phillip to come next weekend."

"It's Thanksgiving," Vicky says, looking up from the table.

Libby places her hand to her heart. "Oh, I do adore Phillip! It will be fun to have him here for Thanksgiving dinner."

"You sure it's okay? I'm ready to close this chapter in my life, and I don't want to go to Seattle."

"Speaking of Thanksgiving, we better get busy with the dinner menu. Since Phillip will be here and the two of you *are* fabulous chefs, I'll host. You two can cook!" Vicky laughs.

• • •

By Saturday, Mel is stronger than he's been in a while. He moves from his recliner to a chair closer to the window, where he can watch the snow float from the sky as neighborhood children play in their front yards. As Jessie starts a fire in the fireplace, Libby comments that it would be a good day to decorate for Christmas.

An hour and a half later, Sam's family arrives with Vicky's crew not far behind. Years ago, as a family, they used to cut down their own Christmas tree, but the tradition stopped when everyone moved out. Sam and Vicky had their own families and were making their traditions. Mel and Libby thought it was silly to do the hard work and instead bought a beautiful artificial one with built-in lights. This year, feeling a little nostalgic, they decide to recreate Christmas from years ago. Sam and Tyson will take the kids to the tree farm east of town to pick up a real Douglas Fir.

After Vicky and Jessie haul up a dozen boxes of decorations from the downstairs storage room, Libby notices they don't have a tree stand. She sends the two girls to the store to buy one along with new lights while she makes a batch of cinnamon rolls.

In the car with Vicky driving, Jessie checks her phone for the tenth time in only a matter of minutes. It's been four days, and she still hasn't received a reply from Zane. It's hard to admit, but she is disappointed. She was hoping he would text her back and convince her to change her mind.

"He called Tyson after you canceled," Vicky said, peering at Jessie out of the corner of her eye.

"Why didn't you tell me?" Jessie asks incredulously.

"You told Tyson you wanted people to mind their own business. I'm trying. But you are glued to your phone for a reason." Vicky responds.

Jessie rolls her eyes. "What did he say?"

"He asked what he should do. I told him he was too irresistible for you to stay away too much longer."

"Vicky!"

"Well, it's true, and you know it."

"It's just coffee."

Vicky nods. Pulling the vehicle into a parking spot, she turns the ignition off. "Coffee, and then what?" she prods as she climbs out of the driver's seat.

"Then nothing. Hopefully, we can be friends."

Vicky arches an eyebrow inquisitively as they walk side by side toward the store. "Friends?"

"I don't get fairy tale endings, okay? That dream disappeared. For Christ's sake, do you really think he would want me after everything? The drugs, the men, and the women, and his dad?" Jessie snorts. "I'm used up and worn out. When I tell him the truth, he is going to see me differently. If he thinks there is something between us, it's a schoolboy fantasy about the girl he used to know, not the girl I am, and vice versa. What we had was beautiful, but we were kids."

"Maybe," Vicky agrees though Jessie can tell she is not totally convinced. "Joan came over for dinner the other night. The hospital called to tell her Ron's condition has worsened."

"Good. There is a sense of pleasure knowing Ron sits there unable to move, unable to control any of his bodily functions, stuck in his own mind with warped thoughts day in and day out. I hope when he does die, it's a slow, painful, agonizing death. He deserves it."

Before they enter the store, Vicky grabs Jessie forcefully by her arm and yanks her to the side of the building.

"Ouch!" Jessie pulls away.

"Do you hear yourself? You're all over the place. One minute you're tired of being angry. The next minute, anger possesses you!"

"Are you going to tell me I shouldn't be angry?" she hisses.

Vicky lowers her voice. "You have every right to be, but it's difficult to watch how much power the anger has over you. Look, what he did to me was messed up in so many ways. Even though you didn't want me to marry Tyson, by doing so and having my family and my happily ever after, I won. He didn't get to take anything else away from me."

Jessie's eyes narrow into slits.

Compassion tents Vicky's features. "I'm not ready to give up on your dreams and I don't want you to either. I know healing takes time, but somewhere along the way you have to realize the anger and blaming others is a comfortable crutch for you to hide behind, but it doesn't work. You can choose any time to stop being a victim and start doing things that might help."

Jessie's face contorts as her hands ball into fists. Vicky's condescending advice and self-righteous attitude are unwelcome. She has the husband who adores her, the perfectly well-behaved children, a comfortable home, and a job and life that feed her soul. She gets to have an uncomplicated relationship with the entire family. Somewhere along the way, she acquired easy-going confidence and tenacity to survive any hurdle that dares to get in the way of her happiness. Vicky became the person Jessie envisioned herself to be before failing at it. Yes, Vicky won. This is clear, and Jessie hates her for it.

The devastation on Vicky's expression tells Jessie the thoughts in her head spilled out of her mouth. Ironically, a moment later, Vicky's face fills with triumph.

"Finally, some authenticity! Being real wears much better on you than the paralyzing apathy that's snuffed you out."

Glowering, Jessie whooshes past her sister and through the automatic door where she grabs a shopping cart.

"You pushed my buttons on purpose," Jessie pouts.

Without a reply, Vicky follows as her to the back corner of the store where aisle upon aisle is full of Christmas ornaments, lights, garland, stockings, and candy. Instantly, Jessie's sour attitude disappears and is replaced by childlike enthusiasm.

Christmas was her favorite holiday growing up, but just like everything post-Ron, she learned to make it through the days never really enjoying or engaging. A.J. loved the holidays, so Jessie tried to muster up some cheer. It was a struggle, and afterward, she was exhausted and raw. Now, as she walks through the aisles taking in the bright colors, festive decorations and recalling memories from the past, she is flooded with warmth realizing this holiday isn't hovering over her like a grey cloud.

• • •

Four hours, a twelve-pack of beer, three pepperoni pizzas, a pan of cinnamon rolls, various cups of hot chocolate and sixteen Christmas carols later, the tree is complete. It is a beautiful sight to behold. Exhausted but smiling, the entire family collapses around the living room, watching as Sam places the Angel on top of the tree and Jillian plugs in the lights.

"Drumroll please," he exclaims, quoting his favorite Christmas movie.

As they all make various noises with their tongues and slap their hands on their thighs in anticipation of the tree lighting, the doorbell rings interrupting the moment.

Tyson jumps up to answer the door as Libby adjusts Mel's oxygen mask and the others look at one another curiously.

"Uncle Zane!" the kids squeal.

Jumping up, they wrap their arms around his legs and torso, eagerly telling him about the festivities of the afternoon. Though he tries to give them his full attention, he only has eyes for Jessie. And she for him.

Suddenly, Libby, without a word to anyone, brushes past him, disappears down the hallway and slams her bedroom door. Mel, who had been fighting sleep and just closed his eyes, opens them to see what the commotion is. Still groggy, he gives Zane a faint smile and wave before he disappears behind his lids once again.

Sam steps down from the ladder, gives Zane a friendly slap on the back, and offers him a beer.

With his gaze still fixated on Jessie, he declines.

"I'm sorry. I didn't realize you were all in the middle of family time. I can come back another day," he says, heading toward the door.

Jessie quickly stands up. "No, wait!"

The room grows silent as everyone stares at her.

"Stay. We were just getting ready to play a game of marbles."

Vicky, Tyson, Sam, and Jillian exchange a knowing look. They are surprised by this announcement, but soon everyone is nodding their heads in agreement. A moment later they shuffle around the room picking up boxes of unused decorations and empty paper plates.

For a brief second, Zane hesitates. He spent most of his day with baby pigs but found himself checking his phone every few minutes to see if Jessie texted again. Frustrated, he called it a day, went inside, and took a shower. While heating leftover meatloaf in the microwave, he stared mindlessly at the wall wondering for the zillionth time what she was doing. Finally, when he could no longer stand it, he got in his truck and drove to town. Before he could second guess himself, he parked in front of her parents' house, not even noticing the number of vehicles parked out front. He punched the doorbell and waited. He was as nervous as a teenage boy going on his first date. He was surprised and relieved to see his brother, but unprepared to walk in on the entire family.

Though he could assume what her reaction would be, it still hurt when Libby left without even acknowledging him. He felt guilty and wanted to disappear. But, with the way Jessie looked at him when he arrived, it would be torture to leave.

Shifting his weight from one foot to another, contemplating his options, he watches them hustle around. He's desperate to stay. He misses this family and the comforts of this home almost as much as he misses her. But it could be awkward spending their first significant amount of time together with everyone else. Finally, Tyson nudges him into the kitchen and hands him a beer.

"You need this," he chuckles.

Popping off the top, Zane takes a long drink.

Fifteen minutes later, everyone except Mel and Libby are seated around the dining room table playing marbles.

Jillian wins the first game, Tyson the second, and as they are about to start a third, Vicky and Jessie's cell phones beep at the same time.

Looking at their text messages simultaneously, the girls stand up.

"Mom needs help getting Dad into bed," Vicky says.

Tyson puts his hand on her arm. "Sam and I'll do it," he says.

Under normal circumstances, Zane would volunteer as well. He'd do just about anything for Mel. However, because Libby could not stand the fact that he was in her house, he hardly thought this would be a way to get into her good graces. But he felt useless staying with the three women.

"I'm going to go outside for some air," he informs them as he slides open the back door.

He steps onto the back porch, and he tilts his head toward the sky in time to see the full moon disappear behind a cloud encasing it in a golden hue. It's a crisp evening, enough so that he can see his breath in the cool night air. He is trying to figure out how he found himself in this scenario when he hears someone behind him. Startled, he turns around to find Jessie wrapped tightly in a sweater holding his jacket out to him.

"I thought you might be cold," she offers.

Jessie moves to stand beside him. She can either make small talk about the beautiful evening or take Vicky's advice. So, she gets right to the point.

"I'm sorry I canceled on you the other day. I needed time to wrap my head around what I want to say to you. I owe you such a big explanation. There is so much…"

"No!" he says, cutting her off.

Stunned by his reaction, she frowns.

He shakes his head. "Sorry, I didn't mean to be so abrupt. I mean, yes, we need to talk. But not today. Let's enjoy this."

She can see the plea in his eyes when he turns to face her. "I want to spend time with you. Can we do that? No pressure, no explanations, no drama."

He reaches a hand out to caress her cheek. Unintentionally, she pulls away.

"I'm sorry," they say in unison.

Zane smiles first. Jessie starts to laugh.

"This is ridiculous," he says. "And awkward. How many times in two minutes can we both apologize?"

Sam pokes his head out. "Hey guys, Jillian and I are heading home. Mom said the kids can spend the night, so we will swing by to pick them up in the morning."

"Look at you two getting a night without the kids," Jessie teases.

Sam raises his eyes brows in acknowledgment.

"Dad all settled?"

"Yeah. We gave him his meds and turned the heat up in their bedroom. It's a cold night. He doesn't need to get a chill. Zane, buddy, good to see you. It's been too long. You should come around more often. Maybe one of those times you take the twins and Shane out riding, we will tag along."

Zane's face lights up. "I would like that. We'll hold out for a week of nice weather. Maybe during Christmas break, if we don't get any more snow."

After a few more minutes of small talk, Jillian appears to say her goodbyes and pulls a still chatting Sam by the arm. Tyson and Vicky follow a few minutes later which leaves Zane and Jessie alone.

"Do you think they planned this?" Jessie asks as he follows her inside.

"Possibly," he says, moving toward the front door.

"You're leaving?" she appears surprised.

"Um, I figured I probably should. I don't want to make you or anyone else uncomfortable."

Jessie waves her hand nonchalantly. "Don't worry about Mom. She's harmless."

She feels more confident and at ease since Zane let her off the hook for an explanation, at least for now, so she invites him to stay. They settle across from one another at the dining room table.

"Tell me about the ranch. I forgot to tell you the other day how amazed I am at the beautiful work you've done."

For the next hour, they share stories of the lives they lived over the last several years, both careful not to make any personal revelations as they skirt around topics neither are ready to address. She tells him about medical school, her decision to quit, and finally attend the culinary program. They talk about the bistro and Phillip, but she purposely forgets to mention A.J. He relays the details of his grandparent's death, the renovations on the ranch and the friends he now considers family.

"You never married," she announces, surprising them both.

His forehead creases. "Neither did you."

"Touché," she smiles sadly, changing the subject. "Tyson told you about Dad."

"I don't even know what to say, Jessie. I'm so sorry. I wish…"

Her eyes brim with tears, and she looks away. "We all wish, Zane."

"He is the greatest man I've ever known. You are all blessed to have him. Shit, you have no idea how grateful I am for the time *I* had with him. He was more of an influence on me than…" he hesitates.

Stricken, Jessie's eyes widen, but Zane quickly recovers.

"Anyone."

They hear the clock on the wall chime.

Zane stands pushing his chair in and shrugs into his coat.

"Thanks for coming over," Jessie says as she walks him to the door. "Hey, why *did* you come over?"

"I came to see you, but I didn't expect to get the entire family," he admits, as his face turns crimson.

When she tips her head back and laughs unapologetically, he feels the tug on his heart. He's missed her unrestrained playfulness and the joy it used to bring him.

"Want to ride next week if the weather is good?" he suggests.

"I really would." She gives him a tender smile. "Can we play it by ear? Phillip is coming to town on Wednesday and staying until Sunday."

Unable to bite his tongue, Zane asks, "Is Phillip more than a friend?"

"Good Lord, no!" Jessie smirks. "The man is a complete womanizer. He's been a good friend."

Moving forward a few inches, he closes the space between them. "I used to be a womanizer *and* your best friend. Things happen," he says as they lock eyes.

"That was different," she whispers on a breath.

The heat of his gaze stirs something unexpectedly blood-tingling inside of her. Flustered, she steps away and clears her throat.

"I'm selling the bistro to Phillip," she announces.

Zane's exhales. Years of wondering, hoping, and longing instantly disappear. Instinct makes him want to sweep her into his arms, twirl her around and kiss her deeply in celebration. Those actions would scare her. So instead, he smiles foolishly and tells her good-night.

"Maybe we'll see you over Thanksgiving then," he calls over his shoulder as he walks to his truck.

Jessie closes the door. "Yeah, maybe," she says quietly.

CHAPTER THIRTEEN

The Wednesday before Thanksgiving, Phillip's flight lands at three in the afternoon, but instead of happy anticipation, Jessie is apprehensive about his visit. She drags her feet when it's time to leave for the airport, and although they already discussed the details of his flight and sleeping arrangement countless times, she is disturbed by a nagging sense of dread.

Could it be that she would rather spend time with Zane than entertain her friend for the next four days? Like a whimsical schoolgirl, Zane has been on her mind non-stop since Saturday night. Everything about him makes her quiver—from the intense way he stared at her, to his sheepish grin, down to the masculine energy that radiates off of him. It's been so long, she'd almost forgotten what lust felt like, but she welcomes it like an old, familiar friend.

Despite her heightened state of bliss, Jessie's anxiety skyrocketed, and on the drive to the airport, she can't help but wish Phillip would have canceled. It was absurd for her not to go to Seattle to settle business. Maybe it's the fact that she isn't prepared for her old life to come in contact with her new life, which frankly seems silly considering A.J. was here last month. But that was before. Now there is Zane to consider, and he is a whole different aspect of her life. The family is one thing. An ex-boyfriend is someplace she isn't ready to go yet, and she can't guarantee the Zane and Phillip won't cross paths.

As the landscape whips past, she taps her fingers nervously on the steering wheel, feeling the tension mount in the back of her shoulders and neck. In an attempt to calm herself, she turns up the radio and sings along to Garth Brooks, but by the time she pulls into terminal parking, her breath is fast and short.

She is light-headed and worried she might be on the verge of a panic attack. She stops to buy a bottle of water. After a few sips and feeling slightly more composed, she walks to the gate. While waiting, she watches the hustle and bustle around her. Moments later, Phillip appears, and the miserable expression clouding his features is her first clue. When she spots the person trailing behind him, Jessie finally understands where her apprehensions stemmed.

• • •

"It wasn't planned, I promise. I avoided her all week for this exact reason, but she showed up at the bistro last night demanding to know what I was doing for Thanksgiving. You know what a bad liar I am. I'm sorry!" Phillip pleads with Jessie while A.J. retrieves her luggage from baggage claim.

Jessie quickly sends a text to her sister, asking her to prepare another bedroom. Phillip brought an unexpected guest.

Her family is not going to be happy about this. It was apparent to everyone when A.J. showed up unannounced over Halloween, that Jessie was not thrilled with the surprise visit. Instead of hurting A.J. with the truth, Jessie kept silent, allowing her irritation to smolder, and as one could imagine, the three days were filled with many uncomfortable walls of silence, curious inquisitions from her family and built up resentment from unspoken words. Instead of simply having a civilized adult conversation about their relationship, A.J. was pouty, possessive and made harsh, sly remarks at the most inopportune times, humiliating Jessie.

At first Jessie tried to make excuses for her, but it didn't take long to come to her senses, and she refused to get sucked into the dysfunctional cycle their relationship survived in. Unfortunately, the less Jessie engaged, the harder A.J. tried to get a reaction. Her family was not impressed.

On the last night of her previous visit, in a desperate attempt to salvage the remaining pieces of their broken relationship, A.J. asked Jessie to marry her. Her explosive outrage to Jessie's negative response dissolved any remaining thread that kept them together. On the drive to the airport the following morning, Jessie dropped the bomb that she planned to sell her half of the bistro to Phillip.

For several days following the visit, Jessie thought about their interactions over the last year. It took being around family and engaging in healthy functional relationships for her to recognize the difference. It wasn't that A.J. was a bad person. They both fell into comfortable roles of A.J. taking care of her in a subtle but controlling type of way and Jessie passively enabling her. A.J. loved to be needed and could be overgenerous. It gave her purpose. She was a nurturer by nature and loved to mend the broken, but when her status in that position was threatened, she exhibited bad behavior.

The two of them spent a significant amount of time with Mel and Libby over the years, but as Jessie looked back, there was always a fight. The week before an upcoming visit, A.J. worried Jessie wasn't going to include her. She made a point of reminding her that *they* were a couple, and *she* was her family. Jessie found this tirade strange since Mel and Libby were nothing but respectful and courteous. While A.J. encouraged Jessie to have a relationship with her parents and heal from her past, Jessie now knows they were just words to appease. What she wanted was Jessie to herself. Without her family's influence, A.J. didn't have to worry about outside interference in the private world they created. Jessie depended on her, valued her opinions, and relied on her for almost everything.

It wasn't until they were apart that Jessie became aware of A.J.'s tendency to manipulate words to sound supportive, encouraging, and loving when in actuality she is critical and condescending. And Jessie easily fell into the trap of consoling or taking responsibility for A.J.'s feelings and reactions.

The ride home is dreadful. Jessie doesn't know who she is angrier with, A.J. for bullying Phillip into bringing her along or Phillip for not having the guts to tell her no or at least give Jessie some warning. Either way, the tension in the car is unpleasant.

Jessie watches in the rearview mirror as A.J. pulls a cigarette out of the pack tucked into her purse. She places it between her lips and flicks her lighter.

"Don't smoke in my car," Jessie says firmly.

A.J. puts the cigarette down, appearing surprised by the tone of Jessie's voice. Her daggered eyes meet Jessie's in the mirror.

"Five years!" A.J. exclaims reactively. "You are willing to throw away a business, a partnership, and me? Do you think once they get to know you, the real you, you will all go back to living your *Leave it to Beaver* life? Don't be so naïve. You're going to be sadly disappointed, and so are they."

Choosing not to engage, Jessie turns up the radio.

Irritated by her passive attitude, A.J. starts to scream. "You wait! Six months from now, when you and your sister can't stand to look at each other, when you come face-to-face with the guy that raped you, when your parents and that boyfriend find out the truth, you are going to come running back to *me* begging for a second chance."

Somewhere in the depths of Jessie's confidence, her power rises.

"Why on earth would you think I would want to be in a relationship with someone who wishes hateful things not only for me but for my family?"

• • •

By the time they arrive at Vicky's, both have calmed down, and Jessie includes A.J. in some lighthearted conversation. A.J. is responsive, even somewhat friendly.

After they retrieve the luggage, they go inside where Vicky and family wait for them. A pot of homemade clam chowder simmers on the stove while biscuits rise in the oven. After introductions are made and Vicky shows her guests to their bedrooms, she pulls Jessie into the laundry room.

"We have a problem," she admits, her voice low. "Tyson invited Zane to dinner tomorrow. We didn't know *she* would be here! We can't uninvite him."

Jessie throws her hands up. "*I* didn't know she would be here! Is he coming? I mean with how Mom is toward him, is she even okay with him being here? I don't want to ruin her Thanksgiving either."

"I thought of that too and asked. She and Dad had a discussion the other night. She did not elaborate but said he is welcome."

"Really? I mean that's great news, but it would have been an easy out."

"He deserves to be here more than *she* does. We are his family. He stayed away out of respect for all of us... especially you. He's taken the brunt of accusations, criticism and been very lonely. He lost everyone he loved."

Jessie groans as she rubs her forehead with her fingertips. Her heart aches as she thinks about what Zane has been through.

"Okay, I will talk to him. If he decides to come, then I will have a conversation with A.J. I don't want to add fuel to the fire if there is no reason. God, this could be the most dysfunctional holiday ever. But it's a mess I created, so I have to be mature and handle it with respect for his sake."

• • •

After dinner, Jessie explains to her guests that she needs to return to her parents' house to help with her dad, which is partially true. She left out the part that Zane agreed to meet her. A.J. offers to ride along but Tyson, aware of Jessie's plan, intervenes explaining that Libby is limiting the number of people at the house at one time.

Although she is disappointed, A.J. relents. Jessie promises not to be gone more than an hour. On her way out she catches Tyson by himself in the kitchen putting dishes away and gives him a quick peck on the cheek as a thank you.

She asked Zane to meet her at eight-thirty, because she thought that would give her enough time to get her dad ready for bed first. His truck is already parked on the side street when Jessie pulls into the driveway at a quarter to eight. As she approaches the vehicle, she can hear heavy rock music booming from the speakers and finds him playing solitaire on his phone. When she taps lightly on the glass, he jumps and then rolls down the window.

"I thought I'd wait here while you take care of business, then we can go get a drink."

"Perfect," she says.

Ten minutes later, a frustrated and irritable Mel is arguing with his wife and daughter. He decided he wanted to take a bath. Typically, someone was around to help Libby get him in and out, but tonight, a bath wasn't on anyone's agenda. The home health nurse left at five, and Libby didn't have the heart to call anyone else for assistance. She tells Jessie that Mel had a good day and convinced her they could do it themselves. Now he sits shivering in lukewarm water unable to help himself out of the tub, his strength depleted. Libby is not strong enough to lift him herself.

"Dad, you have to let me help," Jessie shouts from the open door of the bathroom. "You'll get pneumonia if you stay in there any longer."

"I am not going to let my adult daughter see me naked," he answers weakly.

Libby eventually drains the tub, dries him off and wraps a blanket around him, so Jessie can assist, but each time they feel like they have a good enough grip to support him to a stand, the blanket slips or his knees buckle and he demands to be put down for fear of falling. When his breath becomes labored, Jessie retrieves the oxygen tank and adjusts the nasal cannula in his nose. But it is impossible to balance him and a bag of oxygen at the same time. Exhausted, Libby rubs her lower back.

"Go call one of the boys, Jessie."

Instead, she runs outside and taps on Zane's window. "We need your help."

Although Mel is depleted, his eyes light up when Zane enters the bathroom. In one swift movement, he scoops Mel into his arms and carries him into the bedroom while Jessie follows with the oxygen tank. After placing the tank on the floor, Jessie lingers in the hallway to give her dad the privacy he deserves while Zane helps a tired Libby navigate Mel into his pajamas. Although Libby does not speak to him directly, they work together to complete the task.

Once the mask covers Mel's mouth and his pillows are adjusted, Libby lovingly pats her husband's arm.

"I'm going to go make us some tea," she says, leaving the room.

Zane turns to follow but feels Mel's cold, stiff fingers reach out to touch him. Zane positions himself on the side of the bed, and he takes Mel's hand. Tears roll out of the older man's eyes.

Jessie wonders what is taking Zane so long. She steps into the bedroom and leans against the door frame. She crosses her arms and watches the scene in front of her.

Mel attempts to pull the mask away from his mouth, but his fingers fumble, so Zane reaches down, adjusts the straps, and lays the mask on Mel's shoulder.

"Thank…you," Mel says softly. "Thank…you…for…your…help," he repeats slowly.

"I'd do anything for you, Mel."

"I...know...you...would." Mel nods his head, his intense eyes narrowing. "I believe...you would do... about anything for...this family, Zane."

• • •

Unable to find the right words, Jessie's toys with the lid of her teacup. They didn't say much on the drive. Inside the café, they interact long enough to order drinks, and now they sit across from one another in silence again privately rehashing the earlier events.

With eyes down, Jessie peels back the lid and blows into the steam. "Vicky said you were planning on coming to dinner tomorrow," she finally blurts out.

"Is there a problem with that?" he asks.

Jessie shakes her head, twirling a strand of hair through her fingers.

"Phillip brought someone with him. It was someone I didn't expect to see, and well, it's complicated, but I feel I need to at least warn you in case you don't want to come. At least I will give you a choice," she rambles. "I know we said we weren't going to talk about it or explain anything at this point, but A.J. decided to show up, and now I have a lot to explain."

Zane bites his lip, trying to appear confused at her attempted confession. Granted, he is surprised to hear that A.J. tagged along but the rest—he already knows what's coming.

Unable to make eye contact, Jessie stares over his shoulder out the window focusing on the golden ray of light casting shadows from the street lamp.

"Dating wasn't my forte in college," she smiles tensely. "I made some pretty poor choices. The relationships I did try left me jaded and resentful. And I was single for a very long time."

Her voice shakes as she tells Zane about A.J. and the demise of the relationship over the last year. When she finishes, he leans forward resting his elbows on the table between them.

"Are you a lesbian?"

"I'm a fucked-up individual. That is what I am. There's more to it, Zane, more to why I am such a mess."

"Are you in love with her?"

"No," she admits regretfully, looking down at the napkin she's torn into shreds. "I don't think I was. She was my best friend, and I truly care about her, but love, passion, intimacy?" Jessie's face sours. "I'm not capable of that with a woman or a man. I don't know what that makes me. A spinster for life?"

When he doesn't respond, she peeks at him from under her lashes. His expression is matter-of-fact, which does nothing to put her mind at ease.

"Why are you telling me all of this?" he challenges.

"Because I don't know how she is going to act tomorrow. She can be reactive and irrational. She's a bit toxic, *and* she is not happy I'm selling the bistro. I don't want you to be taken off guard if she makes snide comments."

Zane reaches across the table, placing his hand over Jessie's. This time she does not pull away. In fact, his touch makes her heart flutter.

"I'm not going to lie, the fact that you care enough to share this with me gives me a lot of hope. But I already knew about A.J.," he reveals.

Jessie sucks in a sharp breath. "Tyson?"

"Don't be mad. Since you've been back, he's the one who's talked me off a ledge a time or two when I wanted to do something stupid like see you before you were ready. But can I be honest? I had trouble believing that you wanted to spend your life with her."

She tilts her head to the side inquisitively. Despite the years etched on his face, he remains devastatingly attractive. The curly amber waves fall across his forehead reminding her of the many times she watched him climb out of the swimming pool sopping wet, shaking his head like a dog, as pellets of water hit her while she sunbathed. That boy didn't even compare to the man in front of her now. He is still athletic though she imagines it's years of hard work and labor that sculpted the muscles beneath his tightly fitted shirt. She can't help admiring the taut veins that pop when his hands flex, and a burning fire ignites in her as she recalls those hands moving cautiously and carefully over her body.

He leans further into the small table until they are only inches apart. He keeps his hand locked on hers, his eyes lingering on her face.

"I remember everything about you from the time you were a young girl. I remember the way your eyes would light up at simple enjoyments in life like finding a ladybug or caterpillar on a branch in your treehouse. Remember when we dissected frogs in Biology? The other girls in class were horrified, but your enthusiasm was contagious. You were the one to convince our 5th-grade class to send letters to Rick Thompson's parents after he died in that car accident even though he was two grades below us. You felt everything. You carried joy in your heart and spread it to everyone. You were the most passionate person I ever met, and it was one hundred percent genuine. I remember that passion, that desire. Your ability to give unselfishly. At one time it was for me."

Jessie finds it difficult to breathe. She is mesmerized by his words. His confidence and perception of her leave her speechless.

"Call me silly," he continues. "But whatever you had with A.J., I believe it was circumstantial. I plan on coming to dinner tomorrow because I'm not intimidated by a woman you had a circumstantial relationship with and did not love."

She does not deny or confirm his assessment but instead redirects her focus.

"That's the thing, Zane. She doesn't have a clue about my past and just recently found out I had a boyfriend in high school. She is irritated about the entire thing and could provoke you, or me. I need to warn you."

Zane refrains from asking the dozen or so questions on his mind. "Would it be better if I didn't come?"

Jessie recalls her sister's words. "This is your family. They've missed you, and you miss them."

"I've missed you," he admits tenderly.

Once again, Jessie's heart slams into her chest. Leaning back in her chair, she roughly bites her bottom lip which takes her out of the trance he is putting her in.

Zane puffs out a breath. "Seriously, Jess. I can have dinner out at the ranch with the guys. I don't want to cause you any unneeded stress. I promise if I do come, I will be respectful. I won't hurt you."

A sad smile crosses her features. All the pain she had caused this man, and still, his biggest concern is not hurting her.

• • •

A.J. did not take the news about Zane as well as Zane received the news about her. After everyone else has turned in for the night, Jessie sits on the guest bed watching a distraught A.J. pace the room. With his back against the wall and his feet crossed at the ankles, Phillip quietly observes.

"I'm begging you. If not for me, then my parents. The last thing they need is to have this dirty laundry aired all over the place," Jessie pleads, looking to Phillip for reassurance.

"Do not make a scene!" he warns, glaring at A.J. "You are a guest in this house, and you need to keep your theatrics to a minimum."

"What about me? Does anyone give a shit about my pain? I don't want him here. He can't come!"

Jessie stands up fiercely. "You don't get to make demands. *You* were not invited. He is family. *You* are not!"

Her outburst surprises A.J.

"Do you really want to know who I was before you?" Jessie continues. "I was bubbly and assertive, a go-getter. *I* was a cheerleader. I was strong, confident, influential, and I had a voice, a strong voice. Something horrible happened, and I turned into a mouse who hid from the world, allowing people to bulldoze me and make decisions for me. I allowed everyone I dated, including you, to push me around. What you don't seem to understand is since I've been back here, I have been working on finding my voice. Though I'm not exactly where I want to be, I've made huge strides in not allowing myself to be anyone's pathetic mouse anymore. Nobody, including you, gets to take that away from me."

Slamming the door behind her, she retreats to the living room where she throws herself onto the sofa bed Vicky had graciously pulled out. Although it's comfortable enough, Jessie can't stop the surge of adrenaline. After an hour of tossing and turning, she is still awake. She pulls out her cell phone to check e-mails hoping it will make her tired, but it doesn't work. She moves to the chair where she watches snow fall from the sky while her mind circles back to Zane.

He messaged her before bed.

Thanks for telling me about A.J. I look forward to seeing you tomorrow. Happy early Thanksgiving.

Her feelings, although complicated, are becoming impossible to ignore. The way his eyes bore into her earlier reminds her of the many stolen moments they shared as teenagers—the kisses, the caresses, the promises of a future.

Feeling restless, Jessie gets up for a glass of water, but when she passes by the room A.J. is occupying, she notices a soft light from under the door. With a twinge of compassion, she wonders if they should try to talk again. Jessie is about to knock when muffled sounds stop her. She leans close to the door and hears two familiar voices, one male and the other female. They are not having a conversation. When their moans grow considerably louder, Jessie does not know whether to be irritated or amused.

She tiptoes back to bed and quickly becomes comfortable, falling easily into a peaceful sleep.

• • •

Jessie is standing at the stove in her pajamas whipping up a batch of pancakes when A.J. and Phillip appear, fully dressed and ready for the day. Vicky and Tyson already left to help with Mel. Jessie asked them to take the kids along so she could have a private discussion with her guests. When Jessie told her why, Vicky appeared as delighted and amused as Jessie felt.

When they sit down at the breakfast table, Jessie folds her hands under her chin, studying the other two while they eat.

"How long have you two been sleeping together?" she asks casually.

Phillip gags on his orange juice. A.J.'s face turns white, and her fork drops with loud a clank.

She hurries to explain. "It just happened. I was upset about all that was transpiring. Phillip came to my room to console me. I was vulnerable and well..."

Jessie holds up her hand. "How long?"

"A year," Phillip admits hanging his head.

A.J. glowers at him while Jessie laughs.

"Things between us weren't good," A.J. attempts again, her voice shaking.

"This started before I left? Just because things were not good does not give you the right to sleep with someone else. Were there others?"

A.J. presses her lips flat. "Why would you think that?"

"You are bisexual, after all. There hasn't been much intimacy in our relationship from day one. Who knows where else you get your needs met."

A.J. stiffens. "Honestly, do you even care if I sleep with someone else? Is sex the issue? Or are we having this conversation because it seems like the right thing to do given the circumstances?"

For a moment, Jessie is not sure what to say. As far as she was concerned, despite the problems and lack of intimacy, they had been committed to one another.

Had been being the operative words.

A.J. stands, shoving back her chair. "I don't know when it hit me," she contemplates. "Before you left. When you came home in June. Maybe on the plane ride after Halloween. All I know is that the cloud finally lifted, and I was able to see our relationship through your eyes."

She moves to the picture window and looks onto the street. "You aren't gay. You certainly aren't bi-sexual. You never wanted me for a partner. For some reason, we kept up the charade. How stupid was I?"

Jessie interrupts sternly. "You are not an innocent victim in this. You knew I wasn't a lesbian when you met me, and being with a woman sexually *never* crossed my mind. I told you that."

With a painful grimace on her delicate features, A.J. turns away from the window. "You hurt me. You were emotionally unavailable, and you dragged me down with you. I can't believe you have the audacity to ask me why I slept with Phillip. I was lonely, Jessie!"

Jessie laughs, tossing back her head. "I find your hypocrisy offensive. The guilt you inflicted, the snide comments, the passive-aggressive behavior all the while you were secretly banging Phillip. I wasn't screwing anyone, you realize that, don't you? The only thing I'm at fault for is trying to have a relationship with my family. You couldn't handle that."

Fire rages in A.J.'s eyes, but it doesn't stop Jessie.

"I was a project for you. When we met, I was lost and hadn't a clue who I was. You took advantage of that for selfish reasons. As far as Phillip, if that is what our relationship had come to, despite who was emotionally involved or not, you should have ended things, or at least had enough respect to have a conversation before you decided to sleep with my best friend."

Frustrated, A.J. runs her hands through her short blonde hair until it's sticking up on the ends.

With shoulders hunched, Phillip disappears into the back-guest room. A.J. follows him down the hallway, but when she reaches for the bedroom door, she turns back to Jessie with her eyes full of sorrow.

"You want to know when I knew it was over for good?" She waits for Jessie to say something but Jessie remains silent.

"When you came back to Seattle in the summer. Your eyes sparkled. You were animated and happy when

you spoke about Vicky. For probably the first time, I
saw love in your heart. I realized then you were never
looking for a girlfriend. What you wanted in me was a
sister to replace the one you'd lost."

• • •

A weight lifts as Jessie watches the cab carrying Phillip
and A.J. pull away from the curb. Not long after, Vicky
and Tyson return with their parents. Once Mel is comfortable, with the remote in hand so he can flip from
one football game to the next, Tyson takes the kids to
the backyard for a game of touch football while Jessie,
Vicky and Libby get busy in the kitchen.

As they baste the turkey, brown sausage for the dressing and prepare pies, Jessie gives them the rundown of
what transpired earlier.

"I wish I would have gone through the stupid phases
of exploring my sexuality when I was younger instead
of having a mid-life crisis."

Vicky chuckles, shaking a dough covered finger
at Jessie. "That wasn't a mid-life crisis. You're only
thirty-one."

Sam and his family arrive around two. It doesn't take
long for Sam, Kelsey, and Tanner to join the others in
the backyard while Jillian pours herself a glass of wine.

"Pour me one of those" Jessie insists, taking a glass
out of the cupboard.

"Red or white?

"Surprise me. After the last two days, I won't be
picky."

With a puzzled look, Jillian pours the Merlot as
Vicky recites the short version of the story.

"Hmm, so I guess you aren't a lesbian then?"

"That seems to be the question of the day. "Neutrosexual" is what I am going to call it. Relationships, marriage, sex, men, women, I don't think any of it's for me."

After the words leave her mouth, the front door opens. As if on cue, Zane steps through it, a bottle of wine in one hand, and a grocery bag in the other. His attention drifts to Jessie as if she's the only person in the room. His eyes drink her in. She blushes nervously twisting her fingers around the stem of her wine glass. In the silence, you could hear a pin drop.

"Mmm...hmm," Jillian says, taking a sip of wine. "Neutrosexual...my ass!"

Vicky hurries to unload his arms and thanks him for picking up the whipped cream.

Zane walks to the other side of the house and peers through the back window to find the group running around the yard, tossing a football. He contemplated not coming. Zane was truthful with Jessie the evening before and wasn't concerned about the status of her future with A.J. However, he was nervous about being around the two of them. He didn't know what to expect and if he were to be completely honest with himself, the idea of Jessie with anyone else—past or present—made him queasy.

He turns away from the window and scans the room. His eyes lock on hers. Offering a silent explanation, Jessie shakes her head as a soft, easy smile shapes her lips.

"I'll go get you a beer," she says, disappearing into the garage.

He isn't sure if this is an invitation to follow or not. He doesn't want to appear too anxious. With the eyes of the other three women following every move he makes, he decides to sit with Mel, who is resting comfortably watching the football game.

When Jessie returns, she hands him his beer. "They left. I'll fill you in later."

Later, when the feast is complete, Sam, Tyson, and Zane maneuver the table close the couch to make it more accessible for Mel. The grandkids grab chairs, move them to their appropriate places, and soon everyone takes a seat. Jessie watches everyone grab the hand of the person next to them and bow their heads as Libby says the blessing.

"Dear Lord, we can't thank you enough for bringing us together today. It's a dream come true for Mel and me," she says, her voice cracking.

Out of the corner of her eye, Jessie sees Vicky flick away a tear and feels her own eyes well up.

Clearing her throat, Libby relaxes her shoulders. "You have given us a good life and a beautiful family. Lord, we have had good times and hard times, but through them all, we feel the presence of your grace and love. Let us give thanks not only today but every day for your blessings. Let us go forward and carry them into all we do. In your name we pray, Amen."

To lighten the mood, the grown men make a few wise cracks about the *blessing*. Another of their favorite movie quotes of the holiday season. Soon everyone is laughing. After the delicious meal is devoured, the children pitch in for clean-up. Vicky, Jillian, and Jessie supervise while indulging in another glass of wine.

When their chores are complete, the children run downstairs to play. Mel falls asleep, worn out from the commotion around him as well as the heavy meal. Yawning, Libby crawls in beside him and flips the channels on the television until she stops on the old classic, *It's A Wonderful Life*. She lies her head on his chest and shortly, she too, is fast asleep.

Jessie links her arm through Vicky's. Placing her head on her sister's shoulder, they watch from the kitchen. "How is she going to do this?"

"I have no idea," Vicky says, as a tear runs down her cheek.

A moment later, Tyson sneaks up and wraps his arms around Vicky's waist planting a kiss on the curve of her neck.

"Come on," he whispers, taking her by the hand.

He motions for the others to follow. They grab their winter coats, and they follow him out back where the fire pit blazes to life. A bag of marshmallows lies next to Sam, who is relaxing in a patio chair with his feet propped up. He holds out a stick to each of them.

"We have pie inside," Jessie declares incredulously. "We don't need marshmallows."

"Live a little," Sam says. "You don't have to watch your weight today. Besides, you're just going to run it off tomorrow."

Jessie sticks her tongue out but reaches for a stick anyways. Always aware of Zane's presence, she notices he is not outside with them, but she is too embarrassed to inquire and instead becomes entranced by the dancing flames. She pulls off the hot, gooey mush, and just as she opens her mouth to take a bite, she feels him behind her. She turns around and hands him the stick.

"Mushmeeeow?" she mumbles between bites.

Smirking, he rubs the corner of her mouth with his thumb and walks away. The simple gesture stirs something inside of her. He holds the stick slightly above the flames and roasts his own, but instead of eating it himself, he brings it to her and holds the marshmallow in front of her lips as his dark, alluring eyes tease. Transfixed, she opens her mouth, accepting the delicious treat. He returns to the group while a disoriented Jessie leans against the side of the house to steady herself. It must be the wine and the rich food causing her light-headedness. Deep down, she knows it is neither.

She positions herself between Sam and Jillian at the fire pit, a safe distance away from Zane. While they gossip about high school friends and teachers, she observes his somber expression in the brilliant light of the fire and once again, appreciates what she sees. His striking features are not the only thing that attracted her to him all those years ago. Even then, there was so much more to the complicated boy. Because of her, she can pretty much guarantee, he is an even more complicated man.

Regardless, she is impressed with the person he's become. Lesser men would have succumbed to the pressure of drugs and alcohol, gambling, women, or who knows what else due to his abusive childhood. From what she has learned and can see in the time they have spent together, he is a survivor, a determined man who will not use the traumas of his past as an excuse to hold him back. She admires the hard-working rancher who's built a friendship and partnership with his hired hands and their families, as well as the integrity and control he's shown over the last several months knowing she was in town. The bond he and Tyson share is undeniable despite circumstances that kept them apart, and seeing his patient and respectful interactions with the children touch her heart.

She continues to observe him as he stares intently into the flames. Watching the blaze cast shadows on his face, Jessie senses a sadness within him. She longs to be the one to make it go away but is filled with despair, knowing she's the one that put it there.

"It's cold. Let's go inside and play poker," Tyson suggests.

Once inside, they find Libby awake watching her movie while Mel continues to nap beside her. They invite her to join but understand her desire to stay where she is. The six of them spend the next two hours playing cards, eating pumpkin pie, refereeing disagreements between children and laughing until their stomachs hurt as they relive childhood escapades.

"Do you remember the party Sam had at that crappy little house he was renting?" Tyson asks. "The only way inside was through the back door in the alley. Vicky had just graduated, and I think you two were sophomores."

"Oh God, please don't," Jessie groans.

Sam snorts. "You had gone on two dates with that one guy...what was his name?"

"Robbie Schmidt," Zane states, arching his eyebrow in amusement.

"Yeah, good old Robbie. He was crazy about you," Tyson adds.

Unfortunately, Jessie remembers. He kissed like a pufferfish, and after two dates, she called it off. But Robbie was jealous of her friendship with Zane. He showed up at the party ready for a fight which was stupid because Zane and Tyson were not ones to back down. Tyson had thrown one punch before Jessie stormed out the back door, cast iron skillet in hand, swinging like a madwoman. She managed to break Robbie's nose.

"Bled like hell! I saw him at the store last month, and that sucker never got it fixed. It's still crooked!" Sam laughs as tears stream from his half-closed eyes.

Jessie lifts a hand to shield her embarrassment. "I'm glad I have not run into any of these people."

"Feisty should have been your middle name," Zane grins, holding the beer bottle to his lips. "No one screwed with you."

"They knew if they did, they would have you three to deal with. You would have killed anyone who messed with us," Jessie jokes.

The energy in the room grows heavy as Zane's expression turns grave, and he slams his beer bottle on the table. Warily, he shifts his gaze to Tyson.

Slightly buzzed from the wine, Jessie turns to Vicky. "What did I say?" she asks innocently.

Confused as well, Vicky shrugs, and they wait for an explanation.

Promptly, Sam pushes his chair back and begins to clear the dishes.

"Mom, we should probably get you and Dad home. I think he's had his fill for the day.

"Yeah, besides, aren't you three doing the Black Friday shopping thing early in the morning?" Tyson adds lightheartedly.

"Good Lord, no!" Vicky playfully smacks him in the arm while Jillian and Jessie shake their heads emphatically.

While everyone makes plans to go sledding and attend the Christmas parade the following day, Jessie tosses her paper plate into the trash. She packs up her belongings, anxious to sleep in her own bed. She returns to the kitchen with her bag in hand as everyone is getting ready to leave, and notices Zane's truck is already gone.

CHAPTER FOURTEEN

The next four weeks pass in a whirlwind for Jessie. Between balancing the four catering events she scheduled before Christmas Eve, she is volunteering an extra hour a day in the classroom to help students get ready for the holiday program. There are costumes to put together, songs to rehearse and props to make. Jessie was under the impression that parents pitched in at such times but was surprised to hear that because most parents work full time, it's rare they get involved. This disappoints her. She cherishes the memories of her mother coming to the classroom. She can't imagine not having the opportunity to do it for her kids.

At the thought of having children, a forgotten longing burns deeply. She immediately brushes it aside and glances at the calendar on the table in front of her. Tanner's orchestra program is Wednesday. The twins' classroom party is Friday, which is also the last day of school before break. Kelsey's Girl Scout troop enlisted her help in teaching them how to decorate holiday cookies on Saturday, and Shane has his last basketball game the same evening.

As exhausting as it sounds, she finds it all exhilarating. The negative energy she spent dealing with A.J. and the bistro weighed her down more than she realized. Eventually, she will forgive Phillip. He is the one person over the years who respected and supported her with unconditional love. No guilt. No manipulation. Phillip brought humor into a mostly dull and grey life. She doesn't really care about his sexual relationship with A.J. She finds the situation more amusing than painful. But Phillip is big, dumb, and needs to control his libido. A.J. can be very seductive and knows how to use her sexuality to her advantage, so frankly, Phillip is powerless against her. For now, he can deal with the mess he got himself into.

She calculates a bill for one of her catering clients and smiles to herself. This is what a fulfilled life is supposed to feel like. The one exception is she hasn't seen Zane since Thanksgiving. He didn't meet them at the Christmas parade, and when Tyson told her he extended an invite for sledding, she was sure he would show up. She was wrong. She sent him a text message four days ago asking to meet for coffee but hasn't received a reply. At the time, she hadn't thought much about his abrupt departure. Her concern has grown since she hasn't heard from him, especially since they'd overcome the initial hump with such ease.

She turns the oven on to three hundred and fifty degrees and looks at her phone again, just as she has over the last several days. Frustrated, she tosses it onto the counter. Once she pulls out her mixer and begins adding ingredients, she stays distracted while she makes six dozen assorted cookies for the library's open house.

She sings along to her music playlist but every so often rechecks her phone again.

By the time she returns from making her deliveries, she is discouraged. Unless Zane is out of town on vacation, which she knows isn't a possibility, it's pretty obvious he is avoiding her.

She messages her sister to inquire, wanting to give him the benefit of the doubt.

Vicky writes back a few minutes later saying he just replied to the text she sent him about Christmas. This makes Jessie furious, but it's too late to take a drive out to the ranch tonight which is probably a good thing considering she is irritated. Instead, she comes up with Plan B.

• • •

The school day can't get over soon enough. Jessie breaks up an argument between two boys on the slide who can't decide who is stronger—Spiderman or Superman. With only three days left until Christmas break, the children are bouncing off the walls, and Jessie has a serious case of sensory overload. At times like this, she is grateful she didn't go into teaching and wonders how Vicky does it. Today alone, there was gum stuck in hair, three incidents of roughhousing, one boy wound up with bloody nose, a variety of tears amongst girls who could not find it in their hearts to include everyone in their reading circle and a shortage of Elmer's glue during craft time. Jessie is craving the two-week break as much if not more than the kids.

When her three hours are up, she grabs her winter coat and bolts for the door. Shifting the car into drive, she carefully eases away from the curb onto the slushy street. The journey out to the ranch takes an extra five minutes due to sketchy roads, which gives her time to think about her strategy. It's not like he owes her anything, but it still annoys her that he can't even reply to a text message.

The ranch, all covered in snow, looks like the picture on a postcard. She parks next to Zane's truck, climbs the stairs of the front porch, and knocks on the door. While she waits, she reaches into her pocket and puts a fresh coat of balm on her dried lips. When there is still no answer, she pries the door open and pops her head in.

She calls out, but there is no answer. She clomps her way through the ankle-deep snow as she crosses the yard, thinking he must be in the barn. She pries open the large solid door, peeks her head around the corner, and hears the commotion from inside. On the floor of one of the stalls, Zane, and who she assumes must be Brent and Dawson, surround a very pregnant and agitated sow. As she approaches, Zane throws a vicious glare over his shoulder but turns his attention back to the emergency at hand. Jessie ignores him, trying to make out what is happening. Overdue. C-section. Small litter. Before she knows it, Dawson cuts open the sow's belly. Fascinated, she steps closer and watches as they pull the babies out one by one.

Thirty minutes later, exhausted and covered in blood, dirt, and sweat, Jessie follows a grim Zane back to the house. Once inside, he storms upstairs with Weiser trailing behind him. She soon hears the water running. She is disheartened but unwilling to leave. She circles the living room taking in the familiar surroundings. She admires the large windows, which, along with the open floor plan, brighten up the kitchen and allow the dining room to flow into the now spacious living room. She runs her hand across the comfortable burgundy furniture, thinking she would have picked the same given the opportunity, something they could curl up on to watch movies while giving the home a modern yet rustic appearance.

Enamored, she climbs the stairs taking in the artwork and antique decorations hanging on the wall and without thinking, walks into his bedroom. A large oak bed frame draped with a red and blue checkered comforter faces French doors with a view of the valley as spectacular as anything Jessie has ever seen. A fireplace adorns the wall to the left of the bed and a single oversized dresser matching the bed frame sits opposite of it. She is astonished by his excellent taste. It's a plain and simple room but comfortable at the same time.

She turns to leave, not wanting Zane to catch her poking around his room, but a silver picture frame on the bedside table draws her attention. She picks up the eight by ten frame and holding it close, Jessie gasps. There have to be a dozen small photos unevenly shoved into the collage. There are several of the two of them dressed up on Halloween along with candid snapshots at parties, football games, basketball games, and clowning around the hallways of high school with other friends. There is a picture from the senior prom and another at graduation, both dressed in their cap and gown, Zane is kissing her cheek.

"What are you doing?" His gruff voice startles her, causing her to drop the frame. It hits the corner of the table and clanks to the floor. As she bends to pick it up, Zane quickly snatches it out of her outstretched hand.

"I'm, I'm sorry," she stammers.

She made a mistake. Zane is irritated, and he is standing disturbingly close to her wearing nothing but sweat pants. Brown locks of hair are matted against his forehead and beads of water gather on the smooth olive skin of his bare chest. His broad shoulders are the result of years of hard work, and his taut stomach is absolute perfection as the cut of his muscles disappear mysteriously beneath the elastic of his waistband. Jessie feels her face warm.

She turns to leave, but Zane grabs her arm.

"You're a mess. Take a shower," he grumbles, shoving a towel at her. "I'll ask Tonya for some clothes you can borrow."

He goes to his dresser and pulls a T-shirt out of the drawer. With his back to her, he yanks it over his head. Too stunned to move, Jessie winces as her hand flies to her chest. The scars, an indication of his troubled childhood, are still there. They are a painful reminder of the horrific things Ron was capable of, not only to her and Vicky but to his own flesh and blood.

Once Zane leaves, Jessie locks the bathroom door behind her, removes her clothes and steps under the hot mist. The water rains down, soaking her hair and warming her chilled, shivering body. She leans her head against the ceramic tiled wall, feeling weak and tired. Overcome with grief, she begins to cry. She hurts for the young boy who desperately wanted to be loved by a monster. She aches for the young man who gave her all the love he was capable of while soaking up affection from a family that wasn't his. Mostly, she sobs for the same man who not only risked but lost it all for no reason of his own.

When she has no tears left in her, she washes her hair. On shaky legs, she climbs out of the shower, wraps herself in a large cotton towel, and sits on the floor.

Zane knocks on the door. "You okay?"

"Yeah," she attempts to sound cheerful. "I was cold and didn't want to get out of the shower."

"I'll leave the clothes on the bed."

Jessie wipes the steam off the mirror and glances at her bloodshot eyes. She knows Zane won't ask, and deciding she has nothing to explain, she dries off then dresses in an oversized Montana State sweatshirt and fitted leggings. She heads downstairs with her hair still damp.

Zane hands her a steaming cup before carrying his cup to the recliner where he punches buttons on the remote control. Jessie sinks into the corner of the couch, curling her legs beneath her. She sips on her coffee while watching him out of the corner of her eye. As she was alongside him today in his element on the ranch, intimately aware of his passion and strength, and his vulnerability, it rekindled a yearning that used to make her glow from the inside out.

After flipping through a few channels, Zane turns off the television and tosses the remote onto the coffee table. Weiser moves from where he was lying by the front door to sit beside him and whines as if sensing his master's foul mood.

"Why did you come out here, Jessie?"

She raises her eyebrows in surprise at his curt tone. "You didn't return any of my messages."

He scowls at his cup, refusing to meet her gaze.

A knot grows in the pit of her stomach. "On purpose? I'm confused. I thought this was okay. Respect, no pressure, right?"

Zane shoves a hand through his still-damp hair. When he dares to look at her, his chest tightens. He's been at a loss since Thanksgiving. It's not like he thought any of this would be easy. But why can't he catch a break? He waited, never once giving up on the ridiculous romantic notion she'd return one day, and she did. Over the last few months, he re-experienced what it was like to love her, and he had no idea how he coped for as long as he had. It was apparent she'd changed, but many things hadn't. The way she snapped the gum she was chewing, the small hop in her step when she walked and talked at the same time, and the way she twirled her hair around her finger using it to tickle her ear. She still had the dimple in the right corner of her cheek when she smiled her shy, apprehensive smile, and the animated way she jabbered when she was nervous still made him laugh. The devotion and empathy she showed toward her parents during the hardest time of their life was the Jessie he knew. She came back to Helena to face her demons. It took courage and determination. He loves everything about her, old and new.

She may have gotten used to hiding inside herself, afraid to show the world who she really is, but he can still see her. He saw her again today on the floor of the barn when she jumped right in the middle of the chaos to console the distressed pig.

He wants to spend more time with her and all of them because they are his family. It killed him to walk away, and there were times he entertained the idea of blaming Jessie. It would have been easy enough to hate her because then maybe he wouldn't have spent years loving an absent dream. But he refuses to hold her responsible.

Zane can't explain how much Thanksgiving meant to him. He has no idea why Libby agreed to have him there, but, he was grateful. He'd live the day over a million times if he could, except the innocent remark Jessie made reminding him of the skeleton in his closet. The harsh reality hovered close, and it terrified him.

When she came downstairs a few moments ago, he could tell she had been crying and berated himself for being an ass. All he'd wanted for as long as he could remember was to have her there. Now here she was, and he'd acted like an idiot.

"I'm famished," he says. "You?"

She nods, and he extends a hand to her. When she grabs it, he playfully yanks her to her feet.

"Let's make ourselves a meal."

• • •

Two hours later, they are full, happy, and sitting around the cluttered dining room table, once again lost in conversation about anything and everything that is important, except the obvious. Weiser hops between the two of them appreciative of the attention he is getting with their change of mood.

"You should get a Christmas Tree," Jessie nods toward the front window. "Put it over there."

"I can't remember the last time I had a Christmas Tree," he comments with a faraway look in his eye.

Jessie tilts her head. "Why?"

He stands up to clear the table. "I don't celebrate the holidays here, so there is no sense wasting the energy to put one up. I go over to Brent and Tonya's. They have a tree."

"Let's go get one tomorrow," she claps her hands excitedly. "Christmas isn't for another five days."

"You can't be serious," he chuckles. Opening the dishwasher, he begins to load glasses into the top rack.

One by one, Jessie hands him the plates after she rinses them. "I bet your grandparents left a box of decorations in storage. If they did, knowing you, you didn't have the heart to throw them away."

She couldn't be closer to the truth, he thinks in amazement.

Jessie glances at the time on her phone. "I have cupcakes to decorate this evening. I really should go."

Zane crosses his arms and presses his back against the counter, disappointment biting at him as he watches her clear the remaining dishes. He could get used to this. They complemented each other in the kitchen preparing the chicken enchiladas, as if it were the most natural thing in the world—him sautéing meat and shredding cheese while she diced tomatoes and made green chili from scratch. She gave directions, and he complied, admiring her culinary expertise. They flirted and teased naturally and on several occasions, he caught her blushing. When she reached around from behind him to help guide his hand while stirring the simmering sauce, her body lightly caressing his, it took all his willpower not to turn and take her into his arms.

He takes the glasses and utensils from her hands and sets them on the counter before turning to face her.

Jessie catches a whiff of his aftershave and steps closer. She can feel the heat of energy radiating off of him as she inhales the woody scent. She closes her eyes when his hand cups her cheek. He traces her delicate skin with his thumb until it rests softly over her lips. Her body quivers in anticipation as she places her hand softly on his chest.

Zane wants nothing more than to give her all he is, all he was, and all he can be. Until the fear of losing her again grips him tightly. He drops his arms to his side, rests his forehead against hers and sighs. When their eyes meet, her pain is unmistakable. Not knowing what to say, he tucks a strand of hair behind her ear while the ache in his chest intensifies.

Jessie steps back and wipes at her moist eye. "Tomorrow. Christmas Tree," she announces firmly. "We have to take your truck so pick me up at ten. It will give us plenty of time in the afternoon to decorate."

Zane shakes his head in amusement. "You are just as bossy and demanding as I remember."

• • •

Zane rings the doorbell at precisely nine-fifty-five and waits anxiously, rubbing his sweaty palms together. Libby answers the door, and though her smile is tense, it's not entirely disingenuous.

"Come in, boy," Zane hears a soft, breathless voice call from the living room.

Zane moves to stand beside Mel, who is laying almost flat on his back in the recliner.

"How are you doing today?" Zane asks.

"How...am...I...doing...today...what?" Mel squints with a mischievous smile.

"How are you doing today, old man?" Zane chuckles, using the pet name he and Tyson had for him as kids.

"Much...better."

Libby helps Mel adjust his positioning so he can sit at an angle. When she disappears into the kitchen, he places his hand over Zane's, patting it softly. "Jessie is...on...a...business call. You...can wait...with me."

Mel turns his gaze back to the *The Price is Right* but keeps his hand clamped tightly over Zane's. Zane shifts his attention to the television where Drew Carey receives a bear hug from an overly excited and very burly Navy Seal. Mel lets out a soft laugh. Something stirs inside him, sitting there with the man he loves like a father, their hands wrapped together. He doesn't know how much time Mel has left. In an automatic response, Zane places his other hand over Mel's and squeezes it affectionately.

Zane clears his throat nervously. "Mel, there's something I need you to know."

Mel holds up his free hand and shakes his head. "No!" he says emphatically.

Zane is surprised by his irritation. "But…"

A bout of coughing ends the conversation. Zane places the oxygen mask over Mel's face and adjusts the pillow behind his head. What was he thinking? Now wasn't the time or the place to spill his guts. His intention isn't to break the heart of a dying man the last days of his life.

Zane excuses himself to the bathroom, disgusted with himself. As he makes his way down the hall, he can hear Jessie on the phone in the back bedroom discussing the delivery time for her next catering event. Locking the door behind him, Zane turns on the faucet and splashes cold water into his face. After drying off with a towel, he stares in the mirror. Zane and Mel were a lot alike, and he knew if Mel found out the truth about his daughters, he would never forgive himself. Mel doesn't need that burden.

Zane exits the bathroom as Jessie is shutting the door behind her. His heart melts when she smiles at him. Before they leave, Libby hands them a thermos full of hot chocolate and tells them to have fun. She pats her daughter affectionately on the arm and repeats the gesture with Zane.

• • •

Later, laughing hysterically, they haul the tree up the porch steps and through the front door of Zane's house.

"Oh, you found the decoration! I had a feeling you knew where they would be," she winks.

After she left the night before, he was curious, and he couldn't close his eyes without remembering how it felt to have her close, so Zane searched the closet in the spare bedroom where he kept his grandparents keepsakes. As Jessie predicted, he found the Christmas decorations in the same spot he stored them years before.

They sit on the floor sifting through boxes of ornaments he and Tyson made in grade school and gave to his grandmother as well as others she collected. Zane recalls his mother taking them shopping each year to buy a special angel for her tree, and it looks like she kept them all.

"I had no idea she knew what ornament she was getting because we got her the same thing every year. Boy, did it make her happy. And I loved seeing her happy."

"She was lucky to have you two," Jessie comments, as she stands to hang another ornament. "You were her whole world."

Zane stares out the window at the falling snow.

"My grandparents and your parents saved our lives, you know. If it weren't for them, we would have turned out just like him," Zane's eyes grow dark.

Dumbfounded, Jessie turns to look at him. "What?"

Unsure of why he said what he did, Zane fumbles over his words. "Nothing. I was just rambling."

There is no mistaking the anguish on his face or the hostility in his words. Jessie steps over the box and kneels next to him on the floor, taking his hand in hers.

"You've spent your whole life determined not to be like him. You weren't back then, and you certainly are not now. You can't even make that comparison."

"I have a lot of anger because of him, Jessie. It's gotten worse over the years," he admits.

"Zane, you have got to believe me when I tell you if you were anything like him, I would not be here in your living room putting up a Christmas tree and getting sentimental about your grandmother's ornaments.

I am here because you don't have it in your heart to be like him."

Zane shakes his head sadly. "You don't know what I have in my heart, Jessie. There is a lot of ugliness."

"Well, then, that makes two of us."

Quiet and at a loss for words, they stare at the tree until a knock on the door startles them. With a quizzical look, Zane answers it to find Dawson with his friend, Amanda along with Brent, Tonya, and kids standing on his porch. Brent has a six-pack of beer tucked under his arm. Dawson has two bottles of wine, and both women are carrying cookies, baked bread, and sacks of other assorted goodies. All three kids are bundled up from head to toe and covered in snow as if they were playing outside.

"We saw you bring in the tree and decided it may be a celebration," Tonya said, pushing her way past him into the house as everyone follows.

Bewildered, Zane stammers through introductions, and soon the house is full of energy and holiday spirit. Zane pulls out his cell phone and extends an invite to Vicky and Tyson.

While the men take the rambunctious children outside to make a snowman, Jessie busies herself in the kitchen putting together a tray of cheese and crackers and assorted vegetables. She sends a text to Vicky asking her to pick up avocados and tortilla chips. Luckily, Jessie finds chicken breasts thawing in the fridge and cuts them into pieces before tossing with olive oil and seasoning. As she places the meat along with onions and pineapple chunks onto skewers, Tonya offers to help. Jessie searches Zane's cupboards until she finds paper plates and napkins, while Tonya opens a bottle of wine, pouring three glasses. Zane, bringing in the cooked skewers from the grill, hands the plate to Jessie and grabs himself a bottle of water as he heads outside to join the fun. An array of food soon covers the table.

"I hear you were high school sweethearts," Amanda, who Jessie found out has been dating Dawson off and on for the last few years, comments. "You two are adorable together. How on earth did he let you get away?"

Jessie, shifting plates around the table to make room for the chicken, stiffens. "It's complicated."

"That is exactly what Zane said," Amanda says, oblivious to the dynamics.

Tonya elbows Amanda in the ribs. "Zane says you're going to start a catering business here. That's exciting! Fill us in."

Jessie doesn't miss the delightful and appreciative look in the ladies eyes when she informs them of her decision to stay in Helena permanently.

"That is fantastic!" they squeal in unison.

Jessie raises an eyebrow. "You two sound like sisters."

"Speaking of sisters, here I am with your avocados," Vicky announces, shrugging out of her coat and handing Jessie the plastic bag. Vicky is familiar with the other two. She gives them both a quick hug and pours herself a glass of wine.

"This is strange," Vicky whispers a while later when she and Jessie are sitting on the couch alone.

With wine glasses in hand, they watch through the sliding glass doors as kids jump off the porch into piles of snow.

"What is?" Jessie asks.

"Zane, having people over." Vicky's eyes sparkle. "Look at you, acting all domesticated in his kitchen like the good little hostess you are."

"Oh, shut it!" Jessie swats her arm. "I just happened to be here."

"Yeah? How *did* you happen to be here?"

Jessie is filling Vicky in on the events of the previous day when a crying Sasha bursts through the door.

Vicky jumps up to intervene. "What happened? You have snow all over your face and down your coat! Look at your hands. They are red and frozen. Careful, no snow on the carpet."

Through chattering teeth and tears, Sasha tells on Shane. "He stole my gloves...and...and...pushed me in...the...the...snow!"

Vicky pries open the door and yells for her son to come inside and explain why his sister is crying.

The fathers herd their kids to the front porch where they strip off gloves, boots, and snow pants before going inside. They rush to the table like a pack of wolves and begin to devour the food. No one uses a plate. They stay rooted in one spot, shoving handfuls of food into their mouths, hardly chewing or breathing before something else goes in. Jessie watches in fascination and giggles when she sees the same shocked expression on Zane's face.

• • •

The thrill of the holiday captivates Jessie. Filled with vital energy and feeling rejuvenated, she hums along to carols on the radio while applying finishing touches on a three-tier wedding cake to be delivered early this afternoon for a Christmas Eve wedding. It is her last delivery for the week and after, she will return to help her mom with the Seafood Chowder for the evening dinner.

Despite her good spirits, this holiday is bittersweet. She is ecstatic the entire family will be at their childhood home for both days, like in her memories of Christmas's past. The main reason for this is because Mel is too fragile to leave the house. He drifts in and out of sleep more often than not, is hardly eating anything due to increased nausea and is starting to lose control of his bladder and bowels. The humiliation of this causes him to become irritable and restless.

This behavior is a shock to all of them, especially Libby. She handles it as well as can be expected, but Jessie and Vicky try to intervene when they can. When Sam and Tyson are at the house, the two girls take her on brief walks for fresh air or out to lunch for a much-needed break.

Today, when the home health nurse arrives, Jessie drags Libby along to deliver the cake. On their way home, they make a quick stop to look at another property. As they drive, Jessie shares her vision with her mother. Her bakery will be open from seven in the morning until two in the afternoon. She can cater for special events on the side if something comes up but feels that cookies, pastries, cupcakes, and cakes will keep her plenty busy.

She stops rambling when her mother doesn't respond. Jessie cranes her neck and finds her mom staring glumly out the window with tears falling into her lap. Jessie parks the car in front of a for-sale sign and reaches over the console to grab her hand.

Recognizing they've arrived, Libby promptly regains her composure. She removes her hand from Jessie's and wipes her tears. Without a word, she steps out of the car and follows Jessie inside. Sue shows them around the one thousand square foot home that was previously owned by an elderly couple who bought it in nineteen forty. They lived there until they passed away earlier this year. The house is quaint, inviting, and a perfect location for the new bakery assuring a comforting and pleasant experience for customers.

"This is it!" Jessie exclaims. "I feel it in my bones. Don't you feel like you just walked into your grandmother's kitchen?"

When she turns, she meets her mother's desperate expression.

Rushing to her side, Jessie wraps her arms around her. Libby lies her head on Jessie's shoulder and shakes uncontrollably.

"Will you give me a job?" she blurts out a moment later. "After he is gone…I just don't know what I will do with myself otherwise."

CHAPTER FIFTEEN

The entire family attends the Christmas Eve church service, except Mel who is at home with the nurse watching over him. Upon entering the building, organ music plays familiar carols while people snake through pews searching for seats in the overflowing sanctuary. Jessie feels the same intimate warmth as the last time she was here. As she looks around, she recognizes many faces. A few of her mother's close friends smile their greetings and familiar classmates, home for the holidays, wave hello. Typically, Jessie would attempt to avoid these interactions but finds she does not want to hide anymore. Instead, she responds with a confident smile.

Jessie forgot how much she loved church on Christmas Eve. Even as a teenager, while all of her friends were wrapped up in shopping, decorating, food, parties—Jessie loved the simplicity behind the true meaning of the holiday. It was about family and unconditional love.

With a full heart, her thoughts shift to Zane as they sing "Joy to the World." She doesn't know if he ever went to church or even believes in God at this point in his life, but she casually invited him along tonight. He politely declined. He was going to spend Christmas Eve with his mother but planned on stopping by her parents' house the following morning to watch everyone open presents per Tyson's suggestion.

After they sit, the minister starts his message. At first, Jessie is distracted by the reflection of candles bouncing off the stained-glass windows, but it's not long before she is drawn in by his words.

"Its life-changing to discover God wants to be your friend. He wants to get close and personal, to heal what's broken, giving us a life of love, friendship, and relationship like nothing we've experienced before. God sent his Son into the world to show us how much we are loved. Tonight we celebrate his birth."

Jessie leans forward in her seat.

"When God uses his love to change us, He builds change from the inside out. He does this by the renewing of our mind, our souls, and the healing of our hearts. When we suffer, He suffers. More than anyone, He is aware of the baggage we carry around—the guilt, the shame, the hurt, the brokenness. He doesn't remember the wrongs that we do. He forgives completely, but we, as humans, remember the harm done to us as much as we remember the harm we have done to those we love. *We* carry guilt and shame. He heals us by saying, 'I forgive you. Now it's time to forgive yourself.'

"His grace sustains, nurtures, and feeds us. It gives us energy and power to believe that His Holy Spirit is inside of us to give us confidence, strength, and joy. In knowing His love, we begin to believe what He says is true. We can start to think our lives are worth it. *Your* life is a whole lot more than how you've defined it. Start living with intention, make decisions to get out of your comfort zone, or with God's invitation make a commitment to change. God is good and strong, and He has what the world needs, but some of you have a hard time believing it can be for you. He wants a relationship more than anything. 'I desire mercy,' He says, 'not your sacrifice. I desire your heart, not your religious performance. I don't call you servants; I call you friends.' You are an unceasing spiritual being with an eternal destiny in God's great universe."

Tears well up in Jessie's eyes as he finishes. On either side of her, Sam and Vicky take her hand in theirs. At the comforting gesture, she drops her chin to her chest, and her shoulders begin to shake.

When the children are called to the front of the church to sing *Away in the Manger*, Jessie quietly excuses herself to get a tissue. She walks swiftly to the back of the sanctuary, and she opens the side door but is caught off guard when she finds Zane standing by himself. He, too, is shocked to see her.

"Hi," he says, clearly embarrassed.

"Hey."

Noticing her red eyes, he reaches for her hand. "You okay?"

Linking her fingers through his, she steps to him and nods. "That was powerful."

Zane pulls her close and circles his arms around her.

She rests her head on his chest. "What are you doing here?"

"I have no idea. I was at my mom's, and we were watching *Deck the Halls*. You know that Christmas movie with Tim Allen? All I could think about was how much you would hate it. Tim Allen's character wanted to take a trip to someplace warm to get away from everyone. The neighbors went overboard, treating them poorly because they were going out of town. Everything seemed fake and blown out of proportion. I know how much you love the true Christmas Story. It made me think. There are hardly any movies about it. Every year, people spend hours upon hours watching movies to get them into the Christmas spirit. I was doing the same thing when it dawned on me that the real spirit is here with you guys. I know nothing about all of this," he says, gesturing around him. "All I know is the love your family gave me growing up. In that, I learned to believe in miracles and something bigger than myself. When you left..." His voice catches.

Jessie lightly touches his cheek as his eyes shimmer with tears.

"What he said," Zane nods toward the front of the church. "Do you think it's possible?"

Jessie sinks deeper into his embrace and sighs. "All we can do is hope."

• • •

After church, at Libby's request, Zane picked his mom up and met them at the house. Joan, pleased to be there, gives everyone affectionate hugs. Although she is her quiet, gentle self throughout the evening, her delight is apparent with her face bright and full of enthusiasm. She watches her grandchildren dance in front of the television playing on their *Wii* while they excitedly explain their games to her. She doesn't seem to understand the scoring process, but claps her hands wildly and embraces them in a hug when they win. While she doesn't actively participate in the conversation, Joan listens politely, nodding her head in agreement with the topics. Everyone attempts to engage her, but she is perfectly content observing.

Mel spent most of his day in bed but now rests in his recliner dressed in candy cane pajamas. He still has a lot of fight in him and continues to hang on, one day after another, for just a little bit more time with those he loves.

After finishing every drop of the Seafood Chowder, they all gather in the living room to open presents. Jessie scans the room, taking in the activity around her when her eyes land on Zane. He stares at her with the same intense longing that weakened her knees years ago. She feels a magnetic pull to sit by him, but as she gets up to move, her sister shoves a small box in front of her.

"You're last, little sister," she announces. "You only get one gift this year. We all pitched in so if you don't like it, well...it's too bad," she smiles impishly.

While Libby adjusts Mel's recliner so he can sit up, Jessie tugs the silver bow and begins to unwrap the blue and white paper, carefully. Slowly, she pulls the top off what looks like an earring box and finds a single silver key lying inside. She picks it up between her thumb and index finger and looks at her parents suspiciously.

"Did you buy me a car?" she wrinkles her nose.

Libby clasps Mel's hand in her own and grins from ear to ear.

"A key to an apartment? You ready to have me gone?"

The room is silent as she looks from one person to the next in complete confusion. Finally, Sam breaks the news.

"We all pitched in on the down payment for the house that you looked at earlier today with Mom. She said it's perfect for your bakery. We figured you could work out the rest. If you want it, it's yours."

With wild enthusiasm, Jessie jumps up and runs into her mom's arms. She then leans over to her father and kisses his cheek.

Vicky, who disappeared into the kitchen moments earlier, returns with a bottle of champagne and a stack of plastic cups.

"Time to celebrate!" she announces, popping the cork.

• • •

No one is under the illusion that they will have another holiday with Mel. Therefore, everyone agreed to spend the night, allowing them to be together first thing in the morning. The kids were worried that Santa would not be able to find them, but Jessie explained Santa is aware families visit loved ones and are not always home. Even though he had a large book with names and addresses, he also followed their hearts. She went on to say part of the reindeer's jobs, especially Rudolph's, is to fly around and keep track of where all the children slept.

After Mel is in bed, Libby announces that she is going to take her grandkids for a drive to look at Christmas lights and invites a very eager Joan to join them. The grandmas load up the grandkids in Jillian's mini-van with hot chocolate in hand and carols on the radio. They set off, promising to be home in an hour. The rest head downstairs to play a game of pool.

The first game is husband and wife against husband and wife. Jessie and Zane watch from the couch, sipping on champagne. The losers of the game, Sam and Jillian, take on Jessie and Zane who wind up beating them as well. The two winners square off in the last game.

Jessie hasn't played pool since she was a teenager but quickly picks it up again. After a tense twenty minutes of strategizing, she calls the shot and sinks the eight ball in the corner pocket for the win. With contagious exhilaration, she jumps into Zane's arms. Jessie doesn't know who is more surprised—Zane when he catches her a few inches off the ground with her arms around his neck, her siblings and their spouses who watch in amusement, or Jessie herself for her out-of-the-ordinary, zealous behavior.

Jessie flushes, removes her arms from his welcoming embrace and sinks onto the couch. She picks up her glass of champagne and casually tips it into the air.

"I had a little bit too much to drink," she explains.

"I think everyone's back," Jillian comments, lifting her chin toward the ceiling.

They make their way upstairs where they find the kids busy with new toys and electronics. Sasha and Shelby take turns showing their grandmother Joan their new stuffed animals. Shane and Kelsey watch a video on his new portable DVD player. Vicky picks up the crumpled wrapping paper from the floor and gives the kids a stern fifteen-minute warning. They still need to get ready for bed, put out cookies and milk for Santa, and spread reindeer food in the front yard. Tanner, who at eleven figured out the truth about Santa, looks toward his mom and frowns. She returns his glare with a pleading gaze that says, "Please don't ruin this for the others." Sam and Tyson help Libby clear dishes off the table while Zane walks to the front door to get his mother's coat.

Jessie follows but can't look him in the eye. She's still embarrassed by her earlier display. It had nothing to do with drinking too much. The old Jessie wouldn't have thought twice about jumping into someone's arms after winning a game of pool. She would have danced around in circles and hooped and hollered for a few more minutes. The old, competitive Jessie would have challenged the other team to another game. All week and especially tonight, she'd felt like *that* Jessie. It was wonderful—until she saw the surprise on everyone's face. Now she is ashamed of her spontaneous outburst.

"It's okay, you know, to have a little bit of the old you mix with the new you," Zane says as if reading her mind. "You will eventually find the right balance, and I have a feeling, it will be perfect. The light in you is still alive. It's up to you if you want to make it shine or not."

Jessie does not look up from the floor.

Realizing his attempt to cheer her up failed, he takes a lighter tone. "I miss all of us hanging out. It's like old times."

"It is, isn't it?" she agrees, a smile spreading across her face.

Joan appears, ready to leave. Jessie watches as Zane helps her with her coat. After they say goodbye, she wanders into the living room where she positions herself on the floor next to the twins admiring their artwork as they color a large oversized card for Santa. They drew two stick figure reindeer, one with a red nose. There is a moon and a cluster of white snowflakes. A row of candy canes lines the bottom along with a slightly deformed large, red circle. There are a variety of shapes sticking out of the top and a string hanging from the side. Jessie assumes it must be Santa's bag of gifts. In big, bold print, they have written:

Thank you, Santa. We love you, and we are glad you found our hearts. Love Tanner, Kelsey, Shane, Sasha, and Shelby. XOXOXO

Jessie longs to have this sort of moment with her children someday.

"You want us to sign your name?" Kelsey asks.

"That would be nice," Jessie says, running her fingers through her niece's long blonde hair.

"Get teeth brushed and pajamas on. Then we'll finish up in here. The air mattresses are blown up downstairs. You all can have one big Christmas slumber party!" Vicky announces.

Cheers erupt. After five minutes of organized chaos, they are ready to set out the big plate of cookies and milk Libby prepared. Sam gives each of them a tiny bag containing reindeer food—a mixture of oatmeal and red and green glitter. Curious, Jessie peeks over Shane's shoulder and reads the little note attached to the baggie.

Magical Reindeer Food
Sprinkle on your lawn at night,
The moon will make it sparkle bright.
Santa's reindeer fly and roam;
This will guide them to your home

Bundled in winter coats and boots, the entire family steps onto the front lawn. When Tyson counts to three, the five children take their handfuls of food, toss it into the air and onto the snow. The three girls embrace in a hug while Tanner and Shane give each other a high five.

I look at Vicky. "Who started this tradition?"

"We did about five years ago," she explains as we walk inside. "You think this is new. Wait until I tell you about Elf on a Shelf."

"A what?"

Hanging her coat up in the closet, Vicky laughs. "That's a story for tomorrow."

• • •

On Christmas Day, as the family hoped, Mel was more alert and in a cheerful mood. He watched his grandkids unwrap their gifts while snapping photos with his cell phone, more engaged than even a few days before. He relaxed in his recliner for longer periods of time without napping. Although he didn't have much of an appetite, he ate some mashed potatoes in between sips of his smoothie and enjoyed a few bites of Eggplant Parmesan.

It gave everyone a false sense of hope they would have more time with him. Unfortunately, all the activity was too much, and in the aftermath, Mel begins to decline quicker than anyone could have imagined.

As the New Year approaches, they notice the confusion, common in the later stages of the disease. He's having more difficulty swallowing during meals. His pain and fatigue have increased immeasurably. He is unable to get to and from the rooms with a cane or a walker. Instead, he has to use the wheel chair or be carried. All of this makes him anxious, so he stays in his room more often than not. The hospital social worker, along with the home health nurses, did a wonderful job educating and preparing the family for what lay ahead, but witnessing it firsthand is a different thing entirely.

"Mom, are you sure you will be okay if we go to Zane's tomorrow? We can cancel and come here," Jessie offers.

"Good heavens, no!" Libby exclaims, a look of panic crossing her features. "No offense, but I don't want you here. Your father and I want to have the evening alone. Go, have fun. If I need something, you're only a phone call away."

Jessie doesn't feel entirely comfortable with the idea but decides it's not worth the argument. Instead, she begins to make a grocery list. She hasn't seen Zane since Christmas, but they text daily. It is his idea to have a New Year's Eve party and he ropes her into helping him plan it. She is excited to help and the anticipation of spending the afternoon with him ignites every nerve in her body. Her heart leaps when the doorbell rings.

When she opens the door, she is unprepared at how the pure masculinity of him takes her breath away.

Later they are walking through the grocery store, Zane pushing the cart and Jessie tossing items in the basket as she checks them off her list. The last thing they expected was an unpleasant encounter.

"Now *this* is something I never thought I'd live to see again," a familiar voice from behind them cries out dramatically.

Beside her, Zane groans while Jessie grits her teeth. She would know that sickeningly sweet voice anywhere. She looks over her shoulder at Dawn Kliwicky who studies them intently with one hand on her hip and the other holding the hand of a young boy with a tear-streaked face.

Dawn still has a long thick black mane of hair. Her big round eyes are caked in charcoal liner and thick mascara, while dominant cheekbones are a glaring pink and her pencil-thin lips are bright red. Dawn used to be a cheerleader with Jessie, but the petite young girl was replaced by a voluptuous woman with curves in all the right places. Premature wrinkles appear around her eyes and pinched, drawn skin circles her lips.

Dawn studies her from head to toe. "I heard you were back in town. Been a *long* time, Jessie. It's like you just disappeared."

Jessie's tightly presses her lips together, but Zane quickly intervenes by sticking his hand out to the boy. "Is this your little guy? He's a handsome kiddo."

Dawn blushes as she eagerly takes his hand instead. "Yes. He is my oldest. Luke, can you say hello to Mr. Zane and Miss Jessie? I went to school with them. He's seven and has a younger sister who is four. She's at home with her dad."

Jessie plants a fake smile on her face. "Hi!" she says to the young boy who glares at her from under his pout.

Dawn presses a manicured finger to her lips. "How have you been, Zane? I don't ever run into you."

"Ranch life is a busy life," he says. "It doesn't leave me much time for anything else."

"Well, it must," she looks sharply at Jessie. "Some things will never change, I imagine. Looks like you two are having a party."

"A family get-together to enjoy the holidays," Zane replies.

"Speaking of enjoying the holidays..." She giggles. "You were shocked to see me at that New Year's party in our freshman year of college. It's hard to believe it's been that many years. I guess it was my lucky night we wound up in the same place, *and* in the same bed," she slaps him flirtatiously in the arm. "Those memories are unforgettable."

Jealousy crashes into Jessie like a wave.

With a scowl, Zane places once hand on Jessie's lower back and the other on the cart as he pushes past Dawn.

"Funny, there are many things in life I consider unforgettable, and that wasn't one of them."

• • •

"Want to talk about that?" Zane asks on the drive back to the ranch.

"No," Jessie replies curtly. "I don't think there is anything to discuss."

It wouldn't matter what Dawn did or didn't say, Jessie felt triggered the moment she laid eyes on her. The emotions Dawn stirred up were enough to make Jessie physically ill. Granted, her comments didn't help, but Jessie wasn't ignorant enough to think Zane was completely alone over the years. She just wishes he hadn't found comfort in Dawn's arms.

"Then why are you upset?" he prods, bringing the truck to a stop in front of the house.

Weiser, hearing the vehicle pull up, trots out of the barn to greet them.

"I'm not upset," she says, jumping out.

Opening the cab door, she grabs the groceries and heads inside, ignoring Weiser. Zane pats the dogs head affectionately before retrieving the rest of the supplies.

Inside, he sets his bags down on the counter and watches her storm around the kitchen shoving fruit, vegetables, and various other items into his refrigerator.

"Are you finished?" he asks when the bags are folded and neatly put away.

"Yes. I think you should take me home now," she says, folding her arms.

Zane snickers, popping a grape into his mouth.

"I'm glad you find this amusing," Jessie snaps.

"I do, actually. You're jealous."

"Why would I be jealous of that? You do realize her boobs are fake, right?"

Zane tips his head back and laughs. "Yeah, that was pretty obvious. Jessie, let me explain."

"Please don't," she holds a hand up. "I don't want an explanation. I have no right."

"I think you do," he disagrees.

A part of her wants to cancel the party. She doesn't feel much like celebrating but knows canceling would be childish. Besides, she would only be running away again. If she wants a future with Zane, they can't keep tip-toeing around their complex history. It's time they talk. Really talk.

• • •

They make a truce to curb the subject, agreeing to prioritize the conversation as soon as possible. The following morning, Jessie runs eight miles and feels considerably better by the time she arrives at Zane's later that afternoon to prepare food for the party. She brought extra clothes along in case she gets dirty while working in the kitchen.

Carrying an armful of firewood into the house, Zane shakes flakes of snow off his damp head. After meticulously placing the wood into the fireplace, he strikes a match and the warm fire blazes to life. They make small talk while he helps her prepare stuffed jalapeno poppers and spinach artichoke pastry puffs. She punches the timer on the oven and explains how to cook baked brie with caramelized pears.

"This is a lot of fancy food," he comments from the other side of the kitchen where he is busy chopping vegetables. "Did we need to go to all of this trouble?"

"Are you kidding me?" Jessie's eyes widen. "This is not trouble. It's therapy! Keep cutting. Can you turn the music up while you are at it?"

Grinning, he obliges and clicks the volume button on the stereo remote as the beat of The Black Eyed Peas thumps through the speakers. He returns to his duty, but out of the corner of his eye, he admires Jessie as she begins to move to the music while lost in a trance with her art. He can see what she means, cooking heals her as ranch work does him.

For the next few hours, they fall into the comfortable groove as they shuffle around one another grabbing bowls, utensils, loading the dishwasher and of course, sampling their handy work. At seven-thirty, the doorbell rings. Vicky and Tyson are the first to arrive. With arms full, they shake off the snow, hang up their coats, and move into the kitchen. Tyson stocks the refrigerator with beer and champagne while Vicky plugs her slow cooker into the wall. She opens a bag of tortilla chips and dips one into the pot, scooping up a glob of queso.

"Brilliant!" she exclaims after she is done chewing. "Best I've made so far."

Sam and Jillian are next, and they too have their arms full of food and drinks. Tyson hands Sam a beer and is about to pour his wife a glass of wine when Brent, Tonya, Dawson, and his date arrive. His date isn't Amanda. Jessie politely shakes her hand as Dawson introduces Lily to the group. He notices everyone's confused expressions and explains Lily is his cousin. Amanda, a nurse at the hospital, is working and will join them later. Tyson and Zane stay busy playing bartender while Jessie and Vicky put food onto the table. Jillian answers the door as more guests, mostly coworkers of Vicky's arrive. It's not long before Zane pulls a card table from the back closet to start a game of poker. Meanwhile, the women mingle and chat in the living room.

"You didn't take the kids over to Mom's, did you? They were hoping to be alone tonight," Jessie frowns.

Jillian explains that her mother is in town and offered to stay with them all at their house. She brought along hats, noisemakers, and silly string to have their own party.

Over the next hour, as more alcohol is consumed, the card game becomes louder. Having lost several times, Tyson throws his hand on the table, pushes his chair back angrily, and seeks out his wife.

Dawson is next to fold, then Zane, and after that, the husband of a teacher from school folds too. Sam and Brent are left, taking turns staring at the cards in their hands and eyeing each other suspiciously. Finally, Sam balances on two legs of the chair anxiously and calls the betting. With a grin, he turns his cards over one by one, revealing a full house. Brent shrugs innocently, placing his cards face up. A royal flush. Laughing hysterically, Brent encircles the money with his arms and drags it toward him as Sam playfully curses.

Everyone's attention turns to the front window as headlights pull up the driveway.

"Is anyone else coming?" Jessie asks.

As far as she knew, everyone invited had already arrived, including Amanda who showed up a half hour ago. Squinting, she pushes the curtains back to get a better look, but with the heavy snow, she cannot make out the two figures walking up the steps. When the bell chimes, Dawson moves to answer it but is forced out of the way as a very drunk Dawn and another female, stumble through the door. They hold up bottles of champagne, whoop, and cheer as the house grows quiet.

Zane moves his way through the crowd to meet them.

"What are you doing here?" he says through gritted teeth.

"We were in the mood for a party," she leans toward him and playfully pokes him in the chest. "*You* are having a party."

He lowers his voice. "You weren't invited."

Dawn pushes her lower lip into a pout. "Are you sure about that? When I saw you at the grocery store yesterday, you seemed real keen on having me here."

Jessie takes shallow breaths, watching the exchange from across the room. She remains rooted to the spot, desperate to disappear. But as her gaze scans the people around her, she reminds herself she is a mature adult, and the last thing she is going to do is hide from someone as ridiculous as Dawn.

Jessie moves beside Zane and greets them politely yet with a firm, determined look in her eyes. "Come inside. But keep your coats on, you won't be staying long. We'll call you a cab. The roads are awful and crazy drivers are everywhere. Zane, will you call while I get Dawn and her friend some food."

He pulls the cell phone out of his pocket. Dialing, he disappears into the hallway as Jessie leads the two compliant ladies into the kitchen and hands them a plate.

"Help yourself. It looks like you two could use some substance to absorb the alcohol."

They shovel spoonfuls of food onto their plate. When Zane returns to stand next to Jessie, he casually drapes his arm around her shoulder.

"How about your friend eats in the living room while the three of us talk, Dawn," Jessie urges.

The friend obliges, sensing the tension, and disappears.

After taking a sip of champagne, Dawn presses her hips against the counter as she tries to balance the plate of food in her other hand. When she realizes she can't hold both, she sets the bottle down and picks up her fork.

"What did you think you were going to accomplish by coming here tonight?" Jessie asks calmly.

"To party," she states with wide, innocent eyes. She shoves the fork into her mouth but talks around it. "You going to tell her about us, Zane?"

"There is no *us* to tell."

"But there's a story between you two," Dawn sings, pointing the fork at them.

Her smile dissolves into a frown when her eyes land on Jessie who remains stone-faced and somber with her arms crossed over her chest.

"Zane and I are friends."

"You two were always *just* friends. That's what happened on prom night, right? You were just friends who I was stupid enough to double date with. I am the one who wound up going home alone."

Jessie's wrinkles her nose "Is that what this is about? That is ancient history, Dawn. Let it go."

"I will not let it go!" she cries, throwing her plate on the table, splattering food everywhere. "You two ruined my life. The night I was with Zane after you broke up and left for college, I've been waiting years to throw that in your face so you will know once and for all what it feels like to have someone stab you in the back."

Jessie bolts out of her seat, slamming her hands on the table, fire raging in her eyes.

"Don't you dare sit there and tell me how *your* life was ruined. You think that was a bad night? You have no idea, absolutely no idea what a bad night even is."

"You are being dramatic. It was your choice to break up with Zane, not his. Don't act like it was your heart that broke. He told me why you left."

Jessie spins around glaring at Zane. "What did you tell her?"

"Go ahead, Dawn. Keep digging that hole you're about ready to climb into," Zane replies disdainfully.

Dawn pushes off the counter and approaches Jessie.

"Lots of rumors swirled about you having a guy on the side. Zane found out, and that's why you left. It makes me sick how careless you were with him. You just didn't want *me* to have him. Did you give any consideration to the fact you ruined *his* life? Yes, he was drunk the night we spent together, but it was clear how devastated he was. He took all the blame. He kept saying how much you would hate him if you knew the truth, and he was lucky he wasn't in jail. I knew then he was never going to get over you. Now you're back to toy with his heart all over again."

Jessie narrows her eyes into slits and grabs Dawn by the arm, digging her nails into the pale flesh.

"You have no idea from a drunk one-night stand what Zane has been through," she says through clenched teeth. "You can't even fathom the hell of the last thirteen years, and as much as I loathe you, Dawn, it's something I hope you never have to experience."

• • •

Wrapped in a blanket, Jessie stands on the front porch watching the vehicle pull away. The guests, oblivious to what transpired in the kitchen, continue to enjoy the party, but Jessie is not ready to join in. She sits on the swing with her legs dangling using her toe to push back and forth while her teeth chatter from the cold.

Dawn was surprised by Jessie's outburst. Jessie was surprised by her outburst. Zane, on the other hand, didn't seem shocked. Instead, he stepped between the two instructing Dawn to wait for her cab in the living room. When she left, he pulled Jessie into his arms. In the comfort of his embrace, she stopped shaking. A moment later, she unraveled herself, grabbed a blanket off the back of the couch, and walked outside.

Zane escorts the two unwelcomed guests to the cab after it arrives. When the taillights are no longer visible, he stuffs his hands into his pockets and slowly climbs the steps.

They listen as everyone inside begins the countdown, and a moment later, hear the loud cheers of "Happy New Year!"

"Mind if I sit with you?" Zane asks.

Jessie doesn't answer but continues to stare absently at the inky blackness of the sky.

Defeated, he turns to the door. "Don't stay out too long. The temperature is going to drop."

"This isn't how I envisioned this evening turning out," she says, her voice full of disappointment.

"Me either," he turns back to her.

She stops the swing and pats the seat beside her. When he sits, she reaches for his hand, appreciating the warmth it holds.

"Why were you so nice to her?" Jessie comments.

He squeezes her hand tightly. "The world breaks everyone. She's no exception. She wants to blame us, but it wasn't prom night that ruined her."

The door creaks open and Dawson, Lily and Amanda followed by Brent and Tonya come to say good-night.

They stand up to exchange hugs when the group of teachers trail out couple by couple. They take turns saying thank you before climbing into separate vehicles. Zane places his hand protectively on the nape of Jessie's neck, and they watch their neighbors grow smaller, disappearing into the dark of the night as they walk toward their homes.

"Despite the obvious, did you have fun?"

Jessie leans her head on his shoulder. "I imagine it's been the best holiday either of us had in a while."

"Best I've had in my life," Zane remarks. "Let's help them clean up so everyone can get home."

Zane's hand slides to her lower back as he follows her inside expecting to find their siblings busy at work. But everything has already been put away, and the house is empty and silent.

Zane gives Jessie a skeptical look. "Where'd they go?"

Before she can answer, they notice the slider door is slightly ajar and hear the remaining cars pull away.

"I guess that was their way of saying goodbye and have a good night."

With a weary sigh, Jessie pulls out a chair and collapses into it. Zane sits beside her. He searches for the right words as he takes her hand and begins to toy with her fingers.

"You have no idea how much I wish I could take back that night with her."

Jessie rubs her tired eyes. "I'm mad at myself. If it weren't for me, you wouldn't have been in that position."

"Jess, that's not fair."

"No, Zane, it's more than fair," she replies angrily, pulling her hand away. "I put you through hell. I put my family through hell. Look at all of you, treating me as if I had done nothing wrong. Aren't you mad? Don't you hate me?"

Zane presses his fingertips into his temple and looks away. "Sometimes." he admits. "Hating you might make it easier, but I don't have that right."

She stares at him quizzically. "That doesn't even make sense."

"I could ask you the same thing, you know? If you hate me simply because of who I am."

Jessie doesn't have time to make heads or tail of his innuendo when the melody of a familiar song promptly shifts her attention.

Zane brings her hand to his lips. "This song always reminds me of you," he says, his voice so low, she can hardly hear him.

With a gentle tug, he pulls her to a stand. He places a finger under her chin, tilting her head until their eyes lock.

Her trembling fingers stroke his cheek. Zane turns his head and plants a faint kiss into her palm. On a slow exhale, she leans into his chest where he wraps his arms around her, letting his lips rest on the top of her head. With the soft music playing in the background, they sway from side to side in their rhythmic dance.

Zane moves one hand on the back of her neck while the other makes small, slow circles at the base of her spine. "I love those memories with you, Jessie. The memories are all we seem to have, though. I want to start making new ones."

Jessie fades into him, remembering every sensation he ever stirred in her, loving the security of the old as it mixes with the excitement of the new. Jessie explores him, making sure he is not an illusion. Her hands move up his back until her fingers are tangled in the hair at the nape of his neck. When she moves her thumb tenderly across the rough stubble of his chin and rests it on his bottom lip, Zane releases a long, deep moan. She peeks out from below her lashes, recognizing the hunger staring back at her. There is something else behind his eyes—compassion and loyalty.

Unable to resist the pull he has on her, she places a hand on his shoulder and arches up on her toes until her lips hover inches from his. She lingers for a moment, delighting in the familiarity of his musky scent and warmth of his skin. Closing her eyes, she leans closer, riding on the vitality of his breath.

With one swift movement, he pulls her against him and covers her mouth. Treading lightly at first, he softly grazes her lips only to become consumed with the taste of her he remembers so well. His hands thread through her blonde locks, and he feels her shock melt away as she weakens under his touch. A jolt of passion he denied himself for too long forces him to deepen the kiss.

For weeks, Jessie was unable to compete with the blaze that was barely simmering below the surface. Now that it has jumped to life, she no longer has control. As Zane releases another pleasurable groan, her mouth responds in increased urgency. When she wraps her legs around his waist, he easily carries her into the living room and carefully places her on the couch. He leans over her, his tongue continuing to plunge, explore and entice while his hands vigorously stroke the lean curves of her athletic body.

When the music ends, there is nothing but silence surrounding them, and for some unexplainable reason, this unnerves her. She begins to feel claustrophobic under his weight. When he whispers her name, the sound of his voice breaks the trance, and she begins to hyperventilate.

"Stop, Zane. Stop. I said, stop it!"

She pushes on his chest with all of her strength and quickly rolls out from underneath him onto the hardwood floor. She cowers as visions of being hit invade her mind. She curls into a ball and begins to cry.

Zane feels helpless and shifts into a seated position.

"You don't have to be afraid. I'm not going to hurt you."

"Shit!" Jessie spouts between sobs. "I know you won't. Until the day I die, I know you won't hurt me. I'm screwing this whole thing up."

"There is nothing to be sorry for."

"Yes, there is. I'm damaged goods, Zane. I've been with a lot of other men. I've even been with a woman and this, this sex stuff, I'm no good at it."

Zane slips off the couch onto the floor beside her.

"I don't care who you've been with. We all have a past. I slept with my share in a drunken stupor trying to get over you. I wouldn't chalk any of it up to a good time."

Burying her head in her arms, she cries. "Zane, you were supposed to be my first! It got all screwed up, and then I had all these shitheads, and it was awful. I don't like sex. I've tried, but I just don't. Jesus, look at you! You are hot, and all manly and sexy as hell, and you deserve someone who wants this with you. That's not me. I don't know what I'm doing."

Jessie swallows back a sob as she rests her head on his shoulder.

Zane kisses her forehead while combing his fingers through her hair.

He breaks the embrace and searches her face. "Let's start over, Jessie. I may not be your first, but let me be your last, your forever. Let me love you. That's all I ever wanted, to show you what you deserve. The way *we* are meant to be."

Jessie melts into his arms, tired of denying what she feels. She seeks out his mouth longingly, and when his lips move against hers, she releases a long, liberating breath. He promises to make her feel safe and secure as he gently lowers her to the floor.

Making love with Jessie evokes sensations in him he never knew. Slowly, inch by inch, moment by moment, Zane takes his time to tickle, tease and entice. The way she anticipates and squirms under his touch intensifies the burning hunger. His greatest desire is to bring pleasure to her in every caress and every desperate kiss. He wants to take away any negative experiences before this night.

After all the hurts and challenges, they are finally together, and he knows it will never be enough. He wants to, no, he *needs* to commit their passion to memory. Because if, for some horrible reason, he never gets the chance to touch her again, at least this night will be emblazed in his mind forever.

CHAPTER SIXTEEN

Zane rolls onto his stomach into the middle of the bed and snakes his arm around Jessie's bare torso as she begins to stir.

"Do you have to go home?"

"Sometime, but not right away." Jessie lifts her head, giving him an imploring look. "Why? You have something in mind?"

Fully awake now Zane rolls over until his body is fully covering hers.

"Would it scare you if I asked you to be domestic with me today and help take down Christmas decorations? It's not that I need the help, but I would like the company. And we can do this a little more."

Jessie's heart skips a beat as the previous night floods her thoughts. What he did to her was magical, unforgettable, and deliciously intoxicating! Jessie was pleasantly surprised with herself. Somehow Zane brought out the hidden vixen within her, a part of her she knew she possessed, and even craved exploring as a teenage girl in love, but never gotten the chance to. For too long, she felt dirty and disgusting. She couldn't imagine finding pleasure and satisfaction in an act that caused her suffering. Zane held to his promise. He showed her something different, and he somehow made her forget. He replaced years of horrific memories with thrilling desire and exhilaration. She surrendered to him and allowed the explosion of sexual freedom to flow from her like a freshly uncorked bottle of champagne. After, he held her while she shed tears of relief and intimacy. She never felt so completely connected to another human being.

If there was any doubt in her mind about her love for Zane, it mysteriously disappeared. The unselfish and tender way he handled her...he gave her the very best gift he possibly could, an invaluable display of devotion. She didn't realize two individuals could mold into one, sharing the highest form of consciousness. What she feels for him is indescribable, and despite the complications they still have to work through, she isn't going to let him go.

● ● ●

Zane and Jessie stay in bed until one in the afternoon making love, drifting in and out of sleep, discussing her plans for the bakery, and then making love again. Zane sneaks out a few times to do his ranch chores. Jessie offers to help, but he insists she stay in bed and keep it warm. Finally, after his second round outside, a cold and famished Zane suggests they make breakfast.

In the kitchen, Jessie fries bacon while Zane monitors the waffle maker. He smirks as he shovels the still steaming golden waffle onto a plate. "Voila!"

While they eat, her phone bings announcing a text. She ignores it. Five minutes later it starts to ring. She glances at it before tossing it into her purse annoyed.

Later, they are relaxing in the bathtub surrounded by candles and bubbles up to their necks. Jessie rests comfortably against Zane's chest.

"Did I tell you that I am glad you decided to stay in Montana?" he says.

"I think you may have mentioned it."

"We don't need to talk about it now because I know there are still a lot of things to hash out, but I want you to know my intentions, Jessie. I want all of this, all of you. You bring light into my world where it has mostly been full of dark. Without you, things are just 'blah.'"

"Blah," Jessie repeats. "That's an interesting description."

Zane pulls his hand out of the water flicking droplets onto her face. "I'm serious."

"I know. I appreciate it, but can we curb it for now? I'm not going anywhere, Zane. But I like how light-hearted all of this is, and I'm not ready for serious conversations yet. I need to enjoy you."

Zane kisses the top of her damp head. "You go ahead and enjoy the hell out me as often and as much as you need."

• • •

In the early evening, Jessie finally calls her mom explaining she won't be home again. It's an awkward conversation but, at thirty-one, Jessie isn't going to lie, especially about this.

Zane is bringing boxes and plastic tubs out from storage when she hangs up.

"How's your dad?" he asks, placing the boxes on the stack already sitting on the living room floor.

"No change," she says with a heavy heart.

"If you feel like you need to go home. I'm not going anywhere," he winks. "We can see each other tomorrow or the next day or even the day after that."

Jessie smiles, appreciatively. "I want to be here. The emotional rollercoaster is wearing on all of us. Mom's exhausted, he is exhausted. The break is nice. We've all told him it's okay if he needs to go. He keeps hanging on as if there is something else he's waiting for. We understood with the holidays, but now we aren't sure what that something is."

Feeling somber, Jessie stands up from where was crouched on the floor stuffing Christmas lights into a box. She stretches her arms over her head and then begins to remove ornaments from the tree. Zane wraps his arms around her from behind and nuzzles her neck.

"How about we do the rest of this tomorrow? Let's be lazy and watch a movie instead."

A grateful Jessie agrees and rifles through Zane's DVD collection. He goes to the kitchen to make a bag of popcorn and grabs two sodas out of the fridge. When he returns, he finds the opening credits of *Pulp Fiction* playing on his television.

"Are you serious? You want to watch this?"

"I want to watch a movie that reminds me of you," Jessie replies.

Zane's amusement reaches his eyes as he takes a seat next to her on the couch. She curls her legs up beside her, covers them both with the blanket and snuggles her body in close. As they watch, they are absorbed by the swelling desire they cling to out of fear and desperation. Once again, they become consumed by their love.

• • •

"Shit," Zane murmurs under his breath as he looks at the text Brent sends at seven-thirty the following morning. Zane forgot about a meeting with a butcher from Big Fork who is driving through Helena on his way home from the holiday.

After a shower, he grabs the coffee Jessie has waiting for him in his thermos and a donut. On his way out the door, he gives her a slow, lingering kiss promising he will not to be more than a few hours.

"I'm going to clean up the rest of this Christmas mess, so when you get home, all you have to do is dump that tree somewhere outside."

Radiating in the euphoria of the last few days, Jessie hums to herself as she floats from room to room gathering miscellaneous decorations. On her tiptoes, she reaches above the window frame to remove the strands of garland and then links the wreath from the front door on the crook of her elbow. In the dining room, she stuffs each piece into plastic tubs. After she packs the ornaments away, she notices there is nothing to put the lights in. She makes her way from one spare room to the next trying to remember which closet Zane found the boxes in the day before. Puzzled, she closes the door of his office and checks the hall closet. With no luck there, she goes upstairs to the guest bedroom but again, does not find any empty tubs or boxes big enough to use. She decides to check Zane's bedroom closet. She flicks on the light and proudly grins when she spots a large cardboard box shoved to the very back of a shelf, sitting alone.

It's too high for her to reach, so she considers waiting until Zane gets back. However, she wants to have all of this done, and the house cleaned so they can spend the afternoon in town running errands. Along with supplies for her next catering job, she still needs to sign documents at the bank for her business loan and pick up the home inspection report.

Construction is set to begin tomorrow to expand the kitchen. The work includes tearing down two walls from the dining space and living area to have a more open concept for the customers. Last week, she purchased new appliances, the glass display counter, furniture, and old-fashioned decor. Aside from a few other small loose ends to tie up, Jessie feels confident about the grand opening, set for the week before Valentine's Day.

Maybe that is what her dad is hanging on for, Jessie speculates.

She looks around Zane's room for something to stand on. She spots a rustic footstool made out of a large, piece of cedar. It's heavy, but she manages to move it into the closet where she balances herself on the small round top reaching for the box with her fingertips. As the box moves slightly to the right, she can tell it is not very heavy. She prays whatever's in it is not breakable as she jumps up a few inches to give it a final push and leans back as it tumbles to the floor in front of her. She hops off the stool, squats down and turns the box upside down.

Jessie's chest tightens as she exhales deliberately. Bewildered, her trembling finger traces her embroidered name on the cheerleading bag. She fumbles as she unzips it. After a moment of clarity, her breath becomes rapid, and she begins to gasp for air. One by one the jagged pieces of the last thirteen years shatter while the remaining few finally fall away, disappearing beneath her into an abyss of nothingness.

• • •

He's been calling her name for the last five minutes. He knows she hasn't gone home since her car is still outside, but when she doesn't reply, panic grips him. He sprints all over the house from room to room. He searches until he finally rushes upstairs. His closet is the last place he considered, but once he bursts through the door, practically out of breath, he finds her on the floor curled in a ball. With her hands clenched in fists, her teeth chatter as she rocks back and forth, staring at the blank white wall underneath Zane's hanging wardrobe.

Fear pulses in his temples as he reaches down to comfort her. Jessie recoils at his touch. She sits up and quickly places her foot on his chest. Growling through gritted teeth, she uses all of her strength to push him away.

Zane tries to speak but catches a glimpse of the royal blue canvas bag crumpled at Jessie's side. Dumbfounded, he backs out of the closet until he feels the bed behind his legs. He eases himself onto the mattress while Jessie glares at him, her eyes full of malice and betrayal. The only sound in the room is the ticking of the clock on the hallway wall.

Finally, she breaks the silence. "Where did you get this?" she demands, lifting the bag.

Folding his hands in his lap, Zane's face fills with agony. "You know where I got it."

A whimper escapes her lips. "You know what's in it?"

Zane nods.

"Oh God!" she wails. "You knew!" she tosses out the accusation. "Always?"

He nods. "From the day it happened."

Although her legs are weak and shaky with emotion, Jessie pulls the straps of the bag over her shoulder and pushes herself up. As calm as humanly possible under the circumstances, she darts past Zane, down the stairs, and out the front door, letting it slam behind her.

Zane drags himself to the window and watches helplessly as her car drives away. Grief-stricken, he can't help wondering if, for the second time in his life, he's made a choice that will leave him destroyed.

• • •

She runs. Because this is what she does.

As her car races down the highway and tears fall from her eyes, Jessie once again runs from herself, from the man she loves, from the memories. The desire to escape crushes any rational thoughts. Her brain violently attacks, mercilessly beating her up with a version of history she is unfamiliar with.

Her life could have been different, she thinks, if Zane had just....

Jessie brings her car to a screeching halt in the middle of the road on the outskirts of town. She takes another brief moment to gather her thoughts and calm her shaking hands. She knows what she has to do. Praying she doesn't get pulled over for speeding, adrenaline pulsates through her as she punches the accelerator of the car and races home.

Once inside, Jessie confronts her mother. "I need Zane's letters," she says urgently. "Please?"

In stony silence, Libby disappears down the hall. She returns a moment later holding a large manila envelope with Jessie's name scrawled on the front. Reluctantly she hands it to her. Jessie reaches in and pulls out a stack of unopened letters held together with a rubber band.

She stuffs them into her purse and gives her mom a quick peck on the cheek before she leaves.

• • •

As the winter sun begins to creep methodically below the horizon, Jessie sits in her parked car overlooking the valley of her hometown below. Two hours later, her eyes are blurry with tears as she reads the words over again. The letters are written and dated in September, October, and November of 1996. All of them are an outpouring of Zane's soul. In the first five, he begs her to come home, explaining what transpired on the day they were supposed to meet—that in his snooping around the guesthouse, he was the one who found the videos of the girls. In the letters, he confesses his outrage and blindsided reaction which led him to leave the ranch in search of his father, oblivious to his plans for the rest of the day. He admits that when he arrived at the ranch four hours later, the guesthouse was empty except for the visible signs of what had taken place. In later letters, Zane updates her about his move to Bozeman for college, his roommate, his classes, and the minute details of his day. It's as if Jessie can visualize herself walking beside him, an observer of his life for those short months.

Zane's guilt and shame for not protecting her, apologies for not being more persistent when she refused to see him, along with his undying love, never-ending commitment, and pleas for forgiveness seep onto every page. There is something else, too. In each letter, he guarantees her safety.

My father will never lay hands on another woman again. His reign of terror over all of us...Tyson, me, my mom, Vicky, you, and other innocent girls...it's over, Jessie. His power is dead.

Raw with despair, she stares blankly toward the silver light of the moon as she clutches the final letter to her chest. It's dated December 24, 1996. Unable to stop herself, she reads the words of a desperate young man one last time.

Jessie,

It's Christmas Eve, and I decided not to go back to Helena. No point really. I know you aren't there which is hard for me to understand. This is your favorite holiday. I can't help but wonder where you are and what are you doing tonight. Will you be going to church like you have for the last eighteen years?

I've always felt like you had this special connection with God. I believe you are one of His all-time favorites, and He likes to listen to what you have to say just as much as I do. So, I'm wondering if I can ask you a favor. When you talk to Him, can you maybe say an extra special prayer for me? Can you ask Him to forgive me for not being the man you needed? I have done some horrific things in my life, but these last four months...well, I need you to ask Him to give me some grace. I can probably use some strength too. I feel like I'm floundering here in Bozeman. Everywhere I look and everything I do...I am reminded that you are supposed to be here with me.

Every night after I study, I leave my dorm room and climb the hill behind campus where I sit and stare at the stars, wondering if you might be watching them too. And if you are, if it's somehow possible to reach you over the miles between us. I miss you. I've never felt such complete utter emptiness in my life as I do now. I know the world is unkind, but on the days I don't want to get out of bed, I can't help but wonder why it wants to continue to hurt me. What did I do wrong?

I pray that you have received my letters. I don't know what your lack of response means. Do you think about me and our love? Do you ache for me the way I do for you? Do you even want to put this behind us so we can move forward together?

Or do you hate me?

I don't want to be a nuisance, but it seems these letters have become my crutch, my only hope. That makes me feel even weaker. So I have decided this will be the last one unless I get a response from you. Please understand that doesn't mean I am giving up. I will never give up on you or us. But how does the saying go? If you love someone, set them free, if they come back to you, it's meant to be. We are meant to be, Jessie. Everything in my being tells me that. But I realize, I need to set you free too, so you can take care of whatever it is you need.

I just want to say thank you. You and your family loved me when you didn't have to. You showed me who I want to be, how I want to love, and what mark I want to leave on the world. But I don't want to do it without you. So, I will wait. If and when you decide to come home, Jessie, I will be here. Don't ever doubt that.

There is nothing in this world that can ever change the way I feel about you.

Zane

PS: I know Vicky feels the same. She will be here too.

As the demons she allowed to define her slowly dis-integrate, they are replaced with anguish. Zane knew the truth. And he still loved her. Ron took away her inno-cence, but her own damn stubbornness and pride took away her happiness, her future. No one was responsible for that but her. Vicky was right. God and the world didn't conspire against her. She was the one who kept herself trapped inside the box chained to her irrational insecurities.

Flanked by guilt and consumed with this informa-tion, Jessie doesn't notice the consistent vibrating of her phone or the various text message in her inbox. Instead, she unzips her cheerleading bag and pulls three videotapes from a pile of over a dozen. All three have labels with white stickers on the side. One says Julia, another Carrie, and the last Dawn.

She returns the tapes to the bag, full of empathy. Carefully, she folds the letters, stuffing them into their envelopes and bundles them with the rubber band. Opening her glove compartment, she lifts up the var-ious vehicle paperwork and hides the stack of letters beneath them.

The sound of tires on gravel startles her out of her daze as Zane's truck pulls up beside her. Jessie steps out of her car to meet him but is caught off guard as Zane sprints around the front of the truck taking her by the arms, his face pale and covered in grief.

"Jesus, Jess! We have to go! It's your dad!"

PART FOUR

CHAPTER SEVENTEEN

Mel — 1996

"Don't you look dapper!" Libby exclaims as she drags a delicate hand down my back, straightening the suit jacket.

I shake my head as I stare at myself in the full-length mirror. "I don't know about dapper. That makes me think of Fred Astaire. I am hoping for something more along the lines of Bruce Willis—charming, funny, and sophisticated with a little bit of badass in him. What do you think?"

"Oh, Bruce Willis is good." I see Libby grin over my shoulder. "I never thought of that, but yes, there is a bit of an uncanny resemblance."

Turning around, I take her in my arms. "You ready to see me walk our oldest daughter down the aisle?"

Libby claps her hands around my neck, giving it a slight tug. I lean in to touch her lips.

"I don't think it's a matter of if *I'm* ready. I think it's a matter of if *you* are ready."

I return to the dressing room where I take off the tuxedo placing the slacks and jacket on the appropriate hangers. *Am I ready?* That is a loaded question. Is anyone really prepared to watch their little girl get married? Even to a kid they like?

I say *kid* because that is how I still see Tyson. Twenty-two or not, he's still a kid. I love the boy like he is my own and genuinely could not imagine a better partner for Vicky, but Christ! They are young. Libby and I didn't get married until we were twenty-six and twenty-eight, and looking back on that, at how much we have changed over the years, we were naïve to the obstacles that lied ahead.

All I can do is hope they have good heads on their shoulders to be willing to face the challenges together. They are going to come, like it or not and to make it through to the other side, they have to navigate the most important partnership of their lives.

As I exit the dressing room, I hand the tailor my suit, and he reminds me it will be ready to pick up two days before the wedding. I take Libby by the hand, and we walk to the car. I'm quiet on the drive home. If she notices, she does not say anything. This is one of the many things I love about my wife. When I need time to think, it's as if she can read my mind. She does not bulldoze me with annoying questions or nitpick my feelings. She gives me space and time to work through my thoughts, and then if I feel like talking, I know she is my haven.

I look at my wife, flooded with admiration. Libby is stoic. My rock. She is not what you would call an overly emotional person. Does she feel? Deeply. Does she show it? Not always. Can she express it? Yes, but only to certain people who earn the right. No matter what we have had to face as a family, Libby takes the bull by the horns and deals with it. She does not complain, she does not whine, and she does not create drama.

It's not that her life has been picture perfect. Her father was a severe alcoholic. After he returned home from the war, he turned to the bottle. At the time, veterans were not being diagnosed or treated for the trauma they experienced but knowing what she knows now, it's obvious he suffered from it. He never discussed his experiences in the military, but Libby recalls hearing him wake up in the middle of the night screaming, and watching her mother talk him down after many panic attacks.

Although the drinking helped with the nightmares and anxiety, his anger swirled beneath the surface like a volcano on the verge of erupting. He never laid a hand on them physically, but as children, Libby and her siblings witnessed many violent fits of rage. Sometimes it was something as simple as a vehicle repair gone wrong. His patience wore thin, tools went flying, and things would get broken. Other times when Libby or one of her brothers became defiant, as most children do one time or another, her father grabbed the nearest object such as a full ashtray, a plate of food or textbooks from school. He threw whatever he could against the wall and then turned his rage toward a table or chair, tossing them on their side before storming out of the room. The kids quickly learned to scamper out of the way while Libby's mother made excuses or ran after him in an attempt to deescalate the situation. When he drank, he was impossible to reach.

When he was sober, he was a kind, playful, hard-working, a God-fearing man who doted on his wife and kids. Libby used to fall asleep praying for God to help her daddy, and to this day, she attributes her strong faith and the power of miracles to those prayers being answered.

Five years after the war ended, Libby's father left. Her mother told them he took a job out of town. As a sales rep for a lumber company, traveling was not unusual. Libby doesn't recall the specifics because she was too young, but she thinks he was gone for five weeks. She found out years later that, while drinking at a local bar, he and his brother got into a physical altercation. Libby's uncle was knocked unconscious and taken to the hospital. Drunk and scared, her dad ran to the home of their pastor begging for help. The pastor lived on a ranch sixty miles out of town, and his wife, who was a nurse, helped him while he detoxed. Along with daily prayer and scriptures, he worked around the ranch for a small wage. He returned home a changed man who never touched a drop of alcohol again.

Libby was drawn to Tyson and Zane when they started coming around. In them, she saw the scared kid she used to be because of her experience with her father. Unfortunately, despite the miracle that turned her father around, there was nothing that would change Tyson and Zane's situation. Libby's father was a good man with bad behaviors due to circumstances out of his control. Their father, on the other hand, was pure evil. In his eyes, she saw his pleasure from controlling and instilling fear in others. She sensed his narcissism and knew there was no repentance in his body.

When the boys were at the house, though her heart broke over the things she knew, she kept her emotions in check. While the girls and Sam were aware she didn't particularly care for Ron, she was never critical of him to anyone other than me.

"They are going to have their share of baggage and opinions to figure out. They certainly don't need me to unload mine on them as well," she reminded me often.

I push the button on the garage door opener and watch it rise as I slowly pull in the sedan. Once we are at a full stop, Libby reaches into the back seat to grab the bags of ribbon she bought from the fabric store.

"Do you think this is okay? The two of them getting married in less than a month?" I finally voice out loud before she can open the car door.

"You know it is, Mel. I can't shake the strange feeling, either, but I don't think it's about Vicky and Tyson. I think it has more to do with how awkward it's going to be to share this special day with such a jerk and fake the whole 'bringing two families together' bullshit."

I chuckle. It's rare for my beautiful wife to speak words like that, so when they do leak out, I know it's got to be pretty serious.

Libby places her hand over mine. "You're giving one daughter away and about to see the other head off to college," she says as if reading my mind. "I'd think you were inhumane if you weren't feeling a tug on your heart."

A lump forms in my throat as I nod. I turn to meet her gaze again and feel my eyes well up with tears.

"We have a great family, Lib. We are gaining one hell of a son in law, and I imagine another will follow eventually. I hope those two graduate from college first before they think about anything else, but I am happy with the direction our family is growing."

Libby squeezes my hand affectionately. "You love those boys, Mel. They don't have to marry our daughters to be a part of the family. They were family the first day we met them."

"And you love them too," I remind her.

Libby's smile widens. "That I do."

• • •

I've been holed up in the garage for the last two days. Vicky asked me months ago to build an arch for the ceremony. Although the wedding is at the church, she wants more decorations, more flowers, more pizzazz. The pastor cautioned her not to go overboard, but she always visualized getting married under a cascading arch of sunflowers. Since it's a fall wedding, her mother encourages it, and to be quite honest, I really don't want to deny Vicky anything. She deserves the wedding of her dreams. If an arch is what she wants, an arch is what she is going to get.

I will be the first to admit that I am a sucker for all my children. Next to falling in love with Libby, becoming a dad was the best thing that ever happened to me. Each time she gave birth, a part of my heart I didn't know existed came to life. Parenting came naturally to me. I think it did for Libby, as well. Some of my buddies talked about parenting as a negative obligation, a burden to their lifestyle, something in the way of hunting, sports, and drinking. As for me, I saw my children as a bonus to those other things. I took them hunting, even my girls. At my softball games, I was proud to have my wife and kids there to cheer me on. They were outside with me as I worked on projects and fixed vehicles. The drinking with my buddies didn't interest me anymore because I derived so much pleasure from being with my best friend, my wife. Together we watched our kids' experience life. Whether they were climbing trees, running through the sprinkler, having snowball fights, playing tag in the back yard or riding bikes around the neighborhood, we sat for hours on the front porch completely content listening to their laughter in the wind.

Libby and I were pretty lucky with our kids. For the most part, they were easy to raise. All three had very distinct personalities and interests, but when it came to morals, values, and being all-around good people, we hit the jackpot. Sam was the typical responsible, bossy, pick on your little sisters' older brother. While he could be mischievous and ruthless in his antics with them, he was forever their protector, wore his heart on his sleeve and thrived at taking care of them. He and I did everything together, fishing, camping, and hunting. He was my sidekick. Now, I could not be prouder. He's grown into such a strong, positive role model in our community and his involvement in law-enforcement complements the person he already was by feeding his need to help others.

Vicky was the sweet, soft-spoken, rule-following, mild-mannered daddy's girl. She had this temperament from the day she was born. Vicky wasn't fussy, she was easy to calm, always cooperative, and loved following a structured schedule. In the evenings, she was the first to crawl into my lap and play with the hair on my arm while asking me questions about work. At school, she raised her hand to assist the teacher. She was the friend who included everyone because she hated to see someone's feelings get hurt. At home, she was busy doing her chores while her brother and sister complained. When Sam and Jessie called her a brownnoser, she reminded them the sooner her chores were done, the more time she could spend with me. While she loved to hunt and fish and didn't mind handing me tools when I worked in my shop, there was a part of Vicky that did not always enjoy getting dirty. She liked to ride her bike, but she was not one to jump through mud puddles or race down dirt paths. And when it came to riding horses, she was the person who got on the saddle after everyone else did the hard work.

Then there is Jessie, my spitfire. Vicky is a bit more feminine and ladylike, while Jessie is a tomboy, competitive, and enjoys getting dirty alongside her brother. Her desire for independence was apparent early on. She wanted to feed herself the moment she started eating table food. She wanted to dress herself and refused assistance from anyone after the age of two. When she started kindergarten, she told her mother and me to wait in the hall while she entered the classroom by herself. Even though she never gave us too hard of a time, there was a fierceness in her soul. If someone told her she wasn't capable, she would move heaven and earth to prove them wrong. She was a leader by nature and had no problem vocalizing her thoughts or standing up for something unjust.

All three of our kids have a positive outlook on life, engaging personalities, and were not rude or inconsiderate. I'm not saying this because I am biased. They truly are great. As I think about this phase of raising kids coming to an end, I get a small ache in my chest. But I remember there are even more enjoyments to come.

I strike the hammer down on the nail and then stand back to inspect my work. The arch is almost complete. All that's left is to sand the pillars and paint the pinewood white. I grab the gallon bucket, sandpaper, and paintbrushes out of the cab of my truck and carry them back to my shop. As I get lost in the back and forth strokes of sanding, Libby calls out my name.

I peer out the door to find her leaning on the sliding door tapping her fingers tips on the glass.

"What's up?" I ask, wiping dusty hands on my jeans.

·"I just got off the phone with Sam. Jessie stayed at his place last night, remember? Now he called to say she wants to stay there the rest of the week."

"Why?"

"That's what I asked. Sam said she and Zane got into a fight. She thinks if she stays at Sam's, Zane will give her space. If she is here, he will keep bugging her."

"That's strange. What was the fight about?"

Libby shrugs. "Do you think we should check on her?"

"Nah," I reply. "I'm sure everything is fine. I know she's getting antsy about leaving. She probably wants more independence, and staying with Sam and Jillian is almost like living on her own. What is going on with Zane will blow over. Those two are crazy about each other."

Libby frowns. "Okay," she says with a hint of hesitation in her voice.

Her reaction surprises me. She isn't a worry wart or an overbearing parent.

"Lib?" I call out after her. "What is it?"

She spins on her heel to face me again and purses her lips together.

"I don't know. The strange feeling we talked about the other day, I can't shake it. Maybe it's the anxiety of the wedding and everything else, but I can't seem to get Jessie off my mind."

I step onto the patio and reach for her.

"I don't know if I'm ready to be empty-nesters yet," she whispers.

Clinging to me, she buries her head into my shoulder.

• • •

When I hear Libby's scream my name, I run up the stairs from the basement where I had the washing machine disassembled. She grows hysterical as she shakes the crumpled stationery at me.

"She's gone!

I whip the letter out of her hands and scan it. I retreat to the couch and let the words sink in while Libby grabs the phone and begins making calls. This doesn't make sense; I think to myself. Why would Jessie leave? I saw her at dinner last night, and this afternoon when I came home from lunch, she was cleaning out her car, music was blaring from her stereo. She waved at me as if she didn't have a care in the world. Granted, she was taking her recent break up with Zane hard, but Jessie was a lot like her mother—tough, stoic, a survivor. I don't doubt her feelings for Zane, and I imagine they will work out their issues, but if not, it won't take long for her to bounce back. She's going off to college, and with her zest for life, Jessie won't be down for long.

Dumbfounded, I scan the letter again.

I refuse to go to college with Zane. It's best to make a clean break. I've registered and been accepted to another school. I am on my way there now. I will call in a few days after I get settled to give you my phone number. I DO NOT want any of this information EVER to get back to him. A reconciliation will NEVER be an option. I prefer if you do not tell Vicky where I am, either. There are dynamics with Zane that I prefer not to talk about, EVER. Because of them, I cannot accept Vicky's marriage to Tyson. We discussed this, and she is aware I will not be at the wedding. I am so sorry to hurt you. It is the last thing I want, but I feel it is the best thing for me.

I shake my head. This overdramatic explanation doesn't even sound like Jessie. Vicky, possibly, but Jessie? Not at all.

I step into the kitchen and try to explain how ridiculous this is to Libby but shudder when I see her face.

"I called Sam. He told me to leave this alone," she explains, as she sinks her anguished body into a chair. "How do I leave this alone? How do we find her? I want to call the police, but he told me not to."

I don't have an answer for her. I sit across from her and stare out the window, defeated. We remain like this for what seems like an eternity until I can no longer stand the tension flowing through the room. I shove my chair out of the way and retreat to my shop where I slam the door. I'm powerless to help my wife, I'm powerless to help my daughter, and I'm even more powerless to figure out a solution to solve this whole damn, stupid mistake. This is ridiculousness, and once we can get it all sorted out, our life will go back to normal. Yet from the deep, shadowy recesses of my gut, I know this is more than a mistake.

For the next few hours, I exert my energy completely reorganizing the shop, but the weight of the situation mocks me, reminding me that no one, not even our beautiful little family is immune to suffering.

• • •

I call Sam and Vicky, telling them "just leaving it alone" is not going to suffice and demand they come over to give us a better explanation.

The two of them, along with Jillian, sit side by side on the couch, looking like chastised children.

"Things with Zane didn't end well," Vicky explains. "She's broken, and we just need to give her space."

"What did he do to her?" Libby pleads.

Vicky sneaks a glance at Sam and Jillian out of the corner of her eye as if seeking support.

"It's not my story to tell, Mom. It's hers. To be honest, we don't know all the details anyway. What she wrote in your letter was basically all she told us.

"In this family, we don't run away. That's moronic!" I bite out.

"You think I don't want to have her at my wedding?" Vicky whines. "I know what you're thinking, I should have stopped her from leaving. Have any of you tried to stop Jessie from doing something when she had her mind set on it? You all know she can be impossible."

"What if we postpone the wedding a few months," I suggest. "She's got to realize this was an irrational decision, and once she does, she'll come to her senses. What if I talk to Zane?"

"No!" Vicky and Sam shout in unison.

Sam looks at me with sad eyes. "She's not coming home, Dad. Jessie had a couple of weeks to plan this out. She's made her decision, and its best if we leave Zane out of it."

• • •

It's Saturday afternoon. Four days have passed since Jessie left and no one has heard from her. I can hardly stand the gloomy atmosphere in our house even though I know I'm a fifty percent contributor. Libby and I live on the edge every second of every day, jumping each time the phone rings, hoping it is her on the other end telling us she is safe. It's usually a wedding vendor or a friend of Libby's. The not knowing is unbearable. I escape as often as I can. I work more hours than usual, volunteer to help neighbors around their yards and even offer my services at church when I would typically defer it to the other men from our ministry group. When none of these other things fill my time, I hide in my shop. While I do this, Libby throws herself headfirst into Vicky's wedding plans. Despite the position we find ourselves in, she is determined to make this a beautiful and memorable day for our daughter and her fiancé.

Today they are at the dress shop for Vicky's final gown fitting. Afterward, they will be meeting at the home of one of her coworkers for the bridal shower. No one has inquired about Jessie up to this point but her absence this afternoon is bound to bring about questions. We decide if this happens, we will explain she has a scholarship opportunity that required her to leave a few weeks earlier than planned to attend a medical seminar. As regretful as it is, we agreed she could not pass it up. Any other questions will be ignored or redirected.

I brush one last coat of paint onto the wedding arch. After it's dry, I load it into the back of my truck to deliver it to the church and decide to make a detour by Sam's to return the staple gun he loaned me. I am relieved to see his truck parked out front. It's been a long, drawn-out day with too much time to think. Maybe he'll be interested in having a beer together.

I climb the stairs but hesitate before knocking when I hear elevated voices seep through the crack of the door that is slightly ajar.

"You need to talk to him, Sam. He's going crazy not knowing. At least give him some peace of mind."

"I don't need to do shit, Jillian! Let him go crazy!"

"That's not fair. He is as much a victim in this as she is. Put yourself in his shoes. He has no idea why she stopped talking to him, and now she disappeared without a trace."

"Bullshit! If he wasn't that son of a bitch's son, do you think she would have taken off the way she had? He's as much a part of this as Ron is."

"You know how much he despises that man. You can't make him responsible for his father's actions," Jillian implores.

"No, but he is responsible for not protecting her."

I hear the contempt in Sam's voice as he continues. "And Tyson should have done the same for Vicky. Jessie should never been out at the ranch alone with that man. What Ron did to her...God, Jillian. I want him dead!"

I feel as if I am drowning in the unease of my suspicions. I push the door and stand motionless as it creeks open. A mortified Sam and Jillian stare at me when I step into the apartment.

"What are you talking about?" I insist, my voice is devoid of any emotion.

Sam falters over words while Jillian wrings her hands together nervously, nodding at his excuses.

"Stop it!" I yell.

They sit at their dining room table, watching as I pace the room. A formidable and intimidating silence lingers between us.

"Talk!" I finally demand. "I want to know everything."

• • •

When Sam finishes, I sink to the floor and put my head down, hiding my eyes behind the palms of my shaking hands. I have a mixture of tears, snot and spit accumulating down my cheeks, on my chin, and at my feet. I cannot seem to stop or gain control over myself. I continue to shudder as poison pumps through my veins. Jillian disappears into the bathroom and comes back with a box of Kleenex.

"Would you like something to drink," Jillian asks faintly.

I can't even find the words, let alone my voice. I shake my head while I stare absently at the carpet.

"Dad?" Sam finally says moments later.

Maliciously, I shove myself off the floor and storm out of their apartment. I look over my shoulder and find Sam following me.

"Your mother will never hear about this. Do you understand me?"

"Where are you going?"

I don't answer. I climb into the truck and drive home. I barely stop in front of the house when I slam it into park and jump out. A moment later, I march back to the vehicle with my 9-millimeter semi-automatic pistol tucked in the back pocket of my jeans, oblivious to everything around me. When I jerk open the door, a hand on my shoulder yanks me back.

"What are you doing?" Sam roars.

"What someone should have done a long time ago!"

"Dammit, Dad. This isn't the way to handle this."

I scoff, shaking his hand away.

"Bullshit! You even said you want him dead. That man spewed evil and terror onto everyone I love. He will hurt no one else. I will see to that!"

"I'm coming with you!"

"Like hell you are," I growl, pushing against his chest. "You stay as a far away from that ranch as possible! I'm not too old to beat your ass if you show your face."

I don't bother to look at Sam as I crawl behind the wheel. Tires spin as I pull out of the drive, my fractured mind focused on one thing and one thing only, making someone bleed.

● ● ●

Later that evening, I sit on the back-porch swing staring at the stars, trying to organize my muddled mind and chaotic emotions. Libby came home from the shower a few hours ago. She gave me a brief synopsis of the day and then disappeared into the spare bedroom to be alone. It's the same thing she did every evening this week. I'm silently grateful she is not communicating with me right now because I don't know if I can look her in the eye and pretend that our entire lives have not changed for the worse.

I kick the dirt with my toe, gliding the swing back and forth. My stomach convulses as I go over the day's events for what seems to be the hundredth time. Someone got to Ron before I did. Someone took the wrath of their anger out on him. Someone left him for dead. I have a pretty good idea of who it was.

I wring my hands together, feeling like I am suffocating under my own twisted madness and adrenaline, desperate for the revenge I may never get. A part of me still wishes I could have been the one who beat Ron to a bloody pulp and left him to choke on his blood.

A highly agitated Sam was waiting for me when I got back to the house. He listened to his department scanner after I left and when he heard dispatch request an ambulance to the ranch, he agonized feverishly, until he saw my truck pull into the drive. Heavy with defeat, I explained what I found and who I thought was responsible. Sam used his position as leverage and made phone calls while I put my gun back in the safe. When I returned, he said Ron was alive but in critical condition. I eased myself onto the cement step next to him.

Sam finally spoke. "Dad, I know you don't want to hear this right now, but this is not going to change anything. Jessie is not coming home. There are so many components at play here than just Ron. The Jessie we all know, she is gone. And there is nothing we can do about it. What transpires between her and Zane is between them. We need to stay out of it."

The weight of his words pushed down on me like a boulder crushing my entire existence. What seemed like an eternity later, he placed a hand on my shoulder, giving it a tight squeeze. There was nothing more to say, so he left.

I'm not sure what to do now. The loss I feel is so pervasive, the hopelessness ravages every part of my soul. Libby is in the prison of deep grief, and if I tell her the truth, it will only intensify her pain. I could not save her from the heartache of Jessie leaving, but I can save her from the agony of knowing what Ron did to our girls. I swallow back a sob and squeeze my eyes shut tightly, willing away the hypothetical visuals that invade my mind.

The phone rings startling me. I walk inside slowly, my body stiff and sore.

"I went to the hospital," Sam says. "Ron has a traumatic brain injury as well as broken ribs, broken clavicle, nose, and cheekbone. The bones on his right hand are shattered, and there is damage to his liver and spleen. His injuries are inconsistent with a fall, so they are going to open an investigation."

"Is his family with him?" I ask.

"Only Joan. They can't get anything out of her. Talking to her is like having a conversation with a wall. The officers say she displays the typical signs of an abused woman. They aren't naïve to the rumors about their marriage. They wonder if she had something to do with this, but there are no signs that point to her."

"What about the boys?"

"The police went over to Tyson and Vicky's apartment looking for them. Apparently, they are on a camping trip over by Big Sky. She hasn't heard from them since they left early this morning."

"Dad, the police are trying to figure out who made the anonymous 911 call," he warns. "Is there anything or anyone besides me that can trace you to being out at the ranch?"

I stop breathing for a moment because all I can think about is Libby and what would happen if I wound up going to jail. I say a silent prayer that however this entire scenario plays out, somehow, someway, justice will prevail.

CHAPTER EIGHTEEN

Mel — 2009

It's hard to believe thirteen years have passed since Jessie left home. I wish she was coming home under better circumstances instead of this, but regardless, we are both ecstatic.

Libby cleans the house from top to bottom in preparation for her arrival. I help as much as I can, but I want to cut the grass before I have to sit down and take a break. This is the part I hate—the lack of energy to do what came instinctively before and the amount of rest I need to make it through an entire day. I can't say I ever took it for granted because my physical health was something I always valued, but it's clear to me how the little things that came naturally before I now have to plan out and execute in a specific way, so I have energy after.

I store the lawnmower in the corner of the garage and tell Libby I'm going to lie down before dinner. I crawl into bed and pull the covers up to my chin and shiver. I have lost a considerable amount of weight which probably contributes to the chills I experience. I'm tired, and although a nap sounds heavenly, I can't seem to let myself relax, so I toss and turn but cringe as my muscles throb.

Thirteen years, I think again. At times it seems like everything happened yesterday. Looking back, I can admit despite the tough times, the years were not horrible. Although the logistics were not ideal, we were lucky enough to maintain strong bonds with all three of our children. We've been able to travel often, laugh a lot and the moments Libby and I have shared have been priceless. Every day I wake up and remind myself of the blessings we continue to acquire. This new one is the hope we will have our kids under the same roof together once again.

Still, I wish things would have played out differently. I can't deny the regrets rooted deep below the surface of the brave exterior I show the world, and as sleep eludes me, I remember the secrets buried there.

Vicky and Tyson's wedding was bittersweet, and while a much-welcomed distraction, it was a bit convoluted. As Sam and I agreed, we kept what we knew between the two of us. Despite the absence of her sister and the persistent cloud of tension hovering over us, Vicky and Tyson truly had a wonderful day and appeared deeply in love. The adoration between the two was apparent to everyone present. Ron's absence only enhanced the joy of the day. Joan, used to keeping up appearances and remaining impassive, was quiet but pleasant as she engaged with the bride's side of the family. The only other relatives in attendance for Tyson were his grandparents. He had a variety of friends and coworkers to make up for the absence of family.

Zane remained aloof and somber during the two-day event. Even though he was the best man, he chose to stay out of the way hardly engaging with anyone. Libby's anger toward him intensified the longer Jessie was gone, and she was silently grateful he kept to himself. I, on the other hand, knew the many reasons for his distance. He tried to hide his hands, shoving them in his pockets, but at the rehearsal dinner, I finally got a good look at them. Even though it had been over a week, they were still slightly swollen and bruised. There was a small obtrusive cut at the corner of his lip, and a yellowish mark lingered under his eye. He did a good job covering it up with makeup, so it wasn't obvious.

I chose to ignore him the same way Libby did, realizing the wedding was not the time or place, but hoping I would somehow find the words when the opportunity arose. Unfortunately, the opportunity never did.

Jessie finally reached out to us exactly a week after she left. I can count the number of times I saw Libby cry over the years and this was one of them. Jessie reassured us that she was safe and focusing on school and her future was her only priority. We listened as she confirmed what Sam already warned me about. She was never coming back to Helena. We heard the desperation in her voice as she begged us not to ask questions and as crazy as it sounded, to trust her. When Libby commented that her reaction was a bit harsh, Jessie immediately shut down, abandoning the discussion.

True to her word, she called once a week, sometimes more, but the cycle continued. If we asked a question or brought up a subject she didn't want to discuss, she ended the conversation. Libby and I eventually learned that if we wanted to keep the lines of communication open, there were conversations we were never going to be able to have. The hardest part for me was stepping down from the role I always played as a father—the disciplinarian, the enforcer of rules and respect, and the one who made my kids toe the line. If circumstances were different, I would have chewed Jessie's ass, never allowing her passive-aggressive behavior to control our relationship. That wasn't how we functioned as a family. But this was new territory, and it was a slippery slope.

Eventually, the three of us learned how to navigate it. In time, Jessie invited us to visit. Libby couldn't get on a plane fast enough. We spent five days with her in Chicago after Christmas and made a point to see her three to four other times throughout the year. It was always on her territory. She made it clear she wanted us in her life and vice versa. Once the pressure of unknown and unrealistic expectations wore off, we were able to make it work.

True to her word, she never returned to Helena, but we alternated holidays between visiting her and staying here with our other children. It was easy to find places to meet halfway for long weekends, and we took many camping trips. After a couple of years, Sam, Jillian, and their kids joined us.

But Vicky never did.

As much as we craved our time with Jessie, the easy-going, confident, bubbly young girl full of energy and fire was gone. She was replaced by a quiet, sullen, and cautious young adult who wasn't comfortable in her own skin. She was still as hard-working and determined as she always was, but we saw that Jessie's ambition stemmed from something that looked more like fear and a strong desire to prove herself, rather than the love for life and purpose it used to be. This was especially hard on Libby. It was one thing to grieve over Jessie's absence and put the chapter of raising kids behind us, but it was another entirely to grieve over her lost spirit knowing she may never again be the person she used to be. We desperately missed that Jessie. Like everything after that horrible day, the interactions took time. Eventually, in our presence, she began to feel more comfortable, and we saw glimpses of the girl we always knew.

The upheaval of our family was one of the hardest things Libby and I had ever gone through. The first year tested our marriage in ways neither of us prepared for. Due to the underlying anger we both carried around but never discussed, we fought more often than not until eventually we grew tired and gave in to avoidance. Unable to rely or depend on one another during our grief, we both sought refuge in other things.

When I wasn't at work, I was obsessed with tearing engines apart on cars, trucks, motorcycles, and snow-mobiles and then selling the restored items. I stashed the extra money away with the secret hope that one day I could use it to bring Jessie home. Libby joined a gym and involved herself in so many groups and classes, she was hardly around. Monday, Wednesday, and Friday mornings she attended aerobics and left herself available to substitute teach the other days. Tuesday night was a book club, Thursday was Bunco. Every Saturday morning, she had breakfast with girlfriends and after, a pottery class. On Sundays, we attended church, but I came home by myself while she stayed for her women's ministry group. When we were in the house together, we mostly kept to ourselves. I watched sports or focused on some project while she stayed in her room reading a book or baking in the kitchen.

We were disappointed in the direction our relationship was going, but neither of us was willing to take steps to improve it. It was as if we felt we deserved to punish ourselves by watching our marriage dissolve into nothing.

And then a few months after the first anniversary of Jessie's departure, something changed. It wasn't a drastic epiphany, and there wasn't a long drawn out discussion over our misery. We made a choice. I missed my wife, and she missed me. While sitting in church one Sunday, I reached over and placed my hand on Libby's leg during the sermon. The following week, she linked her fingers through mine while singing hymns. One evening when she was going for a walk, she asked me to join her. The walks together turned into every other evening. At first, we didn't have much to say, but in time we grew more comfortable being together without the topic of Jessie hanging over us. We began to discuss little things—Sam's job, our grandson, Vicky's pregnancy, work, Libby's hobbies, and the extra money I saved. The simple exchanges of our daily routines started to build trust, and soon we were making plans. We began remodeling projects around the house. We started having dinners and game nights with friends and planned camping trips for the upcoming summer.

It was a stormy year, but despite the turbulence, Libby and I weathered it becoming even more secure as partners.

It was after a trip to Chicago for Jessie's twenty-first birthday when Libby and I were finally able to have heart to heart about our daughter. She approached me one night in my shop while I was hammering a dent out of the rear fender of a nineteen seventy-eight Dodge pick-up truck. I found it advertised in a small farming town about a hundred miles away. The seller was only asking a thousand for it, and I could not pass it up knowing that once I restored it, I could sell it for a considerable profit. I wanted to use this money for a surprise trip to Hawaii.

"I want you to know, I am okay," she told me.

Puzzled by her statement, I stopped the pounding to glance up from my work and found her leaning casually against the door frame.

"About Jessie. After she left, I was consumed with these one-sided conversations in my head, hoping one day I would have the opportunity to have them face to face. I had things I wanted to tell her, ways to help her, advice to give her, words of faith and wisdom to support her through whatever she was going through. I wanted to fix her. I was so busy begging God to hear and answer my prayers that I didn't stay quiet long enough to hear Him. I hated the quiet. It was uncomfortable, painful, and lonely, so I made my world noisy. But noisy didn't work, so I stopped. Now I am forcing myself to listen."

"Have you heard anything?" I asked, setting my tools on the bench.

Libby nodded. "I don't *need* to have those conversations with her. That is my ego talking. We did an excellent job raising her and planting the seeds. The foundation is there. I have this overwhelming peaceful feeling that God is working with her, and on his own time, those seeds are going to grow. He's got this. I have to let him have it. He is going to heal her, and I need to trust it."

That day, her words brought me a sense of reassurance as well. From that point forward, Libby and I were able to leave the cloud of sorrow and bitterness behind. We found acceptance in knowing some things may never go away, but we had a lot to be grateful for.

Less than a year after Ron's "accident," the Sheriff's Department closed the investigation. There wasn't enough evidence to pursue the case, and because of

352 PIECE BY PIECE

Ron's reputation along with various rumors about his infidelities and illegal activities, the District Attorney didn't want to touch it. It probably wasn't the finest day for the department, but I know a few of us who will be eternally grateful for the decision.

As time went on, it was always my intention to reach out to Zane, although I had no idea what I was going to say. I could not even conjure up the words in my mind to somehow bring either of us peace, but I felt it was my responsibility not only as Jessie's father but as the only healthy male role model in his life, to support him. He was just a kid when he made a sacrificial choice to enact revenge on his father, the person who not only ruined his life but the life of the one he loved the most. It had to be hell to live with that and lose Jessie at the same time.

But, one year after another passed. Tyson and Vicky kept me informed of his whereabouts even though they didn't hear from him often. We didn't see him at family events. Even though he was invited, he never showed. I guess this made sense considering he had secrets of his own.

I ran into him once at the liquor store after he had moved back to the ranch. It took me a moment to recognize him as he changed so much since I'd last laid eyes on him. The boy I knew and loved as one of my own stood across the parking lot from me as a man. I don't know who was more surprised to see the other. My initial step toward him was a visceral reaction. I stopped just as quickly, recognizing his distress as he looked around like a caged animal searching for an escape. In that split second, I remembered he didn't know what I knew. He thought we blamed him for Jessie's disappearance. I wanted to tell him otherwise. I wanted to reassure him that my love and admiration for him had grown over the years. I wanted to give him a shoulder to rest his burdens on and let him know he didn't have to do this alone. Like I would with any of my kids, I wanted to take him in my arms and hold on for dear life, never to let go. When I tried to speak, my body froze, my throat tightening. A moment later, I turned away and climbed into the cab of my truck. On my drive home, I berated myself for losing out on the only chance I'd been given to right this wrong.

To this day, I continue to allow Libby to believe what she wants about Zane, and I don't try to convince her otherwise. I know she spent years trying to put pieces of the puzzle together, yet none of them fit quite right. It's easier for her to place blame than not have a secure answer. I hate lying to her. It's not just one lie, it's several that I've layered, one on top of another.

I don't have a good excuse for my actions. The only one I can come up with is that I am a coward. Aside from not being able to save my daughter, not being able to save Zane is the second biggest regret of my life.

• • •

As I walk through the kitchen, I hear their laughter float up the stairs from the basement, and my heart practically combusts with joy. My girls are together, and I feel another prayer is answered. There are still a few more to come, but I am confident in the direction this process is taking as well as the outcome.

Libby and I watch as Jessie, Vicky and her three kids play a board game. Their enjoyment is contagious but I grow weary and finally decide to call it a night. I slowly retreat up the stairs and close the garage door before I shuffle down the hall. It is more common to shuffle than not as I continue to lose the strength in my legs. This disease is a bitch, I think as I sit on the edge of the bed looking down at my shaking hands while the throbbing in my head continues. The pain can be unbearable, but I won't let them see that.

I just need a little more time, I pray.

For some reason, I wasn't surprised by my diagnosis even though I didn't have many symptoms. I didn't feel any different aside from the consistent pain in my hips and lower back that didn't let up no matter how much Tylenol or Advil I took. Maybe I was a bit more tired, but at sixty-eight, who wouldn't be? It was when I noticed the blood in my urine that I decided I better get in to see Wilk. He sent me to an oncologist for tests immediately and, low and behold, prostate cancer. After a bone scan, MRI, and CT, we discovered the cancer had metastasized and spread to my lymph nodes, bones, and lungs. The doctors told us that, though there was no cure for metastatic prostate cancer, there were new therapies that could extend my life. Regardless, the outlook was grim. Forty percent of patients survived for a year while one percent survived for five years.

Even though we knew what the outcome would inevitably be, Libby and I spent days discussing our options. We seemed to be in silent agreement that it was easier to focus on what we should do instead of folding in the towel. After two weeks of contemplation, sometimes together and other times by myself in silent prayer, we had to face reality and have the hardest, but most honest conversation we've ever had in forty years of marriage. I knew what I had to do, why I was going to do it, and how this played into God's bigger plan. After we spoke the final decision out loud, Libby and I spent the rest of that day in each other's arms talking about the life we made, the memories, the laughter, the tears and most of all, our children. We cried together, got angry together, and prayed together until we finally fell into an exhausted sleep curled in each other's embrace.

I could have spent the next few months feeling sorry for myself, but I knew there was a bigger hand playing a bigger card in this whole situation. I don't want to look at this as a sacrifice on my part because I feel that is a little narcissistic. But I am able to acknowledge as tragic as my diagnosis is, it was the first in a line of many miracles that began to unfold in our lives. These miracles will determine a future for the people I love that may not have happened otherwise.

Jessie doesn't realize how much I watch her, how I pay attention to the small details of her day, her mannerisms, and her reactions. It's not like I have anything else to do, and having her here with us gives me a chance to get to know her in a new way. I guess I'm making up for the lost time and I am not going to waste any of it.

The first week she was home little things would unnerve her, and although she didn't outwardly react, I could see her wheels spinning as her anxiety exhausted her. She slept often and wandered the house restlessly when she was awake. I imagine this is the first time in thirteen years she hasn't had work, school, friends, or anything else to distract her. As uncomfortable as it is, it's about damn time. She had an exercise machine delivered to the house, and she runs on it like a maniac. She's already too damn skinny and eats like a bird. If she keeps running as she does, I'm afraid she will waste away to nothing.

Keeping a lid on her emotions is starting to prove difficult. A few weeks ago she spent almost two entire days in her room claiming she was sick, but we knew it was a lie. She was a wreck and hardly got out of bed. I'm guessing it had to do with the upcoming apprehension of meeting her sister's kids. We all agreed years ago that the estrangement with Vicky was ridiculous, but like everything with Jessie, we kept our opinions to ourselves. In our hearts, we knew this day would come, and when it did, she would be welcome with open arms. For some reason, Jessie didn't realize that, and her fear of rejection was apparent.

Regardless, my girls are back together.

I turn off the bedside lamp and smile to myself as their laughter, like music to my ears, floats through the vent. I drift into a peaceful slumber feeling lucky enough to have an opportunity to turn back time.

• • •

There isn't much time left. I'm tired. My body is failing me. Talking is hard. Instead, I spend my time listening to every conversation and absorbing every emotion of those I love. I want to leave this world connected to their hearts.

I'm proud of Jessie, and the steps she has taken to heal, and having her here has been a godsend for Libby. It gives her something else to focus on other than being my nursemaid and watching me deteriorate in front of her eyes. It's enjoyable to see them engage so easily again. They work well together as they balance the responsibilities with me, the grandkids, and the small catering business Jessie started.

I'm also incredibly proud of Vicky and Sam. They carried a heavy burden all of these years being the two people Jessie confided in. They continue to rally around her with support and unconditional love while knowing that years of deceit is slowly making its way to the surface. No one in this family is going to be immune to the truth when it comes out. Everyone, except for Libby, has something they are going to have to explain. I wish

I could predict the consequences that will materialize when it happens, but I do believe we are all prepared. It's time to let the secrets die.

I wonder how much Tyson knows. For someone who hasn't had much contact with his brother over the years, Tyson and Zane are awful chummy. I've caught the casual glances and speculative exchanges when they think no one is aware. Granted, Vicky and Jessie picked up again right where they left off, but I sense something different with the two boys. They share a camaraderie that did not disappear over time. Could it be that Tyson was also involved in seeking revenge?

I remember the day Libby came home from a counseling appointment with Vicky. She was distraught, almost hysterical, which I hadn't seen in her since the day Jessie left. Once I got her to calm down, she proceeded to tell me that Vicky was sexually assaulted as a teenager. I thought her admission would be a relief as one of the big pieces of this mystery was revealed. But Libby convinced herself Zane was the perpetrator. She needed answers, and it made sense to her that when Jessie found out, she despised not only Zane but her sister too, which explained her extreme reaction. It also explained why Tyson and Zane have not remained close.

I had the opportunity that day to tell Libby what I knew, but I was blindsided by her assumptions and didn't know how to contrive a believable enough story without unraveling the parts that were not mine to tell.

Libby is going to need a lot of support when this is over. I wish I could spare my wife the pain of the truth. I know she will be disappointed in me. I'm disappointed in myself. If I could turn back time, there is so much I would do differently. Will Libby hate me once I tell her? Will it be too much for her to handle? Will I be able to face my maker knowing the depths of betrayal I had inflicted upon her? It's one thing to experience agony and grief when you know you are going to leave your wife due to your impending death. It's another thing entirely when the possibility of losing her is because of lies and deceit at your own doing.

Libby brings me my protein shake and adjusts my oxygen before placing the straw into my mouth. When I reach up to wrap my fingers around the glass, Libby swats my hand away. I'm not such an invalid yet that I can't do this myself, but Libby wants to take care of me. I do worry about her, though. She has been nothing but strong and has the energy to do this now, but it will eventually wear on her. I've already discussed this with Sam and am confident he will see to it that everyone pitches in when the time comes. No matter what, I want to make sure Libby is taken care of the way she deserves.

• • •

When Zane has the courage to show his face on our doorstep with the entire family present, I know my dishonesty cannot continue. His pained expression from the cold response he received from my wife will forever be in my memory.

Later that night, when we go to bed and are finally alone, I come clean. When I finish, Libby sits on the end of the bed, her shoulders hunched over in silent defeat. I expect to see hate in her eyes. I expect anger like I'd never experienced before. I expect tears at my betrayal.

She surprises me.

"A part of me knew all along, but I so badly wanted to believe the story I told myself," she says remorsefully. "I kept fighting to fit square pegs into round holes. The fight gave me a purpose when I felt completely helpless."

She turns to me with tears in her eyes. "How did we fail at protecting them?"

"We can't do that to ourselves, Lib. There is only one person responsible for this."

"I want to make him pay."

"Someone already did."

On a long exhale, I reveal the rest of the story.

CHAPTER NINETEEN

The emotional turbulence and tormenting fear I experienced leading up to my confession was brutal. I declined quickly, but by the time Christmas rolled around, I was feeling better again. The decorations, the laughter, and the energy around me gave me a surge of unexpected vitality, and I was able to be involved more than I had anticipated.

Now as New Year approaches, I feel worse than ever. The cream Jessie used on me no longer works, so I'm in pain all the time. Smells make me nauseous. It's hard to breathe, let alone talk. I have no appetite. All I want to do is sleep and hold my wife in my arms as much as possible. Of everything, I think that is what I will miss the most. Libby's delicate frame cradled against mine. As grateful as I am to have my children around, I want to spend every moment of every day I have left with my wife, the other half that makes my heart whole.

Zane is here to pick up Jessie. While he waits for her, he sits by me, his hand resting on my arm while we watch television. Over my oxygen mask, I study his expression, but it's difficult to read. As if he senses me watching him, his head shifts until our eyes meet. In them, I recognize a piece of myself.

I slip the oxygen mask below my nose. "If she hadn't come back home, would you have gone to her?"

Zane's somber expression turns to one of bewilderment.

"Next year on her birthday was my deadline," he admits. "But I'm glad it didn't come to that. I don't know if I would have been welcome."

I could tell him, I think. I could relieve him of the burden he's carried and explain how this has played out in God's time, but as desperate as I am to bring him peace it's still not the right moment.

When Jessie appears, and their eyes lock, my heart swells. I may be dying, but I know what I see. The unspoken words they share express more than a mouthful ever could. They are two souls that would be incomplete without the other. I see respect, admiration, and true friendship that did not vanish over time, the very qualities that secure the foundation for any marriage. I see the strength and depth of character to become better than they were before and better than they would be alone. They are no longer children, and through trials and tribulation, they have learned what it means to live life without one another. Now they have an opportunity to take on the world together.

After they leave, my wife leans over me. As she usually does, she places her hand on my forehead, checks the levels on the oxygen tank, pulls the blanket around my shoulders, and kisses my cheek. In a moment she will disappear into the kitchen to make my smoothie.

I will sip on it until I am full and then fall asleep while she sits in the recliner opposite me reading a novel.

Before she can turn to leave, I place my hand on her wrist. I don't have a lot of strength but enough to motion for her to lie down beside me. I remove my mask and turn my face toward hers. Although years are etched into her delicate skin and her eyes are fatigued, she is still the radiant beauty I fell in love with over forty years ago.

Some men consider their wives their weakness. I consider Libby my strength. I'm fully aware of how lucky I am to share life with her and don't take a moment for granted, especially now. It was hard to anticipate the reaction she would have when I finally told her the truth. It took time for her to sort it out in her heart and head, but she found compassion and understanding in my choice. Since then, we grieved the loss of what our family was, but we found comfort in what it's become.

Tonight, I get to ring in the New Year with her. The irony is it will be the most uneventful New Year's we've ever spent together but possibly the most meaningful. I know I won't get to see much of the upcoming year, maybe a few days, or even a few weeks. Tonight I'm not going to let her go, and until my time is up, I'm going to cherish every minute.

I feel her inhale sensually as our lips touch and recall the pleasurable way she used to shudder under my touch. I'd give anything to make love to her one last time, to show her everything I have ever felt for her, to give myself to her in this life and promise her forever all in eternity. I know it's an impossibility so instead, I savor her warmth as our mouths explore.

It doesn't take long before I'm coughing. The fit subsides quickly, but I'm exhausted. Regardless, she crawls beside me, shifting until our bodies are nested together.

Craving the intimacy from a few moments before, she massages my arm while I run my fingers through the strands of her silky hair recalling in detail every inch of her. As we drift off to sleep, I know the memory of this will be engraved in my mind when I draw in my last breath of air.

• • •

"It's time," I tell Libby.

"Are you sure?"

"She came for the letters?"

Libby nods.

"Then it's time."

Libby sends out the text. I am nervous as they arrive. First Sam and Jillian then Tyson and Vicky. I motion for Sam and Tyson to help me into my recliner. Once I'm comfortable, I close my eyes, knowing what I am about to do is going to wipe me of any energy I have left. My stomach twists anxiously. Am I making another huge mistake? What if my admission backfires and my family spirals out of control? Am I causing more pain even though my intentions are pure? *Are* my intentions pure, or am I trying to clear my own conscious?

Finally, Zane and Jessie come bursting through the door. Exasperated, she takes one look at me and burst into tears. Falling at my feet, she sobs. Cradling her head with my hand, I attempt to reassure her as I did when she was a girl.

Libby returns to the living room to sit beside me and explains why we asked everyone over. "This is a difficult conversation for us to have. But first, Mel has some conditions."

"Call it my dying wish," I say with a shallow breath.

"Dad, don't joke about this," Sam interjects.

I put my hands up in surrender as Libby continues.

"Tyson and Vicky," she says, directing her attention to the couple. "Your father insists you two get into marriage counseling first thing tomorrow morning. Promise us whatever you hear today, you will face together. Not apart."

With compassion in her eyes she turns her attention to Jessie. "We love you. No matter what. Your father and I don't care who you decide to spend your life with. Your happiness is what matters. But we want you to bring the whole you into that relationship. The *real* you. Not someone who gets by coping on pieces of a broken heart. You deserve better and the person you share your life with deserves better."

Without waiting for a reaction, she turns to Zane. With tears in her eyes, she takes his hand into hers. "Mel and I owe you an apology. In fact, we owe you so much more than an apology."

CHAPTER TWENTY

It's difficult to say how a person will feel when they get to this point on their journey. I imagine the accumulation of thoughts and emotions are different for everyone. I realize this insight may appear strange considering I am on my death bed facing what some would consider impending doom. The inevitable is staring me in the face; it looms so close that I feel the whisper of God's spirit all around me. It's not a matter of days at this point. It's a matter of hours.

I did a lot of reflecting over the last year, and I was sure I would still be doing it before God decides to take me. But I'm not. Instead, I take comfort in the extraordinary love I'm experiencing. There is an abundant amount of anticipation going on inside of me, and though my body has deteriorated and I can no longer speak the words clearly, my soul is filled with a joy I didn't expect. There is an exhilaration, similar to the one I felt on my wedding day, as if I've been waiting my whole life for this moment, and the best is yet to come.

I no longer have regrets. A week has passed since we came together to divulge years of secrets. In that short time, I've seen even more miracles take place within my wife, within my children, and the men who I consider my sons. Words cannot express what it feels to have Zane back where he belongs. This is what I have been waiting for—to have everyone back together. This family was strong enough to survive the storm and I am confident, they will now find happiness as they dance in the rain.

We all have a purpose. I had no idea what mine was until this exact moment. Even though I was being shaped and molded and made several mistakes along the way, God knew how to use me to do his work, and now my job is complete.

I don't have much pain anymore. I'm grateful for this. It is a challenge to keep my eyes open. I hear conversations around me and delight in the laughter when it is there. There are tears too, but as I told the family last week, this is a time to celebrate God welcoming me home. Despite their sadness, I know they are making an effort on my account.

I feel the warm lips on my cheek and smile inside when I hear the voices of my beautiful grandchildren. What a wonderful experience it has been to share in their love. I may not be able to be with them physically, but my spirit will be at every birthday party, every sporting event, every awards ceremony, and every holiday. I look forward to watching over them as they continue through life.

I feel Libby's body curl into mine. Her delicate fingers caress my temples as she whispers her love in my ear. I want to thank her for saving my soul, but a peaceful contentment like I've never experienced before suddenly washes over me. The glow of the radiant light is beautiful, and it warms my body as the strong hand reaches out to link fingers with mine. Like a lifeline, I cling to the hand of my friend, feeling the power of its pull as I follow the silhouette home.

EPILOGUE

Spring — 2019

Jessie stands on the front porch shivering as the wind hits her face and dust swirls around. She pulls her sweater over her shoulders and watches Zane, astride his horse, gently guide the colt behind him into the coral. She can see his lips move as he gives directions to seven-year-old Melanie and four-year-old Paxton. Climbing out of the saddle, his feet stir up a cloud of dirt. Full of enthusiasm, the children's eyes light up when he places an arm around their waists. Simultaneously, he lifts them off the horse and swings them in a circle. Jessie can't help laughing out loud as their delight reaches her ears. She clutches her chest, amazed her heart is big enough to contain all the love she feels for these three.

She tilts her head to the sky and closes her eyes. A ray of sunshine peaks from behind a cloud, the first glimpse of light on an overcast day. In the warmth, she senses her father's presence more than ever. She smiles, and wraps herself in a tight hug feeling his strong embrace around her.

A moment later, Melanie and Paxton bounce up the stairs and into her waiting arms. Looking over their heads, she locks eyes with her husband. His smile sends tremors along her spine. She kisses the cheeks of her children before ushering them into the house to wash for dinner. As soon as they disappear, Zane reaches for her hand, and she melts into him.

There was a time when having this type of relationship was a distant dream. Marriage is meant to be more than what society defines it to be. It's a oneness, a permanent spiritual union between man, wife, and God, not something easily dismissed or thrown away when people grow apart or face challenges. It sounded great in theory, but she didn't know if she possessed the character for this type of commitment. She had lived a long time with a hardened heart, and Zane had unresolved issues of his own that weighed heavy on their future.

There was the initial shock as all the secrets surfaced. Like their mother, she and Vicky found it hard to hold a grudge against the three men who devoted their lives to loving and protecting them. After Mel's death, it didn't take long for Jessie to realize she wanted to be Zane's wife. But she needed to decide the type of woman she wanted to be in marriage as well as a mother to her children because holding onto unresolved guilt and shame could result in contempt and resentment. *This* would be the biggest enemy to their family. A changed heart for both of them was the only solution. They could not erase their pasts but could learn how to pay attention to it, find forgiveness in it, and heal from it.

Her parents were right. They deserved this, and failing was not an option.

It wasn't a specific moment that inspired overnight healing, but instead, an accumulation of hard work and small daily miracles over time that supported them along the way—therapists, other survivors of abuse, a book given by a friend, authentic conversations with loved ones, powerful messages at church—taking time for prayer and a relationship with God. It boiled down to choosing to change and stop making excuses. They had to be willing to show up, be vulnerable, and open to miracles when placed in their paths. Little by little, the unraveling of chains that had kept them bound began to take place. At that point, they noticed they were bringing something bigger into their lives. Together, they continue to rebuild their life day after day, rediscovering themselves and each other in the most authentic of ways.

Unfortunate events two decades ago put everyone Jessie loved in a position to make impossible choices, but thankfully, they all persevered.

Ron died nine months after Mel. The facility informed Joan, and she made arrangements to have him cremated. The boys didn't want to be involved, so she took care of the loose ends but made sure they received their respective portions of his life insurance.

After two years of discussion, research, and due diligence, the two couples took that money along with the inheritance from Mel and used it to open a non-profit agency. The Heart of Hope Advocacy Center in Helena collaborates with law enforcement, mental health professionals, medical and victim advocates, and spiritual coaches to support adult survivors of abuse, sexually abused children, and their families in their healing process. They still have the ranch and Jessie runs a very successful bakery, but they remain involved with the agency as active board members intent on seeing their vision achieved.

A lot was revealed to Libby in a very short period of time, and after Mel's death, she struggled more than expected. She was grieving the love of her life, and she was reeling with a multitude of emotions—mostly guilt, anger at herself, and sadness for her daughters. When the kids shared the mission of their non-profit with her, she felt like this was her purpose—giving back and finally helping. She was hired on to work fifteen hours a week writing grants and organizing fundraising events. She volunteers another two hours a week for the agencies support groups. Along with this, she remains active and involved in the lives of her children and grandchildren. Her good days are better than her bad days, but when she has them, she reminds herself of the promise she made to her husband; to live every day to the fullest until it's time for them to meet again.

With his hand on her hip, Zane follows Jessie into the hallway where they peek into the guest bathroom to find their children up to their elbows in bubbles dancing and singing enthusiastically.

"I got that sunshine in my pocket got that good soul in my feet…I can't stop the feelin' so just dance, dance, dance." They happily sing their favorite Justin Timberlake song.

He nuzzles her neck as she places a hand affectionately on his cheek, and they continue to observe the kids, enjoying their carefree confidence.

"We need to go through these boxes before I put them in storage," she says as she leads him to the spare bedroom.

At sixty-eight, Joan is in relatively good health but recently opted to put her house on the market to move into a retirement community a few miles from Tyson and Vicky. There was an auction at her home the previous weekend, and Zane and Tyson dropped off the leftovers at Goodwill. Yesterday she arrived with four cardboard boxes labeled "keepsakes." While Melanie and Paxton took her into their playroom for a tea party, Jessie unpacked the car.

Now they rifle through the first three boxes filled with Zane's childhood memorabilia—reports cards, art projects, 4-H ribbons, sports trophies, and class pictures. The last one holds random snapshots of Tyson and Zane through the years. Joan appears in a few, but there are none of the entire family. Sitting on the edge of the bed, Jessie and Zane flip through the photos and reminisce.

When they finish, Jessie stands to leave, but Zane reaches into the box and pulls out a small blanket that covers the bottom. Underneath it, he finds a plastic bag. Giving Jessie a curious glance, he unzips it.

Inside, taped in bubble wrap and still caked in mud, is Ron's pistol.

In 2015, Children's Advocacy Centers around the country served more than 311,000 child victims of abuse, providing victim advocacy and support to these children and their families.

For more information on sexual abuse
against children visit:

http://www.nationalchildrensalliance.org/cac-model/

https://www.cachouston.org/what-we-do/

FACT: The real prevalence of child sexual abuse is not known because so many victims do not disclose or report their abuse.

- One in four women and one in six men were sexually abused before the age of 18 (Centers for Disease Control and Prevention, 2006).
- The primary reason the public is not sufficiently aware of child sexual abuse as a problem is that 73% of child victims do not tell anyone about the abuse for at least a year. 45% of victims do not tell anyone for at least five years. Some never disclose (Smith et al., 2000; Broman-Fulks et al., 2007
- Nearly 70% of all reported sexual assaults occur to children ages seventeenand under (Snyder, 2000).
- Nearly 700,000 children are abused in the U.S annually.
- About four out of five abusers are the victims' parents.
- 34% of people who sexually abuse a child are family members of the child.

FACT: Sexual assault can have a variety of effects on a victim's mental health. Victims of rape or sexual assault are at an increased risk for developing depression, PTSD, Substance Use Disorders, Eating Disorders and Anxiety. (Mental Health America, 2019)

- One in five women and one in seventy-one men will be raped at some point in their lives.
- In the U.S., one in three women and one in six men experienced some form of contact sexual violence in their lifetime.
- 51.1% of female victims of rape reported being raped by an intimate partner and 40.8% by an acquaintance.
- 52.4% of male victims report being raped by an acquaintance and 15.1% by a stranger
- More than one third of women who report being raped before age eighteen also experience rape as an adult.

DISCUSSION QUESTIONS:

1. What was your initial reaction to the book? Did it hook you immediately or did it take some time to get into?

2. The story deals with grief, loss, and trauma. Do you feel the behavior of the characters reflect their individual experiences?

3. What character did you relate to the most, and why?

4. Were there parts of the book you thought were incredibly unique, out of place, thought-provoking, or disturbing?

5. What was your opinion about the sibling relationship between Jessie and Vicky? Tyson and Zane?

6. Dawn is a character that appears off and on throughout the book. Were you surprised about the connection to Jessie that was revealed toward

the end? They were both victims of abuse, yet they handled their circumstances differently. Why do you think this is?

7. Tyson knew about Vicky's abuse. If you were in her shoes, how do you think you would have reacted when you found out Tyson's secrets?

8. How do you think Jessie's trauma impacted her relationship with A.J.? If she had chosen to have a future with her instead of Zane, how do you think the book would have been different?

9. The ending is left open to personal interpretations. What is yours? If you were writing it, how would you have liked to see it end?

10. Was anything left unresolved for you?

11. Every family faces challenges that can make them stronger, or divide them. What challenges has your family faced? How did they affect the interactions? Looking back, what would you have done differently and what would you do the same?

12. The book has a variety of character perspectives that you only see through their eyes. Were you frustrated with how the characters reacted until it was pieced together?

13. Was there a quote, paragraph, or specific moment that inspired you?

14. If the book were adapted into a movie who would you have play the parts?

ABOUT THE AUTHOR

With the encouragement of her family, Hope began writing thirteen years ago as a way to heal from painful experiences. Finding authenticity in her own emotional, physical, and spiritual growth is her passion. With the support and loyalty of genuine relationships on her journey, she has developed a strong desire to support others as they dive into healing and spiritual transformation.

In 2017 she began her business Hope for Health Wellness. Her goal is to inspire, encourage, strengthen, and give hope to others on their journey to live whole-heartedly. Through retreats and workshops, she collaborates with professionals and community members to share holistic resources, provide education through guest speakers, and promote self-care to support the body, mind, and spirit.

Hope's professional background is in human services working with children and families. Currently, she sits on the board of Park County's Collaborative Management

Program. Previously she was the Program Manager of a supervised visitation center and has participated in child protection teams to provide advocacy and support for victims of child abuse.

Hope devotes much of her time to her yoga and meditation practices, going on hikes, watching the latest "binge-worthy" television, doing jigsaw puzzles, and playing with flowers. When she isn't spending quality time with family and friends, you can find her listening to music that feeds her soul and ignites her passions.

ACKNOWLEDGEMENTS

My love, Sky Flansburg. Our love story is one of friendship, faith, heartache, healing, trust, and unconditional devotion. Thank you for being my partner in adventure, dreaming big, and taking risks with a leap of faith. We are the perfect combo to travel this journey together. Your support and belief in me is my rock.

To my daughters. You're the inspiration that motivates me to connect and understand other's hearts and honor their individuality.

My brothers, Rich and Troy Strang. Thanks for taking me along on your adventures, toughening me up, giving me courage and strength, and making me feel that I was capable of doing anything you two were doing.

Carolyn Cline for being the sister I never had. Thank you for sharing our childhood, always knowing my soul, and accepting me exactly as I am no matter how far apart we are.

Lynn Huylar, Director of Safe Harbor-a children's justice center in Cheyenne, Wyoming for being a wonderful friend and mentor. You provided an exceptional work environment as well as, the priceless experience, education, and understanding of child abuse.

Pastor Jim Burgen at Flatirons Community Church for your talent to deliver powerful messages of spiritual transformation. Your words of wisdom and inspiration continue to blow my mind and heal my heart. The seeds you planted were continued motivation as I pieced this story together.

My Beta Readers, Julie, Peter, Rhonda, Lindsey, and Sara. Thanks for cheering me on. Your insight, critical eye, and constructive feedback was essential through this process. The time you devoted to this project is greatly valued.

My editor, Felicity Fox. You made a very intimidating process a powerful learning experience. Your suggestions, knowledge, and thoughtful responses brought me to the next level in my writing. Your belief in my story and positive reminders kept me on track when I questioned myself. Thank you!

Thank you Susan Krupp. Working with you to create my cover design was pure joy. What an enjoyable process starting with your creative vision and artistic talent. Your patience with my requests was appreciated, and my heart soared the first time I saw it. You nailed it!!

Author Academy Elite: This program was a turning point for me. Thank you, Kary Obebrunner, for your desire to change lives and encourage others to believe in the story they have to tell. To the coaches: Abigail, Nanette, Brenda, Tony, and Nicci for your encouragement and wisdom. The Igniting Souls Community and fellow authors for allowing me to have an inside seat in the brainstorming process of your books and businesses. I look forward to future collaboration with this aligned group of people.

My Hope for Health Wellness Retreat and Workshop partners, Jeni Nelson-Fagan, Theresa Hansen, and Sara Peterson. You helped bring my vision to life. Collaborating with you has been a dream, and this is only the beginning. I can't wait to see where this takes us!

Future books by Hope Flansburg

Angel Kisses

Summer 2020

Never Look Back Trilogy: A Family Saga

Book 1 March 2021

Book 2 January 2022

Book 3 September 2022

Empowering Women, Inspiring Women,
Strengthening Women, Women Giving Hope
Your Journey to Spiritual Enlightenment Starts Today!

Hope For Health Wellness Workshops and Retreats

Spend Time Sharing Ideas, Vision, Wisdom and
Abilities While Teaching the World to See Your Value!

Escape to the mountains of Colorado for yoga,
meditation, self-care, healthy meals, guest speakers
and presentations that will reconnect you with your
emotional, physical and spiritual health. Through collaboration and connection, we bring small groups together
to support, guide, teach, and share strategies for spiritual
transformation.

For Upcoming Dates and Registration Information
go to www.hopeforhealth.me
https://www.facebook.com/hopeflansburg4/

CPSIA information can be obtained
at www.ICGtesting.com
Printed in the USA
FFHW011311221119
56070853-62079FF